**Elizabeth Jeffrey** was born in Wivenhoe, a small waterfront town near Colchester, and has lived there all her life. She began writing short stories over thirty years ago, in between bringing up her three children and caring for an elderly parent. More than a hundred of her stories went on to be published or broadcast; in 1976 she won a national short story competition and her success led her onto write full-length novels for both adults and children.

*Elizabeth Jeffrey titles published by Piatkus, in alphabetical order:*

Cassie Jordan
Cast a Long Shadow
Dowlands' Mill
Far Above the Rubies
Fields of Bright Clover
Gin and Gingerbread
Ginny Appleyard
Hannah Fox
In Fields Where Daisies Grow
Mollie on the Shore
Strangers' Hall
The Buttercup Fields
The Weaver's Daughter
To Be a Fine Lady
Travellers' Inn

# *Elizabeth* JEFFREY

## Gin and Gingerbread

PIATKUS

First published in Great Britain in 1989 by Century Hutchinson Ltd
This paperback edition published in 2018 by Piatkus

1 3 5 7 9 10 8 6 4 2



A CIP catalogue record for this book
is available from the British Library.

ISBN 978-0-349-42147-6

Typeset in Sabon by M Rules
Printed and bound in Great Britain by
Clays Ltd, Elcograf S.p.A.

Papers used by Piatkus are from well-managed forests
and other responsible sources.

Piatkus
An imprint of
Little, Brown Book Group
Carmelite House
50 Victoria Embankment
London EC4Y 0DZ

An Hachette UK Company
www.hachette.co.uk

www.littlebrown.co.uk

To my children, Lynn,
Julie and Chris, with love

# *Chapter One*

Abigail reached the door of her father's study and stopped to dab her swollen eyes yet again with her handkerchief, edged in black lace. Then she took a deep breath and knocked.

'Come,' the deep voice from within commanded.

She pushed open the door. The study was a room she rarely entered. It was her father's domain, a man's room, but comfortably furnished in walnut with a Turkey-red carpet and long crimson curtains tied back from the window. A leather armchair and small smoking cabinet stood near the fireplace, where the embers of a coal fire smouldered. Over the mantelpiece a portrait of a woman hung, draped now with black crepe, and on the opposite wall a large nautical chart in a maplewood frame showed the estuary and creeks of the River Colne. Bookshelves lined the rest of the walls and under the window a terrestrial globe rested on its stand. In the middle of the room, behind a large leather-topped desk on which an inkstand and blotter were placed with mathematical precision, sat her father, Henry Chiswell, of Chiswell and Son, Oyster Merchants of Colchester in the County of Essex.

He was a small, spare man for all his booming voice, but he had an air about him, a presence, which commanded if not respect then certainly attention. He was dressed no differently today, the thirtieth day of March in the year 1839, the day after his wife's funeral, than any other day. Henry Chiswell always wore black.

'Yes, Papa?' Abigail waited obediently. She knew perfectly well why he had sent for her.

Henry cleared his throat. 'I suppose you realize that now your mother is d . . . no longer with us I shall expect you, as my eldest child, to run the house, Abigail?' he said brusquely.

She gave a barely perceptible sigh. 'Yes, Papa.'

'Good. Then it comes as no surprise to you.' Henry sighed in obvious relief that she had taken the responsibility so readily. He stared for a moment at the portrait over the mantelpiece. Then he shook his head a little theatrically. 'We shall miss her. I shall miss her. Twenty-five years we would have been married this year.' He turned his attention back to Abigail and said in a more businesslike voice, 'You will have charge of the household keys, of course.' He looked down at the blotter in front of him and straightened it fractionally. 'Er – where are they, by the way? Have you any idea where your mother kept them?'

'In the drawer of the cabinet beside her bed, Papa.'

He nodded several times. 'Ah, yes, of course.' He got up briskly from his chair and left the room.

Abigail wiped away another tear and took the opportunity to blow her nose while he was out of the room. Poor Papa, the business took up much of his time but had he really no idea that she had already been running the household for the past two years? Ever since her mother took to her bed, in fact? She went over to the window and watched a coal cart rumbling up the hill pulled by an enormous shire horse. That reminded her, she must remember to order more coal from Mr Brigg's coal yard at the Hythe.

Her father returned, chinking the keys as he walked. He

handed them to her as if he thought it should have been an act of some ceremony but he wasn't quite sure how to do it. So he contented himself with clearing his throat again and saying, 'Look after them. You know which lock each one fits?'

Abigail allowed herself a little mirthless smile. Probably better than you do, dear Papa, she thought, but aloud she said, 'I think so, Papa,' and fastened them back on to her belt. It said something that her father had never noticed them there in all the two years she had worn them, collecting them from her mother each morning and returning them last thing at night.

'I'm sure you'll manage very well, Abigail,' he said briskly. 'I think it will be a perfectly satisfactory arrangement.' He resumed his seat and leaning back steepled his fingers. 'Of course, I shall still need your help in the business, sometimes. You have a useful aptitude for figures' – he permitted himself a brief self-satisfied smile – 'no doubt inherited from me. It would be a pity to waste such a talent simply on household accounts, important though they are.'

Abigail raised her eyebrows. This was the nearest thing to a compliment she had ever heard pass her father's lips. 'But what about Edwin?' she asked. 'And Pearl?'

Henry sat forward and leaned his elbows on the desk, frowning. 'Pearl is a fine-looking girl,' he said after a moment. 'She's – what? – eighteen, now?' Abigail nodded so he went on, 'I've no doubt she'll soon find herself a husband.'

Whilst I am twenty-three and so plain that no man is ever going to look twice at me, Abigail thought with some irritation. She sighed. But you're probably right. Not even Matthew . . . She pulled her thoughts back to what her father was saying.

'Edwin, as you well know, is being groomed to take over the business, just as I was groomed to take over from my father,'

Henry was saying, with more than a hint of pride in his voice. 'His course is set. Nevertheless, there is much to do, and even with Ezra Carver there as clerk there is still a place for you.'

Abigail's spirits lifted. She had been afraid that her father would dismiss her from Chiswell and Son now that the burden of running the house was completely on her shoulders. She hadn't wanted that. She was far more interested in the oyster business than in running the house. A film of dust on the mantelpiece gave her far less concern than a badly packed barrel of oysters. Not that there was ever a film of dust anywhere; Ellen, the housemaid, was far too diligent to allow such a thing.

'That's all I have to say.' Henry got up from his chair and went over to the window, dismissing her. 'Except,' he added, with his back to her, 'I shan't be in to supper tonight.'

Abigail stared for a moment at his silhouette, framed in the window. 'Oh, Papa, you're not going to begin working again? Not so soon . . . ' An irritable shift of his shoulders warned her not to say more. 'You work much too hard,' she couldn't resist adding before she turned and left the room.

She shivered a little as she crossed the hall on her way to the morning room. It was a large draughty hall and the broad mirror hanging over a gilt consul table only served to emphasize the cold spaciousness by making the hall look twice as wide as it actually was. Even the thick runners placed on the black and white tiled floor did nothing to reduce the chill.

She paused at the mirror and looked at herself critically. Black didn't suit her. She was too pale, sallow even, and her features were plain; her mouth too wide, her nose too big and her face too long. She adjusted the new black lace cap and smoothed her hair. Of that at least she could be proud; it was long and thick and of a rich chestnut colour. She brushed it with a hundred strokes every night and wore it parted in the middle and smoothed into two thick loops over her ears. She peered closer into the mirror. Her brown eyes were still bloodshot from all the tears she had shed over her mother. Her lip quivered again and she bit it and straightened her shoulders. The time for crying was over now. Life had to go on. She turned and headed for the morning room, then changing her mind, took her cloak from the hall stand just inside the door and hurried out. She couldn't help it if people were surprised to see her so soon after her mother's funeral. She needed air.

Henry, still standing at the window, watched her go. He stroked his mutton-chop whiskers thoughtfully. It was a pity she was so plain. Whey-faced, too. He sighed. Her only redeeming feature was the hair she had inherited from her mother. His glance went to the portrait of his wife. My, Edith had had a head of hair! It had been so long she could sit on it. And that glorious chestnut colour . . . Mind, she'd had a temper to match it. Abigail had inherited that, too.

He knew where she was going now. She would be making for the quay. Abigail loved the river and always went there if she was troubled or upset, whereas his only interest in it was in what profit could be made from harvesting its fruits. He gave a self-satisfied nod. Things would work out very well. Abigail would run the house efficiently, he had no doubt of that, and she would continue to be useful in the business. It was no bad thing that no man would ever look twice at her. He stood for a moment longer and then turned and walked over to the tapestry bell pull hanging by the door and gave it an impatient tug. A bell jangled somewhere in the depths of the house and a minute later a slightly breathless maid appeared.

'Tell Wilfred to have Busker and the trap ready in half an hour. And tell Daisy I shall not be in to supper,' he said curtly.

Hetty gave a quick bob and hurried back along the hall and down the back stairs to the warmth of the kitchen where Daisy, the cook, was pouring the coachman another mug of porter.

'You've to 'ave the trap ready in half an hour, Wilfred,' Hetty said, resuming her seat at the kitchen table where she had been cleaning the knives. 'An' master says to tell you 'e won't be 'ome to supper, Daisy.'

Daisy and Wilfred exchanged knowing glances. 'An' we both know what *that* means, don't we!' Wilfred said, wiping the froth off his whiskers.

Ellen, drinking tea at the other end of the table, pursed her lips. 'Indeed we do. Thass shameful. An' 'im with 'is wife not cold in 'er grave.'

Wilfred leaned forward. 'I reckon Busker could find 'is way to that woman's 'ouse blindfolded.' He began to chuckle. 'Did I ever tell you 'bout the time I took 'im to the blacksmith's at Wivenhoe to be shod an' 'e carried on right past the blacksmith's and never stopped till 'e was outside Effie Markham's 'ouse?'

'Yes, you did. Often times,' Daisy said sharply, suddenly remembering Hetty's presence. 'An' thass enough o' that talk, Wilfred Jackson. You better be quick an' finish your drink an' go an' get the trap ready. You know what 'is lordship's like if 'e's kep' waiting.'

It had been a hard winter. For weeks the snow had lain thick, compacted into ice on the ground. The pump at the Hythe, from which the poor took their water, had frozen, forcing them to gather the snow from the rooftops to melt for drinking and when this was gone to gather it in buckets from the fields. Even the river had frozen.

But now only a vestige of the snow remained, in a corner of St

Leonard's churchyard that received no sun. Elsewhere, daffodils were beginning to bud with the promise of spring and primroses peeped bravely through the grass among the gravestones, enjoying the first real sunshine of the year.

If people were surprised to see the little black-clad figure making her way down the hill so soon after her mother's funeral they gave no sign. Those that knew her, and that was most, bobbed a brief curtsey or doffed a ragged cap as she went by, silently acknowledging a sympathy they could share and understand, for death was no stranger to the crowded, poverty-stricken yards and courts that clustered round Colchester Hythe. When she reached St Leonard's Church Abigail paused and looked through the church railings, past the grey stone building bathed in the late afternoon sun, past the primroses and daffodils, to the new grave, covered in wreaths of spring flowers. She bowed her head, and as she stood there, over the clop of the horses on the cobbles, the grind of the cartwheels, the cries of optimistic street sellers, and the shouts and squabbles of passers-by, came the strains of music from inside the church. That would be Edwin pouring out his grief at the organ. She was tempted to go in and listen, she loved to hear her brother play, but she understood that today he wouldn't welcome an audience. He needed to be alone with his music just as she needed the solace of the river. Pulling her cloak round her more closely she hurried on to the bottom of the hill where the river slugged its way between muddy banks past the quay and on towards East Mill.

The tide was out. A line of boats, fishing smacks bearing the letters CK to signify that they were registered in Colchester, were tied up at the quayside, whilst across the river lighters and colliers crowded against the wharves of Hayfield's timber yard and Brigg's coal yard. Along either side of the quay were the makings, the bonding yards and vaults, warehouses for things like tea, coffee, sugar, butter, cheese, a shipyard, a dry dock, a lime kiln, granaries, seed and corn merchants, all in states of decay or repair that accurately reflected the state of business. Among it all, a smart, freshly painted two-storey building bore the legend HENRY CHISWELL AND SON, OYSTER MERCHANTS. It had been started by her grandfather, Old Mr Henry as he had become known, and under his son, her father, it was going from strength to strength.

Abigail didn't stop but made her way slowly along to the end of the quay, savouring the late afternoon sunshine. It was all noise and bustle. Horses stamped patiently as carts were loaded; men shouted to each other as they worked or idled their time away; ragged children, looking to earn a farthing where they could, squabbled in the filth of the gutter, and two flashily dressed women hanging round the door of the Anchor waiting to be taken in laughed raucously as three sailors, who hadn't seen a woman for weeks, fought over who should receive their favours first.

But at the far end of the quay, where there was nothing but an old derelict warehouse, unused for years, it was quiet, and pleasant just to stand and look out towards the bend in the river beyond which were hidden the little fishing villages of Wivenhoe and Rowhedge and further down river the cinque port of Brightlingsea and the estuary rich with the oyster layings from which her father and a good many others made their living. She sat down on the last bollard of the quay. She always thought of it as 'her' bollard because the boats rarely tied to it, it was too far from the busy end of the quay. Here she would come and sit when she wanted to be alone, when she was very happy or very sad, or when she simply wanted to think.

The riverside had its own smell. It was difficult to define. It was a smell of tarred rope, of sawn timber, of coffee, overlaid with the distinctive stink of the makings, of fish left to rot, and of the black mud, popping quietly as pockets of gas escaped. But all the smells, good and bad, were part of the atmosphere of the river and part of Abigail. She never stopped to think whether they were good or bad; they were simply there, as part of her life, a part that she loved and valued.

She folded her arms under her cloak and her fingers touched the keys at her waist. She wasn't particularly sad any longer. Now that the funeral was behind them life would return to normal and wouldn't be so very different. Nevertheless Abigail would miss her mother. She would miss going to her room to settle her for the night and talking over the day with her. There would be nobody to talk the day over with now; Edwin was rarely at home, and Pearl ... she sighed again. She didn't have a lot in common with her flighty younger sister but maybe she and Pearl would draw a little closer together now.

As for her father ... His business was his life. Started as an oyster stall on the quayside by his father it had grown and flourished until now Henry was the biggest oyster merchant on the Colne. And as he had told her, Edwin was being groomed to take over when Henry could no longer work. She shook her head. Sometimes – as with the household keys – her father could be very unobservant. Couldn't he see that Edwin hated the business and wanted nothing to do with it? That his heart was in his music and – something she herself had only recently discovered – journalism? When Edwin could make enough to live on by his pen he would be off, of that she was in no doubt, and she was torn between wanting her brother to be happy and successful and dreading her father's anguish in discovering that his only son didn't care about Chiswell and Son. If only she could inherit the business herself! She would like nothing better. But she was only a woman so it was quite out of the question.

She walked back slowly along the quay, scanning the boats for a glimpse of *Conquest*, the oyster boat Matthew Bateman sailed for his grandfather at Brightlingsea. Her heart gave a little skip when she saw it, moored next to the *Edith*, her father's boat, which Josh Miller, Matthew's uncle, sailed. Matthew was on the foredeck of *Conquest* and when he saw her he raised his hand.

'Afternoon, Miss Abbie,' he called.

'Good afternoon, Matthew.' Abigail felt her colour rise. Matthew was a tall, broad man, about three years her senior, with a face weatherbeaten to the colour of mahogany and unruly dark curls and whiskers. He lived with his widowed mother in a small cottage in Dolphin Yard off Hythe Street. Abigail had known him almost ever since she could remember and she would have stopped and spoken longer, but with a friendly smile and a lift of his cheese-cutter cap he turned away and continued with his work.

With a stab of disappointment she went on her way. Nobody knew how she felt about Matthew, there was no one she could confide in, not even her sister. Her mouth twisted wryly. She could just imagine Pearl's reaction.

'But Abbie, he's only a common fisherman! You *can't* be in love with a common fisherman!' But her look of amazement would not have been because Matthew was a common fisherman but because it would never have occurred to her that poor, plain old Abbie could ever begin to harbour feelings of love for anybody in her breast.

Abigail sighed. How little Pearl knew. How little anyone knew.

She continued on her way along the quay and reached the door of her father's warehouse just as it opened. About half a dozen women and two men came out. She noticed that one of the women was heavily pregnant and all of them had hands that resembled nothing so much as lumps of raw meat. The women bobbed shyly towards her and then went on their way together with one of the men. The other came across, his cap deferentially tucked under his arm. It was Isaac Honeyball, one of her father's dredgermen.

'May I offer my condolences over the mistress, Miss Abbie?' he said quietly.

'Thank you, Isaac' She smiled at him and made to continue on her way.

'Bad winter it's bin, this year, Miss Abbie, and no mistake,' he went on, shaking his grey, balding head.

'It has indeed, Isaac. I'm sure it has caused great hardship to many.'

'I doubt there'll be more as'll suffer, too, Miss Abbie, as a result of it. There'll be precious few oysters next season after a winter sech as this one's bin. There's always a bad spat after a bad winter.' Spat was the name given to the spawn of oysters.

Abigail smiled at him. Isaac Honeyball could never be accused of optimism. He would never see any good in anything if there was a chance things might go wrong. 'I expect we shall survive, Isaac,' she said cheerfully. 'The beds are well stocked.'

'That's as may be, Miss Abbie,' he said, shaking his head. 'That's as may be.' He retrieved his cap from under his arm, doffed it and replaced it on his head as he walked away.

Abigail watched him go. He was probably right. A bad spat always followed a bad winter. But her father didn't depend entirely on oysters for a living. Henry Chiswell was prepared to buy and sell almost anything as long as it had a profit in it. Chiswell and Son would survive.

# *Chapter Two*

The year of mourning was past. It had been a difficult year for everyone, particularly Abigail, who had borne the brunt of the family's discontent.

'I've hated wearing black, it simply doesn't suit me,' Pearl complained for the hundredth time. She peered at her reflection in the overmantel in the morning room, a pleasantly over-furnished room, bathed in late spring sunshine. 'It makes me look – wan.' She pinched her cheeks in an effort to bring more colour into them.

'Nonsense. Of course you don't look wan, as you call it.' Abigail was sitting at the table checking the silver. She looked up at Pearl with her head on one side. 'A little pale, perhaps, but that's because you spend so much time sitting indoors with your head in a book.' She smiled at her sister. 'Anyway, it makes you look interesting.'

'Interesting! Pah! I don't want to look interesting. I want to look pretty!' Pearl snapped, sitting down with a flounce. She leaned back in her chair. 'Not that we've been allowed to go anywhere for the past year to look pretty, or interesting, or wan. And I'm bored silly staying at home.' She yawned and stretched her arms above her head. 'Bored quite silly.'

'You could always check the linen cupboard,' Abigail suggested. 'I believe some of the table linen needs renewing. It's a task I never seem to find time for.'

Pearl stopped in mid-yawn, her arms still outstretched. 'Me? Check the linen cupboard? Don't be ridiculous, Abbie. I wouldn't know a sheet from a table napkin.'

'Then it's high time you learned, my girl,' Abigail said sternly. 'If you can do nothing else you can count everything.'

'Oh, why can't you ask Hetty to do it?' Pearl pouted.

'How can Hetty do it? She can neither read nor write, as you very well know. And I doubt she can even count beyond the fingers of one hand. But we need to know for Papa's dinner party at the end of next week. The mayor will be coming and Mr Hayfield and, oh, I don't know who else.'

'Oh, yes.' Pearl sat up, immediately interested. 'My new dress is nearly finished. It's pearl grey, to match my name, and it's to have a pink rose at the bosom. It will be all right to have a pink rose, won't it, Abbie? We are out of mourning now.'

Abigail looked doubtful. 'We should still be in half-mourning, strictly speaking, Pearl. But, no, I shouldn't think a pink rose would be out of place.' She finished checking the silver and put it back into its baize-lined drawer. 'I must go to the warehouse now,' she said, going over to the mirror and patting her thick chestnut hair. 'I told Papa I would be there at ten and I promised Edwin I would help him make up the end of the month accounts today.'

Pearl regarded her sister with her head on one side. 'You've got such beautiful hair, Abbie. It's really not fair, when mine is so, well, ordinary.'

'Don't be a little goose, your hair is a very pretty golden colour,' Abbie laughed. She turned and looked at her sister. Pearl was nineteen now, a sweetly pretty girl with wide blue eyes, regular features and slightly pouting lips. Her hair, though not as thick and richly coloured as Abigail's, clouded round her face in an attractive froth of golden ringlets. Her complexion was flawless. 'I really don't know what you're complaining about, Pearl.' Abbie fetched her bonnet and put it on. 'You're an extremely pretty girl.'

'I still wish I had hair like yours.' Without another glance at her sister Pearl picked up a magazine and began reading the latest instalment of *The Old Curiosity Shop* by Mr Charles Dickens. 'What time will you be back?' she asked without looking up as Abigail turned to go. 'And does Daisy know what's for luncheon?'

'Yes, she does. And I shall be back in plenty of time to eat my share.' Abigail reached the door. 'Don't forget to check the linen while I'm gone' were her parting words.

But Pearl didn't answer. She was too engrossed in Little Nell's troubles.

Henry pulled out his gold hunter watch, looked at it and then replaced it impatiently in his pocket. He drummed his fingers on the top of his desk indecisively for a few seconds and then picked up a sheaf of papers and left his office – it was marked PRIVATE in gold letters on the etched glass panel – and went across the landing to an identical door opposite – marked OFFICE – and threw it open.

'Is she here yet?' he asked, frowning at the young man bending low over the desk. Henry wasn't sure that he liked the present fashion of wearing the hair oiled so close to the head and then curling at the neck although he had to admit it suited the boy. In fact, he was a handsome young devil. Dressed well, too.

Edwin looked up. 'No, Father,' he replied, 'not yet.'

'Bah!' Henry made a sound of irritation. 'I want these letters done today. She'll never get through them all if she doesn't look sharp. She said she'd be here by ten.'

'It's only five past, now, Guv'nor,' Edwin protested. 'I'm sure she'll be here in a minute.'

'In a minute!' Henry jabbed a finger at his son. 'Time is money, my boy, and don't you forget it.' He looked at his watch again. 'I must go. I've a Commissioners' meeting shortly. Hayfield, across the river, agrees with me that it's time something was done about the river silting up. It's expensive to unload cargo at Wivenhoe and then have to bring it the rest of the way by lighter because the river's become so shallow. And our boats could use more of the tide if the channel was deepened. There's even talk about a canal between Wivenhoe and Hythe . . . '

'But something ought to be done about the town's drinking water supply, Guv'nor,' Edwin said. 'Surely the money would be better spent on that. The river can wait.'

The river can't wait. First things first. Now, where are those papers about the proposed canal, Carver? I gave them to you yesterday, didn't I?'

Ezra Carver looked up from his desk at the far end of the office, away from the light of the window. He was a thin, rather weedy-looking man of about thirty, with receding sandy-coloured hair, and pale eyes, which he now blinked myopically.

'Yes, Mr Chiswell, but I haven't got them now,' he said anxiously. 'You said to let Miss Abigail see them, so I gave them to her.' Ezra gave the dry, consumptive cough that punctuated practically everything he said.

'Bah!' Henry said again and strode over to the third desk in the room, where piles of papers were laid out in a neat orderly fashion. He riffled through them impatiently, littering them over the desk and on to the floor. 'They're not here,' he muttered. He turned to Edwin. 'Did you take them, boy?'

Edwin frowned at the mess his father had made. 'I looked at

them, yes. But I'm sure Abbie brought them back to your office when she'd seen them, Guv'nor.'

'Did she? Oh, I'd better go and look there, then.' Henry put the letters he had brought conspicuously on top of the heap without making any attempt to repair the mess he had made, and left the room. A few minutes later his office door slammed and there was the sound of his feet clattering down the stairs.

Without a word, both Edwin and Ezra hurried over to Abigail's desk and began to tidy up.

'Better not let my sister see her desk in this state, Carver,' Edwin said, shuffling the papers together into some sort of order. 'She'll go through the roof. She's got a temper like a mud-engine. Although perhaps you didn't know that, Carver? Perhaps you've never come up against it.'

Ezra Carver straightened the blotter and inkstand. 'No, Mr Edwin,' he said with a cough, 'I can't say I have.'

Abigail adjusted her bonnet in the hall mirror, put on her pelisse and left the house. As she walked down Hythe Hill, she stopped at St Leonard's churchyard for a quiet moment to put fresh flowers on her mother's grave. They wouldn't be there for long, she knew that. If the little ragged urchins who swarmed the streets didn't steal them, their elders would. Pearl was probably right in saying it was a waste of time to put them there. But Abigail persisted. It was the only thing left that she could do for her mother.

The hill was busy, with horses and carts rumbling up with merchandise unloaded from the boats, and with people who suddenly appeared from the numerous yards and alleys, hoping to pick up anything that might by accident or with a little help fall from the laden waggons.

She hurried on. The quay, too, was crowded. The tide was full, the water sparkling and glistening in the sunlight, giving no hint of the unspeakable things that found their way into it from the open sewers and drains of the town. Boats that had come in on the tide were unloading their cargoes and others, taking to fishing now that the oyster season was over, were preparing to leave on the ebb. There was no sign of Matthew, although his boat, *Conquest*, was there.

The warehouse was empty. The last of the oysters had been gone for some weeks. There would be no more until the season opened again in September; oysters were only eaten when there was an 'R' in the month. From now on the beds would be cleaned ready for the spatting season, when the new young oysters would attach themselves to the old oyster and cockle shells and the bits of old tile and stone, known as cultch, and where they would remain and grow, never moving, until they were three years old and ready to be transferred to the fattening beds.

Abigail gathered her skirts and went up the wooden stairs to the office.

Edwin had heard her coming and looked up with a smile when she pushed open the door. He was very fond of his elder sister. He only wished that he was half as competent in business matters as she was. She seemed to have a grasp of what was going on and a way of handling people that he could only admire. He wished too, and not for the first time, that she had been a brother instead of a sister, then she could have followed their father into the business, leaving him to pursue his interests in music and writing instead of having to wrestle with the problems of finding the cheapest cooper to make the oyster barrels and beating Mr Harvey down over the price of repairing the dredgers. He was simply not cut out for this kind of life.

Abigail took off her bonnet and pelisse and went over to her desk.

‘Who’s been meddling with my papers?’ she asked sharply. ‘I didn’t leave them in a muddle like this.’

The guv’nor. He wanted the specifications for the proposed canal and he couldn’t find them.’

‘But he had them, Edwin. I took them back to his office.’

‘I know. But we didn’t realize that until after he’d ransacked your desk.’ Edwin smiled sheepishly at his sister. ‘I’m sorry, Abbie. We tried to put things straight, didn’t we, Carver?’

Ezra Carver looked up, flushing as his glance met Abigail’s. ‘That’s right, Mr Edwin, we did,’ he said, with his customary cough.

‘Well you didn’t do it very well. I never saw such a hotch-potch.’ Abigail banged her fist on the desk in temper. ‘And what are these?’ she waved the letters her father had left.

‘Letters the guv’nor left for you to write for him. He wants them by tonight.’

She flicked through them. ‘Six!’ she said, aghast. ‘And long ones, too. It really is the limit. He told me there were only one or two.’ She threw them back on to the desk. ‘I’m afraid I shan’t have much time to spend helping you, Edwin. Not with this mess to clear up and all these letters to do.’

Edwin came over and put his arm round her shoulders. ‘How about helping me first, Abbie?’ he said persuasively. ‘I’ve got myself into the most frightful muddle with the bill for those new London people. If you could just spare the time to put me right over that . . . ’ He smiled at her disarmingly.

She frowned and picked up the letters again. ‘Well, perhaps they won’t take me that long . . . ’ She sighed heavily. ‘All right, Edwin, I’ll help you first.’

She went over to his desk. Abigail was fond of her brother and could never be cross with him for long. She thought he was quite the handsomest man she had ever seen, although she felt that the waistcoat and cravat he was wearing today were a little brighter than was seemly for half-mourning. But the cravat was stuck with a large jet pin, so perhaps it was all right.

She began to check through his work. To say he had got into a muddle with the account of Salisbury's, the London fish merchants, was an understatement. His arithmetic was appalling. She shook her head. 'Oh, Edwin,' she said sadly, 'how shall we ever make an oyster merchant out of you?'

Edwin bit his pen and looked up at Abigail miserably. He regarded her as 'a good sort' and he felt sorry for her in that she was so plain compared with Pearl. 'I hate it, Abbie,' he said in a low voice. 'You know how much I hate it, don't you? I hate being cooped up in this stuffy office. I hate dealing with figures, I never was any good at them.'

'What would you like to do, then, Eddie?' Abigail stole a glance at Ezra to make sure he was absorbed in his work and not listening to their conversation. 'Apart from your music, that is. You know you'll never make a living at that, don't you?'

'Yes, of course. I wouldn't want to make a living at it, anyway. It would take away the pleasure if I knew I'd *got* to do it in order to eat. Do you know what I mean?'

She nodded. 'Yes, I can understand that. It's a bit like your writing, I suppose. I know you enjoy that, but . . . '

'You'll never believe this, Abbie' – Edwin looked at her, his eyes shining – 'but I've met this man . . . he works in the office of the *Essex Standard* . . . he says my writing shows promise . . . '

Abigail shook her head. 'You know Father would never agree to you working for a *newspaper*, Eddie.'

'But it wouldn't just be working for a newspaper. I could do so much. I could bring the conditions of those poor creatures living in the yards and back alleys to the attention . . . '

Abigail laid a hand on his arm. 'Oh, Eddie, it's no use. Don't you see? Father would never allow it. You know "your course is set", to use his own words. He's relying on you to carry on the business when he's gone.'

Eddie covered her hand with his own. 'He'd much better look to you for that, Abbie. You're much more interested in it all than I am.'

'But I'm only a woman,' Abigail said, with a slightly bitter twist to her mouth.

'And that's another thing . . . ' Edwin began.

'No, Eddie, not now.' Abigail held up her hand. 'Let's get these figures sorted out or I'll never get to Father's letters today.'

As it was, it was time for luncheon before she finished helping Edwin so she had to return in the afternoon to write the letters for her father. It was nearly five o'clock by the time they were all done.

She put the letters on her father's desk. He hadn't yet returned to his office after his meeting with the Commissioners but she was sure he would look in on his way home.

She left the office and went down the stairs and out into the sunshine. It was a beautiful May day, promising a good summer. She picked her way slowly along the quay among the usual litter of boxes and nets, ropes and waiting carts, to her bollard. Ten minutes to herself wasn't going to hurt anybody at this hour of the day, and there was always a chance that she might see Matthew.

The quay was less busy now. The tide was nearly out, the river little more than a stream between banks of mud where filthy children mudlarked and scrabbled for the odd coin or clay pipe that had fallen in the water. The boats that were moored, fishing smacks, lighters, small cargo boats, were high and dry in their mud berths, waiting for the water to return and lift them to their natural element again.

Matthew was nowhere to be seen, but Josh Miller, his uncle, was on the *Edith*. He waved when he saw her and beckoned to her. 'Hullo, there, Missy! Are ye comin' aboard?'

Abigail looked down at her full, organ-pleated skirts and cashmere boots. 'Not today, Josh. I'm not dressed for it,' she said, shaking her head and smiling.

He left what he was doing and came nimbly from the deck of the boat, up the iron steps let into the quay, to where she stood. He was a big, bluff sailor in his late forties, with a face lined and weatherbeaten to the colour of tanned leather and a thick mop of curly grey hair that extended to cover the lower half of his face in a bushy beard. A clay pipe was clamped between his teeth.

'My Alice was a-sayin' only this mornin' we hadn't seen you lately, Missy,' he said, his pleasure at seeing her now quite obvious.

'I've been busy, Josh,' she said, still smiling. 'But' – she became serious – 'it wouldn't have been right for me to come on the boat with you, would it, not till the year of mourning was up.'

'No, Missy, it wouldn't, you're quite right.' He nodded. His face lit up. 'But it's all right now, ain't it? The year's up. An' the tides'll be right by the end of next week. If the weather holds . . . ?' He looked at her eagerly.

'If the weather holds, Josh, yes, I'll come.' She sighed. 'Oh, Josh, you don't know how I've missed being out on the river with you.'

'An' I've missed takin' ye, Missy.' He rubbed his hands together in evident pleasure. 'Friday week then, Missy? That's the day I've got to go down and check the new layings. It'll be a six o'clock tide that morning so we can leave just 'afore seven and go down on the ebb and be back on the flood soon after five.'

'That sounds just perfect, Josh.' Abigail gave a sigh of pleasure. 'Oh, I shall look forward to it.'

She had completely forgotten that it was the day of her father's dinner party.

Abigail left Josh and continued along the quay on her way home. As she rounded the corner, past her father's warehouse, and into Hythe Street, a bunch of ragged children were busily picking up bits of coal, little more than dust, that had fallen off a cart as it passed. They worked nearly under the hooves of the other traffic, darting to the edge of the road at the last minute and back again as soon as the road was clear. But one child, smaller and slower than the rest, was just too late and when a galloping horse and rider came thundering down the hill he was caught by the flailing crop by which the man ensured a clear path. If the rider saw what he had done he paid no heed, but in a cloud of dust continued on his way over the bridge.

The child lay where he had fallen, blood streaming from a gash where the crop had lashed the side of his face, across his shoulders and down his back. The other children took no notice, but continued picking up the last bits of coal.

Abigail hurried across to him. He was a tiny lad, not more than about five years old, and nothing but skin and bone. She picked him up without any trouble and he immediately set up a howl.

'Where does he live?' she called to the others. 'Does he belong to any of you?'

A girl of about eight hurried over. 'Yes, Miss, beggin' your pardon, he's my brother. But he dropped his coal so I was jest pickin' it up for him. Is he hurt bad?'

'Badly enough. Where do you live?'

'Perseverance Yard, Miss. At the back of the Perseverance. I'll take him, Miss, shall I?' She held out her arms.

Abigail shook her head. 'No, I'll bring him. Show me the way.'

The girl hesitated for a moment and then led the way through an alley by the side of the beer house to a squalid yard where two cottages propped each other up. No sunlight penetrated Perseverance Yard and when she stepped inside the room Abigail had to blink to adjust her eyes to the gloom.

A woman was sitting on a stool by the empty grate suckling a baby. Apart from a table and a chair there was nothing else in the room. The woman hurriedly got to her feet and bobbed a curtsey when she saw Abigail, a frightened look in her eyes.

'Mum, little Joe's been caught by a whip. He's hurt bad,' said the girl, eager to impart the news.

'Not too badly, I think,' Abigail said quickly, seeing the alarm on his mother's face. She turned to the girl. 'Fetch some water, child, and I'll bathe his wounds.'

'There ain't no need, M'lady. I can see to him,' the woman said.

'No, I wish to see how badly he's hurt. Fetch water, girl',' Abigail commanded.

'You'll have to go to the river, Sal, the water in the bucket's all gone, an' the pump won't be unlocked again till tonight.' Her mother gave the girl a cuff. 'And mind your manners. Curtsey to the lady when she speaks to yer.'

The woman laid the baby down on a heap of rags under the table and took little Joe, smoothing the hair back from his grimy and blood-streaked face. His cries, which had dropped to a whimper, immediately started up again. She looked up at Abigail. 'Thank you for bringin' him, M'lady. I'm much obliged, I'm sure.'

'It won't look so bad when we've washed the blood off,' Abigail said reassuringly. 'Have you any clean . . . ?' She looked round. Asking for clean rag was useless, she could see that, so she lifted up her skirt and tore a strip from the hem of her petticoat. When Sal returned with the muddy water she dipped it in the bucket – itself none too clean –soaking it well. Then she washed little Joe, gently cleaning the blood from the long, blue weal.

'Hush, little boy,' she soothed as he set up a roar at the unaccustomed contact with water, and miraculously his cries subsided. 'There. As I thought,' she said to his mother. 'The skin is not broken in many places. But it's bad enough, goodness knows.' She turned to Sal. 'Did you notice who the rider was, Sal?' she asked.

'A gentleman, Miss.' After her mother's reminder Sal bobbed a curtsey every time she spoke to Abigail.

Abigail sighed. Doubtless in their fine clothes they all looked alike to these children. 'Where is your husband?' she said to the woman. 'At work?'

The woman gave a mirthless laugh. 'At work tippin' his elbow in The Perseverance,' she replied.

'Does he work?' Abigail persisted.

'Sometimes he get work on the boats, or unloadin' an' that,' the woman shrugged. 'An' I do a bit o' fish guttin' and scrubbin' oysters in the season . . . M'lady,' she added as an afterthought.

'I see.' Abigail turned to go. 'Have you any food in the house?'

'Oh, yes, m'lady. We've got half a loaf and a bit o' drippin'.' The woman spoke with pride.

Abigail left and went on home to the big house that her father had built, with its lofty rooms, its thick carpets and curtains; its new, modern furniture which blended so well with the solid oak and mahogany inherited from Henry's father. Everything at Hilltop House spoke of comfort and luxury. For some reason, as Abigail let herself into the house, she felt uneasy.

And she didn't feel much better after she had been to the kitchen and instructed Daisy to send Wilfred, the coachman, down to Perseverance Yard with a can of soup.

# *Chapter Three*

When Abigail realized that the day she had agreed to go down river with Josh was the very day of her father's dinner party, she was dismayed but determined not to let anything get in the way of the day out that she was so looking forward to.

'It simply means I must plan ahead and you'll have to make sure nothing is forgotten, Pearl,' she said cheerfully as she sat at the morning room table checking the guest list. 'There will only be twenty people, so it's perfectly manageable.'

Pearl was putting on her bonnet ready to go out. 'Is that nice Captain Griffiths coming?' she asked, a shade too nonchalantly.

Abigail cast her eye down the list. 'Yes, as a matter of fact he is. And also Lieutenant Barraclough, and Alderman and Mrs Stacey, and Mr and Mrs Hayfield . . . '

Pearl turned and sat down opposite Abigail. 'Are you really sure you should go with Josh next Friday, Abbie?' she said anxiously. 'You know Papa doesn't like you going out on the boats with the men at the best of times – myself, I can't for the life of me see why you are so keen to go, heaving about on the water on a smelly old boat doesn't appeal to me in the least. But if Papa knew you were going on the day of his dinner party he'd be extremely displeased.'

'Extremely displeased!' Abigail laughed. That's putting it mildly. He'd forbid me to go. So don't you tell him, Pearl. And I don't "go out on the boats with the men", as you put it. Put that way it sounds as if I'm some kind of nautical camp follower. You know very well that I would never go with anyone but Josh. And the *Edith* is father's boat, so what possible harm can there be?'

'All the same . . . '

'All the same, nothing. Josh looks after me. He's old enough to be my father.' She put her head on one side. 'In a way, you know, I believe Josh and Alice regard me as a sort of daughter. Did you know, Pearl, they once had a little girl, Emily? She died of scarlet fever when she was only four. I don't think they've ever really got over her death, although it was twenty years ago. She would have been my age now.'

'I didn't know that. How very sad.' Pearl sighed. 'I expect Alice has got all Emily's things locked away in a box in the attic and she gets them out every year on her birthday and looks at them.' Her eyes filled with tears at the thought.

'I'm sure she does nothing of the kind,' Abigail said briskly. 'Alice isn't at all like that. It's far more likely that Emily's things were given to some needy family. But never mind that now. I simply want to be sure that if I leave instructions with Daisy you'll make sure that everything is in order. That's not too much to ask, is it, Pearl? After all, I shall be back soon after five o'clock and the guests won't start to arrive until half past seven. If it comes to that' – she gave a little grin – 'Papa needn't even know I've been out.'

Pearl got up and picked up her pelisse. 'All right, Abbie. Just this once. But mind and make sure you tell Daisy exactly what to do, and don't you dare be late back.' She kissed Abigail briefly on the cheek. 'I'm off to see Miss Marchant now, to collect my dress. It really is the most perfect shade of grey. I'm so excited about Friday night. What will you be wearing, Abbie?'

'Me?' Abigail looked blank. 'I don't know . . .

Pearl threw back her head and laughed. 'Oh, you are a funny girl, Abbie. I do believe you're more excited about going out on that old boat with Josh than you are about Papa's dinner party.' She fairly bounced to the door in a rustle of taffeta. With her hand on the door knob she paused and turned. 'You can wear your lilac silk, it's what you wore when we first began to entertain again after mourning poor dear Aunt Eliza, so it's quite suitable.'

'Yes, that'll do.' Abbie picked up her pencil and went back to making lists.

Abigail hardly slept on the Thursday night before the dinner party. She hovered between excitement at her impending river trip and anxiety in case she had overlooked some vital item that would result in a ruined dinner party and her father's wrath and possibly – worst disaster of all – the end to river trips with Josh. Again and again she went over everything. The table was already laid, the napkins folded into bishops' mitres, the epergne placed in the centre only waiting to be laden with the fruit and sweetmeats already laid out in the larder. Elaborate desserts were made and stored in the cool pantry, as were the cold meat dishes. Daisy had her instructions for everything else and she was perfectly capable. Perfectly capable, Abigail repeated over and over to herself until at last she fell asleep.

She woke early and stole downstairs to the kitchen. Daisy was standing at the big iron range, which Hetty had already raked out and black-leaded before re-lighting, making porridge for herself and the other servants while Ellen prepared breakfast trays for the rest of the family. Hetty was now outside in the coal house busily filling scuttles.

'I shall be back soon after five,' Abigail told Daisy, 'so if I've forgotten anything . . . '

'Get away with you, Miss Abbie. You be off and enjoy yourself,' Daisy said, ladling the thick creamy porridge into bowls. 'Anyone 'ud think I'd never cooked for twenty 'afore. We shall manage, never you fret. Thass time you had an hour or two to yerself.'

'Looks like being a beautiful day, too, Miss Abbie,' Ellen said. 'There was a lovely red sky last night an' there's a haze over the garden this mornin.'

'Orf you go, then, and don't you worry about us back here. Everything'll be orl right, don't you never fear.'

'Thank you, Daisy.' Abigail hesitated. 'It's just a pity that it all had to happen today.' She smiled at Daisy. 'But I know you'll manage. You always do. If there are any problems, Pearl . . . '

Daisy made a face. 'There won't be no problems, Miss Abbie.'

'No, Daisy, I'm sure there won't.'

Abigail slipped out of the back gate and down the hill to the cottage in Spurgeon Street where Josh and his wife lived. Their little kitchen was warm and smelled of freshly baked bread.

'Come you in, little maid.' Alice was a tiny, birdlike woman with grey-streaked-black hair scraped high on her head and secured by a snowy cap that matched the apron covering her voluminous skirts. She fussed round Abigail. 'I've laid out your moleskins on the bed upstairs. Will you hev a bite to eat 'afore you go off?'

'Oh yes, please, Alice. Can I have a slice of your delicious bread and dripping?'

''Course you can, my dear. I'll make it ready while you go and get yerself changed. Josh has gone down to make the boat ready. He says he'll be about twenty minutes, so you've got time.'

Abigail went up the narrow stairs to the bedroom under the eaves where the big double bed was covered by a counterpane as white as Alice's apron. For all Josh was a fisherman there was no hint of fish smells in the spotless little cottage. She stepped out of her full skirts and undid the tight laced stays. Then she put on the white frilled shirt, the woollen guernsey Alice had knitted her and the moleskin trousers she had skilfully cut down to fit from a pair of Josh's that he had scarcely worn, swearing to Abigail that they had never been big enough for him anyway. Abbie pushed her hair up into the cheese cutter cap that completed her outfit and went downstairs.

'Mercy me, Missy, you don't look a day older than the little 'prentice cabin boys they get from the poor house,' Alice remarked with a smile as she handed Abigail a slice of bread and dripping.

'Well, I am older, Alice,' Abigail laughed. 'A good deal older. Mm, this dripping's delicious. Some of those little lads are barely twelve years old when they're taken to sea.'

'An' they ain't all treated as well as my Josh treats young Charlie, neither.' Alice became serious. 'Thass cruel the things that happen to some of 'em. Ony last week my Josh was tellin' me about a young lad got washed overboard off one of the smacks.'

'Did they manage to pick him up all right?' Abigail asked anxiously.

'Pick 'im up? I doubt they even bothered to turn the boat round to look for 'im. Plenty more boys where 'e come from is what they'd say.' Alice sniffed disapprovingly. 'I don't hold with sech goins on, meself. Them little boys have got as much right to live as anyone else and they oughta be looked after better than that.' She glanced at the clock ticking on the wall. 'But I mustn't keep you, Missy. Josh'll be waiting to get away. An' thass a lovely day for a trip on the river an' no mistake. Here's your boots, now. Do they still fit?'

Abigail eased her feet into the heavy leather sea boots Josh had acquired for her and that were not much too big. She clumped round the kitchen a few times. 'Yes, they fit as well as they ever did, Alice,' she said with a laugh. 'They just feel a bit strange after all this time, that's all.'

Alice watched as Abigail went off down the road to Josh. She was a lovely natured girl and no mistake. And to think that their Emily might have been just such a one by now . . . and the same age, too. She stood for a moment, lost in her thoughts, then, visibly pulling herself together, with another sniff and a lift of her head she hurried indoors.

It was a perfect day. A faint haze over the water promised heat, yet there was enough breeze to fill the sails and drive the *Edith* smoothly down river. There was no sound but the creak of the boards and the straining ropes and the constant chuckle of the water as they ploughed along, the bow gently lifting and dipping on the waves.

Abigail perched herself on a coil of rope in the bow and gave herself up to enjoyment of the day. There was nothing for her to do but drink in the beauty of the scene and the glory of her beloved river whilst Josh and his mate Dibby Harris, helped by little Charlie, did all that was necessary. This was a day to herself. She turned her face to the sun, determined to savour every moment of it.

The trees and fields were fresh and green as they rose away from the river bank and as the boat rounded a bend in the river the tiny cluster of houses dominated by the pepper-pot church, so named from its shape, heralded the village of Rowhedge. A little further on, on the other bank was the busy quayside of Wivenhoe, with its row of elegant little Georgian houses, and behind them the square tower of the church. After that flat saltings with fields and hedges behind them stretched out like a gently sloping carpet as the river widened, busy with smacks, barges from London, colliers from Newcastle, and the packet that sailed twice a week to the continent. The river was always the same, yet always changing, always interesting.

When lunchtime came they went below and Dibby served up a thick stew with chunks of bread and black tea nearly as thick as the stew. They sat round in the cabin, stuffy from the heat of the stove and the mingled smell of fish, stew, tobacco and bodies, and ate their fill. To Abigail it tasted as good as anything she had ever eaten and she held out her tin dish for more.

'What would my sister Pearl say if she could see me now!' she laughed.

'I don't think you need to worry, Miss Abigail,' Dibby said, handing her another chunk of bread. 'I doubt she'd even know it was you.'

Charlie, wide-eyed, sat in his corner, the saucepan lid holding his stew clenched between his knees by the handle, and said nothing. He'd never seen a real lady dressed up in such a way before. In fact, he'd never been in such close company with a real lady.

'Come on, Charlie, look slippy. Get that stew down you, we've got to look at the layins before we go back,' Josh said, not unkindly. He ruffled the boy's curly head and climbed back up on deck followed by the others. Abigail took up her position in the bow again. She didn't want to get in the way and be told it wouldn't be convenient for her to come again. Added to that, she could see Matthew's boat *Conquest* in the distance. She was watching the way *Conquest* was being handled, the big mainsail and the jib goose-winged to make the best of a following wind, when suddenly she became aware of a flurry of activity on the *Edith*.

'Put 'er about, Dibby. Thass that old submerged wreck we're comin' up on,' Josh shouted. 'Pull 'er round, quick, 'afore she get tangled up. Thass time they shoved a wreck buoy there.'

Thass no good, gaffer.' As Dibby put the tiller over there was an ominous splintering of wood. With a muffled oath he leaned over the stern. 'Thass the rudder. Thass got caught an' sheered the pintle right off,' he called. 'Get the sails down, quick.'

When the sails were roughly stowed Josh joined Dibby. 'Thass done it!' he said, after examining the damage. 'We'll hev to get her into Brightlingsea as best we can. It'd take a month o' Sundays to nurse 'er up the river like this. That'll be bad enough gettin' 'er as far as Brightlingsea.'

Abigail paled as she heard this. She made her way aft to the two men. 'How long will it take?' she asked anxiously.

Josh shook his head. 'Coupla days, perhaps. Might get her done tomorrow, if we're lucky. That was a nasty crack. The rudder must have caught in one of the ribs on the old wreck.' He frowned impatiently. 'I should've realized we were that close. Thass a bit o' bad, that happening.'

Abigail was silent for a moment. Josh had enough to worry about. But she was desperately worried, too.

'Josh,' she said, 'what am I going to do? I *must* get back. If I'm not back for my father's dinner party tonight he'll . . . I don't know what he'll do, but he'll never forgive me. And he won't let me come out with you again. Ever. I'm sure of that.'

Josh turned preoccupied eyes on Abigail. That was another problem. He and Dibby and Charlie would sleep on the boat, but that wouldn't do for the little maid. He scratched his head, half his mind on the *Edith* and half on Abigail.

'Get an oar out of the dinghy, Dibby. Fix it up as a rudder as best you can. That'll fetch us across to Brightlingsea,' he said absentmindedly, his eyes still on Abigail. 'I don't know, Missy, I jest don't know what we're gonna do about you . . . '

'You in trouble, Uncle?' It was Matthew. The *Conquest* had come up on them and was standing off quite close. 'Can I help?'

'No, boy, thass our rudder. We're makin' for Brightlingsea,' Josh shouted. Then his face cleared. 'But yes, hold you on a minute. You bound for Colchester?'

'That's right.'

'Can you take a passenger?'

'Yes. I'll come alongside.'

Josh heaved a sigh of relief. 'There you are, Missy, Matt'll get you back,' he said, glad to have at least one of his problems solved.

Matthew brought *Conquest* alongside as near as he could but Abigail had to jump across from one boat to the other. It wasn't far and Matthew caught her as she landed, preventing her from losing her balance.

'Why, Miss Abigail!' he said as he released her, his face a picture of surprise and embarrassment, 'I never . . . I didn't realize it was you.'

She flushed. 'I haven't been down the river with Josh for a long time now,' she said, talking quickly to cover her own embarrassment. 'And this would happen on the night my father has guests coming to dinner. I thought I'd be back easily . . . he doesn't know I've come, you see. He'd be furious . . . '

Matthew looked up at the sails. 'Winds died a bit now, I'm afraid. But we'll get you back as soon as we can.' He smiled at Abigail, his teeth showing brilliant white in his brown face, and shouted directions to Tolley, the old man who was mate aboard *Conquest*. 'Just you make yourself comfortable over there on that heap of nets, Miss Abigail, and don't worry, we'll do the best we can.' He smiled again. 'That was one reason why I was so surprised to see you, Miss Abigail,' he said, skilfully handling both tiller and sheets, 'I knew there were guests at your father's house tonight. My mother's been called in.'

Abigail nodded. 'Yes, of course.' Sarah Bateman, Matthew's mother, was often called in to wait on table when the Chiswells had guests. She had been in service before her marriage and was glad to earn a little money by helping out when any of the gentry needed extra hands. Sarah had had a hard life, widowed when Matthew was a baby, and as well as working in the kitchen and dining room she went laundering in the big houses. Yet she retained a quiet dignity, learned no doubt from the years she had spent at Renbow Hall before her marriage, that set her apart from others of her station in life. She had brought Matthew up, practically single-handed, to be courteous and well mannered, and had been careful to see that his speech was correct. Abigail had learned all this from Alice. Sarah was Josh's sister and he was very fond of her – although privately, as Alice confided to Abigail, Josh felt that Sarah tried to be a little above herself.

It took a long time, longer even than Matthew had anticipated, to get back to Colchester. Instead of arriving back at five o'clock as Josh had promised, it was well past six as they drew near to Hythe Quay. Abigail hadn't minded. There was nothing she could do, so she had given herself up to the luxury of studying Matthew as he worked the boat, sailing it to get the best possible speed out of what wind there was. He was twenty-seven, three years her senior, but he looked older. Out in all weathers, his face was lined, especially round his brown eyes, where they crinkled against the sun's glare and his jaw, under curly whiskers, had a stubborn set to it. She watched the muscles on his bare arms rippling as he hauled on the sheets. They had grown up together, eating bread and dripping in Alice's kitchen, playing on the *Edith* under Josh's eagle eye, when they were children, unaware and uncaring of the difference in their stations. It was only as they grew up that the gulf had opened up, leaving them awkward in each other's company and almost as far apart as it was possible to be. And nobody knew, nobody must ever know, just how much she still loved him.

Matthew tied up the boat and gave his hand to Abigail to assist her along the gangplank. The tide was full now and it was quite a sharp descent to the quay. She realized with dismay that she must look like nothing more than a ragamuffin to Matthew in her cut-down moleskins and too-big boots. But she summoned what dignity she could and, careful to keep her voice cool lest he should get even the slightest inkling of her secret, thanked him for his help.

'It's been a pleasure, Miss Abigail,' he said formally, lifting his cap and replacing it on his black curls at its usual rakish angle.

She left him and hurried off along the quay to Spurgeon Street, to change and tell Alice of the mishap that would keep Josh at Brightlingsea at least for tonight.

As she passed Chiswell and Sons' warehouse she automatically glanced up at the window of the office and was surprised to see a figure in black step back into the shadows. Her father! She drew in her breath sharply. Surely he hadn't been watching for her and witnessed her late return! And with Matthew, too!

She began to walk a little faster.

'I'm dreadfully late, Daisy,' she said breathlessly, as twenty minutes later she slipped into the house through the kitchens. 'Is everything in order?'

'Everything's goin' fine, Miss Abbie,' Daisy said, although

from the bustle going on all round her the kitchen looked like some steaming inferno. 'Don't you worry about a thing. Sarah's here now an' she's puttin' the finishin' touches to the table with Ellen. Hetty, are them taters ready yet?'

'Comin', Daisy. I've nearly finished 'em,' Hetty called from the scullery behind the kitchen.

There was a clatter on the stairs and Ellen appeared. 'Daisy, when Miss Abbie gets back, the master ... ' She saw Abigail. 'Oh, Miss Abbie,' she bobbed, 'The master wants to see you in his study. He's fairly ... '

'Ellen!' rapped Daisy, 'mind what you're sayin'.'

'Thank you, Ellen,' Abigail went to the stairs. 'Oh, and will you get Hetty to bring hot water to my room, please,' she called back over her shoulder.

'Yes, Miss Abbie,' Ellen called back, adding under her breath to Daisy, 'and he's in a right old temper, too.'

Abigail hurried along the hall from the servants' stairs to her father's study near the front door.

'Come!' His habitual reply to her knock had a hard, impatient ring to it. He was standing at the window and swung round as she entered. 'And what's the meaning of this, Madam?' he asked, his gaze taking in her still slightly dishevelled appearance. 'How dare you go off for the day when you were needed here to supervise my dinner party?'

Abigail lifted her chin. 'I made sure that everything was under control before I went. But unfortunately, today was the only day Josh could take me, Papa.'

'Don't lie to me, girl. Don't try to tell me you've been with Josh. You've been with that young Bateman. I saw you return on his boat. If it were not for this dinner party tonight I'd confine you to your room for a week. You're nothing more than a ... '

'I have *not* been with Matthew,' Abigail retorted hotly, her temper rising. 'I went with Josh, as I said. You know very well he sometimes takes me with him. The pintle on the rudder broke and he's had to put in to Brightlingsea. It was a good thing Matthew was just coming up river and could bring me with him so I wouldn't be late.'

'Wouldn't be late!' Henry pulled out his gold hunter and tapped it. 'And what time do you call this, might I ask? Supposing there had been some last-minute hitch in the arrangements here? You walk in barely an hour before my guests are due and have the effrontery to say you're not late!'

'I made quite sure there would be no hitch before I left.' Abigail's voice was rising to match her father's. 'And I've already seen Daisy. She assures me that everything is going smoothly. You seem to forget, Papa, I have organized your dinner parties for a long time, now, ever since Mama became ill, in fact. I do know what I'm doing!'

Henry shoved his watch back into his pocket irritably. 'That doesn't alter the fact that you were on young Bateman's boat,' he said, glowering at her. 'I won't have you consorting with the likes of him.' Matthew sailed his grandfather's boat and old Zac Bateman from Brightlingsea was Henry's arch enemy.

'You're glad enough to have Matthew's mother in to wait at table,' Abigail reminded him, stung even further by his attack on Matthew.

'Enough, Madam!' Henry roared. 'I will not be spoken to in that fashion by my own daughter. Remember your manners!' He quietened. 'And see to it that when you appear at my table you are improved in temper as well as appearance. You look little better than a fishwife with your face like a beetroot and your hair like a bird's nest.'

'When you give me leave to go I shall attend to it,' Abigail said smoothly. 'I already have water waiting in my room, and growing colder by the minute, no doubt.'

'Then perhaps it will serve to cool your temper, too, my girl. Go now, and make sure you don't disgrace me tonight.'

Abigail left him, careful to close the door quietly although she was hard put to it not to slam it so hard that all the windows in the house would shake.

Henry sat at his desk, gazing at the portrait of his wife. Edith had been a fiery one, too, but he'd known how to tame *her*, once he'd got her into the bedroom. Maybe a man was what young Abigail needed. He pushed the thought round in his head. He couldn't think of any man who would want such a bad-tempered, whey-faced creature, competent and hard-working though she was. Come to that he didn't relish her being competent and hard-working in another man's establishment, he needed her efforts to be in his direction. He would never find anyone else who would work so hard for little more than her keep. Nonetheless, it was marriage and only marriage that would tame her. To the right man, of course ...

As good as her word, Abigail appeared in good time to greet the guests with her father, freshly bathed and dressed in the lilac silk with a spray of violets at the neck, her hair smoothly parted and brushed into two thick and shining coils about her ears, and her face gently sunburned, giving her the colour she usually lacked. There was no hint in her manner of the fiery altercation of less than an hour ago.

The dinner party progressed smoothly. Abigail had played hostess to her father enough times to know precisely how to behave, summoning the servants to serve and clear at exactly the right moment and deferring to her father exactly as she should – not too little, nor yet too much.

Ellen, with Sarah's help, hovered discreetly. The two women worked well together but somehow Abigail was not happy at having Matthew's mother acting as a servant. Sarah had a dignity and an air that somehow transcended her position. It was as if she had been born to better things, although Abigail knew from Alice that she and Josh had come from ordinary fisher folk.

As the dessert was brought in Abigail watched Pearl. Seated halfway down the table she had spent the entire meal flirting gently with Captain Griffiths, the young army officer, engaging in the dangerous game of playing him off against his subordinate, Lieutenant Barraclough. Both men appeared equally besotted by her attentions, Abigail noticed with faint irritation. Couldn't they see she was only playing the coquette? Sometimes she worried about Pearl. It would be a good thing when she was safely married.

Henry too was watching Pearl, but with fond eyes, proud of her beauty. He sighed indulgently. It was always the same, men flocked round her like bees round a honey-pot; that was the reason he always made sure that he included a couple of young, single men in his guest list. Not that he was in any hurry to see his beloved married, but he liked to make sure she enjoyed herself. He smiled as he caught her eye and flushed a little as she blew him a little kiss.

Slightly embarrassed he turned his attention to Edwin. He seemed to be engaged in a fairly heated discussion across the table with Alderman Blackwell.

'But those houses should never have been built, Alderman,' he was saying.

'Rubbish, my boy. The town must expand or it will wither and die,' the alderman said good-humouredly.

'The town will die, anyway, if the water system isn't improved,' Edwin insisted.

'It needs expanding, I'll grant you that,' the alderman agreed. He had wined and dined well and was in no mood for serious discussion.

'It needs *improving*. You must know that the cesspits from those new houses in St Mary's Terrace contaminate the Chiswell Meadow water supply.'

Henry cleared his throat warningly in Edwin's direction. Such talk was totally unfit for the dinner table, particularly with ladies present.

Alderman Blackwell took the hint. He was grateful for Henry's intervention, particularly since he had just bought one of the new houses.

Fortunately, at that moment the port was brought and the ladies retired to the drawing room, leaving Henry to steer the conversation on to the less dangerous but no less controversial subject of the new railway line at present being built between London and Colchester.

Much later, when all the guests were gone, Henry went to his study to enjoy a final glass of whisky before retiring for the night. Despite the altercation with Abigail beforehand, and Edwin's introduction of the indelicate subject of the town's drainage, the dinner party had gone surprisingly well. He sighed. Sometimes, he felt that his two elder children were becoming far too wayward and self-opinionated for their own good. It was fortunate that Pearl, his beautiful, favourite, last-born child, caused him no worries. For that, at least, he was thankful.

# *Chapter Four*

Abigail stood for a moment at the window of the office, watching the activity on the quay. Next week the oyster season would be opened and Josh and Dibby, with Charlie's help, were busily scrubbing and cleaning the *Edith* ready for the event. Then she would be dressed overall before the mayor and all the local dignitaries boarded her for the annual journey down the river to the oyster beds. Abigail wished she could go with them. Edwin went most years and he said it was quite a ceremony, with proclamations being read and gin and gingerbread handed round.

'Why gin and gingerbread?' she had asked, anxious to know all about it.

'I think it's some old wives' tale about gin helping to counteract the ill effects oysters might have on some people.'

'And the gingerbread?'

He'd grinned. 'Goes well with the gin, I suppose. It's very nice, anyway.'

She sighed at the memory of that conversation and turned back to her desk. Autumn was such a lovely time of year for a trip down the river, with the woods stretching away turning all shades of red and yellow and the fields golden with stubble. But there was no chance of persuading her father to let her go with him. Places were strictly allocated. The boat would be full.

Ezra gave his apologetic cough. It usually heralded some remark and Abigail looked up, questioningly, but he was bent over his desk and said nothing.

She studied him with what almost amounted to distaste, although she couldn't decide why. He was neat and clean, and tidy to the point of fastidiousness. She remembered his wife dying giving birth to a stillborn child some three years ago and recalled that he had taken the event stoically, unemotionally, and had continued just as before, with the exception that he now lived alone in his cottage in Charles Place. She wondered fleetingly if Ezra Carver had any real feelings. She rather suspected he hadn't. She felt ashamed because she had never liked him much; and then guilty because he had never given her any reason either to like or to dislike him.

'Do you know where Edwin is, Ezra?' she asked, in an effort to be pleasant.

Again the cough. 'I believe he's gone to see the editor of the *Essex Standard*, Miss Abigail. He said he wouldn't be very long.' Cough. 'That was an hour and a half ago.'

'Oh, well, I'll just have a look at his desk. It looks as if it could do with a bit of tidying and I've finished what I came to do. I might be able to . . . '

At that moment the door burst open and Edwin almost fell in. 'He's taking it!' he shouted. 'The editor of the *Essex Standard* is taking the article I've written.' He pulled Abigail to her feet and began to dance round the office with her in a mad polka.

'Oh, Eddie, I'm so pleased for you,' Abigail said, breathless from his cavorting. 'But put me down, do. Papa . . . '

The door opened again. 'What in the name of thunder is all this noise about!' Henry stood glowering on the threshold.

Abigail patted her hair and smoothed her skirt. 'Edwin has had an article accepted by the *Essex Standard*,' she said proudly. 'Isn't it wonderful, Papa?'

Henry glared at Abigail. 'Wonderful? It'd be a damn sight more wonderful if he put in an honest day's work at his desk!' He turned to Edwin. 'And as for you, Sir. I'll thank you to pay attention to the business. *My* business! *Our* business! What will one day be *your* business if you haven't thrown all I've worked for down the drain with your confounded incompetence by that time!'

'But, Papa . . . ' Abigail began.

'Don't you "Papa" me. You only encourage him in his idleness if you praise him for wasting his time scribbling. Writing for the local rag, indeed. There's some merit in that, I *don't* think.' Henry went out and slammed the door. Then he opened it again. 'Have the new oyster barrels arrived yet?' he snapped.

Edwin went to his desk. 'No, Guv'nor, not yet. But I have the estimates here, somewhere.' He riffled unsuccessfully through the mound of papers on his desk.

'You mean they haven't been ordered yet?' Henry went over and snatched the sheaf of papers that Abigail had surreptitiously handed to her brother.

'Well, you see, Guv'nor, that new firm was cheaper but I wasn't too sure about the quality. And since we've always dealt with Brown's . . . I was going to consult you . . . ' His voice tailed off.

'Then why didn't you, in heaven's name?' Henry jabbed at a letter in his hand. 'This letter is dated the twenty-first of April, and this one the seventh of May. It's now the end of August! God knows you've had enough time!'

Edwin blushed. 'I'm afraid it just slipped my mind, Guv'nor.'

Henry was studying the letters. At Edwin's confession he glanced up and gave him a look of withering contempt. 'Stick with Brown's,' Henry commanded after a moment's further study. 'They're not much more expensive, we know we can rely on them and – more to the point – they'll deliver in a hurry. You'd better go and see them. Now! Order a hundred barrels and fifty half barrels. That'll do for a start.' He thrust the letters back at Edwin and stalked out.

'I'll tidy your desk while you're gone, Eddie,' Abigail promised. 'Just to make sure nothing else has been overlooked.'

Edwin kissed her. 'You're a good sort, Abbie.' He made a face. 'But I do think the guv'nor might have said he was pleased I'd had something accepted for publication,' he grumbled, reaching for his hat.

'He probably would have done if he hadn't known that you'd been neglecting your work here in order to do it,' Abigail chided.

'Oh, well, I might not be here for much longer.' Edwin refused to be downcast for long. He put on his hat and with a cheerful smile gave the crown a smart tap. 'You never know, I may be offered a job on the *Essex Standard* before long.' He winked at her. 'The editor has a *very* nice-looking daughter, too.' He went off down the stairs, whistling.

Ezra coughed. 'He's a very clever young man, our Mr Edwin,' he said. 'Not many people can write for the newspapers. You must be very proud of him, Miss Abigail.'

'Oh, I'm proud of him all right, Ezra,' Abigail said, but her reply was tinged with exasperation. 'I just wish he would make at least *some* pretence of being interested in Chiswell and Son. I help him out as much as I can; I go through his desk to make sure nothing's been overlooked; but he leaves everything in such a shambles that it's no wonder the barrels got missed.' She sighed deeply. 'I should have realized they hadn't arrived, and looked into it.'

'You can't be expected to be behind Mr Edwin all the time, Miss Abigail. It seems to me, if you'll pardon my saying so, that you have quite enough to do without that.' It was a long speech for Ezra and he accompanied it with what, for him, passed as a smile, and finished it with his usual cough.

'You're probably right, Ezra,' Abigail answered absent-mindedly. She was hardly listening, because she had already uncovered a letter that should have been dealt with a month ago.

'I thought it would be nice if you accompanied us this year, my dear.' Henry carefully selected the choicest pieces of roast beef and put them onto Pearl's plate. He handed it to her with the smile he reserved specially for her.

'Me, Papa? On a boat? To the opening of the oyster season?' Pearl looked at him in horror. 'Oh, no thank you. I hate the water. It's cold and it's wet.'

'Nobody's asking you to swim in it,' Abigail said, a trifle acidly, helping herself to vegetables, and trying, unsuccessfully, not to feel jealous that Pearl should have been asked and not her.

'I still don't want to go, thank you very much, Papa.' Pearl shook her golden curls, quite definite in her refusal. 'Take Abbie. She loves boats – nasty, smelly things that they are.'

Henry was disappointed. He had been looking forward to parading his lovely daughter in front of the assembled guests.

'Edwin will be there,' he said encouragingly.

'Good for Eddie. I hope he enjoys it.' Rather inelegantly, Pearl speared a potato from the vegetable dish onto her plate.

'I've reserved a place for you.' Pearl was the only one of his children Henry was ever prepared to plead with. But it cut no ice this time.

'All the more reason to take Abbie. She'll love it. I'd hate it.

Anyway, she knows far more about oysters than I do. I don't even like them.'

'Pearl is right, Papa,' Abigail said. 'And I should very much like to come with you. I've never been to the opening of the oyster season.' She tried to speak pleasantly, to pretend not to notice that she had been passed over in favour of her younger sister. But there was no mistaking the resignation on her father's face as he said, 'Oh, very well. If Pearl won't come I suppose you might as well.'

'Thank you, Papa.' Abigail inclined her head graciously, accepting what she knew was no more than her rightful due, however grudgingly her father had bestowed it. 'I shall look forward to it.'

'Well, mind and dress suitably for it, then,' Henry growled. 'I don't want you disgracing me by turning up dressed like some pauper cabin boy.'

Abigail recognized the reference to her trip with Josh and realized that she had still not been forgiven. 'I shall not disgrace you, Papa,' she said quietly.

Henry looked at Edwin's empty chair. 'He's late,' he remarked, changing the subject. 'He knows luncheon is at one o'clock.'

'Oh, I forgot to say. Eddie told me he might be a little late. He's gone to see Mr Gosling at the *Essex Standard*,' Pearl said.

'Hm. If he paid as much attention to his work at the office of Chiswell and Son as he does to the *Essex Standard* office; the business might run a little more smoothly,' Henry remarked, dabbing his whiskers with his napkin.

'Speak of Lucifer and see his horns. I heard my name mentioned.' Edwin came into the room and took his place at the table. 'I'm sorry I'm late, but –' With a flourish he produced a copy of the *Essex Standard*. 'I waited for this. Hot off the press, as you might say.'

'Oh, Eddie, has it got your article in it?' Pearl clapped her hands in excitement.

'Yes, it has. And you shall all read it. Would you like to read what I've written about the town's water supply, Guv'nor?' he offered the paper to Henry.

'Not until we've finished luncheon.' Henry waved it away.

Abigail would dearly have loved to pick it up and read it then and there, but she knew she would have to contain herself until her father had read it. But throughout the rest of the meal she tried, unsuccessfully, to get a glimpse of her brother's prose.

Henry was not so impatient. He waited until the meal was finished and Ellen had cleared the table. Then he moved to an armchair with his coffee and took the paper. 'I hope you haven't been stirring up a hornets' nest, Sir. Remember, I'm a Channel and Paving Commissioner. If you go raking up things you shouldn't it'll jeopardize my standing with them,' he said, frowning.

'I've only said what needs to be said,' Edwin replied cheerfully.

'But did you say it *tactfully*, Eddie?' Abigail asked, smiling at her brother.

Edwin shrugged. 'How can you say tactfully that the brook running through Knaves Acre allotments, and which some of the poor still draw their drinking water from, is so full of filth and sewage that the allotment holders dam it and spread it on their garden for fertilizer?'

'Oh, Edwin!' Pearl held her handkerchief to her nose. 'How can you speak of such dreadful things?'

'Because they are true, and because if nobody speaks about them nothing will be done to improve them,' he said, quite unabashed.

Henry lowered the paper. 'This is rubbish,' he said, tapping it with his finger. 'Why didn't you point out that most of the town has piped water? Colchester can be proud of its waterworks. People aren't forced to draw their water from the brook. There are stand pipes and pumps for those who don't have cisterns in their own houses. If poor folk are too idle . . . '

'Oh, come on, Guv'nor. You know very well that most of the town hasn't got piped water. It's only the rich that have cisterns. And over half the town pumps are closed now through pollution. I've been digging into history a bit. Did you know that when the army barracked on the Abbey Fields, the effluent from the camp got into the drinking water at Hythe?'

'But things like that don't happen now, Eddie, do they?' Abbie asked anxiously. 'After all, this is eighteen forty. Things are different now.'

'Not as different as you might think,' Edwin insisted.

Henry threw down the paper. 'The Commissioners are doing a very good job. But we shan't be helped by radical young puppies like you stirring up muddy water simply in order to get your name in print. The sooner you stop this ridiculous journalism nonsense and get down to some useful work the better, sir. You'll have me the laughing stock of the Commissioners if you don't stop this damn silly business. I won't have it.' He thumped his fist on the arm of his chair. 'Do you hear me? I won't have it!' He got up and went over to the bell pull, tugging it so hard that he nearly wrenched it off. 'I have an appointment this afternoon. I trust you will give your *full* attention to anything that crops up at the office, sir.' He turned to Hetty, who had answered the summons. 'Tell Wilfred to have the chaise ready in a quarter of an hour.'

Abigail dressed carefully for the opening of the oyster season, determined that her father should be proud of her. Edwin had already told her that it was an occasion of great ceremony and that everyone who attended was, as he put it, 'dressed up to the nines. Especially the ladies, although there aren't usually many of those'.

She chose her best blue taffeta; it was an attractive blue that set off the rich auburn of her hair and gave her pale complexion a creamy transparency. She fastened her bonnet, a darker shade of the same colour, with ribbons that exactly matched the dress. She knew she could never hope to be even half as beautiful as Pearl, nevertheless she was not displeased with her appearance. She picked up her gloves and parasol and went to join her father and brother.

Henry made no comment when she appeared, except to say that she had taken her time getting ready, but Edwin looked at her admiringly.

'My, Abbie, you look absolutely topping. Here, take my arm. All the chaps'll be envious when they see us board the boat.'

Abigail made a face at him, refusing to take him seriously. She was under no illusions regarding her looks. But she couldn't help feeling pleased at his words and her step was light as they made their way down the hill.

'Mr Young will be there today. He's the editor of the *Essex Standard*,' Edwin told her as they walked. 'And I'm hoping he'll bring his daughter with him. Oh, Miss Belinda's a topper, Abbie, a regular topper. You wait till you see her.'

The *Edith* was dressed overall and gay with bunting. Josh and Dibby were dressed in their best guernseys, with *Edith* embroidered in a curve across the fronts. Even Charlie had a new woollen cap for the occasion.

The mayor and the town clerk, in their official regalia, the Commissioners and members of the town council all boarded the boat and were greeted by Henry. More guests were travelling to

Brightlingsea by coach; they would be taken across in small boats to the *Edith* when she was moored in Pyefleet Creek, where the ceremony would take place.

Edwin pointed out Mr Young to Abigail, but to his disappointment Belinda wasn't there. 'She did have a slight cold when I saw her yesterday,' he said gloomily, 'so I suppose she thought it wiser not to come.'

Abigail smiled at him. 'It will give you an excuse to call on her, Eddie. Take her some flowers tomorrow and ask after her health.'

He brightened immediately. 'By jove, that's a . . . '

'Topping idea?' Abigail said mischievously.

'A very good idea,' he grinned. Abigail left him and went to the bow of the boat, where she could give herself up to enjoying the trip down river on this warm, sunny September day. She could hear the constant babble of voices from behind her and a burst of masculine laughter now and then. Apart from the mayor's wife, who refused to leave his side, she was the only woman aboard, but it didn't trouble her. She gazed at the patchwork of fields as they passed, some yellow with stubble, some dark brown from early ploughing, some green pastureland dotted with brown and white cows. Between the fields, hedges and copses were brilliant with the reds and yellows of autumn leaves. Abigail loved the fresh greens of spring but she loved the bright colours of autumn even more; she knew every twist and bend of the river, but the view was always different, always changing.

After Abigail had left with Edwin and her father, Pearl gave up all pretence of being industrious and went back to bed till luncheon. After she had eaten her solitary meal she returned to her bedroom and put on her new afternoon dress of sprigged muslin. She rearranged her ringlets carefully and surveyed herself critically in the mirror. She could find no fault. With a little secret smile she went downstairs to the morning room and picked up a magazine, every now and then glancing at the clock on the mantel.

At precisely three o'clock the big front doorbell jangled.

A few moments later a worried-looking Ellen appeared. 'Oh, Miss Pearl. There's a Lieutenant Barraclough called to see the master. I told 'im 'e was out but 'e said 'e'd wait. I don't know what to do, Miss Pearl. The master won't be back for a long time, will 'e?'

Pearl pinched her lip, as if undecided what to do. Then she said, 'I suppose I'd better see him, Ellen . . . '

Ellen looked horrified. 'But, Miss Pearl, that wouldn't be right . . . I mean . . . '

Pearl laughed. 'Don't be a goose, Ellen, of course it'll be all right.' She glanced round the morning room; it had a comfortable, lived-in look. 'You'd better show him into the drawing room. I'll be along in a minute. I wonder what he wants?'

Ellen left and Pearl got up and looked at her reflection in the overmantel. Yes, very pleasing. Without haste she went along to the drawing room.

'Ah, Lieutenant Barraclough, how nice to see you.' She extended her hand. 'All right, Ellen, you may go,' she said to the maid, still hovering uncertainly near the door. 'I'll ring if I need anything.'

'But, Miss Pearl, it's not . . . '

'I said you may go!' Pearl turned sharply on Ellen.

Ellen bobbed. 'Very good, Miss Pearl.' The door closed behind her.

Pearl went across to Lieutenant Barraclough and held out her arms. 'There you are, Bertie,' she laughed. 'I told you it would be easy.'

*

The *Edith* was crowded. Too crowded. Two boatloads of people had been brought across from Brightlingsea for the opening of the season ceremony and some of them had spent their waiting time in the Rising Sun and were already the worse for drink. It wasn't long before Abigail found herself parted from Edwin and jostled to the edge of the crowd. It didn't worry her; in fact, she was glad to be where she could breathe the fresh air and watch the oyster boats, smacks and skiffs, all bedecked with flags, which had come to be a part of the ancient ceremony. She saw Matthew, in a small skiff today, nipping nimbly in and out among the bigger boats. He had an old man with him – his grandfather, Abigail guessed – a wizened figure with a face like a bewhiskered pickled walnut. He was obviously enjoying himself, calling greetings to all and sundry, a clay pipe clamped between his toothless gums. Even the wheeling gulls and screaming cormorants seemed to recognize that this was a day of some importance. As the little skiff passed, Abigail waved to Matthew and he smiled back.

There was more jostling as space had to be made for the town clerk to read the proclamation, and Abigail was pushed even further back. She stood on a coil of rope and craned her neck but still all she could see was the top of the town clerk's black hat as he read the ancient proclamation which opened the oyster fishing season. She couldn't hear the words, but suddenly the town sergeant shouted, 'God save the Queen, the Mayor and this Corporation!' A great cheer went up from the boats all around and hats were flung in the air. The man standing nearest to Abigail was more than a little drunk and nearly threw his hat into the river, lurching against her as he reached over to catch it.

She was never sure what happened next, she thought she must have lost her footing on the coil of rope and overbalanced. She put out her hand to save herself but there was nothing to hold onto and she found herself falling. Her last coherent thought was: 'I shall drown'.

She nearly did. Her voluminous skirts and petticoats acted as a balloon for a few seconds, holding her up. But then as they soaked up the water they became heavy and began to sink, dragging her down with them. She heard a lot of shouting going on and then only the rushing of the river. As the water closed over her head she managed to fling up an arm. Suddenly, she felt it grasped in a firm hand and she thought she would be torn in half as the river dragged her down and the hand that would not let her go pulled her, up and up. Her waterlogged skirts were so heavy that she was certain that her arm was being wrenched out of its socket but still she was dragged up. Then an arm reached down and caught her under the arms and she was hauled, choking, over the side and into a boat, to lie in a half-dead, bedraggled heap in the bottom.

'That was a smart bit o' work, Matt, me boy,' the old man said. 'A few seconds more an' you'd never have saved 'er. Better get her across to Bright'n'sea, you can't put 'er back aboard the *Edith*.' He shifted his position and took the oars. 'Who is she, anyway?'

'She's Miss Abigail Chiswell, Henry Chiswell's daughter.' Matthew raised Abigail to a sitting position. 'Can you breathe, Miss Abbie?' he asked.

Abigail spluttered once or twice and he thumped her on the back. 'Is that better?'

She spluttered again. 'Yes, I think I'm all right, thank you.'

Old Zac's face darkened. 'Henry Chiswell's daughter? What did you wanta bother with savin' 'er for? Chuck her back in. We don't want any truck with the likes o' the Chiswells.'

Matthew grinned at Abigail. 'Don't take any notice of Grandad. He doesn't mean it.' He relieved Old Zac of the oars.

'Miss Abigail's never done you any harm, Grandad. Anyway, Grannie'll look after her.'

Old Zac grunted and resumed his seat in the stern.

Abigail tried to sit up. 'I'm sorry if I've caused a lot of trouble. I think I must have lost my footing.'

'You were knocked overboard,' Matt said. 'I saw it happen. And now look at them all. They can see you're not drowned so the excitement's over and they've lost interest. All they can think about is getting their share of the gin and gingerbread.'

That was not strictly true. Edwin, separated from his sister and now some distance away, hadn't realized what had happened at first. Then it took him several minutes to push his way to the side of the boat. He leaned over.

'Is she all right, Bateman? What happened?' he called anxiously.

'She was knocked over the side, sir. I saw it happen,' Matthew shouted back. 'But she'll be all right. No bones broken. With your leave, sir, we'll take her back to Brightlingsea. My grannie will look after her.'

'Thank you, Bateman. I'm grateful. Yes, I'm sure that would be the best thing. The sooner she can get out of those wet clothes the better.'

'My missus'll see she don't take no harm,' the old man said, a trifle grudgingly, his prejudice against the Chiswells battling with his innate consideration for his fellows. 'Good job thass a bright day, or she'd 'a ketched 'er death o' cold.'

Abigail sat shivering in the bottom of the boat. She wasn't convinced that even on such a bright day she wouldn't die of cold. She didn't think she would ever be warm again. The heavy petticoats under the blue taffeta clung wetly round her legs and somewhere she had lost a boot. She put her hand up to her head.

Her bonnet had gone, too. She remembered how much trouble she had taken over her appearance only a few hours ago and thought of the sorry spectacle she must present now. It was humiliating. Her father would never forgive her for disgracing him in such a manner. Tears rolled down her cheeks and mingled with the rivulets still draining out of her hair.

Martha Bateman was sitting outside her front door picking shrimps while chatting with her neighbour. When she saw Matthew approaching with a half-drowned object in his arms she nearly dropped her basin.

'Mercy me, what's all this?' she cried.

Old Zac was behind Matthew, rolling along as fast as his short, bandy legs would allow. 'Young woman got pushed overboard at the ceremony. Get you indoors, Mother, an' stoke the fire 'afore she ketch 'er death o' cold.'

Martha Bateman scuttled indoors. The house was not big but it did have the luxury of a kitchen range with an oven. She quickly popped a brick in the oven and commanded Matthew: 'Set the gal down an' fetch the big tin bath an' set it 'afore the fire. Then get you away an' don't come back for an hour. An' you, too, husband. I don't want to see you in this house 'till I've got 'er to bed.'

Matthew looked anxiously at the still frightened Abigail. He would have liked to stay, to reassure her, to look after her, but he knew that would never do. With him there she would never be able to get out of those wet clothes and into the tub his grandmother was preparing for her. Reluctantly, he turned away and followed his grandfather.

Martha helped Abigail out of her clothes, the bedraggled blue taffeta, the horsehair bustle and the thick petticoats. Then she unfastened her stays, tutting over the great red weals left in the girl's flesh by the pressure of whalebone.

'There you are, my pretty. Sit yourself in this nice warm tub while I put the brick in the bed.'

'Oh, that's very kind, but I couldn't . . . ' Abigail's teeth were still chattering so much that she was unable to finish.

'Well, we'll see.' Martha smiled at her. She was a little round dumpling of a woman, with a rosy face and little black eyes that nearly disappeared into the folds when she laughed. She wrapped the brick in a piece of flannel and went off up the narrow, creaking stairs.

The warmth from the bath and the heat from the range were beginning to seep through to Abigail's chilled bones, although she was still convinced that she would never be warm again. She leaned back in the tub and looked round her. The room was not big but it was comfortably furnished. There was a Windsor elbow chair each side of the range and six Essex chairs round the scrubbed table. The tub was standing on a pegged rug. Through the doorway she could see into the front parlour. A chiffonier held several ruby glass dishes and over it hung a picture of the young Queen and her new husband.

Martha came downstairs, panting a little from the effort, and helped Abigail to wash the river water out of her hair.

'My, but that hair is a bonny colour,' she said admiringly. 'Mine used to be thick like that, but dark.' She rubbed it with a cloth. 'There now, are you feeling better? That was a nasty shock you had, fallin' in the water like that.'

Abigail smiled weakly. 'Yes, I think so, thank you. I must . . . '

'You must put on this nightgown and go up to bed. I'll bring you some bread and milk with a drop o' rum in it. That'll help you to sleep.'

'Oh, no, I won't sleep,' Abigail protested.

'No? Well, you jest hev a little rest, then.'

Abigail humoured Martha and went up the steep stairs to the bedroom Martha shared with Old Zac. A large chest of drawers stood at the foot of the bed and over it hung a faded sampler worked with the alphabet and the text GOD IS LOVE. She climbed into the big bed, realizing that she really had no choice; her own clothes were still soaking wet and nothing of Martha's would fit her. She ate the bread and milk and wondered how she would get home with nothing to wear. Martha would think of something, was her last coherent thought as she gave herself gratefully up to the comfortable warmth of the soft feather bed.

'Did everything go well today, my love?' Effie Markham settled Henry in his favourite chair and came and sat at his feet, careful to arrange herself so that he could see right down her loose, low-cut bodice.

But for once his hand didn't follow his eyes. Absently, he played with the unnaturally red curls at the nape of her neck. 'I was humiliated,' he growled. 'I should never have allowed the girl to come with us. I didn't want her and I said so, but I allowed myself to be persuaded.'

'Pearl?'

'Pearl? No, of course it wasn't Pearl. Pearl would never have disgraced me. Pearl would have the good sense to stay away from the edge of the boat and not fall off it into the water.'

'Who, then?' Effie folded her arms and pushed up her ample bosom invitingly.

'Why, Abigail, of course. I sometimes think she does these things to be deliberately perverse.'

'Oh, Harry, surely not. She would surely never have fallen off the boat on purpose. She could have been drowned.'

He sighed. 'No, I suppose not. But what was worse, young

Bateman picked her up. Edwin told me that. Young Bateman, of all people. I can just hear what his grandfather would say – "Chuck her back in if she's a Chiswell". He's a crafty old devil. He knows I'd like to buy him out, but the old rascal won't sell.'

Effie was silent for a moment. Then she said, 'What Abigail needs is a husband, Harry.' She realized that Henry was not yet ready for lovemaking so she got up and poured him a cup of tea from the big silver teapot, one of his presents to her.

'A husband? Who in the name of thunder would want to marry such a whey-faced wench?' Henry took the tea and sipped it thoughtfully, gazing round the comfortably over-furnished room with the spindly walnut furniture and plush hangings that Effie had chosen and for which he had paid. 'Anyway, what would I do for a housekeeper if she were to marry? She's useful at the office, too. I'd be loath to lose her services.'

Effie had her own ideas as to the answer to the first question, but she was careful not to voice them. Instead she said, 'Then you would have to choose her husband very carefully, my love, wouldn't you?' She smiled up at him from the position she had resumed at his feet. 'It would need to be someone who would be happy to allow her to continue to work for you . . . who would even, perhaps, be grateful . . . '

A slow smile spread over his face. 'Yes, Effie, you're right. By God, you're right. And I think I know the very man. What a clever girl you are, Effie my dear. You always solve my problems for me, don't you?' He put his cup down and did what she had been waiting for, sliding his hand under her loose peignoir.

'I try to, Harry,' she murmured, as he slid onto the floor beside her and began loosening his clothing. 'But, Harry,' she began helping him with buttons, 'you haven't finished your tea.'

He began to kiss her. 'Bugger the tea.'

# *Chapter Five*

When Abigail woke the evening sun was slanting through a chink in the blind. She frowned as the memory of the afternoon's events returned and she stretched her limbs carefully, relieved to discover that she wasn't even stiff. Whatever Martha had put in the bread and milk had certainly helped her to sleep. She sat up in bed and her eyes caught the blue gingham dress, draped carefully over a chair, and the square box beside it. She got out and opened the box. There was a complete change of clothes, from stays and stockings to shoes and petticoats. But how had they arrived there?

Puzzled, she dressed herself and fastened up her hair. Then she went carefully down the narrow stairway. Martha was sitting by the window, busy with her crochet hook. Zac was dozing in the Windsor chair opposite, his clay pipe still in his mouth. But as soon as Abigail appeared he got to his feet.

'I'm off down to The Sun, Mother,' he said to Martha. 'I'll come back when your company's gone, an' not until.' He stumped out, completely ignoring Abigail.

'Oh, dear,' she said anxiously. 'I hope I haven't offended him.'

'Take no notice, dearie.' Martha waved his remark aside.

'Thass jest Zac's way. I don't hold with it, meself, but him, he'll carry a grudge to his grave.'

Abigail sat down in the chair Zac had vacated and began thoughtfully pleating the folds of her skirt. She remembered Old Zac telling Matthew to throw her back into the river because she was a Chiswell, but she had never known what the long-standing feud between the Chiswells and the Batemans was all about. She looked up at Martha. 'Can I ask you three questions?'

Martha smiled. 'You can ask, dearie. Chance whether I can answer!'

Abigail ticked off her fingers. 'One, how did my clothes get here? Two, how am I going to get home? And three, what is all this between the Chiswells and the Batemans?'

The old woman laid her crocheting in her lap. 'The first two are easily answered, dearie. Your brother brought your clothes and he'll be back afore long to fetch you home.' She sighed and shook her head. 'The third one's not quite so simple. An' I don't know if it's right for me to rake it all up again. Not that it's ever died down, I suppose.' She looked down at her hands, idle in her lap but still holding the crochet hook. 'But there, I don't see why you shouldn't know. After all, you're not to blame for what your grandfather did.'

'My grandfather? The one they called Old Henry?'

Martha nodded and settled herself more comfortably in her chair. 'You see,' she began, 'when my Zac and Old Henry Chiswell were young men they used to be mates. Henry's people lived in Brightlingsea at that time, in fact the Chiswells and the Batemans lived next door to each other. Well, the boys – Zac and Henry – grew up together and when they were old enough they used to go fishing together and dredging for oysters. Henry always had the business head, my Zac's never had much of a head for figurin', and after a few years he suggested they should club together and buy their own boat. They did this and Henry used to sell the oysters from a stall on Hythe quay – he reckoned he'd get a better price for 'em there.' She did a few stitches of crocheting, then put it down and went on, 'This went so well that after a while Henry moved up to the Hythe an' stopped going down on the boat and left Zac to do all the fishing and all the dredgin'. Well, like I said, my Zac ain't much of a one for figures an' not bein' able to read an' write he didn't realize Henry wasn't paying him anything like the half shares they'd agreed on. But he could see that Henry was getting a bit big for his boots.

'Zac and me were married by this time and I was busy with young Will, my son.'

'That would be Matthew's father?' Abigail said.

'Yes, thass right, dearie. Well, we'd never had a lot of money so I never thought much about it. I still did a bit of fish guttin', like I'd always done, so we got by. After all, a fisherman's life can be a feast and a fast, and the feast is usually when there's a glut of sprats that won't sell, so I was used to being hard up. Never expected to be anything else, tell you the truth. But when Henry got this warehouse at the Hythe for his oysters, and another boat, an' then went an' married a Colchester girl from quite a well-to-do family – posh wedding it was, too, by all accounts – we could see that somebody was making more out of oysters than Zac.' Her fingers busy again, she glanced up at Abigail, who was listening intently.

Martha warmed to her story. 'Well, Zac was never one to make trouble, but I said he should have it out with Henry. After all, it was s'posed to be a partnership, it wasn't right that Henry should be doing so well while we were still strugglin' to make ends meet. Henry, by this time, had gone all posh and lah-di-dah and he said that if Zac wasn't happy with the way things were there was nothin' stopping him from going off on his own. Zac said what about the boat, after all, half of it was his, and Henry said he was welcome to buy him out if he wanted to, because he'd already got two more boats of his own. Well, the price he named made my Zac see red. Henry had made all this money while Zac had done all the work and looked after the boat and now he was trying to screw the highest price out of him that he could.'

'Oh, but that's dreadful,' Abigail said. 'I didn't realize anything like this was the cause of the trouble.'

'Money's always a cause o' trouble,' Martha said. 'Leastways, greed after money is. Anyway, to get on with me tale, we borrowed the money so that Zac could go an' see a solicitor, but you see, nothing had ever been put down on paper so he hadn't got a leg to stand on. Howsomever, the solicitor must've said something to Henry on the quiet because soon afterwards we had a letter from Henry saying Zac could hev the boat for a lot less than what he'd first said. It took some time, but Zac paid up. I didn't think he oughta pay anything, I reckoned we'd bought that boat over and over, but Zac said he wasn't going to be beholden to Henry Chiswell for a brass farthing, so that was that.'

'And is the boat *Conquest*? The one Matthew sails?' Abigail asked.

'Thass right. Thass supposed to be unlucky to rename a boat, but once we'd paid for her Zac wasn't hevin' her still called by the name Henry had chosen when they bought her so he called her *Conquest*. He reckoned that was a good name.'

Abigail looked troubled. Thank you for telling me,' she said. 'I'd no idea it was anything like that. I didn't know my grandfather, but he's always been held up to me as a good man who built up his business from nothing.'

Martha leaned over and patted her hand. 'Don't you fret over it, dearie. Thass all in the past now. Me and Zac have had a good life, we've never wanted for much although we've never been rich. But Zac has his own oyster layings and young Matthew is a good boy, he looks after them now. We've got a lot to be thankful for, an' I don't harbour no grudges.' She spoke as a contented woman. She smiled at Abigail. 'But thass enough o' that. How about a nice cuppa tea?'

They had hardly finished drinking it when Edwin arrived to take her home. They bundled up the sorry mess that had been her best blue dress with the rest of her wet things and put them in the back of the trap. Then, thanking Martha again for her kindness, Abigail got up beside her brother and they started for home.

'We'll go back through Wivenhoe if you're not too tired, Abbie,' Edwin said as he set the pony off. 'I've got a message for Mr Hatchard who lives there and it's not far out of our way.'

The trap bowled along in the evening air, past the tall church set on a hill on the outskirts of the town where it was a landmark to sailors, past the mill at the foot of the same hill and on between hedgerows bright with autumn leaves. Abigail said little, thinking about what Martha had told her. She didn't doubt that it was true and she couldn't help a feeling of guilt to think that the comfort she lived in was, even if only indirectly, at the expense of Matthew and his family.

Suddenly, she said, 'Eddie, Martha has just been telling me the cause of all the trouble between the Chiswells and the Batemans. Eddie, it's dreadful. Did you know about it?'

'Yes, well, I've picked up the odd word, here and there. Grandfather Henry was a bit of a bounder, by all accounts.'

'I should think he was. Eddie, did you know . . . ?'

'Look, old girl, it's all in the past. There's nothing we can do about it so we might as well ignore it. I always get on well enough with Matt Bateman, and as far as I'm concerned there's an end to it. Ah, here we are, Mr Hatchard's house. I shan't be a sec, Abbie.'

Abigail sat thoughtfully waiting for his return. Perhaps Edwin was right; there was no point in dwelling on the issue. It was all in the past. All the same, she couldn't help thinking about it.

Edwin came back and they drove out of Wivenhoe by way of the end of the village known as the Cross. Just past The Beehive Inn Abigail caught Edwin's sleeve. 'Eddie, what's Father's horse doing, grazing on the edge of the heath?' she asked, puzzled.

'Oh, that's not Father's horse, Abbie.' Edwin tried to set the pony at a trot but for some reason the pony had slowed and would have stopped.

'Of course it's Father's horse. I'd know Boxer anywhere, Eddie. And what's wrong with Billy-boy? Why won't he go?'

Edwin looked embarrassed and tried to get the pony moving again. Too late he realized his mistake in coming home this way.

'Eddie, what is all this? Tell me,' Abigail persisted.

Edwin sighed. 'Well, Father comes to – er – visit someone here sometimes.'

'Oh, yes. And who is that?' Abigail asked innocently.

'Oh, just somebody,' Edwin shrugged.

Abigail looked sideways at her brother. He was flushed with embarrassment. 'What is it, Eddie? Why don't you tell me? Is Father ill? Is he visiting a doctor and wants to keep it from us?' Her voice had risen with anxiety.

'No, Abbie. It's nothing like that.'

'Well, what then?' She tugged at his sleeve. 'Tell me. What is it, Eddie?'

Edwin took a deep breath. 'Oh, Abbie, don't you understand?' he said miserably. 'Father has a mistress, and she lives in one of those cottages.' Billy-boy had picked up speed and Edwin concentrated on driving him, too uncomfortable to look at his sister to see what effect his words had had.

Abigail frowned. 'Father? A mistress? I don't know what you mean, Eddie. Surely a mistress is a . . . a loose woman.' Even at twenty-four Abigail was not entirely sure what the term meant. Her notions of what went on between a man and a woman were, to say the least, hazy. But she was quite sure that it was nothing that her father would ever be involved with, although how she explained the plain evidence of his actions in the production of herself and her sister and brother was not clear, even in her own mind. She shook her head firmly. 'Oh, no, Eddie. You must be mistaken. Father would never do a thing like that. Anyway, he's far too busy. All the meetings he has to go to; all the people he has to see on business . . . ' Her voice trailed off.

'Exactly.' Edwin nodded. 'Most of them lead him to Effie Markham's house.'

Abigail was silent. She couldn't believe it. Not her father, a family man, ruling his household with a rod of iron; a member of the church, singing hymns every Sunday, reading the Lesson, looking pointedly at his gold hunter when he considered the sermon had gone on too long; at the office, where she continually tried to share some of the burden of work because she worried that he worked too hard . . .

She bowed her head. She knew these things happened, she knew men 'kept' women, although she had never been quite sure what the term meant, except that it was something not quite respectable, something that was talked about in hushed tones. Not something her father would ever become involved in. Not the upright and respected Henry Chiswell, with his successful business and his smart new house, his position in the town as one of the Commissioners. Oh, no, it couldn't be true.

She glanced again at Edwin. His very silence and stony expression said that it was.

For the rest of the journey she was silent. She had thought that she belonged to one of the most respected and esteemed families in Colchester. In fact, Chiswell and Son *was* respected and esteemed. But today she had heard discreditable things about both her father and her grandfather. How many more people knew that the idol of Chiswell and Son had feet of clay?

The next morning, when Ellen brought Abigail's tea in she didn't leave after drawing back the curtains, as she usually did, but hovered at the foot of the bed.

Abigail sipped her tea. 'What is it, Ellen? Is something wrong?' she asked.

Ellen bobbed. 'Me an' Cook an' Hetty thank God you never took no harm yesterday, Miss Abbie.'

'That's kind of you,' Abigail smiled. 'I say the same thing, myself. And I thank Matthew Bateman, too. He saved me.' She sipped her tea again, raising her eyebrows as Ellen made no move to go. 'Yes?' she asked.

Ellen twisted her hands together and her words came out in a rush. 'It's like this, Miss Abbie. A gentleman called yesterday to see the master. I asked Miss Pearl what I should do seein' as he was out an' she said to show the gentleman into the drawing room an' she went along to see what 'e wanted. It was over an hour, Miss Abbie. 'E was there over an hour. I was going to stay in the room but Miss Pearl told me to go. I told Cook and she said there wasn't nothin' I could do, but to tell you when you got home. I know it wasn't right to leave her there like that, Miss Abbie, but I couldn't disobey Miss Pearl.'

'Who was the gentleman, Ellen?'

'A Lieutenant Barraclough, Miss Abbie.'

'Ah, yes. I remember him.' Abigail nodded. 'It's perfectly all right, Ellen. You did exactly the right thing.'

Ellen bobbed again. 'I thought I should tell you, Miss Abbie, in case I done the wrong thing. I don't want to lose my place.'

'There's no danger of that, Ellen. Don't think any more about it.'

After Ellen had gone Abigail lay back on her pillows and closed her eyes. What was Pearl up to, arranging for young Bertie Barraclough to call and see Father when she knew he would be certain to be away? It was a good thing the recruiting drive would soon be over and the army officers moving on to the next town. There had been an army garrison actually in Colchester up to some thirty years ago, and Abigail could only be grateful it was no longer there, since Pearl seemed to have such a penchant for army officers. It would be a few months before The Wagon and Horses rang with the spurs of the recruiting officers again. And when they did come she was determined to keep a close eye on her young sister.

Hetty brought the water for her toilet. 'The master will see you in the study after you've breakfasted, Miss Abbie,' she said primly, trying to emulate Henry's words, as she poured the water into the basin.

'Thank you, Hetty.' Abigail got out of bed and performed her toilet absently. How would she face this man, whom she no longer felt she knew? This idol who had feet of clay? This Janus, who presented a façade of respectability and probity while indulging in . . . her mind refused to dwell any further on the subject.

She ate very little breakfast and presented herself at her father's study at nine o'clock. He was doubtless anxious to make sure she was none the worse for her ducking in the river. She wasn't sure she could stomach his concern.

'Come.' The usual response to her knock.

She entered, and to avoid having to listen to his expressions of anxiety and concern over her, began to speak straight away.

'Oh, Papa, do you think you could have a word with Pearl? The servants are very worried because she entertained Lieutenant Barraclough alone for over an hour yesterday afternoon. Apparently, he said he had come to see you. I'd speak to her myself but I know she would take more notice of you.'

It was interesting to watch the look of surprise and then the flush of anger that crossed her father's face before he composed it into an expression of complacency. Finally, he gave a knowing nod. 'Yes, I knew the young man was coming to see me . . . '

'When he knew you would be out?' Abigail asked quietly.

'He couldn't have known that.'

'Practically everyone else in the town must have been aware of it.'

'I must thank Pearl for entertaining him in my absence.'

'But, Papa, she was *alone* with him.'

'Yes, yes, a trifle indiscreet, I will own. But no harm done, I'm sure.' Henry brushed the whole affair aside with a wave of his hand. 'But, now, Madam.' He leaned forward and put his elbows on the desk, his voice beginning ominously quietly. 'It's your future I've brought you here to discuss, not Pearl's. What do you mean by disgracing me in front of the whole of the town council and all the Commissioners? What do you mean by being so stupid as to fall off the boat at the ceremony yesterday? Have you no pride? Have you no shame?' His voice had risen with every word, till he banged his fist on the desk as he shouted the last one. He leaned back in his chair. 'God knows, you spend enough time on boats, dressing yourself up in those ridiculous boys' clothes. I should have thought you were at least capable of keeping your footing on one.'

Abigail took a step back in surprise at the venom in his tone. And she had expected him to ask after her well-being!

'It was no fault of mine! I was pushed, Papa,' she said sharply, annoyed and more than a little perplexed by his attitude. 'The man next to me was drunk and he lurched against me and pushed me over the side. Matthew saw it happen. He told me, afterwards.'

'Matthew!' Henry spat the word. 'You can set no store by the words of a common yokel.'

'He saved my life.'

Henry thrust his head forward. 'Am I supposed to be grateful for that? Disgracing me among my fellow Commissioners? I should never have allowed you to accompany me. It was against my better judgement, as I remember.'

Abigail gritted her teeth in fury. To be blamed for an accident that had nearly cost her her life proved beyond doubt that her father had no regard at all for her as his eldest daughter; especially coming as it had after such leniency over Pearl's flagrant indiscretion. She fought back angry tears.

Henry got up and stood looking out of the window with his back to her. 'It's time you were married,' he said bluntly.

'I'm a little old for a coming-out season,' she replied bitterly. 'And as you regarded it as a waste of money to give me one when I was eighteen, I think you've left it a little late. I'm twenty-four now, remember.'

He shook his head impatiently. 'No need for all that coming-out nonsense. I have a husband in mind for you. A man who will jump at the chance of becoming a part of Chiswell and Son.'

Her eyes widened. He couldn't be contemplating 'selling' her to one of his business associates. Even he would never stoop to that, surely.

He looked at her. 'Well, don't you want to know who it is?'

She licked her lips, mentally going through all the men she knew that Henry might choose. They were all either married or elderly widowers.

Henry sat down. 'You'll marry Carver. Ezra Carver. He's a useful man to me and I shouldn't like to lose him. He knows my business as well – better, almost, than I do myself. It will be an ample reward to give him my daughter's hand in marriage.'

'You can't! You can't marry me to that hateful, creepy little man!' Abigail almost screamed, in horror and revulsion. 'I'm not a parcel, to be handed round to whomever you please, I'm your *daughter!*'

'Then it's time for you to behave like my daughter and do as you are told.' Henry held up his hand. 'And we'll have no displays of temper, thank you, Madam.' He indicated that she should sit down on the chair opposite him. Ignoring the fact that she remained standing, he went on smugly, 'You run my house admirably, Abigail, and you are of inestimable help in the business. But I wouldn't want to deprive you of the joys of marriage and motherhood. Married to Ezra you can have the best of both worlds. You will continue to live here, of course, with Ezra, after your marriage. Things will need to change very little, in fact. Moreover, the stigma of being an old maid will be removed from you. It seems to me to be a very satisfactory arrangement. I can't think what you're making such a fuss about.'

Abigail began pacing up and down the study like a caged

animal, her skirts swishing angrily at every turn. 'Have you consulted Carver on the matter?' she asked in a tight voice.

Henry smiled complacently. 'Ezra will be happy to do whatever I say.' He pulled out the gold hunter and looked at it. 'I shall go to the office now and put the idea to him. I'm sure he will be delighted. As I am.'

Abigail stopped her pacing. 'But I am *not*!' it was her turn to bang her fist down on the desk and the inkwell and pen holders rattled. 'I will *not* marry that man. I hate him. I would rather remain an old maid. I don't care if people look at me in pity. They would pity me more married to that . . . that creepy stick of a creature.'

Henry stood up, matching his will to hers. 'You will do whatever I say, Madam. Make no mistake about that.' With that he left the study.

Abigail stood for a moment, staring at the big chair behind the desk. Her father's chair, a symbol of his authority, his respectability, his autocracy. Did he realize, she wondered, that in the past twenty-four hours all her illusions of him as an honest and upright man had been shattered into fragments? She despised him for his association with the woman in Wivenhoe and she was bitterly upset at his blatant favouritism of Pearl, although she knew she should have been used to that by now. But he was still her father and in spite of his threat to marry her off to Ezra Carver, a threat she couldn't believe he would carry out, she couldn't hate him. She was his flesh, without him she would have had no being; it was her duty to love him.

She left the study and went slowly up to her bedroom. It was a light, airy room, with modern bamboo furniture she had chosen herself and silk hangings to match the green carpet. Imagining Ezra Carver even so much as setting foot inside the door made her feel physically sick. She paced up and down, feeling trapped and defeated. There was, it seemed, no escape.

For two days she stayed away from the office, unwilling to encounter Ezra Carver, hoping that her father would have forgotten the whole sorry business. But on the third day she knew she must go. If she allowed the work to pile up it would only increase her father's wrath and remind him of his threat to marry her off.

But Henry had already spoken to Carver. There was no mistaking the subtle change in the clerk's attitude towards her; a fawning smile, a clammy hand that she quickly brushed off her arm, left her in no doubt that Ezra was delighted with Henry's plan for him. Wherever she moved she could feel his pale eyes following her, his dry cough behind her or his clammy hand on her shoulder.

At last she could bear it no longer. She threw down her pen. 'Oh, for heaven's sake stop looking at me! And stop trying to touch me, you horrid little man,' she cried. Then, snatching up her bonnet she rushed down the stairs and out onto the quay.

The tide was full and the air was thick with river smells and the stench of rotting fish. The quayside was busy – the first dredging of oysters was being brought ashore and taken into the warehouse – but for once Abigail took no notice of the people who doffed their caps or dropped a curtsey. She pushed her way blindly on until she was alone at the very end of the quay, where no boats moored and the old wool warehouses lay derelict.

She sat down on her bollard, rocking back and forth in her despair. She had never felt so alone in the whole of her life. Neither Pearl nor Edwin could help her; Henry wouldn't listen to Edwin, and Pearl wouldn't speak for her. She wished her mother were still alive. *She* would never have allowed this terrible thing to happen. She got up and walked to the edge of the quay. It would be so easy to escape. The water here was deep and dark. She would only have to take two steps and it would close over her head, just as it had done when she fell from the boat. Only this time it would be for ever. Hidden by a bend in the river, it was far enough away that no one would see, no one would know until the tide went out and her body was found in the mud. She looked into the brown, murky depths. It was the only way she could think of to escape from Ezra Carver. She took a step forward.

'Careful now, Miss Abbie. I don't want to have to fish you out of the water again today.' A hand on her arm gently pulled her back from the edge of the quay. 'Why, Miss Abigail –' as Matthew saw her bleak face, 'whatever's wrong?'

'Everything's wrong, Matthew.' She turned away from him. 'I can't . . . ' Tears prevented her from saying more.

Firmly Matthew guided her to a pile of old boxes stacked behind the warehouse, out of sight of the bustle on the quay. He had guessed something was wrong when he saw her leave her father's warehouse in such a hurry and had watched from his boat as she pushed her way through the crowds. He had followed her, at a distance, not quite knowing why, uncertain whether or not he should approach her. But when, to his horror, he saw her step forward to the edge, he had broken into a run.

'There.' He sat her down on one of the boxes and squatted down beside her. Immediately, she put her head on his shoulder and wept as if her heart would break. He didn't quite know what to do next. 'Do you want to tell me about it?' he asked, awkwardly stroking her hair, 'or would you like me to fetch Uncle Josh? Or Aunt Alice?' He didn't know what else to say. For Miss Abigail, so far above him in station, to be sitting here with her head on his shoulder, crying her heart out, was something he had never imagined could happen. He felt more at a loss than being at sea in a force nine gale without a rudder. He patted her arm and waited for her tears to abate.

'I'm sorry,' she hiccupped at last, fumbling for her handkerchief and blowing her nose. 'I'm sorry, Matthew. But I can't . . . ' She began to cry again, 'I can't marry that man. My father says I must, but I'd rather die than marry him.'

'Marry what man?' Matthew frowned. He had no idea what she was talking about.

'Marry Ezra Carver. I *can't*! Oh, Matthew, I *can't*!'

Matthew chewed his lip. He knew Ezra Carver – a spineless, weedy-looking chap who looked as if a good puff of wind would blow him away.

'No, I should blamed-well think you can't!' Matthew said, feelings suddenly welling up inside him that he couldn't name. He only knew that he wanted to hold the girl at his side, to protect her and comfort her. 'I don't know what your father can be thinking of to suggest such a thing.' Then, remembering who he was talking to, 'Begging your pardon, Miss Abigail.'

Abigail shook her head, waving aside his apology. 'But what can I *do*, Matthew?' she said, on another sob. 'I've no money. Nowhere to go . . . '

'Marry someone else?' he suggested lamely.

She shook her head sadly. 'Oh, Matthew,' she said, 'that's not as easy as it sounds. I'm not pretty and vivacious like my sister, as my father is not slow to remind me.' Her mouth twisted wryly. 'Sensible, that's what describes me. Sensible and industrious. Not attributes that make me immediately marriageable, it would seem.' She looked down at her hands, screwing her handkerchief into a damp ball. 'Except to Ezra Carver, of course,' she added bitterly. 'And he'd do anything my father suggested.'

Matthew looked down at the girl by his side. 'I think you're wrong, Miss Abbie,' he said firmly. He looked out across the river. 'And I'll tell you this, if only our stations in life were different I'd be honoured to ask you to be my wife.' He shook his head. 'But we're too far apart. I'm only a common fisherman, while you're a lady. But if one of us had been higher born, or the other lower . . . ' He shook his head again. 'But it wasn't so, and can never be so.'

Abigail lifted her tear-stained face and looked at him unbelievingly. 'Do you mean that, Matthew? That you would marry me? That you . . . you . . . like me enough for that?'

'Like you? I love you, Miss Abbie, and always have, ever since I was a young shaver, that high.' He shrugged. 'But I knew it could never come to anything so I've never dwelt on it much.' He spoke without emotion.

'And you'd marry me?'

'Oh, yes. Like I said, if things had been different I'd have asked you years ago. But they're not, so . . . ' Once more the shrug.

She took his hands in hers. 'Matthew, I'm asking you now, will you marry me?'

He loosed one of his hands and took off his cheese cutter to scratch his head in perplexity. 'But it wouldn't work, Miss Abigail, would it? Look at the house you live in and the place where I live. I've got no hope of keeping you in the way you're used to. And another thing, what about your father?'

'My father doesn't come into it. If he's prepared to marry me off to Ezra Carver he can't care about me, can he?'

'But if you married Ezra Carver your father would see to it that your station in life didn't change. It wouldn't be so if you married me.' Suddenly, at the thought of that weedy clerk becoming Abigail's husband, a violent stab of jealousy shot through him.

'So you don't really want to marry me, Matthew, that's what you're saying, isn't it?' she said dully.

'No, it isn't,' he said sharply. 'I'm just pointing out all the problems.'

'But if I don't mind, Matthew!' she said eagerly. 'If I'm happy just to be with you, loving you and sharing your life . . . ?'

'Loving me?' he repeated, incredulous at the idea.

'Oh, Matthew, don't you know I've always loved you?' she said, her eyes shining. 'I'd have married you years ago, if only you'd asked me. And if I'm prepared to accept your way of life – oh, I won't pretend I'll find it easy – but loving each other as we do I'm sure we'll manage.' She lifted up her face to his and smiled. 'If we're going to be married, Matthew, I'm sure it's all right for you to give me a kiss.'

He flushed with pleasure and bent towards her, then, checking himself he took off his cap and stuffed it into his pocket. 'I . . . '

'Don't you want to kiss me, Matthew?' She was still smiling.

'Want to! Oh, Miss Abbie, if only you knew . . . '

She reached up and put her finger over his lips. 'If we're to be married, Matthew dear, you'll really have to stop calling me *Miss* Abbie,' she said softly.

'Yes, Miss Abbie, you're right.' He gathered her into his arms and as he began to kiss her, gently, wonderingly at first, and then with increasing confidence, Abigail felt a surge of emotion such as she had never experienced before and she knew, without any shadow of doubt, that she had found the place where she belonged.

'Where is Abigail?' Henry demanded the next morning at breakfast. 'Still sulking in her room? Pearl, tell Ellen to go and fetch her down. No, better still, go yourself. And brook no arguments. I've had enough of this ridiculous nonsense.'

Pearl did as her father had bidden. Abigail's room was empty.

Her bed had not been slept in. The servants knew nothing and neither did Edwin. It was not until the afternoon that the news filtered through that Abigail was to marry Matthew Bateman.

Henry was in his office when the news was brought to him by Edwin, who was careful to conceal his own feelings on the subject.

'I've just heard it from one of the men culling oysters in the warehouse, Guv'nor,' he told his father, secretly delighted that Abigail had defied the order to marry Ezra Carver.

Henry was beside himself with fury. 'Where is she?' he roared.

'Dunno, Guv'nor. I only know she's to marry Matt Bateman.'

Edwin left and Henry sat at his desk for a long time. Then he took the unprecedented step of visiting Sarah Bateman.

There were four cottages in Dolphin Yard. Two were nondescript, one was empty and one had a clean, scrubbed step and a geranium by the back door. Inside, Sarah Bateman was ironing sheets, which she did for tuppence a sheet. Henry went inside without knocking and Sarah nearly dropped the freshly heated iron right into the fire at the sight of him in her doorway.

'I want my daughter,' he said, by way of greeting. The room was dim and hot, thick with the odour of damp, freshly ironed linen.

'Abigail is not here, Mr Chiswell,' Sarah said quietly.

'Then where is she?'

'That I can't say.' Sarah plucked at the sheet lying on the table, the only sign that she was not at ease.

'You may well cover up for her,' Henry said with a sneer. 'Quite a feather in your cap, isn't it, to think Henry Chiswell's daughter is stooping to marry your son? A common fisherman. I'm not surprised you're aiding and abetting them.'

Sarah lifted her shoulders and looked straight at Henry. 'I'm no happier about this marriage than you are, Mr Chiswell,' she said. 'I had hoped my boy would marry a girl who would be a helpmate to him, who would work with him, not a lady who's never had to lift a finger to help herself and will expect to be waited on hand, foot and finger by him all the time.' She shook her head. 'Oh, no. My Matthew is not marrying your daughter with my blessing, Sir. The Chiswells and the Batemans were never meant to mix and no good will come of it, you mark my words.' She picked up her iron and began to sweep it over the sheet with long, even strokes. 'However,' she went on, 'my boy is determined to have her and so I must abide by what he wants and make the best of it.'

Henry was, for once, nonplussed. This was not at all what he had expected to hear. He took refuge in bluster. 'Make the best of it!' he exploded at last. 'You say you will have to "make the best of it"! It's my daughter your son is marrying, woman, remember that!'

Sarah sighed. 'I doubt I shall be allowed to forget it, Mr Chiswell,' she said wearily.

Henry gave her a withering look. 'And you can tell the girl when you see her, as doubtless you will the minute my back's turned, that either she comes to her senses and returns home straight away or I wash my hands of her. I'll give her twenty-four hours. After that my house will be locked as far as she is concerned.' With that he strode away.

Sarah didn't look up from her ironing. There was no sound in the little cottage but the sizzle of her tears as they fell on the hot metal.

# *Chapter Six*

Abigail and Matthew were married at St Leonard's Church on 4 October 1840 at eight o'clock in the morning.

The vicar had been reluctant to perform the ceremony because he was anxious not to offend Henry Chiswell, a loyal and generous member of his congregation, but since there were no legal obstacles he had no choice in the matter.

Henry, of course, was not there. Nobody had expected that he would be, although Abigail had cherished a faint hope that at the last moment he would relent and forgive her for defying him. She tried not to be too upset at the knowledge that he had disowned her. She had at least not given him the satisfaction of barring her from his house because she had stayed with Josh and Alice until her wedding, going home only when she knew he would not be there to collect a few belongings and say goodbye to the tearful servants.

Pearl had been difficult.

'You're throwing your life away,' she'd warned when Abigail had slipped in one day. 'Fancy marrying a stupid fisherman. And a Bateman, at that. No wonder Father is furious with you. I can't think what's come over you.'

'Matthew may be a fisherman, but he's far from stupid,' Abigail said, sorting through her things. 'And as to what's come over me, it's quite simple. I love Matthew, while Ezra Carver disgusts me. I've chosen to marry the man I love.'

Pearl sat down on the bed Abigail would never again sleep in. 'But if only you had agreed to marry Ezra you would have been able to stay here, with us. Oh, Abbie, can't you change your mind? Marry him and your life would need to change hardly at all.' There were tears in her eyes as she spoke.

Abigail stared at her. 'Hardly change at all? Married to that mealy little man? Would you really condemn me to that, Pearl? Knowing that he makes me shudder? Just so that life can go on here just the same?'

Pearl turned away, shamefaced. 'He might not live long. He looks consumptive.' Then she turned back, her tone changing to one of accusation. 'I think you're being very selfish, Abigail. You know I'm not fitted to run Father's household. You've no business going off and leaving everything to me. It's not fair. You know I won't be able to manage things.'

Abigail's eyes glinted. 'I don't want to quarrel with you, Pearl,' she said crisply, 'but I think it's you who's being selfish. Perhaps it will do you good to take some of the responsibilities. Perhaps it will help you to grow up.'

At that Pearl burst into tears and flung herself into Abigail's arms. 'Oh, Abbie, I'm sorry, really I am. It's just that I'm so frightened at the thought of you not being here. I shall miss you so.'

Abigail bit her lip and tried to keep back her own tears. 'You must come and see me sometimes. I shan't be far away. Dolphin Yard is only at the bottom of the hill.'

'Dolphin Yard!' Pearl began to cry again. 'Oh, I can't bear to think of you going to such a dreadful place.' She blew her nose and sniffed. 'Anyway, Papa might not like me to visit there.'

Abigail sighed. 'Well, I hope you won't let Papa prevent you from coming to my wedding.'

'I'll come if I can. Really I will.'

Abigail wore her mother's wedding dress, which Edwin had sneaked out of the attic for her, promising to put it back later. He had done everything in his power to support his sister and was there at the ceremony, torn between playing the organ and giving her away. In the end he settled for playing the organ, which nobody else could do, leaving Josh the privilege of giving the bride away. Red-faced and beaming in his best black serge, a little tight and green with age, but still surprisingly presentable considering he had worn it at his own wedding over twenty-five years ago, Josh walked up the aisle with Abigail on his arm.

Pearl was not there, her loyalty to her father had won. Pearl knew which side her bread was buttered. Abigail was saddened and bitterly disappointed.

There were four people in the congregation. Sarah was determined not to miss her son's wedding, ill-fated though she considered it to be, and she sat with Alice, who shared none of her sister-in-law's misgivings. As far as Alice was concerned, the two young people she loved best in the world were being joined together in holy matrimony and her tears, unlike Sarah's, were unashamedly of happiness. At the back of the church sat Daisy and Ellen. They had both been up since four to get their work forward so that they wouldn't be missed for an hour, and had left Hetty in charge of the kitchen.

It was a simple ceremony, beautiful even though the vicar tried guiltily to hurry through it. Afterwards, Abigail signed her name in the register and Matthew put a cross against his before they walked out into the late autumn sunshine.

As she left the church on the arm of her new husband, who walked a little stiffly under the unfamiliar constraints of a new suit, her eyes misted at the sight of the two servants from her old home. She stopped and kissed them both.

'Thank you for coming,' she said softly.

'Miss Pearl says we must go back an' tell her *everything*,' Ellen whispered, her eyes bright with tears. 'She dursen't come herself. We shall tell 'er you looked beautiful, Miss Abbie. For so you do.'

'We 'ope as you'll be very happy – Mrs Bateman,' Daisy added, dabbing at her own eyes.

Abigail looked up at Matthew, her new husband, tall and strong by her side, smiling at her with a wealth of love in his eyes. 'Oh, I'm quite sure I shall,' she said. It never once occurred to her that she might be the scapegoat, the sacrificial lamb, the price that fate was exacting for the sin Henry Chiswell had committed against his friend Zachariah Bateman.

Alice had prepared a simple meal for Abigail and her new husband, and Edwin and Sarah came to share it. Sarah, in her best grey, was a tall, gaunt woman, with iron-grey hair that she wore tightly plaited over her ears. She had had a hard life, bringing up her son alone after her husband had been drowned, and it showed in the set lines of her face. Today disapproval had set the lines even deeper, but true to her nature she had been determined to do what was right by her son and she had come to his wedding.

Abigail approached her as she sat in a corner by the door. 'I know you didn't want me to become Matthew's wife,' she said, sitting down beside her, 'I know you think I'm not used to hard work. But you're wrong. I've run my father's household for years now and helped in his business. I won't be a drag on Matthew. I'll help him, too.'

Sarah looked at the girl beside her, at her soft white hands playing nervously with the heavy gold band Matthew had placed there so recently. 'You haven't any idea what you've let yourself in for, my girl,' she said, with something approaching a sneer.

'Then I'll need your help and support, Mrs Bateman,' Abigail said quietly. 'Because I am determined to make Matthew a good wife.'

The older woman gave a sniff. 'You'd better call me Sarah,' she said grudgingly.

At ten o'clock Matthew and Abigail left to go to their own home. Matthew had managed to rent the empty cottage next to his mother's for two shillings a week and he had a window to mend and a bolt to fix on the back door.

Abigail kissed Edwin. 'You'll put the wedding dress back, Eddie, won't you?' she asked. 'I've left it on the bed upstairs.'

'Of course I will.' He hugged her. 'You looked absolutely topping in it, Abbie. I'm glad I managed to smuggle it out for you. I hope you and Matthew will be as happy as larks. And I hope you'll keep open house for your brother for when the going gets too tough with the guv'nor – because I shan't have you to help me out now, Abbie, shall I?' He sighed, suddenly becoming serious. 'Oh, lor, I'm going to miss you.'

Abigail clung to him. 'I'll miss you too, Eddie. But come and see us. Often. And bring your young lady with you, too.'

Edwin looked surprised. 'Miss Belinda? Yes, I will – if she'll come.'

'Well, try to persuade her.' She caught her husband's hand. 'He must, mustn't he, Matthew?'

Matthew nodded. 'Of course. You'll always be welcome, Sir.'

Edwin clapped him on the back. 'And not so much of the "sir" now, Matt. I'm your brother-in-law, remember.'

The cottage in Dolphin Yard was tiny. Two small rooms placed either side of the front door, with two more up under the eaves. Matthew's tall frame seemed to fill the little living room and Abigail realized that the first thing she would have to do was to discard her horsehair crinoline – if the width of her skirts would allow her to mount the narrow staircase.

'Do you think you will manage to live here, Mi . . . Abigail?' Matthew asked anxiously. 'I know it's nothing near like what you're used to, but I've bought furniture from Mr Jacobs at the top of the hill – if it isn't to your liking you must say. He said he'd take it back if it wasn't right.'

Abigail gazed round the living room. A scrubbed table stood in the middle, with four cheap Essex chairs round it. A corner cupboard held some bits of china and two wooden elbow chairs flanked the open fire, where a kettle sat on the hob. A pegged rug before the hearth lent a little colour to the bare boards. There was no space for anything else in the room except the pitcher of water just inside the door. It was rather gloomy; the deep matchboarded wainscot was painted a dark brown, as were the doors and the cupboards built into the recesses either side of the chimney, although above the wainscot dirty yellow paint served to lighten the room a little.

'I – I haven't done anything about the keeping room through there, yet.' Matthew jerked his head in the direction of the other downstairs room. He was watching her intently. 'I thought . . . it being the best room – the parlour, so to speak – you'd want to choose things for it yourself. I've got enough money left for you to have what you want.' These last words were spoken with pride.

Abigail's eyes misted with tears. 'Oh, Matthew,' she said,

seeking the comfort of his strong arms, 'I've got so much to learn. It's all so different from what I've been used to. You will help me, won't you? You won't get cross and impatient when I don't do things right?'

He stroked her hair. 'I'm only sorry that you've had to come to this, my princess. But it won't always be this way. I'll work and work and buy you a big house, even bigger than your father's, if that's what you want.'

She shook her head. 'No, we don't need a big house, Matthew. As long as we've got each other, that's all we need. But I've got to get *used* to it. You do understand that, don't you, Matthew?'

He held her close. 'I love you, my Abbie. And I'll try to make things easy for you.'

'I love you too, Matthew. And I don't want things easy. I just want you to understand.'

He tilted up her chin and kissed her gently. 'I understand. Now, you go along upstairs and wash those tearstains away. I've put water there for you, ready.'

She managed to get up the narrow, uncarpeted stairway in her wide skirts. The first thing she did in the bedroom was to struggle out of the stiff horsehair bustle and two of the thickest petticoats. It was much easier to move around with them gone. Not that there was far to move. The iron bedstead with its feather mattress took up most of the room; then there was a chest of drawers under the dormer window and in the corner a wash stand with a jug and basin, over which hung a small mirror.

She poured water into the basin. It was cold. She sighed. There was no Hetty to bring hot water now, and it would never occur to Matthew to heat water for washing. Bracing herself she put her hands in the water. This was something else she would get used to.

When she had finished and tidied her hair she went over to the window. The four houses in Dolphin Yard stood in pairs, facing each other across a bare earth yard that was littered with bits of wood, broken bottles, scraps of rag and old tin cans. The yard was reasonably dry now, except for a couple of puddles that hadn't dried out, but Abigail could imagine the quagmire it would become after rain. At the far end of the yard stood the privy that served all the houses. Even from where she stood the stench was appalling. Matthew's mother lived in the cottage adjoining theirs and the doors of the two opposite stood open although the only sign of life was half a dozen children squabbling in the nearest puddle. Both these cottages needed a coat of paint and there were several tiles missing from the roofs. The windows were mostly bare, with a token piece of ragged cloth hanging at one of the upstairs windows. But curtains were hardly necessary because all the windows, up and down, were thick with grime. Matthew had worked very hard on number two. The window she was gazing out of sparkled and there were curtains she could close to shut out the squalid view. She tried not to be depressed and told herself she had much to be thankful for.

Matthew had fixed the bolt on the door by the time she got downstairs again and was setting a stew to cook in the pot over the open fire.

'I should be doing that, Matthew,' she protested.

He smiled at her. Tomorrow, my little love. Today is your wedding day, and you'll do no work.'

She sat down in the chair by the fire, shivering a little despite the heat of the little room. She had never imagined that she would feel so completely alien, so completely out of her depth, in her own home. And there was more to come that she felt ill-prepared to deal with. She worried about it all day as she watched

Matthew, her new husband; not daring to ask, not willing to admit her ignorance.

At nine o'clock he raked over the dying embers of the fire. 'We should go to bed,' he said. 'I must go out on the boat tomorrow. There are oysters to dredge.' He smiled across at her. 'You go up first, dear. I'll follow soon.'

She smiled back at him gratefully and went up the narrow, creaking stairs to the bedroom. There she undressed down to her shift and crept into bed, to lie shivering between the sheets and wait for her husband. Matthew. She couldn't imagine that Matthew would ever perform the unspeakable acts that she had only heard hinted at, but that all wives were subjected to by their husbands, or so it was rumoured. But Matthew was kind, thoughtful and tender. Surely, he would never . . . Her thoughts were interrupted by his step on the stair.

She heard him bumbling about in the darkness and then felt the bed sag as he got in beside her. She lay there, rigid, right on the edge of the bed.

He groped for her hand. 'What is it, my little love?'

'N-nothing. Nothing at all.' She tried desperately to control the trembling in her limbs.

He began to stroke her bare arm gently. 'Why, you're shivering. What's the matter?' He rolled towards her and kissed her gently. 'You're not afraid of me, are you Abbie?' he said softly.

'I . . . yes, I think I am. A little.' She was confused. One part of her was frightened because something she only half understood was about to happen to her; an indignity; a violation; whilst the other part ached for Matthew's kisses and longed for – she knew not what.

'You know I wouldn't willingly hurt you, my little love.' Matthew was kissing her hair, her eyes, her mouth as he whispered the words, his hands gently caressing under her shift. 'But it has to be. Just this once.'

He didn't hurry, but talked gently to her as his hands explored her soft white flesh, but at last she gave a little moan as she felt his hard nakedness pressed against her. This was not what she had been led to expect. This was no indignity; this was a joyous, sharing culmination of their mutual love. The pain, when it came, was exquisite.

Afterwards they clung together, spent, until they slept and woke to love again.

'I didn't know it could be like this,' Abigail whispered, stroking the rough hair at the back of her husband's neck. 'I thought it was something a wife had to endure, not enjoy!' She giggled.'I feel quite wanton.'

'And so you are. Quite shameless.' Matthew grinned as his mouth came down on hers again. He became serious. 'But that's how it should be, if you love someone,' he said. 'I don't want simply to take pleasure from you, dear, I want to give you pleasure too. We should delight in each other, just as we do. Don't ever feel that there's anything wrong in that, Abigail.'

Her arms closed round him, holding him close. 'I hope we'll always be as happy as this, Matthew,' she said.

When she woke in the morning and reached for Matthew, he had gone. She opened her eyes. It was no wonder; it was broad daylight. She quickly dressed and used last night's water to splash over her face and hands and then went downstairs. He must have got up very early and gone down with the tide. He had lit the fire before he went but she had slept so late – with no Ellen to come and wake her with tea – that it had gone out.

Abigail looked at the ashes in the grate. She had never lit a fire in her life, but there was no time like the present for learning. She rolled up her sleeves and pushed the ashes about with the poker. It needed more coal. She went to the cupboard under the stairs where the coal was stored and got half a bucket and emptied it into the grate. Then she put a match to it.

The match went out before the coal had caught. She took most of the coal off and tried again, blowing it to encourage a flame. But nothing happened except that she got blackened with soot and smoke. She sat back on her heels and pushed her hair out of the way. This was ridiculous. She could organize a dinner party for thirty, render all her father's accounts, write awkward letters to his customers and sort out grievances among his work force, but she couldn't light a fire! Even Hetty could do that! She tried to think what Hetty did, but the fires were always lit by the time she entered a room and all she had seen was Hetty scuttling away with bits of wood and paper. That was it, wood and paper. She got to her feet and went back to the coal cupboard. There was a neat pile of sticks there but only a few wisps of paper.

She laid the paper carefully in the grate and put the sticks on top. Then she lit it. The flames began to lick round the wood and it began to crackle. Gingerly, she placed small bits of coal on the sticks and watched with bated breath. The fire was alight.

She was still kneeling in front of it, glorying in its warmth and proud of the fact that she had lit it herself when, without knocking, Sarah walked in.

'I should have thought you could have found yourself something better to do than idle your time away in front of that fire,' she said, without a vestige of a smile. 'Took your time in getting up, this morning too, didn't you?'

Abigail got to her feet quickly and brushed her hair back, leaving a sooty mark across her forehead. 'Yes. I'm afraid I overslept,' she said. 'And when I got downstairs the fire had gone out. I've just re-lit it.' She couldn't keep the pride out of her voice.

Sarah was unimpressed. 'You used enough matches to do it with too, by the look of it. You'll have to learn to be a bit more economical than that. Matthew's not made of money, you know.'

'No, I realize that.' Abigail bit her lip. She desperately wanted to make a friend of Matthew's mother, but the older woman was looking round the room critically. All she's come here for is to find fault, Abigail thought. Aloud, she said, 'Well, if you'll excuse me, Sarah, I must get on. I want to make a suet pudding ready for when Matthew gets home tonight.'

Sarah went to the cupboard beside the fire and opened the door. 'You'll need flour and suet for that. And currants and sugar. Matthew's very fond of spotted dick. I often make him one.'

'Yes, I must go to Mrs Wrigley's and buy what I need.' Abigail picked up her shawl – a pelisse was too grand to wear now – grateful that Sarah had unwittingly told her what she would need to buy. This, she realized, was how it would be. She would have to learn to keep house for Matthew as best she could. Sarah, far from offering to help or teach her, was only looking for her to fail.

But if Sarah was no help to Abigail, Alice was only too ready to come to her aid. Willingly, she showed the girl how to make the spotted dick and tie it in a cloth and boil it over the fire.

'And don't let it boil dry, dearie, whatever you do, else it'll burn and won't be fit to eat. But keep the pot on the boil, else it'll be heavy.'

'Oh, dear, so much to remember!' Abigail fetched a pencil and paper. 'I'd better write it all down so I don't forget. And you must tell me how to make the fish stew you were telling me about too, Alice.'

'I'll show you how to do that another day. Young Matt won't be needin' fish stew today, the size o' that pudden you got cookin' there,' Alice laughed. 'You serve it up to him with a bit o' butter and brown sugar an' he'll hev a meal fit for a king.'

Alice was a frequent visitor to the little house in Dolphin Yard. It was she, not Sarah, who showed Abigail how to make lye from wood ash to boil the clothes in; how to black-lead the stove and whiten the step; she taught her how to smoke fish and trim the brass oil lamp that stood on the table. She showed her, too, how to make a stew and a bag pudding at the same time in the big black cooking pot, suspending the pudding over the simmering broth and standing the vegetables on a wooden trivet. Abigail had never realized how much she needed to know to keep a little four-roomed cottage clean and one hungry man fed. She began to appreciate the expertise of Daisy and Ellen, servants in her father's house.

It was Alice, too, who showed her how to mix beeswax with turpentine and a little oil of lavender to make polish for the newly furnished keeping room.

Matthew had taken her to choose the round walnut table and the six spoonback chairs from Mr Jacobs' second-hand emporium, and there was enough money left for a whatnot to stand in the corner and a horsehair sofa. He was anxious to buy her the armchairs to match but they both realized that there simply wouldn't be room in the little cottage, so he settled for a square of Turkey carpet instead.

Abigail was inordinately proud of her best room and couldn't resist showing it to Sarah who, she knew, had watched every stick being unloaded from the cart.

'Hm,' Sarah sniffed. 'That's no more than I expected. Coming to Dophin Yard with your fancy airs and graces, you'd have to have everything better than anyone else, wouldn't you? I can see Matthew working his fingers to the bone to keep you in your big ideas. I expect lace curtains will be the next thing.'

'That's right,' Abbie said crisply, 'but Matthew hasn't had time to fix up the curtain poles yet.' She picked up a sacking apron and tied it round her waist. Then she took the kettle and poured hot water into a bucket before refilling the kettle from the pitcher and putting it back on the fire.

'There,' she said, 'by the time that's boiled I'll have finished and I'll call you back in for a cup of tea, if you want to come.' She picked up a bar of lye soap that Alice had helped her to make.

Sarah stared at her. 'Where are you going?'

Abigail picked up the bucket. 'The night-soil men called last night and I think the privy could do with a good scrub-out.'

Sarah's jaw dropped. 'But surely you don't do that!'

'Why not?'

'But you've got a husband. The man of the house always . . . '

'My husband works quite hard enough on his boat without doing household tasks.' Abigail picked up her scrubbing brush and stalked off to clean the stinking privy. One way or another she was determined to prove to Sarah Bateman that Matthew hadn't married a milksop who was afraid of hard work.

# *Chapter Seven*

Henry paced up and down in front of the fire, dislodging the cat sprawled comfortably on the hearth.

'Shamed me, she has. Shamed me,' he said violently. 'I never thought to see the day when a daughter of mine would marry a common fisherman. And a Bateman, at that.' He spat the last words.

Effie filled his glass and then one for herself with her home-made dandelion and burdock wine. 'And after all you've done for her too, Harry. She's a wicked, ungrateful hussy. That's what she is, a wicked, ungrateful hussy.' She plumped up the cushions on his favourite armchair, of dark green plush. 'But she'll rue the day she didn't take your advice and marry Ezra Carver, you mark my words. He'd have made her a good husband and have been a good son-in-law for you, Harry. But come and sit down, dear. You'll do yourself no good prowling up and down like that.'

'And since she's been gone the servants seem to do what they like.' Obediently he sat down and sipped his wine, staring into the fire. 'Pearl, poor girl, doesn't know how to handle them – I wouldn't expect her to, after all, she's only nineteen. Edwin's hardly ever there; he's always off with his newspaper cronies – and nothing good will ever come of that!' He shook his head irritably. 'I shouldn't have to concern myself with such matters. I'm far too busy with all my business commitments to worry my head about domestic affairs.'

Effie nodded. 'You'll have to get yourself a housekeeper, Harry. That's what you'll have to do, get yourself a housekeeper.' She smiled at him archly, but he took no notice.

'I expect you're right.' He lit his pipe and threw the match into the flames and watched it burn itself out. 'A man shouldn't have to worry himself over household matters, not when he spends all his time earning the money to make the house run smoothly. But a housekeeper – that'll be even more expense.' He turned his gaze from the fire to the woman sitting opposite him, and his spirits rose a little. My, but Effie was a fine-looking woman; not one of your skin and grief types, either, there was plenty of her and she wasn't afraid to show that she curved in all the right places. She knew how to make the best of herself too, with those little red curls falling round her neck, leading a man's eye into the creamy whiteness of her shoulder and throat. The little lace ruffles on her low-cut gown could only have been put there to tantalize a man. She could rouse his feelings simply by sitting there and smiling at him. And she knew it.

'More wine, Harry?' She leaned forward provocatively and refilled his glass.

He held up his hand. 'Not too much, woman. If I have too much all I'll want to do is go to sleep.'

She laughed coyly. 'Then I'd better put the bottle away, because we don't want that, do we?' She came and arranged herself carefully at his feet, resting her head on his knee.

'They've never made much money, you know,' Henry said, idly playing with her curls as he stared once more into the fire.

'Who haven't?' She spoke a little sharply, annoyed that his mind was not solely on her.

'Why, the Batemans. Old Zac Bateman can't even write his name, let alone figure accounts, and I don't think his grandson's any better. And the old man's too pig-headed to ask to join the Fishery Company, so he can't dredge for oysters in the river.'

'Where does he get them from, then?' Effie spoke with a sigh. She wasn't in the least interested in oysters except insofar as they paid the rent for her little house, but if Henry needed to talk about oysters and the Batemans she knew it was not in her interest to stop him.

'From Brightlingsea Creek, mostly. That doesn't come under Colchester Corporation so it can be dredged without a licence.' He shifted his position irritably. 'The devil of it is, Bateman grows the finest green-beards on the Colne, and his oysters fatten quicker than anybody else's too. Something to do with the saltings where his fattening beds are, I think.'

'But he doesn't grow anything like as many as you, Harry. And he doesn't market them like you do.' She stroked his knee encouragingly.

'I know he doesn't. He only sells locally, the silly fool. He's no businessman. Never was. Not like my old father was.' He fell silent, still absently playing with her curls.

'Then you don't have to worry about him, do you?' Effie spoke a little sharply, irritated with the conversation.

'Oh, I've never had to *worry* about him. He just annoys me. And I'm mortally ashamed to think a daughter of mine should have married his kin.'

She stifled a yawn. 'Oh, I don't know. Young Matthew Bateman's a well-enough set-up young man, from what I hear.'

'Bah! He's what he is. A common fisherman and Zac Bateman's

grandson. And that makes him no fit husband for my daughter on two counts. Not that I'll ever own her as my daughter again. I'll have nothing more to do with her. Ever!' He thumped his fist on the chair.

'Now, Harry. There's no need to get so upset.' Effie got to her feet. 'I don't like to see you get upset, it's not good for you.' She sat down on his knee and began to stroke his hair. 'We'll have to see if we can't think of some way to take your mind off it all, won't we?' she said softly, leaning provocatively against him.

Matthew was late. Abigail glanced again and again at the marble clock on the mantelpiece. Edwin had given it to her on her marriage and it had pride of place between the two Staffordshire fairings Matthew had won at St Denis's Fair in October, soon after they had married.

It was eight o'clock; the tide had turned two hours ago so there was no chance now of Matthew being home until tomorrow's flood. She tried not to worry, remembering the time she had been down river with Josh and the rudder pintle had broken. Matthew had probably put into Brightlingsea and was staying the night with his grandparents. Or perhaps he was already tied up at Hythe and doing some odd jobs before coming home.

She sat quietly by the fire listening to the wind shriek and howl round the cottage, sending puffs of smoke into the room. The rain drummed incessantly on the windows and a growing trickle of water was beginning to snake across the floor from where the door didn't fit. She shivered in spite of the fire. It was a filthy night even for those ashore; on the water, with seas as high as a house as well as the driving wind and rain, it would be hell.

She glanced at the clock again. She wished she knew what had happened to Matthew; possibilities, likely and unlikely, crowded through her mind and she twisted her hands in her lap in her anxiety. There was no way of finding out, either. Unless Josh knew.

With no thought for the weather she flung a shawl over her head and hurried out. The yard was a stinking morass of mud and she splashed her way through it to the road, where the usual raucous sounds coming from the warm interior of The Dolphin competed with the wild night. She hurried on past St Leonard's Church and through the little lane known as The Packet to Spurgeon Street, where Josh and Alice lived. It was very dark but she was not afraid. There were few people about and they were too bent on getting to shelter from the filthy weather to concern themselves with the slight figure hurrying along with her head bent against the howling wind.

Breathlessly, she pushed open the door and stepped down into Alice's cottage. The lamp guttered in the draught and nearly went out, but recovered when the door was closed.

'Alice?' Abigail tiptoed over and tapped the older woman on the shoulder. She was kneeling by the table, her eyes shut and her hands pressed together. Her face was drawn and furrowed with anxiety.

Alice opened her eyes at Abigail's voice and scrambled to her feet. 'Why, what's brought you out on such a bad night, Abbie my girl?' she asked, with a wintry attempt at a smile.

'It's Matthew. He hasn't come home. And it's such a dreadful night I wondered if Josh might know if he's put in at Brightlingsea out of the storm or something.' Abigail looked round. 'But Josh isn't home, either, is he?' She caught Alice's arm. 'Oh, Alice, do you think something terrible has happened?'

Alice shook her head from side to side and gave a great sigh. 'I reckon I know jest where they are, the both of them,' she said. 'I reckon there's a wreck.'

Abigail sat down and took off her steaming shawl. 'You mean they've gone salvaging? Oh dear, Alice, and on a night like this, too.'

Alice came over and put her hand on Abigail's arm. 'You wouldn't hev Matthew any different, would you, child? You wouldn't hev him turn his back on them pore hearts stranded out on the sands off the coast, with their boat breakin' up under 'em, would you? I know I wouldn't hev my Josh any different, even though I worry my insides out over 'im at times.'

'But I've heard tales of what it all means.' Abigail's voice rose with fear. 'I've heard men talking on the quay the night after some big storm. I've heard them say how they launch the dinghies off the smacks and take them, with two men rowing and a third steering with an oar, and how they sometimes have to make five or six attempts to get alongside a stranded boat, in seas like the side of a mountain. And how they've watched other boats smashed to pieces against the hull of the boat that was wrecked. Oh, Alice, I've heard their tales and I can imagine the inky darkness, the screaming wind and the roaring sea.' She covered her face with her hands to shut out the picture in her mind's eye.

Alice busied herself warming milk. Then she put lumps of bread in it and sweetened it with sugar. 'That don't do to dwell on what's goin' on out there,' she said briskly. 'Our men know the water off the coast as well as anyone can know the treacherous, shifting shoals out there. Now, eat this sop and calm yerself. Matthew'll be all right and so will Josh. All you an' me can do is pray to the good Lord to watch over 'em and keep 'em safe.'

'That's what you were doing when I came in, wasn't it?' Abigail cupped her hands gratefully round the bowl of milk sop that Alice had surreptitiously laced with rum – the spoils from an earlier wreck, collected in the calm of the following day, when all the grateful passengers and crew were safely ashore.

Abigail stayed with Alice until dawn broke, either talking or dozing fitfully in the chair by the fire that Alice kept bright. Then, at Alice's direction, she went home to light her own fire and make a nourishing stew ready for Matthew's return.

At seven o'clock she heard his step and opened the door. His face was lined and grey with fatigue under his tarry sou'wester but his eyes were bright with excitement.

She clung to him. 'Oh, Matthew, thank God you're safe.'

He patted her and held her close. 'Have you had a bad night worrying, my little love? There's no need, you know. I know these waters like the back of my hand.' He released her and sat down to pull off his heavy leather sea boots, his guernsey already beginning to steam in the warmth of the room.

'Oh, Matthew, you're wet through,' Abigail said, ladling stew into a bowl. 'Do your oilskins leak?'

He shook his head. 'No, I took 'em off. They hamper the work when you need to look a bit lively. Ah, thank you, sweetheart, this'll warm me.' He began to eat hungrily, blowing each spoonful to cool it. 'I don't remember when I last ate. Seven souls we saved last night,' he said between spoonfuls. 'It was a schooner wrecked on the Longsands. She was completely awash. They'd all taken to the rigging and they were clinging on to the ratlines for dear life. We only just got them off in time before she keeled right over. There was me in *Conquest*, Uncle Josh in the *Edith* and Barney Cole in *Sovereign*, with Jim Jolly in *Excellent* standing off in case he was needed. But we managed.' He held out his bowl for more stew and Abigail ladled it in, her eyes never leaving his face as he continued his story. 'I took the dinghy with Tolley – we left Billy Barr on board *Conquest* with young Moses – and we collected

Uncle Josh from the *Edith*. We got alongside without too much trouble and managed to board her at the second try. Then we cut them out of the rigging – they were too perishing cold to let go, their hands were all numb – and bundled them into the boat and got them back to *Conquest*.' He took two or three mouthfuls without speaking, then he went on, 'Seas were a bit high but we got them aboard without too much fuss.' He looked at his hands. They were raw and bleeding. 'It's a bit of a job to row in the pitch darkness in a howling gale, when the seas are over your head one minute and you're twenty feet up in the air the next.'

He finished eating and pushed his bowl away, his eyes drooping from tiredness, a full stomach and the warmth of the room. Before he could fall asleep where he sat Abigail helped him to shed his wet clothes and then he stumbled up to bed, to sleep for a full twelve hours.

After he had gone to bed Abigail set about her daily duties. She had been married for over three months now and although she hated it she was used to her husband being away sometimes for days on end spratting – or stowboating as it was called – when he wasn't dredging for oysters. It was a precarious living, especially as a large share of the price of each catch, be it sprats or oysters, must be given to Old Zac, who still owned *Conquest*. He had made no concessions to Matthew now that he was married, in fact he was even harder on him than before, because he had committed the unforgivable crime of marrying a Chiswell. Although he no longer fished or dredged himself, Old Zac knew what was due to him and he exacted it. Down to the last farthing. It seemed as if Old Zac, having been caught once, was determined not to be caught again, even though it concerned his own grandson.

Abigail often thought bitterly that Old Zac Bateman and Henry Chiswell her father were not so different, arch enemies though they might be. They were both hard, unyielding, unforgiving men who lived on the profit wrested from the sea at the risk of other men's lives. She wondered if Henry had ever given a thought to the misery and anxiety fishermen's wives endured while their men were away, as he sat in his comfortable chair and counted up his profits. Profits, she had to admit, that had kept her in comfort as well as himself. She hadn't understood until she had married Matthew how very different life was for a fisherman's wife.

Christmas had been particularly difficult. Matthew had been at home and Sarah had thawed sufficiently to join them in a meal made from a boiling fowl roasted over the fire. To Abigail's surprise and joy Edwin had paid them a visit in the evening, bringing her a paisley shawl and Matthew a new pipe. It had been her only contact with her family and although she refused to admit it, she had missed the turkey and plum pudding, the exchange of presents, the choosing of gifts for the servants – servants who now lived in greater luxury than she did, she thought wryly as she shouldered the yoke and went to the pump down the road to fetch water. The wind from last night had eased and the rain had turned to sleet and then snow until now it was falling thick and fast and beginning to lay. She queued up patiently with about twenty others for her turn at the pump and then hurried back as best she could to Dophin Yard, anxious to get out of the icy January weather. She set the buckets in a corner of the room and covered them with a cloth. She hoped the pump wouldn't freeze again this year. The last freeze hadn't affected her, because her father had his own cistern that the water carrier came and filled as necessary. Unlimited water at the turn of a tap was something else she had not appreciated until she no longer had it. With a sigh she built up a good fire and put Matthew's wet clothes to dry before it. Soon the little room was filled with a warm, steamy smell that held more than a hint offish. She began to feel sick.

But by evening, when Matthew came downstairs refreshed from his sleep, his clothes were dry and ready for him to put on again. Abigail looked up from where she was sitting at the table, sewing by the light of the oil lamp.

He sat down opposite her. 'That's the picture of you that I take with me when I go out on the water,' he said softly, smiling at her. 'You, sitting in our living room, with the light from the lamp shining on your lovely coppery hair. It's a picture that warms me when I'm cold and encourages me when things are hard.' He stretched across the table and took her hand in his. 'I love you, my Abbie, and I thank God for you every day of my life.' He turned her hand over and looked down at it in his great horny palm. It was red and chapped from housework. He shook his head as he stroked her fingers. 'But I should never have been so selfish as to bring you down to this. You were born to better things, my princess.'

'It was my own choice, Matthew,' she reminded him quietly. 'I married you because I loved you. It's true I've not always found things easy, but I'm learning, and you're very patient with me.' She went round the table to sit on his lap. 'I've no regrets, Matthew. You're all I ever dreamed of. And I love you.' She began to kiss him and as they clung together he got to his feet and carried her up the stairs as if she were no more than a baby. Tenderly he laid her on the bed and made love to her, their joy in each other culminating in an explosion of passion. Afterwards, they lay, warm in each other's love, until they slept.

The next day Matthew prepared to leave, pulling on his leather sea boots. Abigail went over to him and laid her hand on his arm. 'Oh, must you go, Matthew? The snow is already thick on the ground and I fear there's more to come.'

'I'm afraid I must, little love. I didn't get much of a catch last time and with sprats hardly more than fourpence a bushel to lay on the farmer's fields for manure we can't live on air. Grannie's ill, too, so Grandad needs extra money to pay the doctor. To tell the truth I doubt she's long for this world.'

'Oh, Matthew, I'm sorry. I like your grannie. She was kind to me when I fell overboard at the opening of the oyster season. I would like to have visited her more . . . '

'But it wouldn't do. Not the way Grandad is over the Chiswells.' He got up and stamped his boots comfortably on his feet. 'Grandad's a stubborn, pig-headed old fool over some things.'

'Does he have the selling of all the oysters and sprats?' Abigail asked carefully. 'Or do you sell them yourself?'

'Oh, Grandad sells them. He's got his regular customers.'

'Local customers?'

'That's right. He supplies all the local bigwigs in Brightlingsea.'

'What about sending them to London?'

Matthew looked blank. 'I don't know what you mean.'

'What about sending some barrels of oysters to London? Regular orders. Every week, so many barrels on the Friday boat, or the Wednesday boat. Like my father does.'

'Oh, no. We couldn't do that.' Matthew looked faintly alarmed.

'Why not? Don't you dredge enough?'

'Well, no, it's not that.' Matthew frowned uncomfortably as he shrugged on his reefer jacket and reached for his sou'wester.

'What, then?'

'Because it would need invoices and suchlike and . . . well . . . ' He rammed his sou' wester down on his head. 'Damn me, Abigail, you know as well as I do that Grandad can't read and write and neither can I!' He flung the words at her and slammed out of the house.

He was gone a week. During that time there was more snow and Abigail pictured him out on the wild sea, pitching and rolling as he pitted his wits and strength against the elements. She cursed herself for an insensitive fool, because knowing how it shamed him that he could neither read nor write it was unforgivable of her to make him admit it outright. It was no consolation to him to know that she loved him just as he was, for what he was; his pride had been wounded and to Matthew that was far worse than a physical blow.

Never before had he left her without a loving kiss, and she prayed desperately for his safe return, slipping each day into St Leonard's Church, whose interior was no warmer than the street, to kneel and ask God, and somehow through him, Matthew, to forgive her and not to allow his hurt pride to render him reckless.

One morning as she knelt there Edwin began to play the organ. She sat up to listen. It was such a long time since she had heard her brother play. Since the vicar had made it plain that his allegiance was to her father and that Matthew was not welcome at St Leonard's, Abigail had stopped attending the church and had gone instead with Matthew to the Congregational Church at Lion Walk.

Suddenly, Edwin seemed to sense her presence and swung round on the organ seat. 'Why, Abbie, what are you doing here? Is anything wrong?'

She shook her head, unwilling to betray Matthew's weakness. 'I was listening to you playing, Edwin,' she said, by way of an answer. 'I had forgotten how well you make the organ speak. But you sound troubled.'

He looked surprised. 'What makes you say that?'

'Oh, Eddie,' she gave a little laugh. 'Your mood always reflects in your music. Surely, you must realize that.' She became serious. 'What is it? Is it father? Pearl?'

He climbed down from the organ seat and came to sit beside her on the pew. 'It's a lot of things,' he said, taking her hand, 'but mostly it's you, Abbie. The house is just not the same without you.'

She bowed her head. 'But I couldn't stay, Eddie, you knew that. I couldn't have married Ezra Carver.' She looked up, her eyes bright. 'I love Matthew very much, Eddie. I've always loved him.'

He nodded. 'I think I knew that.' He took her hand in his and stroked its rough surface. 'If only father wasn't so unforgiving,' he sighed.

'But what about you, Eddie? Do you still see Miss Young?'

He smiled. 'Oh, yes. I get invited to her soirées quite often. I'm sure she likes me and, well, I think I'm in love with her, Abbie,' he added shyly.

'Oh, Eddie, that's wonderful. When are you going to bring her to see us?'

'I don't know.' He frowned. 'It's a little difficult. You see . . . '

She put her hand on his arm. 'I understand, Eddie. Dolphin Yard isn't exactly . . . '

'Oh, it's not that, Abbie,' he protested quickly.

'No, of course not,' she agreed. But they both knew that it was. 'You still write your articles for the newspaper?' she asked, changing the subject.

'Oh, yes, much to Father's annoyance. He says I shouldn't complain about the water supply because everyone is adequately served, these days. But you know differently, don't you Abbie? You still have to fetch your water from the pump. And it's not good water from that pump, either. I've tasted it.' He turned to his sister. 'I think that water is the reason so many people at the Hythe become ill. I think you should boil it before you drink it, Abbie.'

She laughed. 'Whatever for?'

'I don't really know,' he frowned. 'It's just a cranky idea of mine that it's better if it's boiled before you drink it. Anyway, it tastes better. I've said so in the newspaper, much to Father's disgust. He says I should give up writing and use my energies for the business.' He got up and walked up and down the aisle, then came and sat down again. 'I hate that office!' he said vehemently. 'It stifles me. Ezra Carver sits hunched in the corner turning out copperplate accounts and coughing blood while I wrestle with orders I neither understand nor care about, since Father gives me no real responsibility. I can't stick it much longer, Abbie. As soon as I can find myself a room to live in, I'm off.'

'I can't blame you, Eddie,' Abigail sighed. 'But what about Pearl? How is she?'

'Pearl is what she's always been, the apple of Father's eye,' he replied. 'And he can't – or won't – see what she's up to.'

'What do you mean, "up to"?'

'Well, perhaps I'm being a bit unfair. Perhaps she's just being a bit indiscreet. But she does have rather a lot of young men calling to see her.'

'Edwin! What are you saying?'

'I'm not sure.' He frowned. 'But I do wonder, sometimes. Perhaps if you went to see her . . . '

'You know I can't do that, Eddie.'

'You could if you went when you knew Father wouldn't be there.'

'And how would I know that, pray?'

Edwin took out his pocket watch. 'He won't be there now. I know for a fact that he's arranged to meet Mr Hayfield at half past ten this morning to discuss the canal business yet again. I doubt anything will come of it, but there you are. It's five and twenty minutes to eleven now, so he's sure to be gone. You know what a stickler for time he is.'

Abigail hung back. She had not been in her father's house for nigh on four months and was reluctant to set foot in it now. Edwin caught her hand and pulled her to her feet. 'Come on, Abbie. Talk to Pearl, if only to set my fears at rest. I shouldn't like to think of my little sister going to the bad for want of a word in her ear. *I* can't speak to her, it wouldn't be right; and you know Father can see no wrong in her.'

Reluctantly she agreed to go with him, but she refused to let him take her in by the front door, choosing instead to use the servants' entrance.

Daisy and Ellen both wept over her, shocked at her altered appearance, yet delighted to see her. Hetty was too simple-minded even to realize that she lived in greater luxury than her former mistress.

'Has the master gone?' Abigail whispered.

'Yes, Miss Abbie,' Ellen replied. 'I heard the door slam ten minutes ago.'

'All the same, go you upstairs and make sure,' Daisy said, 'we don't want Miss Abbie gettin' herself into trouble.' She pursed her lips after Ellen had gone and Hetty was back in the scullery cleaning saucepans. 'Come to 'ave a word with Miss Pearl, 'ave you, Miss Abbie?' she said sagely. 'An' not 'afore time, neither. Her goins on are shameful. But thass not our place to criticize, beggin' your pardon, Miss – er, Mrs Bateman.'

'No, Daisy, it isn't.' In her anxiety Abigail spoke with more asperity than she intended. She put her hands to her brow. 'I'm sorry, Daisy . . . I didn't mean . . . Tell me.'

At first Daisy shrugged her shoulders, offended, then she said, 'Well, it's the gentlemen, Miss Abbie. Miss Pearl often has young gentlemen call to see 'er, sometimes two or three at a time. I dessay there's no harm in it, they do say there's safety in numbers, don't they, but it don't seem right to us servants – specially as it's always when the master's out.' She pulled the kettle forward on the hob, more out of habit than necessity, and went on, ''Course, when the military come through the town thass a different matter. That Lieutenant Barraclough, he seems to spend most of his time here when 'e's in Colchester. That beat me how he ever find time to recruit any men to the army, he spend so much time with Miss Pearl.'

'Oh dear.' Abigail realized that Edwin had every reason to be concerned about their sister.

Ellen came back. 'It's all right, Miss Abbie, he's gone. Miss Pearl is in the morning room. Shall I tell her you're here?'

Abigail sighed. 'No, I'll go up.' She went up the stairs to the hall. It seemed as big as a cathedral after what she had become used to. And as cold. She pulled her shawl round her more closely and went to the morning room where Pearl, wearing a peach-coloured peignoir with lace ruffles, was reading a book. A breakfast tray was still on the table, pushed to one side. She looked up when Abigail entered.

'What are you doing here? Father turned you out,' she said rudely.

'I came to see you, Pearl.' Abigail spoke quietly, refusing to be angered by her sister's greeting. 'Edwin thought . . . '

'Edwin can mind his own business.' Pearl returned to her book.

Abigail looked round the once-familiar room, with its thick plush curtains and furniture, the flock wallpaper of the same deep red and the polished tables and chiffonier. The room was littered with books and magazines, dress catalogues and swatches of material. Everywhere reeked of opulence and indulgence; even the tambour-fronted work-box in the corner that had been her own seemed the height of luxury to her now. A pang of something she couldn't explain shot through her, a mixture of sadness, regret and pain, mingled with a sharp sense of guilt towards Matthew, who had tried so hard to give her what she was used to and had failed because it was outside his experience.

She took a deep breath and tried again. 'It is Edwin's business. You're his sister and he doesn't want people all over the town talking about you.'

'Well, people can mind their own business. And so can Edwin. And so can you.' Pearl's eyes blazed. '*I'm* mistress here now. I do what I like. In any case, it's certainly no concern of yours!' She returned to her book, looking up again after a moment. 'Well, what are you waiting for?' Her gaze swept her sister. 'Look at you. What do you think you look like, with your shawl over your head like a common washerwoman and your skirt all loose and hanging round your legs? Have you forgotten what a crinoline is, already? And look at your hands! My God, Abigail, you've sunk pretty low. Yet you have the temerity to stand there and tell me what I ought to do and how I ought to behave! You ought to be ashamed of yourself!' She fished about in her reticule until she found a shilling. 'Here, take that. I expect you can do with it.' She flung it across the table. 'Now get out and mind your own business.'

'You stupid little fool, Pearl. You stupid, silly little fool.' Abigail put her hands on the table and leaned forward, ignoring the shilling Pearl had thrown down. Her voice was shaking with fury. 'Don't you realize what a dangerous game you're playing? There's a name for women like you, and it's not a very nice one. And as for being ashamed, it's you who should be ashamed, not me. I'm a respectable married woman. The only thing I've got to be ashamed of is the fact that my sister is little more than a trollop!'

'Get out!' Pearl's head shot up and she aimed her book at Abigail, missing her and hitting the door. 'I don't wish to speak to you, ever again!'

'One day you may regret having said that,' Abigail replied, her voice deadly calm, a sure sign that her temper was only just under control. 'One day you'll come to your senses. I only hope it won't be too late.' She went out and closed the door, standing for a moment with her back to it, her eyes closed, and her fists clenched in fury. Then she strode up the hall towards the front door.

But before she could reach it the study door opened and her father came out, a sheaf of papers in his hand. He stared at her, his face black with rage. 'What are you doing in my house, girl!' he roared. 'Get out! Get out this minute or I'll call the constabulary. Who gave you leave to come here, I should like to know!'

'I'm going!' Abigail shouted back. 'And, believe me, I never want to come here again!' She reached the front door, but it stuck as she tried to wrench it open. Edwin, hearing the noise, came rushing down the stairs.

'It's my fault Abbie's here, Guv'nor,' he said, going over to her. 'I asked her to come and speak to Pearl about the error of her ways.'

'You asked *her!*' Henry pointed scornfully at Abigail. 'You asked *her* to speak to Pearl about the error of her ways! She's a fine one to talk, I must say!'

'At least she's a respectable married woman and not something little better than a whore! Don't you realize, Guv'nor, what young Pearl's doing behind your back? She's a sight too fond of entertaining gentlemen, especially the military officers who pass through the town.'

'Enough, Sir! Don't dare to speak of your sister in such terms.' Henry was quivering with rage. 'I never heard such nonsense in all my life and I'll hear no more of it.'

'My God, Father,' Abigail said bitterly, 'I always knew you were pig-headed, but I didn't realize you were blind as well. Can't you see? Can't you understand what Edwin is trying to tell you?'

'Don't call me "Father"!' Henry turned on her with what almost amounted to a snarl. 'I told you to get out, Madam. This is a family matter and no concern of yours.'

Edwin put his arm round Abigail to prevent her struggling to open the door. 'Abigail is still my sister, just as Pearl is my sister,' he told his father, speaking quietly yet forcefully. 'Abbie was the only person, as I saw it, who could speak to Pearl and make her see sense, so I asked her to come.'

'Well, now you can tell her to go!' Henry shouted. 'I will not have her in my house!'

'She's your *daughter*!'

'Not any longer, she's not!' Henry went back into his study and slammed the door.

'Let me out, Edwin,' Abigail said through clenched teeth. 'Let me out of this house before I smash the door down with my bare hands.'

# *Chapter Eight*

Abigail told Matthew nothing of her visit to her father's house. Their reunion was even more loving than usual after an absence because it was tinged with remorse and sadness at the way they had parted.

'I'm sorry, my little love,' Matthew said, his fingers twisting a strand of her long coppery hair as it lay spread across the pillow. 'I should never have gone off in such a huff, it was very wrong of me. But' – he buried his head in her hair so that his voice was muffled – 'it shames me so that I can't figure or write.'

'I know, Matthew. I know.' She stroked his head as it lay against her shoulder. 'I've thought about it all the time you've been away. And I've resolved to teach you.'

He leaned up on his elbow. 'Teach me!'

She smiled up at him with shining eyes. 'That's right. And why not? I've already bought a slate from Mrs Wrigley's

'You didn't tell her what it was for?' he cut in anxiously.

'No dear, of course not.' Now was not the time to tell him that visits to Mrs Wrigley's shop were difficult. It was obvious that the old woman didn't know whether to treat her as a lady or common fisherman's wife. In the end she tended to serve Abigail with the minimum of words, uncomfortably anxious to be rid of her presence. Now Abigail pulled his head down and kissed him. 'I shall begin today, so that by the time our son is born you will be able to write his name without my help.'

'Our son! Oh, Abbie, my little love,' he held her close. 'You bring me such joy.'

Through the dark days and nights of winter, and all through the summer, whenever he was at home, Matthew scratched away at his slate or pored over the simple words Abigail wrote out for him to read. He was desperate to learn and for that reason he learned fast. His mental arithmetic was already adequate and it fascinated him to see the figures in his mind translated into figures on the slate and to work sums out for himself and see the results written down.

'You know, you're really very clever, Matthew,' Abigail said admiringly. 'If only you could have been properly educated when you were young you could have been – oh, I don't know – a schoolmaster, or something.'

Matthew roared with laughter. 'Oh, no, wife. I think not. I'm a sailor, born and bred. I don't think I would ever be happy too long away from the sea.'

For some reason she couldn't understand his words sent a chill through Abigail that seemed to reach right into her soul, but she said nothing.

Sarah made no secret of her disapproval. She considered that Abigail was trying to raise her son above his appointed station in life and said so by means of veiled and snide remarks.

'I suppose you'll be getting a piano next, so she can teach you to play that,' she would say with a sniff.

Matthew felt at a loss. He realized that his mother was jealous of Abigail's place in his affections but it never occurred to him that she might also feel inadequate and terrified that in his new learning he would leave her behind and despise her for her ignorance.

As for Abigail, she knew how much her mother-in-law resented her and her unbringing, and she tackled even the most arduous and disgusting tasks with cheerfulness so that Sarah would have no justifiable cause for criticism. And she kept the hot-water can that she had begged from Hilltop House hidden so that Sarah would not jibe at her for being soft. Because one thing that Abigail was determined to preserve was her habit of keeping herself clean every day with hot water in the privacy of her bedroom. Not for her Matthew's habit of dousing himself, winter and summer alike, in a basin of cold water that stood on a table outside the back door, even when he had to break the ice on the bowl to do it.

Sarah, on the other hand, made a great ceremony of her weekly ritual of the tin bath in front of the living room fire, carrying out her preparations for this with noisy activity so that no one in Dolphin Yard could fail to realize what was going on.

Abigail hoped that things would improve when Sarah learned of her pregnancy, but they didn't. It was as if Sarah couldn't bear the thought of yet another person coming between her and Matthew. Abigail, with a maturity beyond her years, could understand this but was unable to break through the barrier of silence that Sarah imposed.

'She won't even speak to me now,' she confided to Molly Jenkins, who lived in one of the cottages on the other side of the yard. 'If I say "Good morning" she simply looks right through me as if I wasn't there.'

Molly sat by the fire nursing her latest baby, her tenth, five of which were still living. She was a scrawny, lantern-jawed woman of thirty-five worn out by poverty and continual pregnancy.

'That'll be better when you get the baby,' she said, pushing aside a strand of lank, greying hair. 'You'll see.'

'I only hope you're right, Molly!' Abigail looked round the little room, empty except for a table and a few stools. It was the same size as her own cosy living room but its stark bareness was shocking in contrast. 'But I shouldn't complain, least of all to you, Molly,' she said guiltily. 'I've got so much to be thankful for.'

'So hev I, if it come to that,' Molly said contentedly. 'My Jack's a good man. He always bring his wages straight home, when he get any, and he never knock me about. Not like pore old Sally, next door. Black an' blue she is, sometimes, after her man's come home drunk. He's a dreadful man, that Amos Carter.' She shrugged. 'But there, Sally reckon she's luckier than some, because at least Amos only knock her about, 'e never touch the children. So there y'are. You can always find someone wuss off than y'are yerself, an' thass a fact.'

Humbled by Molly's philosophical words Abigail heaved herself to her feet and went back across the yard to her own cottage.

Abigail went into labour on 1 September 1841, the day the oyster season opened.

Matthew had promised to row his grandfather out to watch the ceremony just as he had always done and Abigail insisted that this year should be no different, saying, 'This will be no place for you even if you stay at home, Matthew, so you might as well go down river as spend the day on the boat where it's moored.'

'I'll go and fetch Mother before I go, then.' Matthew's face was creased with worry. 'I'm sure she'll come if I ask her.'

Abigail kissed him. 'Yes, I'm sure she will. But I think it's better if *I'm* the one who asks her.'

Matthew looked doubtful. 'Promise me you will?'

She gave him a little push. 'Of course I will. This is something I can't manage on my own.'

He sat down. 'I'm not going till I know.'

'All right, I'll go now. Set a pan of water on the fire while I'm gone.'

Slowly, and a little nervously, Abigail went and knocked on her mother-in-law's door. 'Can you come, Sarah?' she asked, trying to keep the tremor of apprehension out of her voice. 'I think the baby is coming.'

For a moment a look of blank hostility crossed the older woman's face. 'Can't you read a book that'll tell you what to do?' she said sarcastically.

Sarah bit her lip as much against an angry retort as against the sharp pain that knifed through her. 'I need your help, Sarah,' she said 'I – I'm frightened.'

Sarah's expression softened slightly. 'Have you set a pan of water over the fire?'

'Matthew's doing that now.'

Sarah nodded briefly. 'I'll be round in a minute. And tell Matthew to make himself scarce and not to come back till tonight. We don't want him hanging about the place while this is going on.'

The pain got steadily worse throughout the day but Abigail bore it stoically. Molly came across to help and support her through the last agonizing hours, during which, although she bit her lip to ribbons and blistered her hands on the ropes Sarah had fixed to the foot of the bed for her to pull on, not a cry passed her lips.

'She's a brave 'un, an' thass a fact. Looks to be a big baby she's birthin',' Molly said.

'She'll do,' Sarah replied as with a last agonized heave from its mother the baby came into the world. 'It's a boy. A lovely boy.' And even Sarah couldn't keep the pride out of her voice.

As he was laid carefully in her arms Abigail said, 'He's to be William, after Matthew's father, and Zachariah, after his grandfather.'

'They're good names. And if he grows up as fine a man as William, his grandfather you'll have no cause for complaint.' Uncharacteristically, there were tears in Sarah's eyes and she turned quickly away and blew her nose. 'Now,' she said, her voice sharp against her unwonted display of emotion, 'you'd better get some sleep. It's late, and you've had a hard day.'

Matthew was beside her when she woke. He kissed her tenderly, almost reverently, and peered wonderingly at the tiny being their love had made.

'I've brought you a present,' he whispered. 'As it's the first day of the oyster season I've brought you a dozen oysters from the first dredge and the traditional tot of gin and piece of gingerbread to wash them down.' He held her up so that she could see.

'May it be a good season,' she said softly. 'And may our son thrive.'

He bowed his head. 'Amen to that.'

Abigail took great joy in her little son and tried hard to include Sarah in her happiness. But after the first few weeks, when she knew herself to be indispensable, the older woman reverted to her former ways and refused to have anything to do with Abigail.

Abigail went to see Alice.

'She's a very silly woman,' Alice said, pursing her lips. 'Josh's sister and my sister-in-law she may be, but I still say she's a very silly woman.' She looked down at William, nestled in her arms where Abigail had lain him. 'Jest look at what she's cuttin' herself off from.' She stroked the little silky head, already covered with a down that hinted of his mother's colouring. She gave a sniff. 'I mind my little Emily was jest such a one as this, only her hair was black as jet. Jest think, if she'd lived . . . '

'You wouldn't have turned your back on her, would you, Alice?'

Alice shook her head. 'Turn me back? When I'd give all I could see to hev 'er here with me now? No. Never. But we all hev our troubles, lovey, don't we? And we gotta remember Sarah's had a hard life. She brought that boy of hers up all by herself after Will was drowned – 'cause she never got no help from Old Zac, she jest had to get on with it. Then when Matthew was old enough Old Zac come an' offered to take him on the boat with him.'

'I didn't know that,' Abigail said.

'No, don't s'pose you did.' Alice rocked William absently on her knee. 'Of course, Sarah didn't want 'im to go. There was a job goin' for a stable lad at Renbow Hall, where she used to work, an' she wanted 'im to take that. But 'e was mad keen to go to sea, so she 'ad to let 'im go with his gran'father. Up till then she'd never 'ad to share 'im with anyone.'

'And now she feels that I've taken him away from her,' Abigail said thoughtfully.

Thass right.' Alice nodded. Then she frowned. 'But there's more'n that, I reckon.'

'What do you mean?'

'Well, I don't know if I can explain right, but Sarah always talk proper, don't she? What I mean is, she talk more like you than the way the likes of me do. She's always tried to better 'erself. In fact. Josh always used to say that once she got into service she began to put on 'er airs an' graces and play the lady. But, be that as it may, she brought Matthew up well. Now I wouldn't hev you think 'e was a little mummy's boy, 'cause 'e wasn't. He was as big a young rascal as any of 'em, in fact 'e was the ringleader as often as not when there was any mischief to be done. But he never had a patched backside to 'is trousers, like the rest o' the boys, an' she taught 'im to speak nice, even if she couldn't teach 'im to read and write.'

'But he can read and write now,' Abigail said proudly. 'I'm teaching him.'

'Ah, there you are, then,' Alice said, as if it explained everything. 'You're doin' even more for 'im than she ever could. She's only jealous, lovey. Thass all it is.'

Only jealous. Abigail thought over Alice's words as she walked home through The Packet with William on her arm. And suddenly she began to wonder if perhaps the coolness she had sensed as she went about her daily tasks – at the pump, at Mrs Wrigley's shop and when she went to fetch Matthew's porter from the tap room at The Dolphin – was not after all due to the people not quite knowing how to handle her changed situation, as she had thought, but rather to Sarah's poisonous tongue. It was a sobering thought.

But there were other and even more important things to occupy Abigail's mind. She was convinced that Matthew and his grandfather were not making the best of their oyster business and she tried hard to get Matthew to widen their market.

'It's not that you wouldn't be able to manage the invoicing if you sent them to London,' she insisted. 'You can read now and your writing is quite legible. Anyway, I could help you with that.'

'You've got quite enough to do looking after young William,' was his reply.

'Can I come down river with you?' she asked on another occasion.

'Whatever for?' His look was one of astonishment.

'I miss it. I used to go down with Josh. You remember that, surely.' In truth, she wanted to see for herself exactly how they went about their dredging.

'That's as may be. But you've got the baby to see after. What about him?'

'I could bring him with me.'

'No.'

'Maybe your mother would look after him while I'm gone.'

'You're not asking her.' Matthew was disgusted at his mother's behaviour towards his wife and, Abigail had discovered, he was his mother's son in that he also could be totally unforgiving. Living next door as they did it was a difficult and sad situation and one that gave her many sleepless nights.

'Anyway,' he went on, 'Tolley wouldn't relish the thought of taking a woman on board. It's unlucky.'

'Nonsense.'

'I know it's nonsense, but you try telling Tolley that. He'd never cast off if you were aboard.'

'I came up river with you once,' she reminded him. 'Tolley didn't complain.'

'That was an emergency. Anyway, we'd done our fishing for the day.'

She tried another approach.

'These oysters are delicious,' she said, when he brought home the first dredge of the new season. 'I've never seen such fat ones. Does your grandfather still sell them all in Brightlingsea?'

'Yes. Mostly. And since Grannie died he's taken to having a stall down on the hard to sell them. It gets him out of the house and he sells a few. He misses Grannie more than he'll admit, so I wouldn't like to discourage him.'

With a sigh Abigail realized that she couldn't again bring up the idea of selling their oysters in London, even though with the coming of the railway to Colchester six months ago there were even better prospects of transporting them. And with the birth of little Laura, eighteen months after William, she was kept too busy to worry about it.

'She's just like you, Abbie,' Edwin said. He was the only member of Abigail's family who had come to Laura's christening and now he walked back to Dolphin Yard with Matthew and Abigail, happy to take a turn with Matthew in carrying young William on his shoulders.

Abigail laid the baby in her cradle and began to set the table for supper. 'She's a good baby,' she said. 'Not like her brother. I can't keep him clean and tidy for more than five minutes at a stretch.'

'I'm not surprised.' Edwin looked out of the open door at the mud-baked yard, from which a fine dust blew on the gentle summer breeze. 'Oh, Abbie, must you stay in this dreadful place? Can't Matthew . . . ?'

'Sh.' Abigail put her fingers to her lips. 'He'll be down in a minute when he's tucked William into bed. I'm happy with Matthew, Eddie,' she went on hurriedly in a low voice. 'He provides me with the best he's able and I'm content. He's a good man.'

'All the same,' Eddie argued, 'this is a terrible place for you to live and bring up little ones. Oh, I know you've made the cottage very comfortable,' he added quickly, seeing her expression, 'but it's not what you're used to, is it?' He looked at his sister in her plain grey dress, her face paler than ever, with lines of worry etching themselves round her eyes, her hair dragged back out of the way under a plain white cap. Yet he could see that she was happy, and this radiated from her, giving her plain face a beauty it had previously lacked.

'It's what I'm used to now, Eddie,' she said quietly. 'I knew Matthew was a poor man when I married him.'

'But I'm sure – with your help, Abbie – he could do much better with his oysters.'

'Of course he could.' She spoke impatiently. 'Do you think I don't realize that? But his grandfather owns the boat. He takes a share for himself and a share for the boat of everything Matthew catches, be it the oysters he dredges or the sprats he catches in the winter. Matthew and Tolley have a share each.'

'But Matthew should get more than Tolley. After all, he's old Zac's grandson.'

Abigail shook her head. 'Tolley has to feed little Moses, the cabin boy. He lives with him and his wife. Moses sleeps under their kitchen table.'

'It still doesn't seem fair to me,' Edwin said, 'and I'm sure, with your help, he could do better.'

Abigail shook her head. 'It's no good, Eddie. I've spoken to him about it and he says he can do nothing while his grandfather lives. It's Old Zac's business, such as it is, and he insists on running it the way it's been run for the past fifty years. Don't you think it irks me to see the best oysters on the Colne sold for half what they would fetch on the London market? But if I complain too much Matthew will think I'm dissatisfied with him and the home he's made for me. I wouldn't have him think I'm unhappy with the way things are, Eddie. Not for all the world.'

'You really love him, don't you, Abbie.' It was a statement, not a question, but she answered it.

'With all my heart.'

Eddie shook his head. 'Oh, Abbie, if only . . . '

'Are you still keeping your music up?' she interrupted, hearing Matthew's heavy step on the stairs.

'Yes, I manage to find time for that. In fact, I don't know what I'd do without it. It's a sort of, I don't know, outlet I suppose. Do you know what I mean?'

'Oh, yes. I know exactly what you mean, Eddie.' She warmed the brown teapot and measured tea into it. 'I've told you before, I could always judge your mood by the music you were playing.' She poured water into the teapot and then turned to Matthew. 'I could always tell. It was quick and lively when he was happy, heavy and loud when he was cross, slow and haunting when he was anxious or worried.' She laughed. 'I've never known anyone who could play the same piece of music in so many different ways.'

Edwin laughed, but the sound held no mirth. 'You would certainly be able to tell my feelings from the music I play after matins every Sunday, these days.' He shook his head. 'How the guv'nor and his cronies can sit there, week after week, with their smug, self-satisfied expressions, singing hymns and praying to the Almighty, "Thy will be done", while they grow fat on the sweated labour of their fellow men, just beats me.'

'Do you think the canal they're talking about will ever come to pass?' Matthew asked, taking his place at the table. He talked easily to Edwin, his previous constraint, caused by their different stations in life, forgotten in shared Liberal views. 'It would certainly make things easier for traffic between Wivenhoe and the Hythe if there was a canal and wet dock. At least we shouldn't be quite so dependent on the state of the tide all the time.'

'There's still a lot of talk about it,' Edwin agreed. 'And of course my father and Mr Hayfield are all in favour. They're agitating for a loop line from the new railway to come out to the Hythe, too.'

'I can see the wisdom in that,' Matthew agreed. 'The railway's no good to them where it is, nearly three miles away. It's easier to continue sending goods to London by water. Why they built it right out in that godforsaken spot I'll never know. It's miles from anywhere. It should have come to the Hythe in the first place. After all, that's where the industry is.' Matthew shook his head. 'I sometimes wonder if the railways are worth all the fuss and bother, myself.'

'Oh, yes, Matt, I'm sure they're the thing of the future. The country will be revolutionized by them. Imagine, it only takes three hours to send goods from here to London. Oh, yes, they're the transport of the future. For people as well as goods.'

'I still think as far as Colchester's concerned the canal is the best bet,' Matthew said thoughtfully.

Edwin sighed. 'The trouble is, a canal would mean the river itself would silt up even more than it already does. And it wouldn't simply be with mud. The river is already little more than an open sewer, but at least it's tidal, so the filth all gets carried away on the tide. Mind you, Colchester's problems are nothing compared with some of the big towns. I've just read a report by a chap called Edwin Chadwick. The things he talks about make your blood curdle. Places like Sheffield and Manchester, where they've built row upon row of back-to-back houses for the workers in the new industries, with little or no provision for sanitation at all.'

'Yes, you wrote about it in the *Essex Standard*, didn't you?' Matthew said. 'I remember reading it.'

Abigail's heart swelled with pride at her husband's words. The hours spent toiling over the slate night after night had been well spent. 'You still write for the paper, then?' Abigail asked.

'Oh, yes. More and more. In fact, Mr Young, the editor, has asked me to join his permanent staff. And I've agreed.'

'Eddie!' Abigail stopped in the act of pouring out the tea. 'Whatever will Father say? How will he manage without you?'

'He'll raise the roof and I shall have to leave home. But as I've found myself a room in one of the houses that have just been built over near the new workhouse that won't bother me. In fact, I'll be glad to get out. The guv'nor and I simply don't see eye to eye over so many things . . . '

'But what about the business? The warehouse? The shop?'

'Mr Heckford runs the fish shop; he doesn't need any interference from me. And now that Carver is dead . . . '

'Ezra Carver dead? I didn't know that,' Abigail said.

'Oh, it must be about six months since he died. Poor devil ended up in the workhouse. I tried to get him into the new hospital, but they'll only take people who are going to get better, anyway – I s'pose it looks bad to have too many deaths on the records. Father, of course, washed his hands of him when he could no longer earn his keep. I did what I could, and Carver had a woman in to look after him till the money ran out. Then . . . ' Edwin spread his hands.

'Poor Ezra.' Abigail gave an involuntary shudder. 'It's true I never liked him, but I would never have wished him such a sad end.'

'Your father surely won't be able to spare you with Carver gone,' Matthew said, helping himself to more brawn.

Edwin followed suit. 'Oh, indeed he will. He's found himself a man called Richard Cotgrove, a fellow in his early thirties, I should say. *Very* smart fellow, in every sense. Natty dresser and shrewd businessman. Oh, now the guv'nor's got Richard I'm quite *persona non grata*. I'm just about sick of hearing him sing Cotgrove's praises from morn till night and sick of being told it's a pity I'm not more like him.' He shrugged. 'Oh, Cotgrove's a decent enough fellow, I daresay; a bit flashy and over-ambitious for my liking, but not a bad sort. But one tends to take agin a chap who's always being held up as a paragon of all the virtues one lacks oneself, if you know what I mean.'

Matthew drank his tea thoughtfully. 'Richard Cotgrove. Yes, I'm sure I've noticed his coat-tails disappearing up the stairs to your father's office.'

Edwin laughed. 'And that's about all you would see. He whisks about like a ferret in a fit. All done to impress Father, of course.' He yawned. 'But that's enough of that.' He drained his tea and pulled out his pocket watch at the same time. 'I must go. I've an article to finish and it has to be on Mr Young's desk at nine o'clock sharp tomorrow morning. Mustn't blot my copy book by handing it in late, especially as I'm dining with the family tomorrow night.'

Abigail raised her eyebrows. 'Dinner with the family, Eddie?'

'You're really getting your feet under the table there, boy, aren't you?' Matthew laughed. 'Who invited you, Mr Young or Miss Belinda?'

'Neither of them, actually. It was Mrs Young,' Edwin grinned. 'Anyway. I must go. I've promised Pearl . . . '

'Yes, how is Pearl? You haven't even mentioned her.' Abigail handed him his hat and accompanied him to the door.

'Pearl? Oh, she seems to have calmed down, now. She doesn't have quite so many young men calling on her these days. Mind you, she's out a lot.' He grinned. 'Calling on them, for all I know.'

'Oh, Eddie. You don't mean that!'

'No, I don't, although she did go a bit wild after you left home. But she's all right now, I think. Except that the guv'nor still invites the army officers to dinner when they're in the town on a recruiting drive and she flirts like mad with them.'

Abigail sighed. 'Oh, yes, I remember how she was with Lieutenant Barraclough. Does he still visit?'

'No, he doesn't come any more now. Her latest beau is a Captain Sanders, I believe.'

'Oh, I wish she'd marry and settle down.'

'So does the guv'nor, in a way. He'd like nothing better than to give her a slap-up wedding. The only snag is, the man's not been born that's worthy of his Pearl beyond price.' He roared with laughter. 'But Pearl doesn't seem too worried. I think she enjoys herself as things are.'

Abigail watched Edwin walk across the yard, then she went and sat down at the table again.

'You look anxious, my little love,' Matthew said, covering her hand with his. 'But I'm sure you don't need to worry about Edwin. He knows just what he's about.'

She shook her head, staring out into the yard where the rays of the sun were casting long shadows. 'It's not Edwin I worry about, Matthew,' she said sadly. 'It's Pearl.'

# *Chapter Nine*

'No, Papa, I can't arrange a dinner party at any time at all over the next few weeks,' Pearl said to her father on one of her rare appearances at breakfast. 'I've been invited to my friends the Harrises, and to the Saunders, too. Then I have to fit in visits to the Cowells, the Bentleys, the Fitches, the Prentice-Johnsons and the Clarkes. I've so many engagements I simply don't know which way to turn. And then there's the Midsummer Ball at the Three Cups Hotel. You'll be attending that, won't you, Papa? Just about *everybody* will be there.'

Henry sighed. 'I don't know. I haven't decided. I expect so.' He got up and helped himself to more kidneys. 'Pour me another cup of tea, please, dear.' He pushed his cup over to her. 'Oh, and try not to let your sleeve drabble in the milk, dear. I really don't know why you can't get dressed properly in the morning instead of coming down to breakfast in that stupid, frilly thing.' He smiled at her to prove that he was not really as irritated with her as he sounded.

'It wasn't worth getting dressed. My dressmaker is coming at ten.' Pearl poured the tea and handed it to him, knocking over the marmalade jar with her sleeve in the process. Ignoring her father's expression she righted it and reached for a piece of toast without further mishap.

'But your dressmaker came yesterday,' Henry protested. 'And the day before.'

'And she'll be coming tomorrow and the day after.' Pearl smiled her most winning smile at her father. 'Don't you want me to look nice, Papa? I thought you liked me to do you credit.'

'Yes, my pet, of course I do.' He dabbed at his whiskers with his napkin. 'But I wish you were at home just a little more often to grace my table instead of always gracing other people's. Can't you fit in a dinner party for me at any time? I feel I should entertain more than I do. The servants will be kicking their heels with nothing to do.'

'Very well, Papa. I'll look in my engagement diary.' With a deep sigh Pearl got up from the table and rummaged among a heap of magazines for it. 'Ah, here it is. Yes. July the seventeenth. How will that suit you, Papa?'

'Can't you manage something before that? I need to entertain my business friends. I always used to . . .' He checked himself. When Abigail was at home his dinner parties were the envy of the town.

'Yes, you always used to,' Pearl said, reading his mind. 'But that was when Abigail was at home to do your bidding at every turn. But she's gone and I'm not to be trampled underfoot like a doormat. If July the seventeenth won't do then you must make arrangements to entertain your friends at The Red Lion or The George, or else find someone else to act as hostess.' Pearl flounced back to her chair and bit, not very daintily, into her toast.

'Very well, my pet, the seventeenth it shall be,' Henry soothed. 'I had simply hoped that it could be sooner because the officers would have been in town then, recruiting for the army. But they'll be gone by the seventeenth and won't be back again for some time.'

'Oh!' Pearl's interest was aroused and she reached again for her engagement diary. 'Oh, yes. I had overlooked the tenth. And look here, the fourth, too. How silly of me. What about those dates?' She looked up at her father, the picture of helpfulness.

Henry nodded. 'The fourth will do very well, my pet. Can I leave all the arrangements to you? I think we'd better make it quite lavish as we haven't entertained for some time.' He didn't add that he was anxious that his business friends should not be aware of how much he had lost speculating on the railway. He had put a lot into the Eastern Counties line, projected to run from London to Norwich, little suspecting that it would take all of seven years simply to reach as far as Colchester and would cost a cool million and a half to do it. Then there were the vast sums in compensation that had been paid to wealthy landowners over whose territory the line passed so that they should not raise objections that might reach unfriendly Parliamentary ears. And the fiasco last March when the line was finally opened! Two thousand excited people gathered to cheer the great event of the first train to arrive! Only it didn't. It was two whole days late! If that was a foretaste of the way the railways were going to be run it didn't bode very well for the future. Henry was beginning to wonder if they were such a marvellous thing as George Hudson, the so-called Railway King, made out. He couldn't see the Eastern Counties line getting as far as Ipswich, at the rate it was going, let alone Norwich. Turning from such gloomy thoughts he brought his mind back to the matter in hand.

'I'll make up the guest list, but shall we say thirty? Must give the servants something to do now that there is only you and me here, mustn't we, dear?'

Pearl made a noise that was something between a grunt and a snort and left the room, annoyed with herself that she had allowed her father to persuade her into organizing his dinner party. Not that she had much idea of how to go about it; she would leave that side of it to Ellen. But it was interesting that the officers were back. Which ones had come this time, she wondered.

Effie was sympathetic when Henry told her of his conversation with Pearl.

'She's ungrateful. That's what she is, ungrateful, Harry,' she said, pursing her tiny mouth in disapproval, 'and after all you do for her, too. She should be pleased to do whatever she can for you. It's the least she can do. She ought to realize which side her bread is buttered and be thankful.' She pushed over a silver dish of tiny cakes, making sure to lean well over the table in the act. 'Have one of my maids of honour, Harry. They're delicious. I made them with my own fair hands. And you know how good I am with my hands, don't you, Harry?' She winked, knowingly. 'Perhaps I ought to have called them maids of dishonour. What do you think?'

He began to sweat slightly. 'I don't think I want . . . '

'Oh, go on, have one.' She leaned over a bit further and gave a little wriggle. 'Surely, you can wait five minutes, Harry? Surely you don't want me to waste this nice pot of tea I've made? Or would you like me to make a fresh pot? Later?' She took him by the hand and led him up the stairs.

Even as he undressed her Henry was filled with mixed feelings. He had been visiting Effie Markham for nearly ten years now, ever since Edith had turned away from his attentions. He suspected that Edith had known and had turned a blind eye, realizing that a man had needs and being content because he had been a good husband and father in every other way.

Effie was a plump, fluffy woman, shrewd enough to know how to keep a man satisfied, but other than that –Henry sometimes wondered if her mind worked on any other level. She talked in platitudes and agreed with everything he said. She had no opinions of her own. She was really quite dull and boring. At one level.

But on the other – he stopped regarding her objectively and gave himself up to enjoy yet again her expertise in keeping him happy.

As he rode home afterwards, having stayed just long enough for the ritual of the tea and maids of honour, which were as dry as chaff, with pastry fit for boot soles, he congratulated himself that he hadn't given in to the inclination that had been teasing his mind of late. And that was to install Effie Markham as housekeeper at Hilltop House.

He'd given it serious thought. Abigail, curse her, had been gone three years now. As far as he was concerned she no longer even existed. Edwin had spread his wings and flown. And not before time, either. The arguments that had raged over the dinner table between them because of his ridiculous Liberal ideas had given Henry more dyspepsia than he had ever suffered from in his whole life. That boy's radical views would land him in trouble before he was finished. All this talk about Sir Edwin Chadwick and his sanitary reports. People had got mighty fussy, all of a sudden, noticing and complaining about the sights and smells that always had been a part of life and always would be.

Henry dug his heels into Boxer's sides and the horse walked a fraction faster for a few minutes. Having disposed of his two elder children, Henry turned his thoughts to Pearl. She was pretty, flighty and – he had to admit it –empty-headed. The plain fact had to be faced up to that she had no thought in her head beyond the latest fashion and calling on her friends and acquaintances. She enjoyed having her own carriage to drive around in and having plenty of money to keep up with the right people. As long as there was always a string of young men dancing attention on her, Pearl would be happy. In lower circles there was a name for women like her. No. Henry checked himself. That was not true. Pearl was mildly flirtatious, that was all. He sighed. Perhaps it would be better if she were to be married. But then he would be left alone.

Once more his thoughts turned to Effie Markham.

Abigail bought a little cake for William's second birthday and stuck two little candles in it. There was no money for any other kind of celebration. But William, so like his father in looks but with a shock of coppery hair, had been excited because he had been allowed to blow the candles out; he was never allowed to touch the candle that lit him to bed each night. He was in bed now, cuddling the peg doll that Alice had made him from a clothes peg and some bits of rag and Abigail smiled at the recollection of the circle of candlelight reflected in his eager, button-bright eyes as he had puffed out his cheeks in order to quench the little flames. Laura was asleep in her cradle on the hearth and Abigail sat with her sewing in the open doorway to catch the last of the daylight. She could see the children from the other cottages in the yard, ragged, dirty and verminous, squabbling on the patch of dirt that was the only playground they had, and she sighed. It was easy enough to keep William clean now, but soon he would beg to be allowed to play with them. And what then?

She put down her sewing to watch the wretched little urchins and was surprised to see a smartly dressed woman enter the yard from the alley beside The Dolphin. The woman paused, as if unsure if she was in the right place, and called to one of the children.

Abigail recognized her voice even before the child had a chance to point to her cottage. 'Pearl!' she called excitedly. She held out her arms. 'Oh, Pearl. You've come to see me. I'm so glad ...' She got no further as Pearl flung herself across the yard into her waiting arms and burst into tears.

'Pearl. My dear, whatever's wrong?' Abigail drew her sister into the cottage and closed the door, for she knew the people from the other houses would be agog to know what such a fine lady was doing visiting the Batemans. 'Now, sit down and tell me. Is it Father? He's ill?'

'No. No, it's nothing like that.' Pearl shook her head impatiently and sat down as best she could at the table, hampered by her voluminous skirts in the small room.

'Take your bonnet off, dear. It's all askew,' Abigail said gently. Then she sat down opposite her sister, waiting.

With an effort Pearl pulled herself together. 'What a poky little room,' she said, looking round. 'And so dark, too.'

'I'll light the lamp.' Abigaïl fetched the oil lamp and placed it in the middle of the table. 'There, is that better?'

'Not much. It's still a hovel. We've got gas lights now, you know.' Pearl sniffed and peered into the cradle where Laura lay sleeping. 'Is this your baby?'

'Yes, and William is asleep upstairs. Today is his second birthday. Unfortunately his father is out in his boat. It's the beginning of the oyster season, you know. Matthew takes his grandfather out on the river to watch the opening ceremony.'

'Yes. I know it's the opening of the season.' Pearl brushed the remark aside.

Abigail waited, watching her sister. Pearl had taken her gloves off and was screwing them up in her hands. 'I know you must be wondering why I've come here, when I treated you so badly last time we met,' she said, not looking at Abigail. 'I'll be quite truthful. I wouldn't have come now, but I don't know who else to turn to. And after all, you're still my sister, so it's your duty to help me.'

Abigail bit back a retort reminding Pearl that she had felt no dutiful feelings towards her, Abigail, when she had been in trouble.

Pearl looked up. 'You see, I don't know what to do. I'm to have a child.'

Abigail received the news in silence. Deep in her heart she was shocked, but, she had to admit, not altogether surprised after what Edwin had told her. 'Who is the child's father?' she said at last.

Pearl's eyebrows shot up in surprise. 'What difference does that make?'

'All the difference in the world, I should think, since he'll have to marry you,' Abigail said dryly.

'But can't you ... ? Isn't there anything I could take? You're married. You must know ... ' Panic showed in Pearl's tear-stained face.

Abigail shook her head. 'There's nothing I can do and nothing that I know of that you could take. And I wouldn't tell you if there was. It's too dangerous. People have died ... '

'But what am I going to do?'

'Tell the father, whoever he is, and if he's any sort of gentleman he'll marry you without delay.'

Pearl pouted. 'I'm not sure I want to marry a soldier. Oh, the uniform's nice, but he'd have to keep going away.'

Abigail went round the table to her sister. 'Don't be ridiculous. Of course you'll marry him. And soon.' She gave Pearl's shoulders a shake. 'Do you want Papa to turn you out into the street?'

‘He would never do that.’

‘Don’t be so sure. Look what he did to me.’

‘Yes, but that was different. You deserved it, marrying that stupid Bateman.’

‘Don’t speak like that of Matthew or you’ll have to leave,’ Abigail said sharply. ‘And remember, whatever I did I wasn’t bringing the shame of a bastard child on him.’

Pearl got up from the table. ‘I thought you’d help me to get rid of it. I’m disappointed in you, Abbie.’

‘Not half as disappointed as I am in you, both to think you should have got yourself into such a mess and then to think I’d get you out of it,’ Abigail snapped. She went with Pearl to the door. ‘You must speak to Papa and tell him he must arrange for you to be married to . . . ?’

‘Captain Brightwell,’ Pearl mumbled. ‘Although I’m not sure I want to spend the rest of my life tied to Percy Brightwell.’

‘You should have thought of that before you took him to your bed,’ Abigail said unsympathetically. ‘Anyway, it’ll be better than spending it on the streets or in the workhouse.’

‘I suppose you’re right. I’ll tell Percy tomorrow that I’m to have his child.’

‘And Papa. You must tell Papa, too.’

‘Oh, Percy will have to do that.’

‘There’s not time, you little goose. You must tell him yourself. And you’ll have to tell him why the wedding must be soon.’

Pearl looked stricken. ‘Oh, Abbie. I couldn’t tell Papa. He’d kill me.’

‘He’s got to know.’

‘You tell him, Abbie.’

‘Me? When he won’t even speak to me? It’s no good me trying to tell him, he’ll never listen.’

'Well, you must make him. Please, Abbie, I beg you. Do it for me.' Pearl turned and hugged Abigail, her eyes filled with tears again.

Abigail sighed deeply. 'Very well, I'll try. Oh, Pearl, why did you get yourself into such a mess? You must have known where it could lead.'

Pearl shrugged. 'I was only having a bit of fun, and, well, it went too far. That's all.'

'That's all!' Abigail repeated, exasperated. 'And quite enough, too, I should think.'

Pearl kissed her. 'I'm glad I came to see you, Abbie. It doesn't seem half so bad now. And I'm sure it's the right thing to marry Percy. He's quite nice really.' She stepped back into the cottage and looked in Laura's cradle. 'Yes, it might be quite nice to have a little baby. I think I shall quite enjoy it.' She smiled at Abigail and went off, picking her way carefully across the yard.

Matthew arrived home with a dozen of the first oysters of the season and a tot of gin and piece of gingerbread, a habit he'd kept since William's birth. He received the news of Pearl's visit tight-lipped. His only comment was, 'Ah, yes, she'll run to you quickly enough when she's in trouble, won't she?'

'But I must help her if I can. You do see that, don't you, Matthew? After all, she's still my sister.'

'And you're hers. But I thank God you've got more charity in your soul than she has, my little love.' He kissed her. 'I wish you well when you visit Henry Chiswell, for he's a hard man.'

The next afternoon she made her way up the familiar stairs at the warehouse to her father's office, a pale figure in her limp, darned dress, the paisley shawl Edwin had given her round her shoulders more for support than warmth because the day was sunny and cloudless. Yet her hands as she clutched the shawl round her were clammy and her heart hammered uncomfortably in her breast. It took all her courage to climb the stairs.

Before she could reach the top the door opposite her father's office opened and a man of medium height, neatly dressed, with a rose in his buttonhole, sleek, dark hair and a small moustache, came out.

'Yes?' he asked, not quite rudely. 'What do you want?'

'I want to see my father, if you please,' Abigail replied with dignity.

He was clearly surprised to hear such a well-modulated voice coming from a person of such humble appearance and even more so to hear the words she uttered. He stared at her in evident astonishment for several seconds.

'My father,' she repeated. 'I wish to see my father. My name is Abigail Bateman. You, I believe, are Richard Cotgrove. My brother Edwin has spoken of you.'

There was a certain admiration in his eyes as he regarded the small, shabby woman on the stairs: to think she had the temerity to visit Henry Chiswell after, as everyone knew, he had declared he would have nothing more to do with her. He shook his head. 'I'm afraid it's no use,' he said, with a tinge of regret. 'I'm afraid he won't see you, even if I tell him you're here.'

'Then don't tell him.' Abigail took a deep breath and marched straight into Henry's office without knocking, leaving Richard gaping on the landing.

'Ah, Cotgrove, have you brought those papers I asked for?' Henry said without looking up. 'Put them . . . ' He glanced up. 'My God, what are you doing here? How dare you walk into my office unannounced! Get out. Get out this minute, before I call the constable!' Purple with rage Henry stood up, nearly overturning his chair.

Deliberately ignoring his outburst Abigail pulled up a chair and sat down. 'Not until you've heard what I have to say,' she said, with a calmness she was far from feeling. 'And you will listen to me' – her voice rose as he began to bluster – 'because it concerns Pearl.'

Still he continued to order her out and she had to raise her voice still further. 'Will you be quiet and hear me?' she shouted at last. 'Or are you happy to let the entire neighbourhood hear me tell you that Pearl is to have a child?'

At that he fell back in his chair, his mouth open, staring at her as she told him of Pearl's visit. 'A lavish wedding, if it can be arranged quickly, will allay any suspicions. Captain Brightwell being in the army, a hurried wedding will not appear strange. And if the child is a little early – well, seven-month babies are not unheard of.'

She stood up and looked down at her father. The purple hue of his rage had given way to a strange greyness and he seemed to have shrunk in his chair. She discovered that far from being afraid of him as she had been when she arrived she felt nothing but pity for an old man whose children had all failed his hopes and aspirations. 'If it's all done quickly there is no need for there to be shame or disgrace,' she said quietly, adding – she didn't know why – 'If you need me, just send for me.'

He looked up, his lip curling. 'I want no interference from you, Madam.'

After Abigail had gone Henry reached down into a drawer for the whisky bottle and poured himself a liberal shot. Then he sat staring at an inkstain on his desk. It was shaped a bit like a heart, he registered with a corner of his mind. A heart. That was appropriate. A symbol of love. He loved Pearl. Was he jealous to think she might love this army captain? He was a nice enough fellow, a bit weak-chinned, perhaps, but other than that . . . He took a gulp of whisky and refilled his glass. Come to think of it, was Brightwell's relationship with Pearl any different from his with Effie? Good God, he hoped so. Effie was no more than a lustful convenience; there must be more to it than that for Pearl. No, it was nothing like that, the man must have forced himself on the girl. And he'd pay for it. By God he would. He'd marry Pearl if Henry himself had to frogmarch him to the altar.

He emptied his glass and sat for a long time staring at the ink-stain. He didn't know what to do; where to go. Usually if he had any worry he would pay Effie a visit. Not that he ever told her any of his business and financial problems but she always knew if he was worried and she knew how to take his mind off things. No, he didn't want to see Effie today. In fact the thought of her amorous athletics made him feel slightly sick. He didn't want to think about sex at all.

But he must. He must talk to Pearl and then he must see young Brightwell before the recruiting officers moved on again. If they'd already moved on to Chelmsford or Ipswich he'd have to go after them. Whatever happened, Pearl's good name must not be tarnished.

He got up from his chair and reached for his hat and cane.

The house was quiet when he reached it, the servants shut away in the basement, probably enjoying an afternoon nap or gossip. For once he was glad they weren't busy about their tasks upstairs. It meant he could talk to Pearl without fear of interruption. He went to the morning room but she was not there, nor in any of the other rooms downstairs. Fear clutched at his heart. Surely she hadn't eloped with the young puppy! He took the stairs two at a time to see if her things were still in her bedroom.

Flinging open the door he went inside. Pearl was there, in bed, her face the colour of the pillow and her eyes closed. She dragged them open as she heard him enter.

'Pearl, my dear little girl. You're ill.' All thoughts of what he'd been going to say to her left his mind as he rushed to her side. 'What is it, my child? Has the doctor been called?'

Pearl shook her head almost imperceptibly. 'Too late,' she whispered, through white lips. 'I tried to be rid of it ... Percy said I must ... He couldn't marry me ... a wife already ... ' She closed her eyes again, gathering strength to finish. 'He said he knew where I could go ... In Vineyard Street ... ' She rolled her head from side to side. 'I think I'm dying, Papa.'

'Nonsense, child.' He patted her hand nervously. 'I'll send for Doctor Green right away.' He went briskly out of the door, glad of something positive he could do. When he came back into Pearl's pretty, frilly pink and white room he went and sat by the bed and took her limp hand in his to wait for Doctor Green.

'Papa ... ' It was hardly more than a sigh.

'Hush, my child. Don't try to speak. Save your strength.'

But there was no strength left. By the time Doctor Green arrived Pearl was dead.

The doctor was a big, ungainly man with great hands that could be surprisingly tender. He pulled back the covers and surveyed the mess. 'Those bloody back-street butchers ought to be hung, drawn and quartered,' he growled. But he covered Pearl over gently. 'Poor little girl,' he said quietly. 'What a terrible waste.'

'There'll be no scandal,' Henry said anxiously. Even in his grief he thought first of his good name. 'I trust that you'll make sure my daughter's name isn't besmirched.'

'If you mean am I going to put on her death certificate that she died of a back-street abortion that went wrong then you can rest assured, Mr Chiswell. I've eaten too often at your table not to couch it in more delicate terms than that. I shall see to it there's no breath of anything untoward.'

Doctor Green did what he had to do and left Henry to his grief and to the shattering realization that his youngest child hadn't been as pure and blameless as he had always deluded himself.

Naturally, it fell to Edwin to tell Abigail of Pearl's tragic death and they wept bitter tears together.

'She came to me for help and I did nothing,' Abigail wept bitterly.

Edwin, strong now, put his arm round her. 'You told her she must be married. And soon. You weren't to know that the blackguard was already married. I've since discovered he's not only married but got four children into the bargain, the swine. He'd better not set foot in Colchester again or I'll kill him with my bare hands, I swear it.'

'I shall go to her funeral,' Abigail said.

She waited at the gate of St Leonard's churchyard, her shawl pulled closely round her. She heard the clop of the horses' hooves before the undertaker's mute appeared out of the icy fog, followed by the shadowy forms of black-plumed horses pulling the black-curtained funeral carriage. She followed the coffin into the graveyard, slipping in behind all the other mourners and standing a little apart until Edwin's hand under her elbow propelled her forward to the edge of the grave. 'You're her sister,' he whispered. 'You have every right to be here.' When the service was over and Henry, weeping as Abigail had never seen him, had thrown a handful of earth down on to the last remains of his youngest child, the mourners all left. Henry, Edwin and Abigail remained at the graveside.

The old man, who had aged twenty years and looked seventy, looked up and saw Abigail. With the tears still wet on his face his expression hardened. 'What are you doing here, Madam?' he said, his lip curling. 'If you're thinking to crawl back into my favour because Pearl is . . . is gone, then you are greatly mistaken. How many times do you need telling that I want nothing to do with you? NOTHING.' He squared his shoulders and walked away without a backward glance.

Edwin took Abigail home.

# *Chapter Ten*

Pearl's sudden, tragic death caused a flurry of interest in Colchester and was the talking point in all the salons and assemblies for several months. But Doctor Green had been as good as his word and in spite of speculation from all quarters no hint of any kind of scandal ever emerged, despite Pearl's reputation among people of her set of being somewhat fast.

By comparison, the death of Old Zac Bateman, Matthew's grandfather, two years after Pearl's, passed almost unnoticed.

He died quietly and without fuss as he wheeled his oyster barrow down onto the hard at Brightlingsea one cold November morning in 1845. He left his boat and everything he possessed, which amounted to nearly two hundred pounds, to Matthew.

'I shall miss him,' Matthew said as he sat by the fire with Abigail and the children the day after the old man had been laid to rest in the churchyard on the hill overlooking his beloved river. 'He was an awkward, stubborn old cuss – and mean, too. I had no idea he had so much money. Mind you, apart from a pint of porter and a bit of baccy he never spent any. I never saw him in anything but sea boots and that old reefer jacket he'd worn for years. All the same, I was fond of the old rascal. He taught me all I know about fishing.'

Abigail smiled sadly. 'But he never forgave you for marrying a Chiswell, did he? He wouldn't even let you take the children to see him. Just look at what he missed.' She gazed fondly at the two children, William, four now, and his sister Laura, two and a half, as they played together on the hearth.

Matthew frowned. 'It wasn't so much that he never forgave me, although it's true, he didn't, but he simply refused to recognize the fact that I was married. As far as he was concerned nothing had changed. If I as much as spoke about you or the children his face would go completely wooden, as if he'd never heard a word I'd said.' He smiled at Abigail. 'But I soon learned not to take any notice of him. He was a "rum ole cove", to use his own words. How Grannie put up with him for all those years I just don't know.' He stared into the fire, puffing at his clay pipe, while the children played on the hearth and Abigail sewed by the light of the lamp. After a while he went on, 'Right up till the day he died I could never make him realize what a blessing you are to me. He just pretended he hadn't heard what I'd said. But I'm sure that the reason he refused to let the oysters go to London to be marketed was because he guessed it was your idea. Cussed old devil.' But he said the words with affection.

'Oh, you did suggest sending them to London, then?' Abigail said, surprised.

'Oh, yes. Many, many times. But I knew it was no use. Once he dug his toes in over anything he never gave in. He'd have starved rather than agree.' Matthew laughed. 'Mind you, seeing what money he left there was never any danger of that!'

Abigail laid her sewing neatly on the table. 'But there's nothing to prevent us sending oysters to London now, is there, Matthew?' she said quietly. 'We could buy that old warehouse at the end of the quay with some of the money he left you. It would make an ideal packing shed. Bateman's green-beards ... the best in the land ... What do you say, dear?' She looked at him, holding her breath, willing him to agree with her.

Matthew puffed his pipe thoughtfully for a moment. Then he grinned. 'You mean you'd set up in opposition to your own father? Shame on you, Mrs Bateman.'

'Oh, I don't think we'd ever be as successful as my father,' Abigail said, taking his words seriously. 'He's the outlet for the Colne Fishery oysters. They're all sold through the fishmonger's shop in the Market Place that Mr Heckford runs for Father, or they're barrelled and sent to London from his warehouse on the quay. Add to that his own dredging smacks that earn him yet another share from the fishery and – well, it's no wonder he's a rich man.'

'I don't really understand this Colne Fishery business,' Matthew said with a sigh. 'It's never affected Grandad and me, except that we knew we weren't allowed to dredge in the river itself. But it never bothered us overmuch because our layings in Brightlingsea Creek kept us going.'

'I can tell you about it,' Abigail picked up her sewing again. 'The Colne Fishery, as it's called, belongs to Colchester Corporation and has done from time immemorial. The ancient charters go back to something like the twelfth century. What it means is that you must become a Freeman of the river – that is, hold a licence from the corporation, before you can dredge Colne. I think it was about forty years ago that the Freemen formed themselves into the Colne Fishery Company. They work together, more or less, and pay the corporation ten shillings a dredge and sixpence for the town clerk's fee – or two guineas for four dredges, which amounts to the same thing. It might pay us to apply to join the Company now that your grandfather is dead, Matthew,' she finished thoughtfully.

'Never!' Matthew banged his fist down on the table with such force that it made the lamp splutter. 'That I'll never do.'

The two children scrambled to their feet at his words and clutched at Abigail's skirts. They were not used to such a display of anger from their gentle father.

Matthew's face had darkened. 'Your father is on the licensing board. Do you think I'll go crawling to him for a licence, only to have my application refused on some jumped-up excuse? And don't try to tell me he has no influence, Abbie, because that I'll never believe. No, we'll carry on as we are. My layings are good, there are plenty of oysters and my fattening grounds produce good green-beards. We'll do very well on our own, my girl. We've no need to go grovelling to Henry Chiswell and his cronies.'

Abigail had never seen him so furious. 'Just as you say, dear,' she answered meekly. 'But we'll market in London?'

'Yes. We'll market in London.' He shook his head as if to clear it. 'I'm sorry, princess, I shouldn't have lost my temper like that.' He looked at her. 'How do we go about it?'

'Let me put the children to bed and then we'll talk about it.' A small smile played about Abigail's lips. At last, she was getting her way.

When the children were safely asleep they talked and talked, far into the night. Then, next morning Matthew took some of the money his grandfather had left him and went to see Mr Hayfield, who owned the old wool warehouse at the end of the quay.

Silas Hayfield was taken by surprise to discover that it was young Bateman who wanted the old warehouse and at first he had a mind to refuse this man, who had had the audacity to marry the daughter of his friend Henry, and to drag her down to his level. But the warehouse was old and leaky, and it stood at the wrong end of the quay. It was earning nothing as it stood there, rotting, and Silas was not one to miss up on a chance to turn an extra shilling. So he named a price far in excess of what it was worth and was surprised again when the young man, politely but firmly, offered him a more realistic sum. After Henry's harsh words regarding the man Silas found himself unwillingly impressed by his open, honest bearing.

'What are you plannin' to use it for, then, boy?' he asked, swivelling in his chair and picking his teeth.

'Packing oysters and sending them to London,' Matthew answered truthfully, after a slight hesitation, knowing how friendly this man was with Henry Chiswell.

'Settin' up in opposition to your father-in-law, are ye, ye cheeky young bugger?' Silas eyed him thoughtfully. It wouldn't please Henry if he sold the warehouse to Bateman, but somehow he'd taken a fancy to this young man. Perhaps he wasn't as black as Henry painted him; at least he hadn't tried to hide the purpose for which he wanted the warehouse. And from what he had observed over the years young Bateman was a hard-working fellow, although it was unlikely he would ever amount to much. He worked too hard to make any money. 'All right, you can have it,' he nodded, bringing his chair to a standstill. He grinned, but it was a grin that turned his mouth down into his beard instead of up, and narrowed his eyes into shrewd slits. 'But forget I asked you what you were going to use it for. It's best I don't know that.' He watched while Matthew counted out the sovereigns on to the desk. Then he made out a receipt. 'I'll get my clerk to look out the deeds for you,' he said, handing Matthew the receipt. He hesitated a minute, looking Matthew up and down. Then he added, with an unusual display of generosity, 'If you want timber to repair it, see Jakes, my yardman. There'll be no charge for it.'

Abigail was elated when he told her and together they visited the old warehouse.

'It won't take much more than a couple of days to make it weatherproof, if Tolley and Moses give me a hand,' Matthew said excitedly. 'We can do the rest when the season's over and we've got a bit of time to spare.'

'And I'll go and see Mr Grimes and order barrels,' Abigail said, her face shining. 'Oh, Matthew, you don't know how I've longed for this day.'

'We'll need someone to do the sorting and packing.' Matthew scratched his beard thoughtfully. 'I'm afraid Grandad's money . . . '

'We don't need to spend money on that. Not yet, anyway. I can pack oysters. I've seen it done hundreds of times. And I've helped.' She hugged his arm. 'You bring me the oysters, I'll get them packed and sent to Billingsgate. Let's see. Shall we aim for the Friday boat next week? That'll be just right for the weekend market and it'll give you time to repair the warehouse before you go down river. And it'll give the cooper time to deliver the barrels. Shall I order twenty barrels to begin with? We mustn't neglect your Brightlingsea customers. But they'll have to start paying a better price, Matthew. We can't sell to them for sixpence a wash like your grandfather did.'

'Oh, Abbie, my little love, you think of everything. Whatever would I do without you?' Matthew swung her up into his arms and did a little dance with her round the derelict warehouse, with its leaky roof and plain earth floor; the place where their hopes and dreams were about to start coming true. 'Is it really all going to happen?'

'Yes, it's really all going to happen.' She laughed as she hugged him and kissed his weatherbeaten face. 'Now,' she scolded happily, 'you must put me down. I've got work to do.'

He put her to her feet and she staggered as the place spun round her. 'There,' she said, clinging to his arm, 'all that dancing around has made me dizzy.'

But it was not the dancing around that had made her dizzy and she knew it. Now, when there was so much she must do to help Matthew, was a most inconvenient time to discover that she was pregnant again.

'Twenty people the master's got comin' next Thursday – an' quails' eggs, 'e's arst for, if you ever heard the like,' Daisy grumbled as she lumbered down the stairs and into the kitchen. 'Thass all the new housekeeper's fault, if you arst me.'

'Housekeeper, indeed,' Ellen said primly. 'Thass not the name I'd give Mrs Effie Markham. Whoever heard of a housekeeper's room bein' right next door to the master's?'

Daisy sat down heavily. Her feet were bad today. 'Quails' eggs,' she repeated gloomily. 'I don't know nothin' about cookin' quails' eggs.'

'I'd better check that the silver was all cleaned after that big party 'e 'ad jest before Miss Pearl . . . ' Ellen nodded instead of finishing the sentence. Even after all this time the servants couldn't bring themselves to speak openly about the tragedy of Pearl's death.

'But that was over two year ago.' Daisy looked amazed. 'That shoulda bin checked long enough ago.'

'I know. But there was the business of Miss Pearl soon after an' that got forgot. An' Mrs Markham don't seem to bother, so I don't see why I should.' Ellen spoke a trifle truculently as she poured a cup of tea for herself and Daisy and a mug for Hetty, who was peeling potatoes in the scullery.

'Come'n drink your tea, Hetty,' Daisy called, leaning her

elbows on the table which Hetty had scrubbed till it was white. 'An' give Wilf a call. I dessay 'e could do with a cup time we got the teapot on the go.'

Hetty dried her hands and scuttled about doing Daisy's bidding. Then she took her place at the foot of the table and wrapped her chilblained fingers round her mug.

'I could do with a bit of help upstairs when the master has these do's now,' Ellen said, cutting them each a piece of slab cake. 'Now Sarah Bateman don't come in to help thass a lot for one person to do.'

'You can't wonder she don't come.' Wilfred sucked tea through his whiskers. 'Although I was never sure whether the master stopped askin' or whether she refused to come any more.'

'Bit o' both, I reckon,' Daisy said. 'I reckon 'e knew right well she'd refuse so 'e made sure she was never arst.'

'Well, it wouldn't be right, would it?' Ellen said, helping herself to sugar, 'He couldn't nicely hev 'is daughter's mother-in-law waitin' on 'is table, could 'e? 'Twouldn't be right. Though from what I hear' – she leaned forward and her voice dropped – 'Miss Abigail don't hev anythin' to do with Sarah.'

'You sure that ain't the other way round, Ellen?' Daisy asked sharply. 'Thass not like Miss Abigail to be standoffish, and that I will say.'

'Well, thass what I heard in Mrs Wrigley's shop,' Ellen insisted. 'That seem to be all about down the bottom end in Hythe Street that the young Mrs Bateman put on 'er airs and graces an' won't hev nothin' to do with 'er mother-in-law. An' that she's got 'er place all decked out with bits o' china and sech-like that pore folk can't afford – an' she leave 'er door open so everybody can see what she's got.' She leaned back in her chair to see the effect her words had on the others.

Daisy shook her head. 'Well, I never did,' she said after a while. 'That don't sound like Miss Abigail. That don't sound like 'er at all. She musta changed a powerful lot since she got married an' went down in the world.'

'Poddin' up again, too, I hear,' Ellen said. 'That'll be 'er third, won't it?'

Daisy nodded absently. 'That don't sound a bit like Miss Abigail, treatin' folk like that,' she repeated.

'I see Miss Abbie the other day, Daisy,' Hetty said, from her end of the table, anxious to add her piece to the conversation. 'She looked ever so ill.'

'She never did carry much colour,' Ellen said.

'I know. But she looked right ill,' Hetty insisted. ''Er eyes was all sunk in, with big black rings under 'em.'

'Funny thing that, if thass true,' Wilfred remarked.

'That *is* true, I *seen* 'er.' Hetty, for once, refused to be put down. 'I spoke to 'er an' she arst me how I was an' I said, "Very well, thank you kindly, Ma'am".'

'Well, then thass a very funny thing,' Wilfred went on, 'cause now Old Zac Bateman's dead young Matthew's come into a tidy sum o' money, from what I can hear. Anyway, thass enough to buy that old warehouse at the end o' the quay an' make it all shipshape. Dunno what 'e'd want to go buyin' that for, though, I'm sure.' He got up and wiped his whiskers on the back of his hand. Thanks for the tea, Missus. I'd better be gettin' back to me work. Though the master don't heed to be callin' for Boxer to be saddled these days, do 'e?' And he gave a ribald chuckle before stumping off, his gaitered legs bowed as much by his rotund body as by early rickets.

Ellen got up and poured more tea for herself and Daisy. 'You get back to your taters, Hetty,' she said, not unkindly. 'I think I'll hev to start trainin' you to help me wait on table. Thass no good. I can't do everything meself.' She dropped her voice. 'An' the way things are, I'll very likely be lookin' for another place before long. I don't much care for the goins on here, now.'

'What go on upstairs ain't for you an' me to question, Ellen,' Daisy said primly. 'But that don't stop Hetty from learnin' to wait on table.'

'Ooh, I'd like that,' Hetty said eagerly. 'I'll work ever so hard, Ellen.'

'You'll hev to,' Daisy told her sharply, ''cause you'll still hev your jobs to do down here.' She began to sip her tea absently. 'I don't like the sound o' Miss Abigail, Ellen,' she said, after a minute. 'That don't sound like 'er at all. I think I'll pop in an' see 'er on my next half day. That won't do no 'arm to go an' ask after 'er.'

Ellen nodded. 'I was thinkin' the same thing meself, Daisy,' she said.

It had been one of Abigail's better days. She had not been able to eat anything but at least she hadn't been racked with the terrible retching that had persisted right up until now, the fourth month of her pregnancy.

She sat down at the table, weary after a day spent in the packing warehouse at the end of the quay, sorting the oysters and giving them a final wash after Tolley and Moses had dry-cleaned them as Matthew sailed the boat back up the river; scraping the shells with a special knife called a cultac to remove any blemishes that would make the shells look unsightly. Then she had graded them and packed them into the barrels, their rough shells grazing and cutting her hands until she could barely hold the pen to record their dispatch to London. But the work was paying off.

Even in the few months they had been sending to London, profits had increased by over half as much again. And now they only had to be shared three ways: a share for Matthew, a share for Tolley and a share for the boat – and it was Matthew's boat.

She watched the children as they played on the hearth. William had a new toy boat that Josh had whittled for him from a piece of driftwood. It bore a striking resemblance to *Conquest*. Not to be outdone, Alice had made Laura a rag doll. 'Mustn't treat one different to t'other,' she'd said. Abigail didn't know what she would do without Alice's goodness and support. She was always ready to mind the children when there was work to do at the packing shed, saying it was better for them to play in her warm kitchen than in such a cold, draughty place. Abigail had been grateful for that as she had worked there throughout the winter, her fingers so numb with cold that she didn't even feel the cuts and bruises from the oysters on her hands as she packed them, her whole body stiff from the icy atmosphere. And all the time feeling so tired and ill that sometimes she almost wished she could die. Neither of her other pregnancies had made her feel so wretched. It was ironic that it should be now, when she needed so much to be well and strong to help Matthew build the business that could make him successful. Sometimes she wondered if it was because she thought so much about Pearl that she felt ill. Pearl would have had to go through the same process of pregnancy if only she'd lived. If only she'd lived. Abigail still grieved for her sister and her own pregnancy wouldn't let her forget the tragedy of Pearl's death, which only added to her misery.

After a while she dragged herself to her feet. It would soon be dark and there was still water to be fetched before the pump was locked. If only Sarah were friendly she could have left the children with her while she took the buckets to the pump. But her door was always closed fast against them. It was a sad situation and one Abigail didn't know how to combat.

She reached for their coats and her shawl just as there was a knock at the door. It was Daisy.

'I've brought you some broth, Miss Ab . . . Mrs Bate . . . M'm.' Daisy, flustered and shy, held out a covered basket. 'I heer'd you wasn't well an' I knew you always liked my special calves' foot . . . ' her voice petered out, unsure whether she should even speak of her young mistress's former life.

'Come in, Daisy.' Abigail stood aside for the older woman to step in. 'William, Laura, say good afternoon to Daisy. She's an old friend of mine. Sit down, Daisy. I was just going to fetch water from the pump, but it can wait. Would you like a cup of tea?'

'No, thank you, Miss Abbie.' Abigail's words had put Daisy at her ease and she looked round the tiny living room. It was plainly but comfortably furnished and spotlessly clean, but there was no oven and none of the gadgets that made life in the kitchen at Hilltop House easier. And water from the pump! To stand all day in a bucket in the corner! Daisy thought of the sink at Hilltop House, where you only had to turn a tap and water gushed out from the cistern. Luxury indeed, compared to this! She looked at Abigail. The girl looked serenely happy, despite her gaunt face and tired voice and her already swelling body. 'Will you take a little of my broth, Miss Abbie? I made it specially.' She nodded encouragingly.

But Abigail shook her head. 'Thank you all the same, Daisy, but it's best if I eat nothing. Then I'm not so sick. At least, not always. But the children . . . '

'I made it for you, Miss Abbie. It's special. It was always the first thing you arst for when you'd been ill as a child. Jest try a little.' Surprised at her own temerity Daisy uncovered the broth.

'Come on, now. Thass still nice an' hot. You need to look after yourself if you're goin' to birth a strong babby,' she said firmly.

'It does smell delicious,' Abigail admitted. 'It takes me back . . . ' She turned away as her eyes filled with tears. 'I'll get bowls for the children, too. I'm sure they'd like some.'

Daisy watched with satisfaction as the three of them ate the broth with evident relish. It had been made with all the best ingredients Henry's kitchen could provide and she'd even risked creeping up to his study for the brandy bottle he kept there in order to lace it well.

'Oh, Daisy, that was delicious,' Abigail said when she had finished. 'I don't know when I've enjoyed food so much. And look at the children – no, William, take it from the spoon, like your sister. It's very bad manners to drink from the dish. Your papa would scold you if he was here.'

'But it's lovely, Mama. I don't want to waste any.'

'Then I'll give you a piece of bread to mop it up with.' Abigail turned to Daisy. 'Anyone would think they'd never eaten! But they've only just returned from Alice and she feeds them on dumplings and all manner of good things.'

'They certainly look well enough, Miss Abbie. Two fine children, they are. An' the one so like you an' the other the image of his father, yet with your colour hair. An' what will you do when you're a man, Master William?'

'I'll have a boat, like my papa,' the boy said, with no hesitation at all.

'We'll see about that.' Abigail ruffled her son's hair. 'You may change your mind when you've been to school and learned about the world.'

Daisy got up to go. 'You're lookin' a little better already, Miss Abbie. You got a little colour in your cheeks, too.' She hesitated, cleared her throat and looked away from Abigail. 'Excuse me. Beggin' your pardon for arstin', Miss Abbie . . . ' She cleared her throat again and then said in a rush, 'I know it's none 'o my business, an' I dessay I shouldn't be so bold as to arst . . . but . . . do you get enough to eat, Miss Abbie? For you look half starved.' She flushed to the roots of her hair, mortified by her own boldness.

Impetuously, Abigail stepped forward and hugged her old cook. 'Oh, Daisy, you are a dear. And, yes, there is plenty to eat here, but I have no appetite as a rule. When I've cooked a meal for Matthew or the children I can't face eating it, myself.' She smiled at Daisy, whose plump, pink face was creased with concern. 'I know I look ill. But it's only because my condition is making me so tired and nauseous.' She sighed. 'And it's at a time when I do so need to be well so that I can help Matthew.'

'I shall bring you more broth,' Daisy said firmly.

She left then and went back up to Hilltop House, wondering just how much of Henry's best French brandy she would be able to take before he began to notice.

# *Chapter Eleven*

Abigail's pregnancy dragged on as the cold winter gave way to spring and then the heat of summer. Matthew, on the one hand elated by the success of his first season and the good spat that had followed, worried and fretted over Abigail's listless suffering which, try as she might, she couldn't hide from him.

With his new-found wealth he bought her the choicest tit-bits of food that he could find and cradled her in his arms when the sickness assailed her, all the time cursing his lust that had brought it upon her.

'Forgive me, my little love,' he whispered as he held her. 'It shan't happen again. I swear it shan't happen again. I'll never cause such suffering to come upon you again.'

'No, Matthew, you mustn't blame yourself. This is only a passing thing. When the child is born I shall be well again. You'll see. And the baby is there because of our love. My love as well as yours. We'll love again. And if there is another baby perhaps it will be easier next time.'

'No!' he said violently. 'No more. I'll never put you through this again.' And he held her close to his heart.

It was on a sultry night in late July that Abigail's second son was born. It was a difficult birth and Molly Jenkins from across the yard, who was with her, sent Matthew for the doctor in the middle of the night, an unheard of occurrence in Dolphin Yard.

'I couldn't save the child,' the doctor told Matthew afterwards, 'but I doubt it would have lived, anyway. Its head was too big for its body. It's fortunate that your wife is strong. She'll live. But there must be no more children.' And with the understanding of one husband to another he took Matthew aside and told him what Abigail could use to guard against future pregnancies. 'It's expensive, mind,' he finished gruffly. 'But worth it if you value your wife's life.'

'Then it'll be worth every penny,' Matthew answered fervently.

Abigail was devastated. Her grief was made worse by a senseless feeling of guilt because she had regarded the illness of her pregnancy as a hindrance to her work at the warehouse; fuming because she felt so wretched; fretting when she couldn't find the strength to continue. Added to that, thoughts of Pearl were always at the back of her mind. This baby, although it could never replace Pearl, was somehow to atone for her untimely death. All these feelings were mixed up in Abigail's mind, some of them not even put into coherent thought, as she dragged herself about the tiny cottage and looked out onto the squalid yard beyond.

The one thing that kept her going was her determination to see Matthew's oyster business thrive. She insisted on visiting the warehouse although she could no longer wash and barrel the oysters. But Molly was glad to earn a few shillings doing this and when things were busy she brought along Sally from the cottage next door and her sister from Perseverance Yard. Abigail recognized Liza from the day she had rescued her little son from under the horse whip. Little Joe had been barely five then – he was eleven now, and a nimble and quick messenger boy despite legs bowed by rickets.

'We must take advantage of the railway now,' she said to

Matthew in her new, tired voice, when the loop line joining Colchester's main station to the Hythe was opened. 'Now that it's so handy and near to the quay it will be very much quicker to send the oysters to London by rail. And we shall be able to send them every day, instead of only three times a week by boat.'

'We shan't be the only ones to think of that, Abbie my love,' Matthew said sensibly. 'Why else do you think your father has been so active in pushing for it? The price of oysters will drop like a stone.'

'Nonsense.' A flash of Abigail's old enthusiasm and energy showed for a minute. 'The price of Bateman's oysters won't fall. Our green-beards are the best, the fattest, and they'll be the freshest. I shall see to that myself.' Her thin, pale face was so full of determination that it tore his heart, knowing that she was still far from well though it was six months since the birth of the stillborn child.

But Abigail was right. Bateman's oysters never failed to sell well, and all through the winter the dredging was good.

Edwin visited his sister and her husband as often as he could, but one summer evening he sought Matthew out down at the warehouse. It had taken Matthew every spare moment when he was not tending the oyster beds to put the old warehouse into good repair, but now, with new timber replacing rotten and a new tin roof and new doors it was, if not warm, at least weatherproof for the next winter. He was inside making duckboards to keep the packers' feet dry and above the quagmire that resulted from water inevitably spilt and splashed about.

'And when I've finished this I'm going to make a barrow so the barrels can be wheeled along to the railway siding,' he told Edwin. 'It was Abbie's idea. We'll be able to load two or three barrels at a time instead of hefting them along one at a time on our shoulders. And even young Moses will be able to trundle the barrow.' He straightened up and laid down his hammer. 'That railway has made a world of difference to us, you know, Eddie. But I'm not so sure about the canal idea . . . ' He lifted the cheese cutter he habitually wore and scratched his head.

Edwin perched himself on a low bench, first inspecting it to make sure it wouldn't dirty his trousers. 'I don't think that canal will ever be dug, Matt,' he said, 'despite the fact that the guv'nor has already sunk more money in the scheme than I suspect he can afford. And for two reasons. One, the river would become even more silted up than it is already – and it wouldn't simply be with mud, even now it's little better than an open sewer, so you can imagine what it would be like if it was dammed – it'd be as bad as the brook over by the allotments, where they dammed it deliberately so they could shovel the muck onto their gardens for fertilizer. And two, look at the people it would benefit most. Mr Hayfield, for one. Look at the property he owns on the other side of the river. It would be invaluable to him not to depend on tides to get his timber up river. And my father, marketing the oysters for the Colne Fishery' – he looked at Matthew – 'and I suppose you, too, Matt, to a lesser extent,' he said in some surprise. 'You're becoming quite a businessman, aren't you?'

Matthew shrugged. 'The business of the canal won't really make that much difference to me. I work the tides well enough and I reckon I can get my smack along when most others can't. My old grandad taught me every trick he knew and I'll swear he could get a boat to sail in a flat calm. As long as there's just enough water to keep her afloat, I can get *Conquest* up river, even if I have to pole her up – and I've done that, many a time. Mind you, I'll agree the river needs dredging, the channel is getting narrower and narrower so there's hardly room to tack. I reckon it needs that more than we need a canal. It'd be cheaper, too.'

'I'm glad you think like that, Matt, because I, for one, would oppose the canal. As I said, look at the people it would benefit most. Mr Hayfield, my father, and one or two others who've already got more money than they know what to do with. Why should ratepayers' money go to feather their nests even further? There are much more urgent calls on public money that would benefit the whole town. Something still needs to be done about the water supply, for a start. Do you know, Matt, the water works – such as it is – supplies piped water to less than a quarter of the town? And then only for a few hours three days a week? But they're better off than the rest of the people, who have to fetch it by the bucketful from the pump. It's disgraceful.'

Matthew nodded thoughtfully. 'Yes, and Abbie told me she had to queue for over half an hour at the pump the other day.' He was quiet for a few moments. He got his pipe out and stoked it, then he paced up and down the warehouse a couple of times. At last he said, 'Which brings me to something I've been wanting to ask your advice about, Eddie.'

Eddie spread his hands in an expansive gesture. 'Ask away, brother-in-law. You know I'll help if I can.'

Matthew squatted down on his haunches, with his back to the wall. 'Well, it's like this. I – we've done very well with our oysters, this past couple of seasons, and with what I've got left of Grandad's money – which is still a tidy bit – I've got quite a good sum laid by. I reckon it's nearly enough to buy a nice little house for Abbie and the children. Abbie doesn't seem to pick up like she should, she's still pale and thin, and I was thinking . . . well, I was thinking that it's time she had something better. I don't like her having to queue for water the way she does.'

Edwin went over to Matthew and clapped him on the back. 'I think that's a capital idea, Matt. To tell you the truth I think that half the cause of her being so tired and ill is that yard where you live. What with the stench from the yards around and from The Dolphin – people aren't too fussy where they relieve themselves when they come out of any beer house, and The Dolphin's worse than some. I've read Edwin Chadwick's report. He's convinced that bad smells cause disease. And I'm sure he's right.'

'Do you really think so, Eddie? It's not something I've ever given much thought to, myself. But if you say so, then the sooner I can find another house the better it'll be for Abbie.'

'You couldn't have decided at a better time, Matt,' Edwin said, delightedly. 'Mr Young, my editor's elderly father, has just died. He lived in a sizable house at the end of St Leonard's Street – four bedrooms, attics, garden, earth closet, water cistern – how would that suit?'

'Oh, I don't reckon I could afford a place like that, Eddie. Anyway, what about you? You'll be thinking of setting up house soon yourself, won't you? Don't you want it?'

Edwin grinned. 'Hold on, Matt. I don't think I'm quite ready to take the plunge yet. Goodness, we're not even engaged.' He wagged his head. 'But give us time. Give us time.' He went over to the door. 'Come on, I'll take you to see Mr Young. At least I can put a word in for you. And there's always the bank to lend you money. I'm sure we can arrange something.'

Matthew and his family moved into the Corner House just before Christmas. Almost immediately Abigail's health began to improve. She delighted in her new home, going from room to room, twitching a curtain here, straightening a bed cover there, moving a chair two inches and then putting it back where it was before.

'Do you like it, Abbie?' Matthew said unnecessarily, his own face reflecting the joy in hers.

'Oh, Matthew, I can't believe ... oh ... come and see!' She

caught his hand and pulled him along to the kitchen, where they watched together as water gushed out at the turn of a tap. 'And the size of this kitchen! It's big enough to dance in!' She did a gavotte round the table. 'And just look at the kitchen range! It's almost as big as the one we had at home – at my father's house,' she corrected herself quickly. 'I'll be able to . . . '

'You'll be able to have a maid,' he said, watching her face.

'Oh, no, I'm sure we can't afford that.' She shook her head.

'But you'll need someone to look after the house and children, my love.' He kissed her. 'You know very well I can't manage the business without you, and you've said yourself that Alice finds the children difficult now she's troubled with arthritis.'

'That's true. All the same . . . ' She frowned.

'All the same, I've asked Molly Jenkins if her eldest girl would like to come and live in.'

'Peggy? Oh, she's a dear little scrap. And good with children, too, for all she's so tiny.'

'I'm glad you like her because she'll be along later today, so she's all settled in before Christmas.'

She flung her arms round his neck and kissed him. 'Oh, Matthew, I do love you!'

It was a modest house compared with Hilltop House but to Abigail it was little short of a palace. Inside the front door there was a long, somewhat narrow hall, from which the stairs rose. Off the hall to the right was a square dining room, with the kitchen behind, and on the other side the drawing room stretched the whole length of the house. Upstairs were four good-sized bedrooms, and two further small ones were in the attic. The furniture from the little cottage in Dolphin Yard looked lost in the Corner House, so Matthew had insisted that Abigail should go and choose whatever else she needed, recklessly demanding that everything should be of the best and adding on anything else that took his fancy. He tried not to think of the sum he owed the bank and thanked heaven that his oysters were the best on the Colne.

Christmas came and with the help of Eliza Acton's cookery book and Matthew's strong arm, Abigail cooked her first turkey. Josh and Alice came to dinner, beaming proudly on the two people they loved best in all the world. Edwin came too, stamping the snow off his boots as he arrived, laden with presents for them all.

Afterwards they roasted chestnuts and Edwin played the piano that had been Matthew's extravagant Christmas present to Abigail and they all sang carols, while the children played with their new toys round their feet.

After William and Laura were in bed the five of them sat round the fire and talked.

'I asked Mam to come and be with us for Christmas,' Matthew said. 'Abbie said it was only right that we should ask her, specially as it's our first Christmas in our new home.'

'But she wouldn't come?' Josh shook his head. 'She's a funny gel, an' always was. Can't forgive and can't forget.'

'I don't see what she's got to forgive,' Matthew insisted. 'She knows Abbie is a good wife to me. She knows we're fond of one another and we've got two fine children. What more could she ask?'

'What more, indeed.' Alice sat twisting her gnarled, arthritic hands together in her lap. She had no patience with Sarah and had told her so when she had gone to complain of Matthew's marriage: 'You've got a fine son, Sarah, an' the little maid'll make you a fine daughter-in-law. You'll hev grandchildren, too. Me and Josh lost our little girl. We got nuthin'. Nobody to foller after us. Nuthin'. So don't you come 'ere carryin' on about your troubles, Sarah Bateman, 'cause they're all of your own makin'. An' thass the last I've got to say about it.' Alice was not given to long speeches as a rule and she had hoped that her words would bring Sarah to her senses. Instead, they had caused Sarah to cut herself off from her brother and sister-in-law, as well as from her son.

'I wish there was something I could do, for Matthew's sake,' Abigail said, frowning. 'I've tried. And at first I thought we might become friends. But after William was born she became worse and refused to speak to us at all. She must be very sad inside. Do you think there *is* anything we can do, Josh? After all, she's your sister.'

Josh shook his head. 'She was always a funny one, even as a littl'un. Jealous as fire is hot if anybody had anything she didn't hev. A rare trial she was to Muther, I can tell ye. Leave 'er alone, thass what I say. Jest leave 'er alone. I heerd she was workin' to help out at Mr Hayfield's over Christmas, so she won't hev been alone.'

'Well, at least she can't say we didn't ask her,' Abigail said.

Edwin got up to go at eleven o'clock. Josh and Alice had gone at nine, refusing to stay the night. 'No, we've always slep' in our own bed and don't see no reason to change now,' Josh had said. 'That don't snow much an' we ain't got far to go.'

'Why don't you stay, Eddie?' Abigail said. 'We've a spare bedroom now, so there's plenty of space. And you've already said you're not due at the Youngs till midday tomorrow.'

Matthew got up and pulled aside the thick blue plush curtain and moved the lace one out of the way. 'Look at that. It's like a blizzard out there. Good thing Alice and Josh went when they did. Better stay the night, man. No sense in you plodding all the way back to Balkerne Lane.'

Edwin joined him at the window. 'Aye. Looks as if it's nearly a foot deep already. I hope we're not in for another winter like the one in thirty-nine.'

'I hope we're not, too.' Matthew said. 'That was when the

pump froze down the road. It was a bad spat, that year, too. Oysters don't like it when it's too cold,' he added in a low voice.

As they had feared, the winter was long and hard. Abigail had cause to be grateful for her new, spacious house, with a fireplace in every room and thick curtains at the windows to keep out the icy winds. She looked out at the bleak winter landscape, where frost rimed the trees and bushes and red-nosed people hurried along, wrapped in old sacks and whatever they could find to keep the icy cold out, their boots – if they had any – ringing on the frozen road. Some hopefully carried buckets. Abigail pitied them most of all. She knew the long wait they would face at the pump if it wasn't frozen, and the disappointment if it was. She offered up a fervent prayer of thankfulness that she no longer had to wait her turn there.

But her thankfulness was tinged with anxiety. Matthew had said nothing and his fattening beds were well stocked for the winter, but she knew that a bad spat usually followed a hard winter and this winter was very hard. She feared for the oysters.

'It's all right, my little love,' Matthew assured her when she voiced her fears. 'The oysters are safer in the shallow, still water, even though it's only three feet deep, than they would be in the deep river, where the current is constantly shifting. We're having a good season. Don't worry. Just you concentrate on getting well. That's all you have to do.' And he kissed her and held her close. 'You *are* feeling better, Abbie, my love, aren't you?' he asked anxiously.

'Yes, Matthew, I am quite well now.' She laughed and leaned back from him. 'Can't you see how well I am?'

He looked at her and grinned. 'Yes, I believe you are. The Corner House plainly agrees with you. You're growing quite plump, in fact,' he teased. Then he became serious. 'All I want is for you to be happy, Abbie. I love you very much and everything I do is for you. This house . . . Everything. And one day I'll make you rich.'

It looked as if it might be soon, too. Bateman's oysters had become well known and were in great demand. All through the hard winter Matthew and Tolley, with Moses the cabin boy, fished fat, green oysters and they were barrelled in hundreds and sent on the train within hours to be sold on the London market.

But Abigail's fears had been justified. A bad spat did follow the cold winter and the oysters that had survived, already weakened by the cold, were attacked by a sponge which bored into the shell and sucked out the meat. In one season Matthew's oyster layings were in ruin.

He was not downcast, although his new-found wealth had encouraged him to employ men to cull and barrel the oysters and he had spent money to put *Conquest* in first-class order; money that Mr Andrews at the bank had been only too happy to advance on top of the mortgage needed to buy and furnish the Corner House. Matthew had been careful to conceal from Abigail the full extent of his borrowing because he knew she would worry and disapprove.

'It'll be all right, my little love,' he assured her in his habitual way. 'There's no cause for alarm because my layings have failed. We'll just have to go further afield for oysters. We'll go round the corner to Cardigan Bay, or over to Jersey. There'll be plenty about. And they'll still fetch a good price after they've spent a month or two in our fattening beds, because the bad spat was general on the east coast. There'll be precious few oysters fished from these parts until the beds can be re-stocked.' He kissed her. 'If the worst comes to the worst I can always go out with the skillingers for my oysters.'

'Oh, Matthew, no!' She shook his arms. 'It's much too dangerous. Remember you've got a wife and family.'

He threw his head back and laughed. 'Rubbish. All those tales you hear from the skillingers are only stories to stop other folks going. There are rich pickings to be had on the Terschelling Bank.'

But Abigail didn't laugh. She knew that the skillingers, as the smacks that went to the Terschelling Bank off the Dutch coast were called, never went singly, but always in a fleet of at least twelve because of the treacherous seas and capricious weather. Queer tales had been told of skillingers; of cruel storms and mountainous seas, of freak waves coming out of the flat calm seas to smash down and splinter a boat to matchwood. Too many skillingers had failed to return for Abigail to disregard their stories, and she dreaded the day when Matthew would decide to sail with them.

As for Matthew, he was only too happy to try his luck further afield. *Conquest* was in good shape, refitted and with a new suit of sails; Tolley was a first-class mate, and he had recently taken on a new hand, Guy Sainty, a Yarmouth man of his own age who had lost his boat in a storm off the Longsands when he was out salvaging. Guy knew no fear and was ready for anything. He worked hard, and there was no task, great or small, that he wouldn't tackle with energy and enthusiasm. And there was young Moses, who must be going on fifteen, although neither he nor anybody else knew his exact age, who was a useful deckhand now.

Throughout the summer *Conquest* fished the Channel Islands' rich deep-sea beds of Jersey in company with about sixty other smacks from Essex and Kent so the supply to Billingsgate could be kept up, and Matthew's layings could begin to be re-stocked. But when the next winter came there was again need to go further afield and despite Abigail's misgivings, *Conquest* joined the intrepid skillingers.

She was smaller than the rest of the fleet by some eight feet overall, but Matthew was not worried about this. He knew that she was seaworthy and he trusted in his own seamanship and that of his crew. The first trip was a good one; the weather was kind and the trip yielded over two thousand oysters. Matthew was elated. Whatever he did was successful. He couldn't go wrong.

'It's because of you, my little love,' he told Abigail as he swung her off her feet and enveloped her in a great bear hug. 'You bring me luck.' He put her down and held her at arm's length, his gaze sweeping her from head to foot, taking in her shining coppery hair under its snowy cap with the lace lappets, her redingote of green striped silk, narrow waisted and crinolined, and the matching kid slippers. She was clear-eyed and her complexion was like the bloom on a peach, a very different sight from the sickly wife he had brought to the Corner House from Dolphin Yard. And now that she no longer had to deal with sorting and packing the oysters her hands were soft and white. He caught her to him again. 'You've suffered much being married to me, my little love,' he said, 'but you've never complained, although at times it must have been very hard for you, I realize that. But I swear you shall suffer no more. That I promise you.'

Abigail said nothing. While he continued to go out with the skillingers her heart would not rest.

Matthew made two more trips to the Terschelling Bank. The first was uneventful but the second was not. Three boats out of the fleet of fifteen were lost with all hands in a storm that sprang up from nowhere. *Conquest* went to the rescue of a fourth, where the crew clung on, waiting for the opportunity to jump to safety as *Conquest* was smashed again and again by the roaring sea against the side of the sinking smack by waves that towered high above the mast one minute, and threatened to suck them under the foundering vessel the next. But all hands were taken off, except the mate, who in his terror had gone below and cut his throat rather than face an icy, watery death.

In the midst of it all, in the torrential rain and the screaming gale that tossed the boat around like a cork, the deafening noise of the wind in the shrouds and the rain lashing icy needles into faces, nobody saw young Moses lose his footing on the heaving, slippery deck and slide to his death in the boiling sea.

Matthew, haggard from exhaustion and the scenes he had witnessed, had tears in his eyes as he broke the news to Abigail. 'He was such a lively little lad. Willing, too,' he said, with a break in his voice. 'And excited to think he was joining the skillingers. I know he was only an orphan lad, but we were all fond of him. We shall miss him playing his Jew's harp below deck when he was off watch. Poor little beggar, we used to shout to him to give it a rest. He could never get a proper tune out of it but it didn't stop him trying.' He shook his head. 'It was my fault. I'm the skipper. I should have watched out for him better.' He signed, a great weary sigh. Tolley's wife's going to be upset.'

'I know,' Abigail said, 'she was fond of him. And so was Tolley.'

Matthew nodded. 'He used to say it was nice to have another man about the house. He has six daughters, you know. And most of his grandchildren are girls.' He ate the food Abigail had prepared without even noticing what it was and drank a mug of porter. Then he went to bed, shocked more by the death of Moses than all the other dreadful events he had witnessed on that fateful voyage.

When he woke it was dark and Abigail lay beside him in the warmth of the big bed. Silently he reached for her and took her to him hungrily, almost savagely, his frustration over Moses' death venting itself in fierce, almost brutal passion.

When it was over he held her close. 'I'm sorry, my little love. I was rough with you. Forgive me.'

'It's all right, Matthew. I understand,' she whispered, tangling her fingers in his thick, wiry hair, that even now held the tang of the salty, capricious North Sea.

For a long time they lay close and she thought he had gone back to sleep. But suddenly he said, 'I shall never go back there. Never. I've got enough brood to re-stock my layings now and if the good Lord sees fit to prosper them I shan't fly in the face of providence by venturing further afield. I've got you and the children to consider, Abbie. What would you have done if I'd been drowned, like young Moses? Oh, no, for your sakes I can't afford to risk my life deep-sea fishing when I can make a good living hereabouts.'

'Oh, thank God for that,' Abigail whispered, with tears in her eyes. She turned to him and this time he was gentle with her.

The next day was 18 March, Laura's sixth birthday. It was a bright, sunny day, holding more than a hint of spring so Abigail took both the children down to the quay, where their father had already gone, with Tolley, to inspect *Conquest* and see if she had sustained much damage in the storm. The quay was, as always, thronged with people, although the tide was at its lowest, when it revealed all the rubbish that had been thrown into the river and left behind on the mud by the ebb. Ragged little boys were mudlarking to see what treasures they might uncover and sell, fighting over a farthing or a broken clay pipe.

*Conquest* lay in her berth at the far end of the quay near to the warehouse but Matthew's keen eyes picked out his family from the rest of the crowd and he took off his cheese cutter and waved to them from his vantage point at the top of the mast, where he was freeing a jammed halyard.

'Look, children, can you see Papa at the top of the mast? Wave to him,' Abigail said, pointing and waving herself. The children took off their own hats and waved excitedly. 'Do you think Papa would let me climb up there with him?' William said excitedly. 'I'll wager he can see for miles and miles.'

'Perhaps. When you're older.' Abigail smiled fondly at her son in his smart sailor suit. 'And little boys don't wager, dear.'

'What does it mean, Mama? Wager?' Laura asked. Then, without waiting for an answer, 'I should like to climb the mast, too. After all, it's my birthday.'

'Oh, I don't think that's a thing for girls to do even on their birthday,' Abigail laughed. Then her laughter died, because striding towards them, dressed in his habitual black, was her father. With him was Richard Cotgrove, handsome and clean-cut, a snowy handkerchief showing a perfect triangle from his top pocket and a rose in his buttonhole. Abigail wondered idly where he managed to get a rose so early in the season.

She thought at first that her father hadn't seen her, and then that he was going to ignore her presence. But as he and his companion drew level he stopped, looking first at the children, who returned his gaze with innocent curiosity, and then at Abigail.

'So you've come up in the world,' he said with a sneer, taking in her braided merino gown and the pelisse and bonnet trimmed to match it. 'A new house, too, I hear. Well, don't get too big for your boots, Madam. Just because your husband has come up in the world, don't imagine he can't go down just as quickly. Businesses that mushroom overnight often wither in the morning. It was a bad spat last summer, but don't think you can come crawling to the Colne Fishery to recoup your losses because it'll do you no good. While I have anything to do with the company I'll make it my business to see that no jumped-up Bateman ever gets a licence to dredge the river.'

'We shall not seek your assistance, never fear.' Abigail's voice was quivering with rage. 'And in spite of what you say Bateman's oysters are doing very well, thank you.' Her chin lifted. 'But, believe me, we would starve – I would take my children to the workhouse – before we would ever come to you for help.'

'Good,' he rapped. 'Because if you did come you wouldn't get it. Come, Cotgrove, we haven't time for idle chat. We have work to do.' Henry moved off. Richard Cotgrove lifted his tall hat and inclined his head politely, giving Abigail a glimpse of a dark head of hair. She noticed that his eyes were very blue and that he looked a shrewd, capable man who wouldn't suffer fools gladly. Abigail could see why Edwin couldn't work with him. He was every inch a businessman, which Edwin most definitely was not. Edwin was far too compassionate for his father's cut-throat world. Her father. He hadn't changed much. He was a bit heavier, his face was a trifle more florid, his hair a trifle more grey, but his manner was as hard as ever. Henry had a heart of flint.

'Who was that man?' William looked up at her. 'I didn't like him much. He was rude to you. I shall tell Papa he was rude to you.'

'I didn't like him too, Mama. Who was he?' Laura always copied her brother.

'He ... he's ...' Abigail got no further as suddenly a cry went up from the crowd and out of the corner of her eye she saw something flutter to the ground like a rag doll from the top of *Conquest*'s mast to the deck thirty feet below. 'No!' she screamed. She pushed forward, clutching a child in each hand. 'No! No! No!'

The crowd parted to let her through and she ran to kneel at the quayside looking down on the deck, where Matthew's crumpled figure lay. Tolley was crouched over him. 'It's all right, Missus, he'm alive,' he called up to her. 'Guy, send one of the boys there for the doctor. Tell 'im to say there's bin an accident an' 'e better come quick.' He looked back at the still figure on the deck. 'We best not move 'im till the doctor say.'

Guy came up off the boat, taking the rungs of the iron ladder set into the quay two at a time. He fished in his pocket for a coin but Abigail forestalled him and thrust a penny into the hand of a grubby urchin hovering near, anticipating that there would be an errand to run. 'Fetch Doctor Green,' Guy ordered. 'An' look lively!'

'If you're back with the doctor within five minutes there'll be another tuppence for you,' Abigail added desperately.

Guy nodded and turned to Tolley's eldest granddaughter standing by. 'Marley, fetch these two childer back to the Corner House, this is no place for them here, beggin' your pardon, Missus. Is somebody at home there?'

Abigail nodded dumbly, her face ashen. She relinquished the children, who were clinging to her. 'Peggy. Yes, Peggy's there. Yes, go with Marley, William. Laura. She'll look after you. I'll be home with Papa directly.'

'Will he be all right?' William asked anxiously.

'Is he dead?' Laura said.

'Of course he isn't dead.' Anxiety gave a sharp edge to Abigail's voice. 'Of course he'll be all right. Now go with Marley.' She managed a brief smile at the girl and fished in her pocket for another penny to give her. 'Ask Peggy to give you all some milk and a gingerbread man.'

The children went off with Marley and Abigail climbed down the iron rungs onto the deck where her husband lay. He hadn't moved.

'Is he very bad, Tolley?' she whispered, crouching down beside him.

'Can't tell, Missus. An' we dursen't move 'im till the doctor come, in case there's anything broke.'

'At least he's still breathing.' She took off her pelisse and draped it over him as best she could to try and warm him. His hands were like ice.

Guy appeared with a door that he'd wrenched off its hinges and with two other men they manoeuvred it down to the deck. 'We shall need a stretcher to move 'im when the doctor's given 'im the once-over,' he said, propping it against a hatch.

Doctor Green arrived, panting, within six minutes. As he examined Matthew, Abigail turned away and gave the boy who had fetched him the twopence she had promised. 'Well done,' she said. 'You must have run hard.'

The doctor finished his examination and supervised the careful lifting of Matthew's inert body onto the makeshift stretcher. He groaned once but didn't open his eyes.

'Is he . . . ? Will he . . . ?' Abigail began.

'Careful with his leg, there,' the doctor said sharply. Then, to Abigail, 'I'll examine him again, properly, when they've got him home.'

Several men had come to help and between them they managed to lift the door with Matthew strapped to it up onto the quayside. Then four of them, taking a corner each, carried it along the quay and up the hill to the house in St Leonard's Street, with Abigail walking beside, holding her husband's limp hand in hers.

They got him to bed and he regained consciousness just as Doctor Green bent over him.

'What in the name of all that's holy am I doing here?' he demanded in a dazed voice. 'I'm in *bed*! How did I get here? And what are you all doing, standing round looking at me as if I was a prize fish you'd just landed?' He scowled weakly at his crew and Doctor Green.

'You took a bit of a tumble,' Doctor Green said, in a masterpiece of understatement.

'You fell from the top o' the mast, Skipper,' Tolley said. 'We thought you was a gonner.'

'I think you'd all better leave, so that I can examine him again. I want to look at him properly and find out exactly what the damage is. Yes, you too, Mrs Bateman.' He pulled back the blanket. 'Are you in much pain, Mr Bateman?'

Matthew rolled his head from side to side and flexed his fingers as they lay on the coverlet. 'Bit stiff and sore. That's all.'

Tolley and Guy led Abigail from the room and down the stairs. 'Well,' Tolley said, 'all I can say is, he's blamed lucky if 'e's got away with no more'n a few bruises and a bit o' stiffness. Did you see what 'appened, Guy?'

Guy shook his head. 'Not really. Far as I could see he leaned too far out an' slipped out of the sling. But I couldn't say for sure.'

'I'll make some tea,' Abigail said, more to keep her hands busy than because anyone wanted it.

They were sitting round the table in the kitchen drinking it when Doctor Green came into the room. Abigail got to her feet. 'Well?'

The doctor shook his head. 'I'm going to call Doctor Jacobs in to confirm my suspicions, but it's only a formality because I'm certain . . . ' He looked at Abigail with great sadness in his face. 'I'm sorry, Mrs Bateman. My examination has confirmed what I suspected when I saw him on the boat. Your husband's back is broken. Matthew will never walk again.'

# *Chapter Twelve*

It took a week for the truth to dawn on Matthew, because not even Abigail had the courage to break the dreadful news to him outright.

His rage and frustration were terrible to behold. He swore and shouted and wept tears of bitter anger. He even called for a knife to cut his throat and end it all.

'If I had to fall, why couldn't I have landed on my head and be killed outright instead of being condemned to this living death?' he wept. And Abigail held him close and wept with him.

'No, Matthew,' she said at last, trying to be strong for both of them although she thought her heart was breaking, 'I thank God you're still alive, crippled though you may be. We still have a life together. We can work together, live and love each other as we've always done.' She kissed him. 'As long as we're together, Matthew, and I know I have your love, I can face anything.'

He turned away from her. 'I can't. I can't face a life where I can never feel the tang of the sea on my face and the swell of the waves under me; a life where I can never take my children by the hand and wander through the Botanical Gardens or take them to St Denis's Fair . . . '

'Oh, Matthew,' she managed to smile through her tears. 'You've never, ever done that, so that's not a thing you'll miss.'

He banged his fists on the coverlet till the bed shook. 'But I can't do it now even if I want to!' His voice dropped. 'And I shall never feel the warmth of your body against mine, my lovely wife, as I have so many, many times as I've taken you to me.' He turned his face to the wall and refused to be comforted, or to comfort her in the anguish she shared with him.

She went to see Sarah.

'I thought you'd want me to come and tell you the truth about Matthew,' she said. 'No doubt there are all sorts of rumours abroad.'

Sarah hesitated, torn between giving herself the satisfaction of shutting the door in her daughter-in-law's face and anxiety to know whether her son really had lost his wits and become a gibbering idiot. 'You'd better come in,' she said.

Abigail went in and sat down at the table in the middle of the room. It was covered with a plush cloth and an oil lamp with a pink shade stood on a tin tray in the centre, ready to be lit.

Sarah sat in the Windsor elbow chair by the fire and pulled the kettle forward. 'I daresay you'll drink a cup of tea,' she said grudgingly.

'Gladly,' Abigail replied, resting her elbow on the table and leaning her head on her hand. 'Oh, Sarah, you don't know how I've longed to make a friend of you over the years. This estrangement has been none of my wish.' She waited as in complete silence Sarah warmed the teapot, measured tea into it and poured the water. Then she went to the cupboard by the side of the fire and fetched cups and saucers of cheap china; the best she possessed. Abigail sighed as she watched the tea being poured. 'I suppose you'll say I've only come now because I need something from you, but I can't help that. Now that Matthew's legs are useless there is nothing he can do to repair the rift between us . . . '

'Legs? Matthew's legs useless?' Sarah's head shot up and Abigail noticed absently that her hair was liberally streaked with silver. 'I heard it was his head. That he'd lost his wits.'

'Oh, no.' Abigail shook her head. 'Matthew is very much in command of his senses. Too much in command, you might almost say. He realizes he'll never walk again, never work again, never sail his boat again.' She paused. 'I think that's the biggest blow of all, the thought that he'll never go to sea again. I remember he told me once he could never be happy too long away from the sea. I only hope to God it isn't true.' She began to cry, sobbing in a way she had never allowed herself to do in Matthew's presence. 'Oh, Sarah,' she wept, 'what am I going to do? How shall I ever manage to keep him contented? How can I make up for what he's lost? How can I be strong for him when I'm so weak myself? Oh, what am I going to do?' She put her head in her arms and cried till there were no tears left.

Sarah sat and watched her, making no move to comfort or console. When Abigail at last lifted her tearstained face and blew her nose, Sarah pushed a cup of tea over to her.

'You'll feel better now you've had a good cry,' she said. 'It was how I was when my William died.'

'You're saying I should be thankful I've still got Matthew,' Abigail said.

Sarah shook her head. 'I'm not so sure about that. There may be times when you'll wish in your heart that he'd gone the same way as his father, my girl, instead of being left crippled and useless. It's a hard row you'll have to hoe. Matthew won't be an easy man to nurse. But once you've faced up to that and learned to live with it you'll find it easier.'

'You'll come and see him?'

Sarah took several sips from her tea. 'If he asks for me.'

'You're a hard woman, Sarah Bateman,' Abigail said wearily.

'I've had a hard life.'

'Parts of my life haven't been easy. And you've done nothing to make them any less hard.' Abigail stood up and looked down at her mother-in-law. 'I would have been your friend, Sarah, if you'd let me, but you turned against me. You even set your face against your own grandchildren through your stupid pride and jealousy. Well, I'm offering you the hand of friendship now. If you reject it there won't be another chance.' She pulled on her gloves and went to the door.

There was a long silence and she waited, with her hand on the latch. At last Sarah looked up. 'I'll come and see my son.'

Life was not easy at the Corner House in the months following Matthew's accident. Frantically, ignoring the expense, Abigail consulted doctor after doctor but the prognosis was always the same; he would never walk again.

As for Matthew, he lay in his bed alternately swearing at the fate that had reduced him in a few seconds from a man to a useless hulk, and sunk into depression to think he would never sail in *Conquest* again.

Abigail had a bed brought downstairs for him and Tolley rigged up a system of ropes whereby he could haul himself to a sitting position. But this only added to his misery; handling the rope was too much like handling a halyard and he railed against the Lord who had condemned him to this half life instead of letting him be killed outright and be done with it.

Nothing pleased him. The sound of Laura tinkling on the piano, a sound that used to fill him with delight – 'Listen, Abbie. She's going to be a pianist like her Uncle Edwin. Won't that be grand? Our little Laura making music like her uncle? Maybe she'll learn to play the church organ, too' – now irritated him beyond words and he would roar at her to stop the noise. William would bring his books and slate to show his father proudly what he had learned at school, only to be told that the scratching of the slate pencil got on his nerves.

As for Abigail, nothing she could do was right. If she sat with him he wanted to know if she'd nothing better to do; if she told him how the business was doing, why did she torture him, knowing he could no longer be a part of it; if she didn't speak, why sit there mumchance? had the cat got her tongue; but if she was absent for more than half an hour, he was left to rot with nobody caring a tinker's cuss whether he lived or died.

Sarah came to see him, a tall, pale figure in a shabby but spotless grey dress, a shawl round her shoulders clutched with hands that showed white knuckles, the only sign of the strain she was under.

She stood at the foot of the bed and gazed at her big, brawny son, the child she had struggled and fought single-handedly to bring up; the man who looked so like her William, the husband she had loved and lost, and who now lay there, reduced to the helplessness of a baby. Nobody knew, nobody would ever know, the anguish she felt in her heart.

'All right, woman, there's no need to stand there gawping like that,' Matthew said bitterly. 'Haven't you ever seen a helpless cripple before?'

'It's only your legs that are useless, so stop feeling sorry for yourself,' she replied, her voice sharp. 'There's plenty you can do. You don't have to lie there and mope.'

Abigail, standing behind her, drew in a quick breath. She knew how fragile Matthew's hold on his temper was now.

But he looked up at his mother and for the first time since the accident he smiled. 'By God, Mother, you don't change. You're still as hard as nails, aren't you?'

'I've had a hard life,' she said briskly. 'I've learned the hard way that you don't always get what you want, so you have to take what's given and make the best of it. You've still got a lot to be thankful for.' Her voice dropped. 'At least you can read and write, so you can keep yourself occupied.'

With that she turned and marched out of the room. Abigail followed and was just in time to see Sarah dab her eyes fiercely with a corner of her apron before she said, 'Don't let him feel sorry for himself. Self-pity never did anybody any good.' With that she pulled her shawl more closely round her and left.

Thoughtfully, Abigail went back to Matthew. He had hauled himself into a sitting position and, miraculously, was smiling. 'She's a rare woman, my mother,' he said. 'You can't help admiring her, can you? Hard as nails, she is.'

Abigail sat on the bed and for once he allowed her to take his hand in hers. 'I don't think so,' she said, shaking her head. 'She might like people to think so, but I don't really think she's hard at all.'

And if she could have seen Sarah, sobbing her heart out at the plight of her only son in the privacy of her own home, she would have understood that Sarah's hard exterior was only a veneer against being hurt. A veneer that occasionally cracked.

After that Sarah visited Matthew every week, staying longer each time. He was always more amenable for a day after she had been to see him. But only for a day. After that he would revert to the see-saw between rage and depression that Abigail was sadly becoming used to.

One afternoon, as Sarah was preparing to leave, Abigail called her into the room that served both as a dining room and drawing room now that Matthew's bed occupied the smaller room on the other side of the hall.

'Sit down, Sarah, I want to talk to you.' She went over to the bell pull. 'I'll get Peggy to make some tea for us.'

'I don't want . . . ' Sarah began.

'Oh, Sarah, sit down and don't argue. I'm too tired to argue. I have enough of that with Matthew.' Abigail passed her hand wearily over her eyes and sat down at the table opposite Sarah.

Peggy brought in the tea, a short, neat girl, tending to plumpness now that she ate regularly. While Abigail poured, Sarah surreptitiously took in the cosy comfort of the room, crowded now with too much furniture, too many pictures and pieces of china, with the piano, Abigail's pride and joy, pushed into the only corner where there was room for it.

'Matthew needs something to do; something he feels is important,' Abigail said as she handed Sarah her tea.

The older woman sipped it. 'I don't see it, myself. He's always got a pile of books beside his bed, he can keep himself happy reading.'

'Oh, yes, he reads a lot. And when Edwin comes they talk and argue about all sorts of things. That's good for him, I'm sure. But he needs something else . . . some purpose . . . ' Abigail frowned. 'Do you know what I mean?'

'No, I can't say as how I do.' Sarah's face was wooden.

'Well.' Abigail watched carefully to see what her mother-in-law's reaction would be. 'I wondered if you'd let him teach you to read and write.'

For a split second Sarah's stern, unyielding mask slipped and her face lit up. Only for a split second, but it was enough. Abigail knew now that her guess had been right and she had found the way to Sarah's friendship. 'I could suggest it to him,' she went on carefully, 'in such a way that he'd think it was his idea and that he'd be helping you. But really, it would be doing him a lot of good. It would make him feel useful again, wouldn't it?'

Sarah shrugged, careful not to let the mask slip again. 'Well, if you think it might help him we'll give it a try. I don't know that I'll ever have much use for that kind of learning, I've managed without for near on fifty years, but if it'll help Matthew . . . ' She shrugged again.

Abigail wasn't in the least deceived by her offhand remarks. She had seen that Sarah desperately wanted to learn but had been too proud to seek help. Now that it had come to it, it was difficult to see whom the venture would benefit most, Matthew or his mother. Abigail was well pleased with the idea that had come to her in the small hours of yet another sleepless night.

But it was not only thoughts of Matthew that occupied her when she lay awake. The oyster layings in Brightlingsea Creek had been partially re-stocked with brood from Terschelling, but it was too soon to know whether it would be successful, let alone whether there would be any significant income from the venture. Tolley and Guy went out into the Blackwater and fished oysters, bringing in enough to keep the fattening beds stocked, but they missed their skipper, or gaffer, as they affectionately called Matthew. Tolley was a first-class mate, but on his own admission he needed someone to direct him, and Guy, coming originally from Yarmouth, was more used to herring fishing than oysters. They both missed young Moses and his Jew's harp, too. All these things pressed on Abigail's mind, together with the need for money to service the hefty repayments to the bank. Matthew, reckless in his new-found wealth, had not allowed for disaster to strike.

Abigail talked about it to Alice and Josh when they had been to see Matthew one Sunday evening. Summer Sunday evenings, after church, when Alice's arthritis was well enough, was their time for visiting their nephew and his family, and Abigail looked forward to seeing them and receiving the benefit of their plain common sense. She always felt better after a visit from them.

Josh listened carefully to what she had to say, then he took a draught of porter and wiped his whiskers. 'You'd find life a lot easier if you was to apply for a licence to dredge the river,' he said. 'At least the men 'ud get a reg'lar wage an' you'd get a share-out at the end of the season.'

'I doubt Matthew wouldn't want that.' Alice shook her head. 'An' he's a rare pig-headed boy when that comes to it.'

'Beggars can't be choosers, woman,' Josh said sternly. 'He ain't in no position to shout.'

'It's not only Matthew,' Abigail pointed out. 'My father . . . '

'Your father couldn't stop you if you was to apply for a licence. He wouldn't hev a leg to stand on if he tried. You gotta serve a seven-year apprentice 'afore you can hev a licence to dredge and be a freeman o' the river. Well, Tolley musta bin with Matthew at least ten year or more, an' Matthew musta done much the same with his grandad, so that take care o' that.' He paused and drained his mug. 'An' if I was to come an' skipper the boat that'd clinch it. I'm already a freeman o' the river. I got a licence. They can't stop me dredgin', long as I pay me dues.'

The lines of worry cleared from Abigail's face as if by magic. 'Would you do that, Josh? Could you? No.' She shook her head and the lines returned. 'My father wouldn't let you go. Who'd skipper the *Edith*? And if he did and you came to me, supposing we couldn't make a living? What would you and Alice do? Well, you could come and live with us, I suppose – but if we had to sell our house . . . ? No, Josh.' She shook her head again. 'I couldn't let you. It's too risky.'

'Me an' Josh've got a fair bit put by for a rainy day,' Alice said, her voice proud. 'We keep it under the mattress. So there ain't no call for you to worry over us. I reckon that'd be the best thing all round.' She leaned forward as far as her arthritic joints would allow. 'Josh don't get on with that Richard Cotgrove too well, tell ye the truth. An thass tellin' ye. Thass right, ain't it, Josh?' She turned to her husband.

Josh shrugged. 'He's all right. Nice enough cove, I dessay. But he's a landlubber. An' I 'on't hev a landlubber tellin' me how to run my boat. No, Abbie my dear, I'd be ony too happy to come over to *Conquest*. I've knowed Tolley a good many years and always got on well with him. An' Guy seem decent enough. Good sailor, too, from all accounts.'

'What will Dibby do?' Abigail asked.

'Dance a jig, I should think. He's bin itchin' to step into my shoes for years,' Josh said dryly.

'Matthew won't like it.' Abigail shook her head. 'He won't like to think of anyone else skippering *Conquest*.'

'Matthew ain't in no position to like or dislike it,' Josh said with blunt sadness.

'How on earth shall I tell him?'

'You leave that to me, dearie.' Josh got up and left the room.

Matthew was pretending to be asleep when Josh went in, so he sat by the bed.

'Hev you thought about wass goin' to happen to *Conquest*, with you laid on one side?' he asked thoughtfully.

Matthew opened his eyes. 'Do you think I haven't worried myself sick over that?' he said. 'Stuck here in this bloody bed, when I should be out on the river. And no, I don't know what's going to happen. Tolley and Guy can't manage on their own, they need another hand. Oh, Christ, I suppose I'll have to sell the lot and we'll end up in the workhouse. I can't see any other way . . . ' He turned his face to the wall.

'Don't be such a silly fool.' Josh was never heard to swear. 'Thass stupid talk and you know it. You got some trouble an' somehow or other we've got to get round it. Young Abbie's workin' her fingers near to the bone. That ain't easy for her, ye know, runnin' the house, runnin' the business, seein' after Tolley and Guy an' the oysters, an' nursin' you. I don't wonder she's nothin' but skin an' grief. An' what do you do to help her? Turn your face to the wall an' give up. You oughta be ashamed o' yourself, Nephew.'

'All right. What do you suggest, then?' Matthew hauled himself into a sitting position with his ropes. 'I can still haul on a rope, as you can see. That must be some help on a boat, even if I haven't got legs.'

'Ain't no call to be sarcastic,' Josh said mildly.

'Sorry, Uncle.' Matthew gave a deep sigh. 'But it's bloody hard, lying in this bed when I should be out on the river skippering *Conquest*. There's nobody else to do it. Neither Tolley nor Guy . . . '

'There's me. I'm ready to.'

Matthew looked at him open-mouthed. 'You, Uncle Josh?'

Josh nodded. 'I've talked it over with my Alice an' your Abbie. We're all agreed thass the best thing. You can't, so I will. I'll be glad of a change. I'm fed up with takin' orders from that smart arse, Richard Cotgrove. He's a funny bloke. There's somethin about 'im I can't take to. I dunno what it is, but I can tell ye I'll be only too glad to part company with him.'

Matthew turned away, his face working. When he'd got

command of himself he turned back. 'If I can't do the job myself there's no one I'd rather trust *Conquest* to, Uncle.' He held out his hand and Josh shook it.

'Thass that, then,' Josh said. 'Now, I'll bid you goodnight.' With that he got up and left the room.

Henry hurried up the stairs to his office, threw down his hat and cane and slumped into the chair. After a moment he opened the bottom drawer of the large mahogany desk and took out a whisky bottle and glass. Soon the warmth from the fiery liquid spread through him, making him sweat in the heat of the summer day. He loosened his cravat slightly and leaned forward and rang the bell that stood on the corner of the desk.

Seconds later Richard Cotgrove appeared.

'Sit down, man,' Henry said impatiently. 'I want to talk to you.'

Richard sat down and crossed his legs, resting his hands lightly on his knees. 'Yes, sir?'

Henry poured himself another whisky. 'Josh Miller's packing up. We'll have to find another skipper for the *Edith*.'

'Dibby can handle her,' Richard said smoothly. 'I don't see any problem there. And young Charlie's nearly out of his time, so he can take Dibby's place as mate. All we need to do is get another cabin boy. I'll go along to the workhouse and see if they've got a likely young orphan boy.'

'Thank you, Richard. Yes. Well, I can leave it all to you, then. I'm sure you'll deal with it very well.' Henry gulped his whisky. 'I don't know why Miller has suddenly decided to give up. He's not that old. God knows what he intends to live on.'

'Don't you know, Sir?' Richard's eyebrows shot up into his hair. 'He's going to skipper *Conquest*. Now that young Bateman's had that fearful accident she needs a skipper, and of course Josh is Bateman's uncle, so what more natural. But isn't Matthew your . . . ?'

'He's nothing to do with me. Nothing. And they needn't think they'll get a licence to dredge the river, if they apply for it. I'll do everything in my power to stop it.'

Richard stroked his moustache thoughtfully. 'They've already applied, as I understand it. And I can't see there's anything you can do to stop them getting it, Sir. After all, Miller is already a freeman of the river – the fact that you will no longer pay his subscription won't alter that fact, as long as he pays it himself. And as long as he pays his two guineas a year he's entitled to his four dredges, whether they be on your boat or Matthew Bateman's.'

'There must be something I can do!' Henry reached for the bottle, changed his mind, then reached for it again and replaced it, with the glass, in the drawer. 'I won't have a Bateman boat in the Colne Fishery Company. I'll find some way to stop it! I'll see Jonas Crabbe, he's chairman of the Commissioners.'

'I've already spoken to him, Sir.' Richard got to his feet. 'There's nothing you can do.'

'Bah!' Henry waved his hand impatiently, pushed his chair back and got to his feet. 'Oh, I can't work with this on my mind. I'm going out.'

Richard handed him his hat and his cane. 'To Wivenhoe, Sir? It's a lovely afternoon for a drive into the country.'

'Mind your own damned business.' Henry snatched the hat and cane and went off down the stairs.

As Abigail had predicted, Matthew was furious to think a licence had been applied for, but he laughed aloud when it was granted.

'I'll wager that's put old Henry Chiswell's nose out of joint,' he said gleefully, 'to think that my grandfather's *Conquest* will dredge beside the *Edith*.' He became serious. 'I wish I could see *Conquest* again. To think I never shall . . . that I shall be stuck in this bed . . . seeing nothing but these four bloody walls . . . ' His voice rose higher and higher and he thumped ineffectually on the coverlet.

'That's just where you're wrong, my love,' Abigail said, her eyes shining. 'Because I've got a surprise for you.' She went to the door. 'Come on in, Tolley, Guy, show him what you've got.'

There was a bit of a scuffle, a muffled curse and a guffaw, and then through the door came Tolley, steering himself in a wicker wheelchair, with Guy pushing from behind.

'The missus ordered it a month ago, and we've jest fetched it. All the way from Thorrington,' Tolly beamed. 'We took it in turn to push and ride. Thass very comfortable, Gaffer. Come on, let's get you out o' that bed and down to the quay. Thass a lovely sunny day.'

Matthew could hardly contain his excitement as they shoved his useless legs into trousers and buttoned up his shirt. Then the two men lifted him into the wheelchair.

'You'll hetta larn to steer it yerself,' Guy said in his Norfolk drawl. 'Look, thass simple enough. Twist the handle this way an' you'll goo to port, and that way for starboard. You'll soon get the hang of it.'

'An' here's the brake. You jest push this lever an' that'll jam the back wheels.' Tolley was as excited as Matthew. 'Right you are. Are we ready to cast off? Let's be on our way down the hill, then. Are you a-comin' along too, Missus?'

'No,' Abigail said, smiling through tears of joy. 'You three men go.'

'I dessay we shall fetch up at The Anchor,' Guy said.

'Well, make sure you come out sober enough to push him home,' Abigail laughed.

It was the most cheerful she had seen Matthew for nearly six months.

He was very drunk when they brought him home and they put him to bed, where he fell asleep immediately.

Tolley and Guy were relatively sober, but their faces were red with excitement. 'Can we talk to ye, Missus?' Tolley said. 'Me an' Guy hev got a idea to put to ye.'

'You'd better come into the kitchen,' Abigail said intrigued. She led the way. Peggy was there, ironing. 'Leave that, Peggy,' she said, 'and go and see what the children are up to. They're playing in the attic'

Peggy took the hint and went, and Abigail sat down at the table and gestured to the two men to follow suit. They did so, awkwardly twisting their woollen caps in their hands, the bravery of the beer house, egged on by Matthew, disappearing now that they were confronting the real skipper, female though she was.

'Go on, then, Guy. Tell the missus. That was your idea,' Tolley encouraged.

Guy sat up a bit straighter. 'Well, see here, Missus, thass like this. I'm a herren man, meself. Afore I lost me boat I used to go driftin' for herren orf Yarmouth. Now, there's herren off the Blackwater – shoals of 'em. I seen 'em.' He leaned forward. 'An' I reckon we could do a nice little trade in 'em, partickly if we was to smoke 'em.' Having said his piece he leaned back, nodding.

'Herrings? Smoke them? I didn't know they could be smoked.'

'Ah, Missus, thass jest it,' Tolley said. Thass a pretty new game. An' if we could get in on it . . . '

'But how?'

'I can tell ye how,' Guy said. 'You need a smoke house . . . '

'But that's going to cost money.' Abigail bit her lip. 'It's no good, we can't afford . . . '

'The gaffer's right keen on the idea,' Tolley put in.

'But what about Josh? He's skipper now.'

'Oh, you know Josh. He'll hev a go at anything,' Guy laughed.

Abigail frowned. 'Could it be worked with the oysters?'

'Don't see why not. Herren season's fairly short. Three months at the most. If we'd got the nets we could start right away. Sell 'em fresh this season, then get a smoke house set up ready for next year. Bloaters, thass what they're called. Bloaters. Make a fortune, we could, sendin' 'em to London.' Guy grinned and twisted the single gold earring he wore. It was there to ensure that if he was lost at sea, when his body was washed up there would be the price of a decent burial, but he often twisted it as a good luck charm.

'Talk to the gaffer,' Tolley said encouragingly.

Abigail nodded. 'All right. I'll talk to Matthew. When he's sober.'

Matthew was so enthusiastic that, against her better judgement, Abigail agreed to fit *Conquest* out for herring fishing. That meant a trip to see Mr Andrews at the bank in Head Street.

Unwilling to let her go alone, much to her annoyance, Matthew enlisted Edwin to accompany her. Even so, Mr Andrews was polite but unhelpful, pointing out that there was still a considerable amount owing on Mr Bateman's account.

Abigail, furious at the smug little man's indifference to her problems, stood up and leaned over his desk. 'You do realize that my husband has had a serious accident, don't you?' she said. 'And that somehow I've got to pull everything together again – with or without your help.'

He looked up at her and smiled blandly. '*Without* my help, I'm afraid, Mrs Bateman. I'm not in the habit of making the same mistake twice. I think your husband rather overstretched himself in the first place. Even without the accident he would not have found it easy, I fear, in spite of all his assurances to the contrary, which, against my better judgement, I listened to.'

'You'll get your money back, Mr Andrews, never fear. If I have to sell the clothes off my back you'll get every penny. I'll find some way.' She turned with a swish of her skirt and left the room.

Edwin followed her. 'I don't know why Matt was so anxious that I should come with you,' he said with a smile. 'You managed the old skinflint perfectly well without any help from me.' He took her arm. 'Come on, I'll buy you tea at the new tea rooms. You look as if you could do with it.'

He led her along Head Street and into High Street. It was market day. High Street was filled with the noise and stench of animals; of squealing, bleating and bellowing, of the constant shuffling and scraping of hooves and the shouts as the occasional pig or bullock escaped and ran amok among the stalls and street sellers. The whole street was crowded and colourful with people selling and people buying. It seemed that the only people quietly going about their business were the pickpockets, oozing their way along the pavements. Everyone else was shouting the odds.

Even inside Bank's restaurant the cacophony could still be heard. Edwin found a table by the window where they could watch in comfort, and over tea and crumpets he said, quite suddenly. 'How would it be if I lent you enough money to get started on this herring business?'

'*You*, Eddie? But aren't you saving up to get married?' she asked. 'What about your Belinda?'

He made a face. 'What about her, indeed! Things aren't going too well in that direction, I fear.'

'Oh, Eddie. What's happened?'

'Well,' he shrugged, 'I got fed up with her prissy little soirées, with their stupid, inconsequential chatter, and I told her so. That was after she'd begun to introduce me at her silly little gatherings as "Edwin Chadwick's disciple", in a very sarcastic and derogatory tone. She's not interested in the conditions of the poor. All she worries about is the lace on her gown,' he finished gloomily.

'But what does Mr Young say about it? After all, he is your boss and she's his daughter.'

Edwin laughed. 'I think secretly he agrees with me, although he can't say so openly or he'd have the wrath of his wife down upon him. But suffice it to say that he's already told me my job is safe.'

'Oh, Eddie. I am sorry.'

'Don't be, old girl. I think I've had a lucky escape, to tell you the truth.' He leaned forward. 'And I'll tell you this, Abbie, I shall be very careful before I get involved again. It's once bitten twice shy for me from now on.' He took a crumpet and buttered it liberally. 'However, that's not what we came here to talk about. We came to talk about you and your business. Now, if you want a couple of hundred I'm your man. I get quite well paid, you know, and I also do a bit of freelance work, so I have a bit to spare, especially now that I'm not thinking of setting up home. So what about it?'

'Oh, Eddie. I don't know what to say.'

'Try "thank you" and then pour me some more tea.'

'Oh, Eddie, thank you.' She poured tea for them both from the silver teapot and handed him the delicate china cup. He raised it before putting it to his lips. 'To bloaters. May they prosper.'

To bloaters,' she said, copying him. 'May they prosper indeed.'

# *Chapter Thirteen*

Edwin was as keen and excited over the prospect of expanding into the bloater trade as Abigail and Matthew. Each week he scanned the local newspapers for auctions of goods salvaged from wrecks along the coast. These were held from time to time and there were often bargains to be had. It wasn't long before he sent word of one and Abigail dispatched Guy, who would know what to look for, to see what he could get. He returned in high spirits with exactly the nets that were needed to catch the silver herring.

And so *Conquest* began yet another career. Fishing for herrings. Some days when they went out they caught nothing and came home despondent; other days the catch was so big that the hold was full and more were piled in baskets on the deck. On those days *Conquest* was accompanied up river by an orchestra of screaming, wheeling, hopeful gulls. If she saw the boat was accompanied by the gulls Abigail, waiting on the quayside with Matthew in his chair, would know that there was work well into the night, gutting and cleaning and packing the catch ready for the train to Billingsgate.

Guy had shown them how to gut the herring with a sharp knife and Tolley had constructed a bench to go over Matthew's chair so that he could play his part, along with Abigail and the women from the yards around the Hythe, who were willing to do anything to earn a few coppers. At first Matthew was enthusiastic, but he had only to let the knife slip and fall to the floor and, instead of asking for it to be picked up, would stare down the river and curse the fate that had imprisoned him in the chair that he had received with such excitement but had soon come to loathe.

The season was short, three full moons, as Guy put it, but profitable, and plans went ahead to build the smoke house essential if next year's catch was to be transformed into the even more profitable bloaters. Guy spent more and more time ashore, overseeing the work, watching as the lofty smoke house rose and towered beside the warehouse, with its series of wickets, or wooden shutters, set high on the wall under the roof to control the smoke from the fires lit below. When it was built it was divided into louvres, frames extending from near the floor to the ceiling, about three feet apart, on which the spits of herring would be hung. Abigail listened, fascinated, as Guy explained the whole process to her, a process that had been in his family for several years.

Matthew listened at first, then grew impatient. 'If he's so interested in it, why didn't he go back to Yarmouth?' he said peevishly as Abigail helped him settle for the night before going upstairs to her own bed. 'Our business is with oysters, not bloody herring.'

'We've got debts to pay off,' Abigail reminded him, her hold on her temper slipping. 'Another bad winter and we could be ruined if it resulted in a bad spat, even though we've joined the Fishery Company. It's a gamble, I know, but if we can only get started ... it'll be another string to our bow so we're not so entirely dependent on a good oyster season. And bloaters are becoming very popular, you know. They'll fetch a better price than herring. Guy says ... '

'Guy says, Guy says,' he mimicked. 'That's all I hear these days. Guy says this, Guy says that. You're getting a sight too fond of Guy, methinks, now you've only got half a husband.'

'Oh!' She thumped his pillow and jerked his sheet straight. 'That's a despicable thing to say and you know it.' She went to the door without giving him his customary goodnight kiss. 'I can't talk to you when you're in such a mood. Perhaps you'll be in a better frame of mind in the morning. You could hardly be in a worse one.'

'Wait. Abbie, come back.' Matthew struggled up onto one elbow and held out his hand. 'I'm sorry. I shouldn't have said what I did.'

Reluctantly she came back to the side of the bed and he took her hand and held it against his cheek. 'It's true, you know. People always behave worst towards the ones they love best. I don't know why it is. It's not your fault I'm in this mess, but I always seem to take it out on you. I don't mean to, my little love. Truly, I don't.' He looked up at her, and she saw that his face had already grown thin; the healthy tan from the sea had gone leaving it white against the curly black whiskers. 'Sit down, Abbie. No, better still, lie down beside me. There's plenty of room. Please, Abbie. I promise I won't rant at you.'

She smiled down at him. Here, at last, was a glimpse of the old Matthew, the man she loved and had married. Eagerly, she slipped off her shoes and got onto the bed beside him, to be held close in his arms.

'Oh, my little love, I know I've been terrible to live with and I'm sorry, truly I am,' he said, his voice close to her ear. 'But the thought of spending the rest of my life . . . of not being able to . . . of never being able to take you to me as a husband should – as is your right and mine – sometimes it's all too much to bear.' He began to kiss her, his lips tender on her face and neck. 'I love you so much, Abbie.'

She cradled him to her, their faces wet with mingled tears, as he went on, 'I had such hopes, such plans, for you and the children, and suddenly, in the twinkling of an eye, it's all come to naught.' He gave a great sigh. 'And it didn't even happen in a storm. I came through storm and tempest, salvage and wreck, without so much as a scratch. And then, for such a thing to happen in harbour . . . leaving you with a useless husband and a pile of debts.'

She kissed him as she felt the tension building again inside him. 'We'll manage, Matthew. We'll survive. Remember, God makes the back to fit the burden. As long as we have our love for each other we'll be strong enough to face whatever comes.' When he was calmer she added, 'It's only when you shout and rave and treat me as if you hate me that I feel I can't go on.'

He gathered her to him again. 'Oh, Abbie, my little love, I'm sorry. Forgive me. I promise I'll try to be more patient with you. With everybody.'

She stroked his hair and he fell asleep with his head on her breast. For a long time she stayed there with him, grateful to have found the old Matthew again under all the pain and frustration. It was past two o'clock when she finally extricated herself from his embrace and settled him in a more comfortable position. Then she went stiffly up the stairs to her own bed, to breathe a prayer of thankfulness for the past precious hours.

For a few weeks Matthew seemed happier, as if he had resigned himself to his fate. Josh, knowing how badly the money was needed, took *Conquest* spratting when the herring season had finished, and salvaging whenever there was the opportunity. The law said a boat was not a wreck while there was man or dog alive on it, and to some of the more unscrupulous life was cheap when pickings were rich, but Josh and his crew, which always included Guy when they went salvaging, were concerned with saving lives above all else. However, once all hands were saved there was nothing to stop them going back to see what else could be salvaged. The men had made or collected together a weird selection of tools which they kept down in the fo'c'sle, always ready in case they were needed. Such things as grapnels, and axes that they called tomahawks – useful for smashing open crates or clearing away wreckage –mauls, crowbars, hooks for slinging casks up out of the hold and iron-framed nets for fishing up waterlogged coal. Nothing defeated them, and if the odd keg of brandy or tobacco should find its way into *Conquest*'s hold in the process, they regarded it as no more than their just reward. Salvaging was a very lucrative sideline and Josh and his crew were experts.

Abigail tried to prevent the men telling Matthew of their more hair-raising exploits, but he was desperate to hear, indeed he seemed to have a masochistic need to twist the knife in the wound of his helplessness.

Inevitably he grew bitter again. One afternoon he shouted at his mother because she stumbled over a word in the book she was reading aloud and then tore the slate from her hand and threw it across the room, smashing it against an oak chest, all because her slate pencil squeaked.

'I don't know how you put up with him, Abbie,' Sarah said, coming out of the room with the pieces in her hand. 'He's like a bear with a sore head again today.'

Abigail, sitting in the kitchen, paused from rubbing grease into her hands, chapped from the interminable cleaning of oysters and gutting offish. 'Life is hard for him, Sarah. We have to make allowances. I try to understand.' She sighed. 'But I agree, sometimes it's not easy.'

Sarah went across to the range and pulled the kettle forward. She had gradually begun to make herself more at home when she came to the Corner House. 'I'll make a cup of tea; I expect you could drink one.'

'Yes, Peggy has taken the children to the shop, they won't be back for a while. I thought I might look at the accounts. There are bills that need paying, I think we've made enough on the herrings to clear some of them . . .'

'You're a good girl, Abigail.' Sarah reached down the tea caddy and spooned tea into the teapot. 'I never thought to say it, but my boy couldn't have made a better choice for a wife, particularly the way things have turned out.'

'Thank you, Sarah.' Abigail knew how difficult it must have been for Sarah to make that little speech for the older woman was not given to compliments. It was with a new sense of friendship that the two women sat together over the teapot.

Late into the night Abigail was still wrestling with her accounts, trying to decide which bills needed paying most urgently, trying to see the right way forward. It was a burden she shouldered alone. She had tried sharing it with Matthew but seeing just how much money they needed only served to increase his feeling of uselessness, making him even more painfully aware of his own inability to provide for his family. So she felt it wiser to work on the books alone, usually late at night when everyone else had gone to bed. It suited her very well; it was better than lying sleepless, dog-tired though she might be, aching for the secret, physical love that Matthew was no longer able to provide.

It was a terrible night outside. The wind howled round the house, gusting round the chimney pots and sending puffs of smoke into the room. Somewhere in the distance a shutter banged. As always on a wild night, Abigail offered up a fervent prayer for those at sea.

Although she didn't know it, among those at sea that night were Josh, Tolley and Guy in *Conquest*. With a fleet of salvagers they had been among the first to rally when the cry went up that there was a schooner aground on the Longsands, a notorious place for wrecks. She didn't find out until noon the next day, when Guy knocked on her door with a sack of oranges and a man wrapped in a blanket.

'Didn't know what else to do with him, Missus,' Guy whispered under cover of getting both man and goods into the house. 'He seems too ... well ... gentry-like, for any of us to take 'im 'ome.'

'I don't wish to trouble you, Madam. Perhaps there's a hotel ...' The man, teeth still chattering from shock and cold, looked round him, bemused.

'He ain't fit to see after 'imself yet,' Guy whispered.

'No, of course not. Come this way.' Briskly, Abigail led the way through to the kitchen and Guy followed, helping the man along. They sat him by the fire and Abigail gave him a mug of hot soup. She stayed with him while he drank it, cupping his hands round the mug as if to draw extra warmth from it, his teeth chattering still. 'I don't think I'll ever be warm again,' he muttered between mouthfuls.

'Yes, you will,' Abigail assured him. 'Peggy has taken the hip bath up to the spare bedroom and she's filling it with hot water. That will help to take the chill out of your bones.'

'Oh, it was terrible. Terrible,' he kept saying, staring into the fire. 'And those men – they don't seem to know any fear.' He looked up at Abigail and she noticed that his eyes were an unusual shade of grey-green. 'Without those men we should all have surely perished.' He shuddered. 'I shall never forget it. The pitch darkness – That was the most frightening thing of all, I think, the darkness; things are never quite so bad if you can see what's happening. And the noise! The noise of the wind and the sea! It was deafening. And the way it screamed through the rigging – like some wild, demented creature. And all the time the boat was being hammered further and further onto the sands where we'd gone aground. Every wave that hit us I felt sure the boat would splinter into matchwood under us and we'd be lost.' He drank some more of his soup and Abigail waited, watching his tired, gaunt face. He needed to talk, to relive his nightmare experience, or he would never rest. She knew this and was content to listen.

He began to talk again. 'Then we heard shouts close at hand. I thought at first I was delirious, but they were calling to let us know that we weren't alone in that hell. Salvation was at hand if we could only hang on until daybreak. I couldn't believe my ears. I didn't think there could be any other living thing within miles. My hands and arms were numb from hanging on – I don't know what I was clinging to, but I knew if I let go I should be swept into the sea. Even so, the waves kept hitting me – some of them went right over my head. It was so cold.' He shuddered again. 'And the power of the sea as it sucked back. I could scarcely hold on for the pull.'

Peggy came back into the kitchen. 'The gentleman's bath is all ready, M'm. An' I've put a brick in the bed, an' laid the master's clo's out, like you said.'

'That's good. Thank you, Peggy.' Abigail smiled at her.

The man got to his feet clutching the now steaming blanket round him. He was tall, as tall as Matthew, she noticed. 'It's most kind of you,' he said. 'I am, indeed, very tired. Perhaps after a short sleep I can find a hotel . . . '

'We'll see,' Abigail said. 'But for now, I think you'll find everything you need in the bedroom. This way . . . '

It was quite late in the evening when David Quilter reappeared. Shaved and dressed in Matthew's wedding suit, which hung on his spare figure, he looked refreshed and had lost the haunted look of earlier in the day. Abigail took him in to meet her husband.

In the daytime Matthew sat in an ordinary Windsor elbow chair, well padded and cushioned, which Tolley and Guy had modified by shortening the legs and mounting it on a wheeled platform so that he could be pushed from room to room in the house. The wicker wheelchair was kept for expeditions out because it was much bigger and more cumbersome. He was sitting by the fire when Abigail brought David in and introduced him. The two men took an immediate liking to one another although they were totally unlike. David was probably a few years Matthew's senior, as fair as Matthew was dark, clean-shaven where Matthew was darkly bewhiskered, with smooth fair hair that insisted on waving in spite of being oiled down. Matthew had a thick mop of unruly black hair that he never attempted to tame.

While David told Matthew of his experiences in the storm and the bravery of the Essex salvagers, or 'Swin Rangers' as they liked to be called, Abigail was able to take stock of him. He had a long thin face, rather pale, with a high forehead and grey-green eyes under long dark lashes and thick eyebrows. His nose was a shade long but when he smiled, which was not often, his whole face seemed to light up, wrinkling his eyes at the corners and showing good, sound teeth. His hands, moving descriptively as he spoke of the boat he had been on, were long and well kept.

Abigail took all this in as she listened to what he was saying, suddenly realizing that she had been staring at the man. Almost as if he sensed her gaze David Quilter looked up and met her eyes before she could turn back to the dress she was altering for Laura. Embarrassed, she could feel a flush spreading over her face and there was a fluttering in her heart that she didn't understand. Quickly, she got up and left the room.

When she returned Matthew said, 'David must stay with us for as long as he likes, mustn't he, Abbie?' He spoke with more than a trace of his old ebullience. 'He's talking about finding a hotel, but I won't hear of it, especially as he's got nothing but the clothes he stands up in. And they're mine!' he added, roaring with laughter.

'Yes, of course you must stay.' Abigail spoke warmly, but for some unfathomable reason she was unable to meet the stranger's green-grey eyes.

'You're very kind. I'll arrange with my office in London for money to be sent so that I can reimburse you before I leave.' He seemed quite content to stay.

David Quilter was with them a week. In that time he told them that he was in the fruit trade and that he had been travelling back on the fruit schooner *Chance* from the Mediterranean to see if the Yarmouth fruit schooners were as fast and efficient as they were reputed to be; to see how the fruit was handled and if it arrived at its destination fresh. 'We were doing extremely well until the storm blew up,' he said. 'The fruit schooners are built for speed, they have beautiful lines. They can compete with the tea clippers any day, in my opinion. But they carry too much sail to cope with those North Sea gales, I fear.'

'Of course, it's the fact that they carry so much sail that makes them so fast, but as you say, it's also hazardous in a strong blow,' Matthew said. 'They can be blown aground before they can get the tops'ls furled. But that's the risk you take if you want speed.'

The next day David took Matthew down to the quay in his wicker chair to see the smoke house, nearly completed now, with a pile of well-seasoned oak stacked nearby ready to make the fires for smoking the herring. Now Matthew was able to share his knowledge of oysters with his newfound friend and David was keen to learn of the differences between the native Pyefleet oyster, fattened in the creek from which it took its name because of the properties of London clay found there, and the coarser Portuguese oyster, a voracious eater. 'You can get oysters from all round the coast but you won't find a better oyster than Colchester Natives,' Matthew said. He became morose. 'My luck ran out in the winter of forty-seven,' he said, with some of his old bitterness. 'I lost all my oysters then and my layings have never picked up properly since although I restocked the beds from the Terschelling Bank. But the men don't tend the beds as I would myself,' he went on unjustly. 'They don't keep them raked and clean so that the new young oysters have a clean surface to cling to. Not like I would myself.'

'That's not fair, Matthew.' Abigail had come up beside them, bringing the children with her as the day was bright. 'Josh and Tolley know exactly what's needed to keep the beds healthy, and Guy is learning, too. They work very hard for us and I won't have it said otherwise. They're three good men and we've cause to be grateful to them.'

'Oh, yes, we must be grateful to the men who do the work I should be doing myself if I wasn't tied to this thing.' Matthew thumped his chair. 'My wife has great admiration for them, you'll notice. Especially for Guy,' he added heavily, 'the handsome one, who has persuaded her with his smooth talk to run us into further debt with this.' He gestured towards the smoking house. 'I only hope he's right and there is a market for bloaters. But Guy can't be wrong, can he, Abbie?' He threw the last remark over his shoulder to Abbie, the sarcasm heavy in his voice.

Abigail sighed and shook her head. 'Take no notice, Mr Quilter,' she said in a low voice. 'He doesn't really mean what he's saying.'

At the end of the week as he sat by the fire with them one evening David said, 'I must go back to London tomorrow. My money has come through so I can pay you for all your kindness to me.'

'Nonsense, man, there's no payment needed. We've enjoyed your company, haven't we, Abbie?' Matthew said expansively. 'And I hope you'll visit us again soon. Often, in fact.' He nodded towards David. 'And I mean that, I'm not just being polite. I've enjoyed our games of cribbage. Abbie will never play it with me, she's always too busy, so you come and play it with me again. You do me good, man.'

David smiled one of his rare smiles. 'You're very kind. Yes, I should like to come back and see you again.' He turned to Abigail. 'You too, Mrs Bateman. You've been most kind to me, even lending me your husband's clothes.' He looked down at himself. 'But I must say it's nice to wear a suit that fits again.'

Matthew was beginning to nod drowsily. 'I think I'll go to bed,' he said. 'But don't forget, Quilter, if I'm not up when you leave tomorrow, I shall expect you to visit us again before long.'

Abigail went through with Matthew. It took her about half an hour every night to get him undressed, helping him pulley himself into bed and settling his useless limbs. At one point her foot slipped and it jarred his back.

'Mind what you're doing, woman,' he shouted. 'Can't you be more bloody careful? I'm not quite a sack of coal, you know.'

'I'm sorry dear.' She bit her lip against an equally angry retort. 'Is there anything else you want?'

'No, just leave me alone. Yes, bring me a glass of water.'

She took him the water and then went back to the living room, standing for a moment with her back to the door as she closed it, her eyes shut against threatening tears. She hadn't seen David Quilter in the armchair by the fire until he stood up at her entry.

'Life can't always be easy for you, Mrs Bateman,' he said sympathetically.

'Oh,' she sniffed and pressed the back of her hand to her mouth. 'I didn't realize you were still there, Mr Quilter. I thought I heard you go upstairs.'

'I went to my room to get a book.' He held it up. 'I'm afraid I keep rather late hours.' He smiled his rare smile. 'In any case, it seemed a pity to leave this lovely fire.'

She went over to the fire and stretched out her hands to warm them. 'Yes, Peggy makes sure it's well stoked before she goes to bed. She knows I rarely go up before midnight.'

'Because if you do you can't sleep,' he added. A statement rather than a question.

She turned her head in surprise. 'What makes you say that?'

'Because I know exactly what you're going through,' he said simply. 'My wife died last year after an illness that lasted over three years.'

'Matthew isn't going to die!' she said sharply.

'No, of course not. But some of your problems are the same as the ones I experienced, I'm sure.'

Abigail sighed and sank down on a little tapestry stool, her favourite seat late at night, where she would sit and gaze into the dying embers of the fire, with the house quiet and still around her, the lamp turned low, wondering what the next day, the next year, would bring; and praying that she would have the strength to face whatever fate might have in store. Sometimes she thought of Pearl, her poor, pretty, misguided sister, and would weep tears of pity and frustration at the futile waste of a young life; and sometimes she would think of her own lost little baby. But mostly she thought of Matthew, her husband, who had been so young, energetic, vibrant with life, and was now wasting away in the next room.

She looked up and saw David Quilter's green-grey eyes watching her. 'Tell me about your wife,' she said.

'Miriam?' He sat down in the armchair again and leaned forward, his elbows on his knees. 'She was dark, vivacious, and quite beautiful,' he began, staring into the fire. 'We were married for ten years. Right from the beginning we hoped for a child, but as the years went on we began to think that it was not to be and we accepted the fact. We had each other and that was enough. We were very happy. Then, when she was thirty-four, to our amazement Miriam found that she was to have a child. You can imagine our joy.' He smiled wryly at the memory. 'But things went wrong right from the start and at four months, most of which she had spent in bed, she miscarried.' He spread his hands in a gesture of helplessness. 'After that she was never well and in constant pain. Eventually the doctor diagnosed cancer.' He paused for several minutes. Then he went on, 'I had to watch her die over those last months, knowing there was nothing I could do. I watched her personality change as she became more and more dependent on the drug she took to kill the pain.'

'Oh, how dreadful for you.' Abigail's eyes were full of pity.

He nodded. 'One of the worst things I had to bear was the guilt. I felt it was all my fault. It wasn't, of course, the doctors assured me that it would have happened whether or not she had miscarried, but it still persisted. Perhaps it was mixed up with the awful feeling of inadequacy; of not being able to do anything; not being able to take the burden of pain on myself. I'd always tried to shield her from life's more unpleasant aspects, but here there was absolutely nothing I could do.'

Abigail looked up at him. 'Oh, I can understand that, exactly,' she said. 'I feel just the same. I feel so useless when it comes to helping Matthew. Even in trying to shoulder all the responsibility, in looking after him, in keeping the business going, all that sort of thing, it only twists the knife further into the wound for him. Because my strength only serves to show up his weakness, and he was always the strong one. Yet where would we be if I wasn't strong? No' – she wiped away a tear – 'that's not true. If I didn't pretend to be strong.' She put her chin in her hands and sat staring into the fire. Then suddenly she found herself telling David Quilter all the worries and anxieties, all the irritations, petty though some of them were, that were slowly eroding her relationship with Matthew; things she had never before told anyone; things that she hadn't admitted, even to herself. 'I'm sorry,' she said when she had finished, shaking her head as if to clear it. 'I shouldn't be burdening you with all my problems, Mr Quilter. I don't know what came over me.'

'It's my privilege to have listened,' he assured her gravely. Thank you for taking me into your confidence. It's often easier to talk to someone you don't know very well and I'm only too happy if I've been of some help. Though I can hardly call listening to you a recompense for all the hospitality you have shown me because I've enjoyed your company, so the debt again is mine.'

They sat for a while in companionable silence until he said, 'Your eyelids are drooping. I think you should go to bed.'

'Yes. And I really feel I might sleep. It's done me so much good, talking to you, Mr Quilter.' She looked up at him and smiled. He got up and held out his hand to help her to her feet. 'I hope you will always feel you can talk to me, Mrs Bateman,' he said quietly. 'I should like to think you could regard me as a friend.' He covered the hand he still held with his other one before, almost reluctantly, releasing it.

'Thank you, Mr Quilter. You're very kind.' For some reason she couldn't meet his eyes again and with a hurried 'Goodnight' she went swiftly from the room.

That night she fell asleep not worrying about the money still owed to the bank, nor the best way to deal with Matthew's frustration and petulance, but remembering the pressure of David Quilter's hand on hers and the unmistakable warmth she had seen in his green-grey eyes.

# *Chapter Fourteen*

David Quilter was as good as his word and visited them as often as he was able. Abigail looked forward to his visits with mixed feelings. On the one hand she longed to see him and talk to him, because she found she could tell him things that she couldn't speak of to anyone else. It helped so much to unburden herself from time to time to someone who, having been through a similar experience, would understand and sympathize. Yet in another way she dreaded his visits. She knew that their conversations, late at night, when the rest of the house was sleeping, were fraught with danger. She had recognized an attraction for this man from the first time she had seen him and the attraction was growing. She suspected, too, that it was mutual, because he was as reluctant as she to break up their quiet fireside talks. Not that they ever did anything but talk. Never did he so much as touch her hand, but she wished he would and she knew he would have liked to. At times she even went so far as to wonder whether it was possible to be in love with two men at once. She still loved Matthew, difficult though he was at times, but, deep in her heart, although she hardly admitted it, even to herself, was the knowledge that she was in love with David Quilter.

The knowledge gave her no joy. She only knew that when he came the house suddenly seemed lighter, happier. Matthew was better tempered, the children better behaved. She probed no further into why she looked forward to his visits and why the gaps between them seemed long, even if it was only in reality a few weeks. She didn't dare.

When he did come he always brought fruit with him – oranges, lemons, pineapple or bananas – and he would tell the children about the exotic places he had visited and seen them growing.

Laura couldn't believe that oranges and lemons grew on trees just like apples and she laughed delightedly when he demonstrated that bananas didn't hang at all, but grew upside down, in bunches.

William, on the other hand, was more interested in the boats that brought the fruit to England, those fast schooners, heavily canvased for speed. He wanted to know all about them and even got his father to draw one for him from David's description.

The sea was in William's blood. He was never happier than when he could go down river with Guy, Josh and Tolley. By the time he was nine he could cull oysters as well as a man, using his own small cultac that Tolley had fashioned from a full-sized one to clean them; and under Josh's expert eye he had brought *Conquest* up river, reading the ripples on the water to get the best out of the wind, knowing just how far to go before turning on the tack. Josh said he was a natural seaman, but it was a constant source of worry to his parents that his single-minded love of the sea was leading him to neglect his education.

'You don't know how lucky you are, boy,' Matthew would roar at him. 'I'd have given my eye teeth when I was your age to have gone to school and learned Latin and Greek! Latin and Greek – I couldn't even write my own name till your mother taught me. She was the one who taught me to read and write, God bless her.' He reached over and squeezed Abigail's hand. Then he turned back to William. 'Yet, here you are, with every chance to learn mathematics, history and all about foreign countries and such-like and you don't even care!'

'But I don't want to *read* about foreign countries, Papa, I want to *visit* them,' William protested.

'I know, son. But first things first,' Matthew said, less harshly. 'It costs money to send you to school, William, and it's money that we gladly spend to give you an education. But your books are a disgrace.'

William hung his head. 'If you knew how I hate school, Papa, you wouldn't make me go. I hate being cooped up in a stuffy old schoolroom that stinks of camphor and mouldy text books. It's a terrible smell, Papa. Rotten fish smells better. Anyway, I'd far rather be out on the river with Tolley and Guy and Josh any day.'

Matthew looked at his son with sympathy. 'I know, old chap. I know just how you feel. I hate being cooped up in this chair. I'd rather be on *Conquest*, too, with the wind on my face and the feel of the swell under my feet. But we can't always have what we want. Stick at it until you're sixteen, lad, then you can join the men on the boat, if that's what you want. David could probably fix you a trip on a fruit schooner, too, if we asked him. But you must finish your schooling first. It's only another few years, boy.' He banged his fist down vindictively on the arm of his chair. 'It's not a bloody lifetime.'

William hung his head in shame. 'I will work harder, Papa,' he promised.

By the time of the September full moon the smoke house was ready to receive the first catch of herrings. *Conquest* was kept hard at work, both fishing the new season's oysters and going further out into the North Sea for the herring that shoaled there. Guy was in charge of the herrings. He even got Scots fisher girls to come and show the local women how to clean and gut them and he personally oversaw the salting and washing before they were hung on long pointed sticks, called spits, about twenty-one to each spit, the spit piercing the gills and coming out through the mouth. Then they were hung in rows in the smoke house to be smoked over well-seasoned oak. There was employment for laid-off woollen workers while the season lasted and Abigail was kept perpetually busy with the paper work, arranging for the boxes of bloaters to be sent to Billingsgate; making sure the oysters were properly cleaned and packed, with a layer of seaweed on top before the barrels were sealed; and paying each man and woman their due at the end of every day. It was hard, demanding work for all of them, and when the herring season was over they caught sprats, which were sold fresh or smoked and packed in boxes and sent to London, and the surplus sold by the cartful to farmers for manure. If it came out of the sea and was edible then Bateman's would sell it. And those who bought Bateman's products knew that they got the choicest, cleanest, best-packaged fish or oysters on the east coast. Before long business was booming again and Bateman's owned two more smacks beside *Conquest*, the *Good Intent* and the *Faith*. But Guy still worked *Conquest* with Tolley and Josh, both of whom complained that they 'weren't as spry' as they used to be. Nevertheless, their knowledge of Colne water and the estuary beyond was second to none and their value as seamen when there was any salvaging to be done was in no way diminished. 'They're like Bateman-cured bloaters,' Guy would laugh to Abigail. 'They'll be good for ever.'

Abigail hoped and prayed that he was right.

She quite often came into contact with Richard Cotgrove, her father's right-hand man. It always amazed Abigail how impeccably turned out the man was, with the triangle of handkerchief peeping from his top pocket and the rose in his buttonhole whatever the season. He had lately taken to wearing a monocle, too, although Abigail couldn't see how an eyeglass screwed into one eye could possibly improve his sight.

But in spite of the fact that he must have been well aware of her father's feelings towards her and also that they were now rivals in business, he was always pleasant and polite.

Occasionally she would ask after Henry, but not often, because she sensed a reluctance on his part to say anything that might be construed as being disloyal to his employer. However, one afternoon when they were both overseeing the loading offish on to the railway she ventured to speak of her father.

Richard hesitated for a moment, then he said confidentially, 'Well, to tell you the truth, Mrs Bateman, I'm getting a little worried about him. I'm afraid he's becoming a sight too fond of the whisky bottle. And as for that so-called housekeeper of his, well . . . ' He cleared his throat. 'But it's not my place to carry tales. You're doing well with your bloaters, I believe, Mrs Bateman?'

'Yes.' She didn't press him further. 'Fortunately, it's been a gamble that's paying off. They seem very popular with the people in London.'

'No doubt due to their keeping qualities. It's difficult to get fish to London absolutely fresh, isn't it?'

'I wouldn't say that, Mr Cotgrove. We can have fish caught out at the Bench Head at three o'clock in the afternoon at Billingsgate by the next morning. You won't get fish much fresher than that.' She turned away to check the barrels of oysters, marked Bateman in red paint, before returning to the warehouse.

Matthew was sitting outside when she walked back along

the quay. Either she or one of the men wheeled him down to the quayside every day because whatever the weather he hated to be cooped up in the house. Today was one of those late March days when, although the wind was chill, the sun was bright and the trees flanking the river beyond the quay seemed to be covered in a green mist of bursting buds. Even the river, at full flood, looked clean and sparkling as the sun reflected pinpoints of light on the ripples, putting a thin veneer of well-being on the rubbish and filth that would be left behind on the ebb.

She smiled at Matthew as she came near. He was much thinner now and despite his useless legs he looked healthy to the point of being weatherbeaten, from the amount of time he spent outside, wrapped up well in rugs against the cold. 'That's the last of the oysters gone, dear,' she said, taking his hand in hers. She always treated him with loving cheerfulness although sometimes, most times, in fact, he responded either with a sharp, sarcastic remark or not at all.

He let his hand lie in hers but he didn't return her smile. 'Two years I've been in this chair,' he said. 'Two bloody years.'

'Then you should be used to it by now,' she said crisply. 'Are you ready for me to take you home? Edwin is coming this evening to play cribbage with you.'

He pulled his hand away irritably and looked up at her. Then, with a sudden change of mood, he chuckled. 'Oh, you're a hard woman, Abigail Bateman. You won't even let a man feel sorry for himself, will you?'

'No, I will not. Now, have you finished cleaning those last few oysters? I promised Eddie I'd have some for him tonight.'

'I did some of them. Then I dropped the cultic.'

She sighed. 'Couldn't you have asked someone to pick it up for you, instead of sitting there moping?'

'I wasn't moping, woman. I was counting all the different colour greens I could see on the trees and fields. That view down the river would make a nice picture with the smacks coming up on the tide.' He fished down the side of his chair. 'Look, I've made a sketch.'

Abigail looked at the sketch he had made on the back of an old bill with a stub of pencil. She was no judge of line or form, her only thought was to find something that interested Matthew and would keep him happily occupied. 'It looks very good to me,' she said, standing away and looking down at it. 'I think you should try painting. Perhaps Guy could make you a kind of easel that you could fix over your chair. We'll have to ask him.'

She pushed him back along the quay and up the hill to the Corner House. It was hard work and by the time she reached home she was quite out of breath.

Indoors she helped him manoeuvre himself from the wicker wheelchair to what he called his 'indoor' chair by means of the strongly developed muscles of his arms and shoulders. Then she poured out the tea Peggy had brought in. She put his on the table in front of him then automatically reached for a pencil and paper and began jotting down figures.

'For God's sake put that away, woman,' Matthew scowled. 'You whisk here, flit there, hurry somewhere else. What's the matter with you? You're like spring-heeled Jack, all I ever see of you is a whisk of your petticoats as you scuttle about. And when you do manage to sit for five minutes you've either got a pen or a bit of sewing in your hands. Can't you just sit still and drink your tea for once?'

She looked up at him in surprise. He was smiling at her. It was obviously one of his good days. 'I'm sorry, dear' – she pushed a stray strand of hair back under her cap – 'but I was just trying to calculate . . . '

'Well, stop calculating and sit.' He leaned forward and put his hand over hers. 'What's the matter, my little love? Has life become so difficult for you that you can't even stop for a minute?'

She made a conscious effort to relax. 'It's just that there are always so many things to think about, Matthew. So many things to do.'

'But the business is fine. If I ever thought it couldn't run without me I've been well and truly proved wrong. We're doing remarkably well, aren't we? The bank's paid off and we've settled up with Edwin, so what are you worrying about?'

She sighed. 'I don't know.' She got up and went and sat at his feet. 'I suppose I've grown so used to worrying now, so used to having too much to do, that I don't know how to stop.' She laid her head on the rug that covered his legs.

Gently, he took off her cap and loosened the pins in her hair.

She lifted her head. 'Matthew, what are you doing?'

'It's a long time since I saw you with your hair down. It must be uncomfortable, always having it screwed up under that cap.' He began to run his fingers through it.

'Oh, Matthew you can't. I look a sight.' She groped for the pins.

'You look like my own dear Abbie.' He put the pins out of her reach. 'Your hair is so beautifully thick and such a lovely colour it's a shame to keep it hidden like that.' He began to plait and unplait it and she gave in and gratefully rested her head back on his knees, soothed by the movement of his fingers through her hair. It was so quiet and peaceful, with no sound but a log shifting on the fire and the rhythmic tick of the clock on the wall. She sat at his feet, half asleep and half awake, content to be companionably close to him. It happened so seldom these days, with his unpredictable moods and temper.

Suddenly the door burst open and Laura came in.

'Be quiet,' Matthew whispered sternly. 'Your mother is asleep.'

It was not strictly true but Abigail was wise enough not to move, and watched through half-closed lids as her eight-year-old daughter, so like Pearl but much more serious-minded and with her father's dark, unruly hair, stood at the other side of the table with her head on one side.

'I only came in to do my piano practice,' she said. 'Uncle Edwin will be here tonight and he always wants me to play to him. I like to make sure I get it right,' she added, frowning.

'Later, my poppet,' Matthew said, a term of endearment he only used when he was in a particularly good mood. 'When your mama wakes up.'

'Has Mama got a headache?' Laura asked anxiously.

'No, I don't think so. Why?'

'Because her hair is all loose. It's pretty like that, isn't it, Papa?'

'Very pretty. Now, run along and ask Peggy to give you your tea early. Then you can come and play your piano pieces to Mama and me. Is William home?'

'No, I expect he's still on the quay with Uncle Josh and Tolley. He never plays with me. He always wants to be down where the boats are. I don't think he likes dolls much, but I'm always willing to play hide and seek with him.' She went off muttering about the inadequacies of her brother.

'She's beginning to play the piano quite well,' Abigail said sleepily. 'We should encourage her.'

'And so we will, my little love. But later. This time is ours, yours and mine.' And he bent forward to kiss her.

Edwin came every week to see Matthew for a game of cribbage, which Matthew greatly enjoyed, although often, if he was in a bad mood, the game would be played in complete silence.

‘I don’t know why you keep coming, Eddie,’ Abigail said with a sigh after one thoroughly bad-tempered session when Matthew had thrown the cribbage board onto the floor, losing the marker pegs underneath the piano, and then gone off to his room in a huff.

‘It’s only once a week, Abbie. And I enjoy coming to see you and the children,’ he said good-naturedly. ‘Anyway, if I continue to come he can’t accuse me of leaving him to rot as he did once when I missed a week. He doesn’t mean to be so unpleasant, you know, Abbie. It’s just the terrible frustration that builds up inside him. It must be pretty awful for him, you know.’

‘Yes, I do know, and I try to be patient, but sometimes it makes him very difficult to live with, Eddie,’ Abigail said sadly.

But today was one of his good days and he greeted Edwin cheerfully and sat with a proud smile on his face as Laura played ‘The Merry Peasant’ without a mistake.

‘Very good, Lolly. Very good indeed,’ Edwin said, using his pet name for her. ‘We’ll have you playing the church organ yet.’ He swept her up in a big hug.

‘Really, Uncle Eddie? Will you teach me?’ she said as he put her down.

‘Yes, I will. When you’re big enough to reach the pedals. Because you play the organ with your feet as well as your hands, you know.’ He sat down and gave a demonstration, using the table as a keyboard for his fingers and at the same time moving his feet around, as if on organ pedals.

‘Oh, I don’t think I’ll ever be able to do that.’ Laura shook her head as she watched him.

‘Of course you will.’ He gave her another hug. ‘Now, off to bed with you. It’s time your papa and I got down to the serious business of the evening.’ He pointed to the pack of cards already waiting in the middle of the table.

Abigail got out her sewing and sat contentedly by the fire while her husband and brother played a friendly game of cards and Edwin gave Matthew all the latest news.

'A lot of money was lost over that canal business,' he said. 'I always said it would never come to anything. Mind you, I think the guv'nor got his fingers burnt over it. He invested in it quite heavily, from what I can gather. If he did, then he'll have lost the lot, I fear.'

'Has it all been scrapped at last, then?' Matthew asked. 'I could never see the sense in spending all that money on a wet dock, myself. I've always said that dredging the river is all that's needed.'

'You're probably right at that, Matt,' Edwin nodded. 'Of course, this latest business, of Peter Bruff and William Hawkins buying the water works will set the town by its ears. Peter Bruff's a great engineer, you know; quite heavily involved with the railways, too.'

'And you think he'll get things moving?'

'I'm sure of it.'

'Well, I only hope Peter Bruff's system works better than the present one. Supplying water for a few hours three days a week is hardly worth the effort and expense. And didn't you say a frog jumped out when someone turned a tap on, the other day?'

'Oh, that's only hearsay,' Edwin said with a grin. 'You know how things get exaggerated. Although it's true, the water doesn't always come through as clear as a mountain stream. But it'll improve, you'll see. And what's more, if Bruff looks after the water supply it'll leave the Commissioners free to concentrate on the problem of proper sanitation for the town. The sooner we get an adequate sewage system – saving your presence, Abbie – the sooner we can say goodbye to the scavengers who tour the streets every night with their stinking, leaking night-soil carts.' He gave a laugh. 'You'll never believe this, but I've heard they congregate on the fields beside East Bridge to eat their breakfast on their way to sell their putrid cargos to the farmers for fertilizer. You wouldn't think they could stomach the thought of food, would you?'

'They spend most of their time drunk, anyway,' Matthew said. 'They're a rough lot.'

'Well, before long all that may be a thing of the past,' Edwin said. 'The cholera epidemic in London a couple of years ago frightened everyone and now they're beginning to listen to Edwin Chadwick. He's certain that bad smells breed disease although nobody's certain just why and how. But if we could get rid of some of the stinking dung heaps we'd be well on the way . . . But enough of that. It's your deal, Matt.'

'You spoke of Papa losing money over the canal. Do you see him very often?' Abigail asked while there was a lull in the game.

'No, not often. I don't visit Hilltop House now he's got that woman living there as his housekeeper. Housekeeper, indeed. I don't know who he thinks he's fooling.'

'I was talking to Richard Cotgrove the other day. He seems to think Papa is getting a little too fond of the whisky bottle, too,' Abigail said with a worried frown. 'Do you think it's true?'

Edwin sighed. 'I don't know. But I must say it wouldn't surprise me. Pearl dying like that hit him pretty hard, you know.'

'It hit us all,' Abigail said. 'Poor little Pearl. I still blame myself . . . '

'I don't know why you should,' Matthew cut in. 'You didn't know the fellow was already married, any more than she did.'

'But you knew Pearl was a flighty piece,' Edwin continued. 'You hadn't blinded yourself to what she was. Not like the guv'nor had. He's never got over the fact that his fairy princess, his Pearl beyond price, was human – and tarnished, at that. It must have come as an even more terrible shock to him than it did to us. And I don't think he's every really recovered from it.'

'Perhaps I should go and see him,' Abigail said thoughtfully.

'What good would that do? He would only order you out of his house and you'd come home even more upset,' Matthew said.

'Matt's right, you know, Abbie,' Edwin said, shaking his head. 'Better to leave him to the ministrations of his lady love. No doubt she has her ways of dealing with him.'

Abigail said nothing but she felt slightly sick at the thought of the woman her father had installed in his house and she wondered if he treated her as harshly as he treated members of his own family. Somehow she doubted it.

# *Chapter Fifteen*

David came to see them again. His visits always cheered Matthew although on the surface it would have seemed that the crippled fisherman and the well-turned-out, slightly aesthetic London businessman had little in common.

This time he brought pomegranates, which neither Abigail nor the children had ever seen before.

'Ugh, they're nothing but pips,' Laura said, ungraciously, spitting them out in disgust. Whereupon he produced oranges, which were much more to her liking.

After she had played her latest piano pieces to him and he had been genuinely impressed by her talent, William showed his expertise with the fruit schooner he was modelling from a drawing his father had made for him.

'That's coming along very well, William,' David said, admiring the sleek lines of the wooden hull. 'It looks as if you've got the proportions exactly right. But don't forget she'll be heavily rigged. Who's going to rig her for you?'

'I shall do it myself, Sir. I can go and see Mr Barr at Brown's shipyard. He's their rigger. He'll put me right.'

'You're a sensible lad, William,' David said thoughtfully.

'You'll go far, I shouldn't wonder.' He gave the boy back his model but said no more.

After the children had gone to bed David produced yet another present. It was a chessboard and a set of chessmen carved from ivory and ebony. 'It's a present to both of you,' he smiled. 'I thought you might be a little tired of cribbage, Matthew. Would you like to try a game that I might have some chance of winning, for a change?' he added with a laugh. He turned to Abigail. 'And it's something you might enjoy, too, Mrs Bateman.'

'I don't really have much time for that sort of thing,' Abigail said with a tinge of regret.

'Then you'll have to make time, because when David has taught me I shall teach you.' Matthew spoke in a tone that brooked no argument. 'Come on, man, set the board up. How do we begin?'

Abigail picked up her sewing as the two men hunched over the table, oblivious to everything but the game in hand. Kings, queens, knights, castles, bishops, pawns, the names washed over her in complicated explanations. She would never put her mind to it, of that she was sure, and that would make Matthew irritated with her. She foresaw stormy hours over the new present.

Every evening when David paid a summer visit to them he took Matthew for a walk, pushing him for miles in the wheelchair, exploring parts of the town that David had never seen and that Matthew had almost forgotten existed.

As they walked they discussed the topics of the day, including the cholera epidemic, which mercifully hadn't reached Colchester.

'Edwin is convinced that bad smells breed disease,' Matthew said. 'I don't know whether he's right or not. You're always going to get a certain amount of stink about the place, I don't see how it can be avoided. Most people don't take any notice of it.'

'Yes, I've heard that Chadwick fellow say something similar about smells breeding disease,' David agreed. 'The fact that there's been hardly any cholera in Colchester might bear that out, too – compared with London, Colchester smells like a flower garden. The Thames on a hot summer night forces everyone within miles to close their windows. It's quite sickening. But I think the cholera epidemic is over now. All the talk in London is about the Great Exhibition. The Queen opened it last month and it seems to be causing great excitement everywhere. Something like thirteen thousand exhibitors, I believe, and all housed in the new Crystal Palace, as they call it.'

'Have you seen it?'

'Yes. I went last week. The Crystal Palace itself is a wonderful construction, and worth a visit for its own sake. It's all been built of glass, on a cast-iron framework. The way it sits in Hyde Park like an enormous bubble is really something to behold. Over sixty feet high, I'm told. I was very taken by its construction. Apparently the chap who designed it is really a botanist. What's his name? Paxton. I think he got the idea from a greenhouse he designed at Chatsworth House in Derbyshire. Quite remarkable it is. Quite remarkable.' He pushed Matthew on in silence for a while. Then he said, 'I would very much like to take your children to see it all, Matthew. William in particular would be very interested in some of the exhibits – they come from all over the world, you know – but I think Laura would like it, too.'

Matthew was full of enthusiasm. 'I'm sure they'd both love it,' he said. 'They've never been to London.'

'But what about Abigail? Do you think she'd let them come? Mothers can be, well, a little over-anxious over their offspring, can't they? Not that I'm suggesting that Abigail pampers William and Laura. Far from it.'

Matthew thought for a few minutes. 'Why not ask Abbie if she'd like to go too? She's never been to London and she could do with a little holiday. She never seems to stop working, as you must have noticed. What do you think?' He twisted round as far as he could in his chair to look at David.

David looked down at him. 'If you're generous enough to let her come with me, Matthew, I'd be more than willing to take her,' he said. 'But do you think she would?'

Matthew grinned. 'We'll ask her.'

Abigail fussed uncharacteristically. She couldn't leave the business; she couldn't leave Matthew; she'd got nothing to wear. But the real reason lay deeper than that and she knew it. She was nervous, shy, of meeting David on his own ground and she was afraid that the tenuous, unspoken, unadmitted bond between them might be broken if they met in different circumstances.

But this was not something she could use as an excuse and the weak arguments she put up in its place were soon overruled. Edwin readily agreed to come and live at the Corner House while she was away and Guy, Tolley and Josh between them could manage the business for a few days. Sarah would keep an eye on Peggy. There was really no reason for her not to go.

'I shall be all right, woman,' Matthew growled. 'It's only my legs that are useless, not my brain. Go and enjoy yourself. Forget you're burdened with a crippled husband for once in your life.' He plucked tetchily at the rug covering his knees. 'God knows it'll be a treat for me too, not to have you continually fussing and whining around the place. It'll be like a holiday for me to be free of petticoat government for a few days.'

Abigail sighed. While he was in a mood like this she might as well go to London, for there was no pleasing him. She knew she'd get nothing but shouts and complaints if she stayed behind. Matthew's good humour was always short-lived.

Laura and William were almost beside themselves with excitement as they boarded the early morning train for London. Abigail was proud of her new flounced skirt of green sprigged silk, with its matching jacket bodice. Little Miss Prentice had sat up all hours to finish it in time but now Abigail feared for its safety among the smuts and smoke of the train, a rattling, roaring monster belching forth black smoke as it carried them noisily along on metal rails at a frightening speed and not much comfort. She was almost surprised to arrive at their destination safely.

David met them. Abigail's heart gave a little skip when she saw his tall figure waiting for them and his smile was full of genuine pleasure as he greeted them.

'We'll go straight to the Exhibition,' he said. 'I've got a cab waiting.' He looked down at the children. 'I'm sure you don't want to waste any time, do you?'

William and Laura could hardly answer; they were, for once, almost speechless with excitement as they clambered into the cab, and they gazed with awe at the great buildings they passed.

Everything was new, everything was exciting.

For Abigail, the most striking thing was the noise. Above the clop of the cab-horse's hooves was the clop of a hundred other hooves, the rattle of pattens on the pavements and the shouts of the street sellers. It seemed there was nothing that couldn't be bought on the London streets, from flowers to fish; from bonnet-boxes to ballads; from dog-collars to last dying speeches. And every seller tried to outshout and outsell his neighbour. They saw a cat's-meat man in a brawl with an umbrella-mender over a promising pitch in a doorway, and noticed that passers-by gave the chimney-sweep, with his two blackened, half-naked, half-starved, bleeding little boys trailing behind him, a wide berth.

At last they reached Hyde Park, where the huge glittering façade of the Crystal Palace dominated the landscape in the bright July sunshine. They left the cab and walked through formal gardens laid out with flowers and green lawns, and adorned by statues of all shapes and sizes, to the steps of the Crystal Palace.

If it had been hot outside it was sweltering inside the building and after wandering around for over two hours Abigail was glad to find a place to sit among the cool fountains and greenery. David went on, escorting the children from one gallery to another, missing little of the eight miles of display.

When they came back, exhausted but still full of excitement, they nearly fell over each other in trying to tell their mother what they had seen.

'We saw this enormous steam engine . . .'

'And sets of false teeth! What do you think of that, Mama, false teeth!'

'Didn't you see the artificial legs, Laura? They were better than those old teeth.'

'Yes. And I saw the dearest pair of little scissors, all twirly and ornamented, with mother-of-pearl handles . . . And what do you think, Mama? There was a piano! And it was from Colchester. From Mr Aggio's shop. It was all gilt and ivory – Mr Quilter said that's what it was – with a white satin front. Oh, Mama, it was beautiful. You must come and see it.' She tugged at her mother's hand.

Reluctantly Abigail got to her feet. 'I'm sure I don't know how you'll ever find it again,' she laughed. 'I've never seen so many people all together in one place in the whole of my life.'

'They estimate that it will run into millions by the time the Exhibition closes,' David said. He was obviously delighted at the pleasure he was giving the three of them and he smiled at Laura's bright, excited face and William's darting eyes that missed nothing.

At last it was time to leave. Another hansom cab took them by a devious route to David's house in a small square overlooking a little park. 'I thought everyone in London was rich,' William whispered to his mother as they travelled along. 'But look at those ragged boys with brooms. What are they doing?'

'They're crossing sweepers. They sweep a path across the road for a copper so that the ladies' skirts shan't be muddied and dirtied,' David explained.

'And look at those little urchins over there. They're even more ragged and dirty than the little mudlarkers on the quay at home. What are they doing?' Laura pointed to a clutch of half-naked, filthy little creatures scrabbling around in the gutter.

'Searching for scraps, I shouldn't wonder. They look half starved,' David said.

Abigail reached in her pocket and fished out a coin. 'Should we . . . ?'

'If you must,' David said doubtfully, 'but I fear it'll only go on a penn'orth of gin.'

'All the same . . . ' Abigail threw the coin at the scrabbling children and then wished that she hadn't for they immediately began to fight and claw at each other for possession, till one, bloody but victorious, scampered off to the nearest gin shop and the others returned to what treasures they might hope to find in the gutter.

'I'm afraid London is full of scenes like that,' David said, seeing her distress. 'I fear one gets hardened to it.'

They reached his house, a tall red-brick house in a terrace of tall red-brick houses, all with white-painted windows and black iron railings leading up to wide black front doors.

Kingsley, his manservant, opened the door to them.

'Mrs Kingsley has the children's supper ready in the dining room as you ordered, Sir,' he said, taking their hats and gloves. 'This way, if you please, Madam.'

As the children ate the substantial supper Mrs Kingsley had prepared for them, their eyes drooping with tiredness, Abigail was able to take stock of the room they were in. It was a cool, elegant room, decorated in green and white in the style of Adam, with a green carpet and highly polished mahogany furniture, delicate porcelain, and gleaming brass fire irons in the white marble fireplace. She couldn't help contrasting it with the room they lived in at home; it was dining room, morning room and drawing room all rolled into one, now that Matthew had his bed downstairs. With a stab of guilt she realized that this was the first time she had thought of her husband all day.

The children finished their supper and went to bed, Laura in a pretty room furnished in the latest walnut style and William in the room next door that was plainer and more to his taste.

Abigail saw them settled and then went downstairs again. David was waiting for her at the bottom of the stairs.

'Now,' he said, holding out his hand to her, 'the rest of the evening is ours, yours and mine. I must confess that this is what I have been looking forward to, all day.' There was no mistaking his pleasure as he led her over to the table and pulled out a chair for her. 'First, we'll dine, and then I've booked seats for us at the theatre.'

'The theatre? But what about the children? I can't go out and leave them,' Abigail said in alarm.

'Of course you can't,' he smiled. 'I realized that and I've

arranged for Mrs Kingsley to keep an eye on them. She's had three children of her own, although they're grown up now. But I can assure you she's perfectly capable.' He smiled again. 'Not that they're likely to wake after such an exhausting day. I should think they'll sleep like logs.'

Kingsley brought in the soup and David poured wine for her.

'I've wanted to do something to repay you for your hospitality for a long time, Abigail,' he said. 'You were so good to me after that dreadful shipwreck. I really don't know how I would have got through the week after that without your help. I feel I've found real friends in you and Matthew. Please let me give you this one evening. Let me indulge myself in entertaining you.'

'You're very kind, David,' Abigail said.

'It's my pleasure, believe me.' He held up his glass. 'To you, Abigail, and to a pleasant evening.'

She held up her own. 'To a pleasant evening.' But for some reason she couldn't meet his eyes as she said the words.

They ate guinea fowl followed by roast beef and then syllabub and at the end of the meal Kingsley placed on the table a bowl of exotic fruits, mangoes, passion fruits, peaches and pineapple. Abigail couldn't help feeling she was in a dream, it was all such a far cry from gutting fish and cleaning oysters.

When the meal was over he took her through to the drawing room. 'We've half an hour before we need to leave for the theatre,' he said, 'so we've time for another glass of wine.'

'A very small one, then,' she said. 'I already feel I've had quite enough, although I'm not sure whether it's the wine or the excitement of the day that's making me feel so lightheaded.'

'A little of both, I shouldn't wonder,' he smiled.

She leaned back in the comfort of the armchair. 'You have a most beautiful home, David,' she said, looking round her. The drawing room was a golden room, with heavy brocade curtains and chair covers and a carpet of deeper gold. None of the rooms that she had seen in the house were large, yet the way they were furnished gave an impression of uncluttered space.

'Miriam did it all,' he said from the depths of the chair opposite. 'She had an eye for colour and I gave her a free hand in designing the rooms.' He gazed round. 'Yes, I think it's quite tasteful. But not particularly homely,' he added, taking a sip of his wine. 'I must say I find it a little too formal, these days. I think it's since I came to your house that I've become a little dissatisfied with mine.'

At that she threw back her head and laughed delightedly. 'Oh, David,' she said, 'and I'd just been comparing this with my house and wondering what on earth you must think when you visit us. Although I must confess that until I saw yours I thought my furniture was quite the last word!' She became serious. 'Of course, since we've had to make the dining room into a bedroom for Matthew the drawing room has become a bit cramped. Not that I mind,' she added hurriedly, 'because it makes it so much easier for him. He couldn't possibly go upstairs.'

'You're very fond of Matthew, aren't you? Even though he's sometimes so awful to you?' David was watching her intently.

'He's my husband,' she answered. 'What he suffers, I suffer. I still love the man in him that once was' – she gave a rueful smile – 'even though I don't get many glimpses of him nowadays.' For some reason she felt uncomfortable under his gaze and she got up and went over to the window. It looked out over the park, where couples were strolling in the cool of the evening. Suddenly, the knowledge that she could never again stroll arm in arm with Matthew hit her afresh, more forcibly than ever, perhaps because she was on unfamiliar ground and could stand back and appraise her situation with new eyes. 'Sometimes life can be very cruel, can't it?' she said in a low voice.

'Indeed it can.' She hadn't heard him come up behind her and she turned quickly. Too quickly. In a brief unguarded moment she caught the naked longing in the green-grey depths of his eyes, a longing that touched a response deep within her. It was only a flash and then it was gone, but in that second she recognized something inside herself that she hardly dared give a name to and she knew that the feeling was mutual. Quickly, she turned back to the view, tinglingly aware that he was still standing behind her although he had made no attempt to touch her. A moment later he moved away.

Afterwards Abigail could hardly have told anyone what she saw at the theatre. She had an impression of glittering dresses, flaring gas lamps, red plush, noise and applause. Looking down at the programme in her hand she saw that they were watching Shakespeare's *The Merchant of Venice*, but she hardly took in a word. All she was conscious of was the man beside her, of his arm touching hers, and of the feelings he had disturbed in her; feelings that she had mistakenly thought she had managed successfully to extinguish.

She kept as far away as possible from David in the cab returning to his house. She wanted this man and she had briefly recognized an equal need in him. But there was Matthew. Resolutely she turned her thoughts to her husband, helplessly bound to a wheelchair. It was bad for him, too. She could never do anything that would hurt him, however cruelly or indifferently he treated her.

The cab reached the house and David gave her his hand to help her out, but she refused to let him guide her up the steps to the door, her one thought was to get to her room where she would be safe; safe, she had to admit, from herself. She could only think she had had too much wine, that these dangerous feelings were coursing through her. As for David, whatever his desires might be he had behaved impeccably throughout the evening.

'It's very late,' he whispered as he closed the door quietly behind them, 'we must be quiet. The Kingsleys sleep at the top of the house but they don't keep late hours. Now, would you like a last nightcap before you go to bed, Abigail?' His voice held a pleading note, as if he couldn't bear the evening to end.

She shook her head. 'No, David. I think it's better not. It's been a long, exciting day. I'll just look in on the children and then I'll go to bed, if you don't mind.' She didn't look at him as she spoke. 'Thank you, for the most memorable day of my life, David,' she said softly as he moved forward to help her off with her wrap.

'And thank you, Abbie, for the most memorable evening of mine.' Their eyes met in the hall mirror.

The next moment she was in his arms. She could not have said who moved first, whether she turned to him or whether he pulled her round, only that it was inevitable that it should happen. He kissed her gently, wonderingly at first, and then with a hunger that found answer deep within her.

'No,' she protested, her mouth still under his. 'David. No.' But she still clung to him and it was he who in the end had the strength to release her.

'No, you're quite right, Abbie,' he said, turning from her. 'It was unforgivable of me. I'm sorry. But, God help me, I love you so much.'

'And I love you, David,' she murmured, her eyes full of tears. 'I knew it before I came here today. I should never have come, I knew that. But I couldn't resist the chance to spend the day with you. I should have known ... ' She stumbled away from him blindly and began to mount the stairs.

'Wait,' he said quietly, 'I'll turn the gas up. You can't see where you're going.'

But too late. As she turned at the first bend in the stairs she caught her foot and fell. David caught her halfway down.

'Oh, darling, are you hurt?' The term of endearment was out before he could stop it.

'No. A little shaken, that's all. I'm all right. Really.' She staggered a little and put her hand on the banister to steady herself.

Without another word he swung her up into his arms and carried her up the stairs and into her room, laying her gently on the bed. 'Are you quite sure you're not hurt?' he repeated softly, still bending over her.

'Quite sure,' her voice was little more than a murmur as she put her arms round his neck and pulled him to her. She had no thought, no feeling other than the overpowering need to consummate the love she felt for this man, a love she knew was returned with equal fervour. She felt no shame, no regret, as he began to kiss her again, kissing her eyes, the soft, smooth curve of her neck and the pink tip of her ear. Then he found her mouth again and all the time his hands were busy gently exploring and exposing the milky whiteness of her body. He did not hurry but explored every inch of her with a gentle, wondering love until at last they came together in an act of indescribable sweetness and delight. Afterwards they lay for a long time, locked together until she slept, to wake and respond joyfully again to his urgent seeking.

The next time she woke he was gone and dawn was breaking. Quickly she covered her nakedness with her nightgown and slipped between the sheets. Oh, God, she thought frantically, burying her face in the pillow, what have I done?

*

'The master sends his apologies, Madam. A messenger came early for him, something has cropped up at his office that needs urgent attention,' Kingsley said, explaining David's absence at breakfast. 'He has left orders that I am to see you safely to your train.'

Thank you, Kingsley, I shall be grateful for that.' 'The master says he will be at the station to see you off if he possibly can.'

Abigail sat down to breakfast and helped herself to toast while Kingsley poured milk for the children. David wouldn't be at the station to see them off, she knew that, and she was relieved that he was not here now. In the cold light of morning she felt embarrassed and ashamed at her own behaviour last night; at how willingly and shamelessly she had given herself to him. And yet she could feel neither regret nor disgust at the beautiful thing that had happened between them. She was convinced that he loved her, just as she loved him. It was just that it was too soon. They should have waited. But waited for what? For ever?

She pushed her plate of half-eaten toast away. The very thought of food choked her.

'Are you not well, Mama?' Laura broke off her discussion with William as to what was the most exciting thing they had seen yesterday and looked at her mother. 'You haven't eaten your breakfast.'

'*I* have,' William said proudly. 'I've had two boiled eggs and four slices of toast and marmalade.'

'I expect you'll be sick,' Laura said interestedly.

'I sincerely hope not.' Abigail managed a smile. 'We've got quite a long journey ahead of us.'

Kingsley came back into the room. He cleared his throat. 'I've ordered a cab for half an hour's time, Madam. Is that all right? It should give ample time to get to the station in time for the Colchester train.'

'Yes, thank you, Kingsley. We'll be ready.'

Abigail went back to her bedroom to collect her things. She sat down for a moment at the dressing table and studied the room through the mirror. It was a beautiful room. Dark blue velvet curtains hung at the two long windows and a matching carpet covered the floor. Two little armchairs and a footstool were covered in a velvet of a paler shade of blue, the same shade as the silk hangings at the head of the bed and the counterpane. The walls were a pale blue-grey with the mouldings picked out in white. Everything was of the finest quality, from the mahogany wardrobe and matching wash stand to the silver filigree-backed hair brushes and the ornate silver knob on the door. She looked round it again, savouring every item. She would remember this room for the rest of her life. She turned back to the mirror and gazed at her own reflection. The woman there gazed calmly back at her, giving no hint of the turmoil of emotions this weekend had produced inside her. True, she had little colour, but Abigail was always pale, her skin creamy and unlined save for a few wrinkles round her eyes. At thirty-five her flaming hair showed no sign of losing its colour and no hint of grey and her figure was still good, as slim as a young boy's despite having borne three children. It was not a pretty face that stared back from the mirror, but a face that had character, a face that had already learned to turn a serene countenance on the world, whatever troubles had befallen. A face that wouldn't betray her now.

She got up from her seat and with a straight back left the room to go and fetch the children.

# *Chapter Sixteen*

September came and with it the opening of the oyster season.

'I don't see why we shouldn't take the gaffer and the missus down river to the opening ceremony,' Guy suggested to Josh in his Norfolk drawl. 'That seem to me he could do wi' takin' outa hisself a bit. He's a right tartar these days if things don't go jest so.'

'Thass a good idea. We could lash his chair down right well on the foredeck there. That wouldn't be in the way o' the jib if we set it right. An' I know little Abbie'd be pleased to come,' Josh said.

'We'd hev to rig up a block an' tackle to get 'im aboard,' Tolley said, staring up into the rigging.

'No. If we manhandle the chair aboard I'll chuck 'im over my shoulder an' carry 'im down. There ain't two penn'orth of 'im, these days.' Guy's face was beaming with his brilliant idea.

Abigail was immediately enthusiastic, Matthew less so, but nobody took any notice of that. Tolley fixed stout eyelets into the decking for lashing the chair and Abigail went to see Alice to find out if she could still wear the little moleskin trousers Alice had made her so long ago.

The old lady was very bent with her arthritis now but she

never complained. 'I've got a lot to be thankful for, dearie,' she frequently told Abigail. 'My Josh is a good man. He see after me when 'e's home. An' when 'e's away I've got rare good neighbours. I don't want for a thing an' I thank the good Lord for his mercy towards me.'

She was as delighted as Abigail to find that the little moleskin trousers and shirt still fitted. 'The boots are still a bit big,' Abigail laughed, 'but I'm sure I can find a pair of Matthew's old sea-boot socks to wear inside them. They'll fill them out quite nicely.'

'You mind you don't go fallin' overboard this time,' Alice warned, smiling. 'Young Matthew won't be able to pull you out this time, pore boy. Not like 'e did afore.' Her smile faded and she shook her head sadly.

Abigail packed up the moleskins and shirt and kissed Alice. 'I'll be careful,' she promised, 'but if I do fall in at least I shan't be hampered by skirts and petticoats.'

She made her way home with her bundle under her arm. There had been no word from David since the visit to the Great Exhibition but this was nothing unusual. Months sometimes passed between his visits and they had never been in the habit of corresponding much. Abigail wasn't sure whether she was glad or sorry; she only knew that she both longed and feared to see him again. Once the terrible dread had passed and she knew for certain that there would not be a child from their stolen union she tried to put it to the back of her mind and only bring the memory out to comfort her in the bad times, when Matthew was particularly difficult. For the rest of the time she could almost pretend it had never happened; that it was just a dream-wish that she had imagined coming true. It wasn't difficult to persuade herself that it had all been a dream, her ordinary day-to-day life was so far removed from the evening she had spent with

David that the whole incident had taken on a Cinderella-type fantasy in her mind. But most of the time she was too busy to think at all.

The trip down river was a disaster. Far from pleasing Matthew it reminded him at every turn of how his life had changed. It began when he saw Abigail dressed ready for the trip. His expression softened and he said, 'You don't look a day older than the day I brought you up river in *Conquest* because Uncle Josh had to put in to Brightlingsea with a broken pintle. You looked like a young lad in your moleskin trousers, but yet so comely. Oh, I was just about bursting with pride to think I'd got you aboard my boat. I blessed that broken pintle, I can tell you, and I wished the wind would drop so that we'd get becalmed and the journey would last twice as long.'

'Yet you hardly spoke a word to me,' Abigail laughed, surprised.

'Of course not. I didn't dare. You were Henry Chiswell's daughter – my fairy princess.'

'And now I'm your wife.' She reached for his hand.

But he shrugged her away, the mood gone. 'Hardly my wife, these days,' he said bitterly. 'More like my keeper.'

'Matthew. It's no use talking like that. We have to . . . '

'Come on, if we're going let's go.' Impatiently he cut her words short.

It was the same throughout the trip. The feel of the wind on his face brought bitter tears to his eyes at the life he could no longer lead, and when they copied the mayor and all the local dignitaries on the official boat, celebrating the opening of the season with the customary gin and gingerbread, he dashed his to the deck. 'What have I got to celebrate,' he shouted, 'except another bloody year in this chair?'

'We only aimed to please you, Gaffer,' Guy said regretfully as they tied up back at the Hythe.

'Well, if you aim to please me get me off this bloody boat and back onto dry land. Lashed up here I feel like a bit of useless deck cargo. That's right, throw me over your shoulder, helpless as a bloody babe.'

Abigail exchanged sympathetic glances with Guy as he climbed the ladder with Matthew over his shoulder as easily as if he were a sack of corn and put him back in the chair Josh and Tolley had hauled back onto the quay. 'It was a mistake to bring him,' she said in a low voice as Guy gave her his hand to help her up the iron steps. 'Everything that's happened has only twisted the knife in the wound for him.' She bit her lip against threatened tears. 'Oh, if only there was something I could do. If only he could accept his life as it is we could still be happy. But this bitterness is eating him away.'

'I know, Missus, and I'm sorry. I wish I'd never suggested you comin' today.'

'Oh, don't be sorry, Guy.' She managed a smile. 'I've enjoyed it, even if Matthew hasn't.' She glanced in Matthew's direction. 'I must go. He's waiting to be taken home.'

'I'll push 'im up the hill for ye, Missus. Thass a heavy ole chair for you to push, an' you so little an' all.'

'Thank you, Guy.' She walked up the hill beside Matthew, with Guy pushing behind, talking about the river trip, the people they had seen, the landmarks that had altered, occasionally addressing a remark to Guy. Matthew maintained a morose silence.

Later, back on *Conquest*, Guy remarked to the others, 'He's a miserable bugger these days. I don't know how the missus puts up with 'im, straight up, I don't. An' 'er sech a kind, sweet, patient crittur.'

But the kind, sweet, patient creature was at the moment being neither kind, nor sweet, nor patient. As soon as Guy had gone she snatched off the boy's cap she was wearing and flung it on the table.

'My God, you behaved yourself badly today, Matthew Bateman,' she said, rounding on him. 'The men only did it to please you. How could you have been so rude and ungrateful to them?'

'It's all very well for you to talk. You weren't the one tied to the deck like some fancy bloody figurehead gone wrong,' he shouted. 'How do you think I felt, stuck up there like a wart on a pig's arse for all to see and pity? Poor old Bateman,' he mimicked, 'lost the use of his legs, poor bugger. Look at him sitting there. They've brought him out for an airing. Of course he's no good. Can't *do* anything any more. Quite useless . . . '

'Stop!' Abigail screamed. 'Stop! Stop! Stop!' She put her hands over her ears. 'It wasn't like that at all. People were pleased to see you and the men genuinely thought you'd enjoy a trip down river again. They won't take you again, of course, not unless you behave yourself better.' She leaned over the table towards him. 'You don't *have* to be useless if you don't want to, you know. It's only your legs. God, what's the matter with you, man? You can cull oysters with the best, but no, drop the cultac and that's you finished, too sorry for yourself to ask anyone to pick it up for you. Another thing, Tolley spent hours making you an easel to fit over your chair so that you could paint, but do you ever use it? No, you'd rather sit and stare into space.' She sat down and wrenched off her boots and then stood up again, more diminutive than ever in her moleskin trousers. 'And instead of opening a few letters and then casting them aside until I've got time to deal with them you could take over the book work for the business.' She took off her belt and threw it on the table. 'You're perfectly capable of doing it and it would give me time for other things . . . '

'Like stoking up the fires in the smoke house with Guy Sainty, I suppose,' he cut in, his voice overlaid with sarcastic double meaning.

'How dare you!' She rounded on him and brought her hand across his face with a sharp crack. 'Guy Sainty has always behaved in a perfectly gentlemanly fashion towards me and I won't have you even hint at anything else. He's a good man. God knows where we'd be without him. But if he heard a remark like that he'd be off like a shot out of a gun.'

As she was speaking he put his hand up to his face, where a livid mark was spreading across his cheek. He stared at her, his eyes narrowing. 'By Christ, my girl,' he said, his voice full of deadly venom, 'if I could get out of this bloody chair . . . ' He held out his hand. 'Come here.'

She stood opposite to him, her eyes on his face, not moving.

He raised his voice. 'I said, come HERE.'

Slowly she moved round the table. As soon as he could reach her he pulled her over to him and threw her across his knee. The moleskin trousers were little protection against the blows he rained on her backside. When he had finished he gave her a push and she rolled onto the floor, sobbing.

'I'll show you who's master in this bloody house,' he shouted. Then, looking down at her crumpled figure on the floor he put his head in his hands. 'Oh, God, Abbie, what have we come to?' he said miserably. He leaned over and pulled her to him. 'I'm sorry. I'm sorry, my little love.'

She clung to him. 'I'm sorry too, Matthew. I understand how you must feel, really I do. I know how hard it is for you and I shouldn't get impatient.'

They clung together, their tears of anger, sorrow and frustration mingling together. 'I know how hard it must be for you too, my little love,' he murmured, his lips in her hair. 'I'm jealous. I admit it. I'm jealous when I see Guy, the man I was, the man I ought to be, talking to you. And I'm jealous when I see you with Henry Chiswell's man, Richard Cotgrove. He's such a well-set-up young chap. And I haven't missed the way he looks at you.'

Abigail put her hand over his mouth. 'But have you ever seen me look at either of them in a way that gives you any cause for anxiety, Matthew?'

He shook his head and gave a great sigh. 'No, Abbie, I haven't. But I couldn't blame you if you did.' He held her close for a long time. 'I know I'm a rotten swine to you, my little love, but I *do* love you, with all my heart. I know it can't seem like that sometimes, but it's there, deep down inside, under all the jealousy and misery, all the time. I love you very much, my Abbie.'

'And I love you too, Matthew,' she said, her face still wet with tears. She laid her head on his shoulder. Oh, if only we could always be as close as this, she thought, we could still be as happy as we once were.

Neither of them had mentioned David.

The winter passed in peace and tranquillity such as hadn't been known for years at the Corner House. Matthew took an interest in the accounts and helped Abigail as much as he could with the business. He designed and Tolly made a gadget that would enable him to pick up the cultac – or anything else for that matter – if he dropped it, and he spent long hours culling the oysters, grading them and packing them carefully in the barrels, then covering them with a layer of seaweed before one of the men sealed the lids down. Sometimes, on those rare, crisp sunny afternoons he would get someone to push him to a sheltered corner beside the smoke house and there he would set up his easel across his knees and paint the river scene; always the same scene but many different aspects. He painted it at high tide, with the trees and hedgerows golden and yellow with autumn, the boats in full sail arriving; at half tide, when the trees were bare and rimed with frost, and at low tide, when the river was barely more than a trickle and gulls strutted and squabbled on the mudbanks, the trees and hedgerows little more than a blur in the mist. He would often paint till his hands were too numb with cold to hold the brushes and Abigail made him half-mittens so that he could carry on, muffled against the cold, pleased that he had found something that kept him happy and contented.

He seemed more resigned to his lot than ever before and Abigail offered up a grateful prayer of thankfulness that their terrible quarrel had resulted in this change in him.

In the winter evenings they often played chess on the board that David had given them, but without the friction she had anticipated when it had first arrived. To her the change in Matthew was little short of a miracle.

'We shall soon be hearing from David, I should think,' Matthew said one evening as they sat by the fire, the chessboard on a small table between them and the gas throwing a pool of light around them. 'He doesn't usually leave it more than six months without paying us a visit. Come to think of it, we didn't even have word from him at Christmas, did we?'

'No, I don't believe we did. Your move, dear.' Abigail knew very well there had been no word from David. And she had begun to understand why. He wanted nothing more to do with her after her shameless behaviour in London. She could understand his disgust at the way she, a respectable married woman, had allowed – no, invited him to make love to her. Even now she went hot with embarrassment and shame at the memory. Yet she was honest enough with herself to admit that if she saw him again, God help her, she would have no defence against him if he wanted her again. She still loved him. But it was better by far that he stayed out of her life, much though she still longed for his presence.

'How long is it since you took the children to the Great Exhibition?' He fingered the intricately carved ebony bishop. 'Must be almost seven months now, mustn't it?'

'Yes, something like that.' She moved her knight. 'Check.'

'Blast! I've taught you too well, my girl, I can see that.' Matthew grinned at her. 'But what about this?' And he took her knight with his bishop.

'You're still too good for me,' Abigail sighed in mock despair.

'No, I'm not good enough, princess.' In all seriousness he took her hand and kissed it.

'Am I interrupting something?' Edwin came into the room. 'Far be it from me to come between the intimacies of domestic bliss.'

'It's nothing private,' Matthew said with a grin. 'I was only telling your sister what a wonderful woman she is.'

'Ah yes, well, we're all agreed on that, aren't we?' Edwin gave her a friendly peck on the cheek.

She smiled up at him. 'I'm glad you've come, Eddie. Now you can play cribbage with him. I'm losing this game of chess so I'll be quite happy to give it up.' She got up from her chair and went and sat at the table in the centre of the room.

The men got down to the serious business of their cribbage game and Abigail took out her sewing, more contented than she had felt for a long time.

'Is Papa well?' she asked Edwin when there was a lull in the game.

'Couldn't say. I don't visit there now that Effie Markahm rules the roost.' Edwin spoke through a haze of expensive cigar smoke. 'It's not like home any more, Abbie. I don't know how Daisy and Ellen stick it, being ordered around by La Markham all the time.'

'Oh, dear. As bad as that, is it? Poor Papa.'

'Oh, you don't need to worry about him,' Edwin laughed. 'He's got all his creature comforts under one roof now so he doesn't have to go hotfooting it off to Wivenhoe at every turn, lecherous old ram.'

'Edwin! It's Papa you're speaking of!'

'It is indeed. Your turn, Matt, me lad.' Quite unrepentant Edwin turned back to the game in hand.

After it was over and they all sat round the fire drinking the ale Abigail had mulled for them Edwin said, 'I've won two tickets in a lottery for lunch at The Three Cups Hotel next week.'

Abigail frowned. 'Oh, Eddie, you haven't been gambling!'

'No, this was a lottery.'

'I can't see the difference, myself. Who will you take with you?'

'You, I hope, Abbie. If Matt doesn't mind.'

'But I'm your sister. Haven't you found yourself another lady friend yet, Eddie? I know you were unlucky with Belinda Young but that was ages ago. It's time you found yourself a wife and settled down.'

'Oh, I'm far too involved with my work now for anything like that. I travel about quite a bit now and I'm also trying to write a book. I don't think a wife would put up with my odd hours.'

'Don't tell me you're a confirmed bachelor?' Matthew said with a twinkle in his eye.

Edwin winked. 'That's it. I'm a confirmed bachelor and I intend to bring my children up the same way.'

'Oh, Eddie, what a thing to say.' Abigail pretended to be

shocked. Then she added complacently, 'I expect you'll settle down eventually.'

'Maybe. But I'll tell you this. It'll have to be someone extra special, who'll put up with my crusades. I fear such a person won't be easy to find.' He grinned. 'Not that I don't keep looking,' he added airily. 'However, that's in the future. Next week is what's under discussion at the moment. Can you spare your wife for a few hours, Matt?'

Matthew smiled at Abigail. 'I should think so. Just for a few hours.'

In fact, Matthew seemed as excited about the expedition as Abigail and insisted that she should have a new outfit to wear for the occasion. 'We can afford it,' he said when she protested. 'We've had a good season with the oysters and the bloaters have been an even bigger success. Anyway, I want to see you looking extra-specially nice.'

Eventually she gave in to him and chose a dress and jacket of a rich, blue-green velvet, piped with a darker green, with a wide, pleated skirt and tightly fitted bodice. With it she wore a loose green pardessus with a matching bonnet and a fur muff.

'You look quite beautiful, my little love,' Matthew said as she presented herself for his inspection. 'Come here and give me a kiss.'

Before they left, Edwin and Abigail wheeled Matthew down to the quay. It was a beautiful crisp day in late March and he was anxious to finish a painting he was doing. 'It's the river in early spring at full tide,' he said, the carpet bag that held all his equipment balanced on his knees.

'Oh, Matthew, is there any state of the river you haven't painted in any weather?' Abigail laughed as she walked beside him holding his hand whilst Edwin pushed the chair.

'Well, I want you to have a set. Then you can hang them all the way up the stairs and think of me as you go to bed.'

She squeezed his hand. 'I think of you anyway, dear. All the time.'

They left Matthew in his own sheltered corner at the end of the quay, promising to collect him again when they arrived back.

'Oh, don't worry about that. Tolley or Guy will bring me home – if we can get past The Anchor,' he added with a grin. 'Now, off you go and enjoy yourselves.'

Abigail kissed him and went off with her brother.

The lunch at The Three Cups was substantial although not to be compared with the lavish dinners served there in the evening. Abigail really enjoyed herself and at the end of it felt just a little light-headed from the wine she was not used to. Edwin insisted on ordering the chaise that was used by the hotel to meet their passengers from the train to take her home.

'Aren't you being rather extravagant, Eddie?' she said with a little giggle as the chaise bowled along the crowded High Street to Queen Street, past the church of St Botolph then round the corner and down Hythe Hill to the house on the corner of St Leonard's Street.

'Well, it's not often I have the privilege of taking my favourite lady out,' he replied, grinning.

The chaise pulled up outside the house and he helped her out, knocking her bonnet awry as he did so.

'Oops,' she straightened it. 'I mustn't go in with my hat all crooked or Matthew will think I've had too much to drink.'

'Which, of course, you have.' He took her arm.

'Eddie! I haven't!' she protested.

'No, Sis, of course you haven't. I was only teasing.' He looked down at her fondly.

She pushed open the door. 'We're home,' she called gaily.

'Master's not back yet, M'm,' Peggy said, poking her head round the kitchen door, and Laura left her piano practice to come and say, 'Oh, Mama, you do look nice. But your bonnet's a little crooked.'

'Oh, dear, is it still crooked?' Abigail went to the overmantel and straightened it. 'Oh, dear,' she said again, 'my face is a bit red, too. What will Matthew say, Edwin, to me coming home flushed like this?'

'He'll probably say he's glad you've enjoyed yourself,' Edwin laughed. 'We'll go and fetch him, shall we? It's nearly five o'clock. He must either be a bit chilly by now or else he's in The Anchor and in a worse state than you are. Coming, Lolly?'

'No thank you, Uncle Eddie. I must finish my piano practice. I'll play you my pieces when you get back. I always play them to Papa.'

'Good. I'd like that.'

Edwin and Abigail went off down the hill. *Conquest* had already gone down river on the ebb tide and the warehouse and smoke house were both deserted although there was still a good deal of loading and unloading of cargoes further back along the quay. Abigail hurried to the spot that was becoming known as Matthew's corner, but he wasn't there.

'They must have taken him with them on *Conquest*,' Edwin said as he joined her.

'I don't think he would have gone without telling me,' Abigail said, shaking her head, 'especially as they'll be gone all night and won't be back till tomorrow afternoon's flood.' She went to the edge of the quay and shaded her eyes to look down towards

Wivenhoe. There was no sign of *Conquest*. She hadn't really thought there would be, because the tide was receding rapidly now. She turned back, but as she turned she glimpsed something out of the corner of her eye and she screamed, a shrill piercing scream that seemed to tear the very air apart.

'Abbie! Abbie! What's wrong?' Alarmed, Edwin was beside her in a second. She clung to him, speechless and shivering, as she pointed to the wheel that was just becoming visible on the ebbing tide. 'Oh, my God! It can't be . . . It's Matt's chair!'

By this time a crowd had jostled their way along to see what all the noise was about. Edwin held Abigail while two burly men fished the chair out with Matthew's lifeless body still strapped into it, filthy from where he had fallen, face down, into the mud. They unstrapped him and laid him gently on the quayside. Then the crowd parted as Abigail took a step forward and collapsed in a deep faint, her head resting on her dead husband's heart.

# *Chapter Seventeen*

Everyone said it was an accident and Abigail didn't argue. Matthew deserved better than to be buried in unconsecrated ground, his memory tarnished with the stigma of suicide just because he had taken his own life. Although that was what he had done. His death was no accident and she knew it.

Lying in her darkened room, unable to sleep, or eat, or face anyone, Abigail went through the events leading up to her husband's death and cursed herself for not realizing what was in his mind.

He had taken the opportunity to plan his death from the moment he knew she would be lunching with Edwin, and even the elements had conspired to assist him; the day had been sunny and bright and the tide had been early afternoon.

She recalled how he had insisted on her having a new outfit for the occasion – 'I want to see you looking especially nice,' he had said. And he had told her he had wanted to finish a painting, one of a set – 'so that you can hang them all the way up the stairs and think of me as you go to bed'. But that painting had already been finished. It was propped up in his room. All that had been found in his carpet bag was a pencil and a few rough sketches.

She knew why he had done it, too. He had done it because he loved her too much to continue the half-life they led. He could no longer bear to be less than a full man, striding the streets and riding the waves. In a queer paradox, the closer they had become over the past few months the more intolerable he had found his life and the more determined he had been to release her from the burden she bore. How mistaken he had been. In taking his own life he had taken the better part of hers and she was desolate, her grief too deep for words, too deep even for tears. And the bitterest pill was that he had died while she had been out enjoying herself with Edwin. She felt she could never forgive herself for that.

After three days she summoned the strength to leave her room, but she left all the funeral arrangements to Edwin, who was a tower of strength. The distance to the churchyard where Matthew would be laid to rest was only a few yards so the plumed horses and curtained hearse were dispensed with and the undertaker's mute led the coffin, carried by Guy and Edwin, Josh and Tolley, tears running unashamedly down the weatherbeaten furrows of the two old seamen's faces. Abigail walked behind with Sarah and the children. She had raised a gasp of astonishment when she appeared in the new blue-green velvet instead of wearing the customary black, but she didn't care. Matthew had said he wanted her to look extra-specially nice and she was determined that he should be proud of her. Her only concession to custom was the heavy black veil that covered her face; a face that had aged ten years in the space of a week.

'That beats me how the accident could've happened,' Tolley said as they sat eating the customary funeral fare of ham when the ordeal of the burial was over. Now that the tension was eased, relief was loosening tongues and conversation flowed freely. 'We was about the place, all of us. Why didn't 'e shout when the brake failed? Thass what I should like to know. We might've caught 'im afore 'e went over the side. An' if we wasn't quick enough for that we could've fished 'im out afore ... ' He left the rest of the sentence unfinished.

'An' to think we didn't even miss 'im from 'is corner,' Josh said sadly. He was sitting with Alice, who had been brought direct to the house because she couldn't manage the walk to the graveyard.

'Well, I thought Tolley 'ud fetched 'im home. I thought thass what 'e told me was goin' to happen,' Guy said.

'An' I thought 'e said you was goin' to take 'im,' Tolley said. 'So that was a right mix-up all round.' He shook his head. 'We shouldn't hev gone down the river so cheerful-like in *Conquest* if we'd knowed the gaffer was lyin' in the mud not fifty yards from where we cast off,' he said with a break in his voice.

Abigail said nothing. The men's words all added to her conviction that Matthew had taken his own life. She could picture him, pretending to sketch but at the same time carefully watching his opportunity to release the brake and propel himself the few feet to the edge of the quay. It wouldn't have made much of a splash when he went in. It was a spring tide so the water would have been almost level with the quayside and anyway, with all the noise and bustle that there was along the wharf another splash wouldn't have been noticed. But let them think the brake failed; let them think it was an accident. It didn't matter any more. Matthew was dead and at peace. Now, somehow, she had got find the strength to put her life together and go on living without him, She took a deep breath.

'Thank you, Sarah.' She even managed to smile at her mother-in-law, who was coping with her grief by keeping frantically busy, and accepted a piece of fruit cake, the first food that had passed her lips for a week.

Sarah stayed with Abigail and the children after the funeral and Abigail would often find Laura sobbing in her grandmother's arms. She was glad. It did the child good to release her grief, and Abigail wished she could do the same. But her grief was locked in her heart and no tears would come. They said she was brave, but she wasn't; she was dead. Dead inside.

She wrote a stiff little letter to David, telling him what had happened. She hoped he would come; it couldn't hurt Matthew, it didn't make her love for him any less, nor her grief any easier to bear. She didn't even feel guilty any more. She didn't feel anything – not anything at all – so she could face David. If he came.

Every day she looked for his reply and when it didn't come she wrote again, unwilling to believe what she knew in her heart must be true, that his silence was really due to his disgust at her shameful behaviour in London. In the meantime, she tried to drag the remnants of her life together. She hung Matthew's paintings up the stairs as he had wished, remembering what he had said as he painted each one, her misery dry in her throat. But still no tears came. She was an empty shell, a puppet, going through the motions of living.

'We must alter the rooms,' she said briskly one morning. 'There's no need for Matthew's bed to remain downstairs any longer. We'll turn his room back into a dining room. Where's William? He can run down to the warehouse and ask a couple of the men to come and take these pulleys down and help us move the furniture.'

'He's already gone down to the boat. He spends all his time there when he's not at school,' Sarah said. 'He's so like his father when he was a lad.' And she sniffed and wiped her eye with a corner of her apron.

'Yes, I know. I think it helps him. He doesn't say much, but

I know he misses Matthew.' Abigail had taken to speaking in short, sharp bursts and Sarah looked at her anxiously. It was as if there were a tightly coiled spring inside her, held firmly in check, and Sarah often wondered and worried as to what would happen if the spring suddenly broke free. But she was wise enough to say nothing.

'Laura will go,' she said now. 'She never minds running an errand when she's at home.'

Guy came back with Laura and a young fisherman called Isaac. 'Didn't seem right to ask Tolley or Josh. They're not as young as they were,' he said. 'Isaac'll help, though. He's as strong as an ox.'

'Good. Then he can help you to carry the piano upstairs,' Abigail said.

'You can't do that, Mama,' Laura protested quickly. 'I need it for my practising.'

Abigail put her arm round her daughter's shoulders. 'That piano is mine, dear,' she said, as gently as her new, brittle voice would allow. 'Papa bought it for me and I want to have it in my bedroom.'

'But, Mama, you can't even play it.' Laura was near to tears.

'I know. But that doesn't matter. It's still my piano.' Abigail put her hand up to silence Laura as she was about to protest again. 'I intend to buy you a piano of your own, dear. A small grand, I think. When we've finished rearranging the furniture there should be plenty of room for it. I've already spoken to Mr Aggio, as a matter of fact.'

'Oh, Mama!' Laura flung her arms round her mother's neck. 'Oh, how wonderful. When will it be delivered?'

'When there's room for it. So the more you help the sooner it will be.'

'Yes. Oh, yes. What do you want me to do?'

'You can begin by clearing the ornaments off the top of *my* piano, then the men can get it upstairs.' Abigail smiled as Laura busied herself. She was not usually very helpful in the house but today she would have moved mountains.

More help was enlisted and finally the piano was safely installed in Abigail's room. It was large, and she used it now as her own private sitting room, so the piano didn't look at all out of place there. She sat in the little velvet-covered armchair by the hearth and gazed at it, recalling the Christmas Matthew had bought it for her. He had been full of health and vitality and reckless high spirits then. It was typical of him to have bought her a piano which she couldn't play and when she had no time to learn. Typical, too, that he couldn't really afford it. Matthew had never had much money sense. But, oh, how she had loved him.

She sniffed. It didn't do to take anything for granted. Life could be changed overnight. As hers had been. Twice. She got up from her chair. It didn't do to dwell on what might have been, either. Life was for living; or at least of making some pretence at it. She got up from her chair and squared her shoulders and went downstairs to supervise the rest of the furniture moving.

They were just taking down Matthew's bed, under Sarah's eagle eye. 'I can see Peggy hasn't reached far under the bed with the broom lately,' she remarked. 'Goodness me, look at the fluff. And what's that over there?' She went over and picked it up. 'Look at this. A letter, never been opened and dated before Christmas. Well, now! Every picture tells a story, doesn't it? I'd have a word with Miss Peggy, Abigail, if I was you. That's downright slovenly, that is.'

'She has a lot to do,' Abigail replied absently. 'I've often thought I should bring someone else in to help her, but somehow I've never got round to it.'

'But how would a letter have got there?' Sarah handed it to her. 'It's addressed to you, too.'

'Oh, Matthew used to open the letters, if we had any, before he got up in the morning. I expect he put it to one side because it was for me and it slipped down between the bed and the wall.' Abigail slit it open and glanced through it as she spoke. Then without another word she put it in her pocket and went back up to her room.

There, she sat down on her bed and took out the letter again. It couldn't be true. What she had read couldn't be true. She read it again, slowly and carefully.

Dear Abigail,

I shall shortly be going abroad on business and I don't yet know when I shall return; it could be that I shall be away for several years. I would come and visit you and your family before I go but I think you may prefer that I do not. My ship sails on 31st January. I will not contact you again unless I hear from you.

I am, your obedient servant,
David Quilter

The thirty-first of January. That was two months ago. She fell back against the pillows and stared up at the ceiling. David had writen like that because he knew she would be too ashamed of her behaviour to see him without warning. And now it was too late. She wondered if he would ever receive the letters she had written, telling him of Matthew's death. And if he did whether he would reply or whether he would regard it as a just retribution for her actions last July. For that was what it was. Retribution. Maybe Matthew had sensed – realized – understood what she had done without ever having been told and had taken his own life rather than be tied to an unfaithful wife. And now she was alone. Because even if he knew of Matthew's death David wouldn't want her. He had been reluctant even to pay them a visit before he went abroad. Had he been afraid she would throw herself at him? Oh, God, no, surely he couldn't have thought that. Not in her own home, with Matthew lying in the room below. She covered her face with her hands. She felt so ashamed. So guilty. So alone.

At last she began to cry, with huge sobs that racked her whole body and shook the bed where she lay. She cried for a long time, washing away at last the shell of ice that seemed to have formed round her heart. Finally, when she was drained of tears and of all emotion she fell into an exhausted, dreamless sleep.

Sarah, passing her room, heard Abigail's sobs, and nodded. Thank God for that,' she whispered to herself. 'Now perhaps her grief can begin to heal.'

A new, calm, gentler Abigail emerged from her room some time later. She had lost the two men she had loved best in all the world; one was dead and the other might as well be dead for all the chance she had of ever seeing him again. But she must go on living.

She put all her efforts into Bateman's. It would never be hers, she knew that; she was simply holding it in trust for William to take over when he came of age. But she was determined that he should have a thriving business, when the time came, and in the meantime it would keep them in comfort. Because it was doing well.

The oysters were fat and plentiful again since the beds in Brightlingsea Creek had been re-stocked. Sometimes she went down river with the men and watched them clean the beds. They always did it on the flood tide, wrapping chain round the dredges and dragging them across the bottom to disturb the mud and clear it away from the cultch where the new oysters lay. Occasionally she went with them to cull the oysters, too, watching each dredge as it came up to be sorted, the brood and cultch being thrown back in together with the partly grown oysters, known as half-ware, whilst the ware or fully grown oysters were taken to the fattening beds, where in just a few months they would grow as succulent as they had been in Old Zac's time. But Abigail made sure that they were sold where they would fetch the best prices. She had a better head for business than Matthew's grandfather.

The bloaters, too, did well in their season. Guy was totally responsible for that side of the business and he supervised every step of the way with meticulous care, from the gutting of the herring to the important building of the fires in the smoke house. This he always did himself. He knew that the secret of a succulent bloater lay in the well seasoned old oak in which it was smoked and he trusted no one else to build the fires under the tiers of hanging fish.

Abigail found Guy a tower of strength and she suspected he would like to be more to her but she gave him no encouragement. In some ways he was too like Matthew for her ever to consider marriage to him although sometimes she was lonely for companionship. But there was a buxom Scottish fisher girl called Morag who came every year at herring time and had her eye on Guy, and Abigail was delighted when at last they married and settled in a little cottage behind the gas works.

Of Edwin she saw little, although he visited her when he could. His time was mostly taken up with a crusade, through his newspaper, for better conditions for the poor, a crusade which, he told her ruefully, did nothing to improve his relationship with his father.

'But, you see, it's all very well for him,' he confided one night as they sat over a cold supper. 'He's had Hilltop House put on the piped water supply. He doesn't have to worry about buckets and cisterns. He doesn't care about the hundreds who still queue at the well with their buckets and jugs. He'd rather the money was spent on improving the river than on supplying the town with clean drinking water. The Commissioners are still more concerned with watering the roads than with providing decent drinking water for the town. Do you know, they're trying to negotiate with Peter Bruff now to provide tanks full of perfectly good drinking water for watering the streets to keep the dust down? Sometimes the streets are watered twice a day! Yet at the Hythe you can see some fifty or sixty people every morning queuing with their buckets as they wait for the pump to be unlocked. It's a disgrace and I'm determined to do something about it.'

Abigail got up and went over to him and kissed him. 'You're a good man, Eddie,' she said, resuming her seat. 'It's a pity there aren't more like you. And I agree with you. I've stood queuing at the pump in the bitter cold enough times. I know what it's like.' She gave a shudder. 'I pray I never have to return to such conditions.'

'I pray so, too, Abbie. And I pray that the poor creatures that still endure such a life may see an improvement. And soon.' He picked up his hat ready to leave, and put it on at a rakish angle that belied his serious mind.

Abigail went with him to the door. 'Oh, look at you. You've got a button off your coat, and you're the one who used to be so smart. I worry about you. Come back in and let me sew it on for you.'

'Oh, it's all right. I'll attend to it when I get home. It's not important.' He shrugged impatiently.

‘You need a wife, Eddie,’ she said anxiously. ‘I wish you’d . . . ’

‘Now don’t start that again.’ He bent and kissed her. ‘I’m all right, I tell you. Perfectly all right.’ He grinned. ‘But you never know, one day I might surprise you. When I’m not too busy with other things.’

He went off whistling, and Abigail watched him go, shaking her head affectionately.

# *Chapter Eighteen*

Matthew had been dead for well over a year. Abigail was sitting in the garden enjoying the cool evening air after a blisteringly hot day and she recalled how he had loved to sit and listen to the birds singing although he had never been very interested in the flowers she had planted. She had not been sitting there long when Peggy came out to her.

'It's Daisy, M'm,' she said, with a worried look. 'Daisy from Hilltop House. She says it's important. She come to the front door, M'm,' she added, as if the eighth deadly sin had been committed.

'You'd better show her out here to me, Peggy.' Abigail was unwilling to leave the cool of the garden to go back into the house, which she knew would still be stifling even though every window and door was flung wide. 'I wonder what she wants?'

A moment later Daisy appeared. Abigail got up to greet her, shocked at the older woman's appearance. Daisy was, she calculated, about fifty now, and her hair, which had been thick and black was now quite white. Once she had been rosy-cheeked and fat, but today her face was lined and her clothes hung on her, several sizes too big.

'Daisy, my dear, are you ill? Come and sit down.' Ignoring the difference in their positions Abigail drew her down onto the seat beside her. 'What's wrong?'

Daisy shook her head, her mouth working. 'We didn't know what to do, me an' Ellen, Miss Abbie,' she said at last, reverting to the name by which she had always known Abigail. 'So we thought if I was to come to you you might be able to tell us.'

'Tell you what, Daisy?'

'Tell us what to do about Hetty, Miss Abbie.' Daisy twisted her hands nervously in her lap.

'Oh, Daisy. She's not . . . she hasn't . . . '

Daisy shook her head impatiently. 'No, Miss Abbie. Nothin' like that.'

'Then what?'

Daisy took a deep breath. 'Well, ye see, thass like this, Miss Abbie. Jest after Christmas Mrs Markham accused Hetty of not doin' her job properly because she let the fire go out in the mornin' room, an' the master sacked 'er on the spot. Mind you, that wasn't right, no matter how you look at it. After all, Mrs Markham was sittin' there, in front of it, so she could've rung the bell an' said, couldn't she? An' Hetty wasn't to know the fire needed more coal on because Mrs Markham used to get riled if the pore girl kep' poppin' in to see, so whatever she did wasn't right. Anyways, she could've made it up herself, that wouldn't hev hurt her, she don't do a hand's turn in any other direction.'

Abigail frowned, trying to follow Daisy's garbled story. But Daisy didn't notice and went on, with a righteous shrug, 'Howsomever, a minute's notice, thass all Hetty got.' She looked up at Abigail. 'That was a cruel way to treat the pore little mawther, an' 'er with not a soul in the world, an' not bein' very bright, neither. Me an' Ellen was Hetty's fam'ly, we was all the fam'ly she had an' now she was bein' turned out in the street at that woman's whim.'

'When did you say this was, Daisy?' Abigail asked.

'Jest after Christmas – well, beginnin' o' Jan'ry. In all that cold frost and snow we had for a coupla weeks.'

'Oh dear, you should have come to me then, Daisy. Do you know where she is now, poor girl?'

'Oh, yes, Miss Abbie. I know where she is, all right. She's livin' in that room up aloft the stables. We've kep' her there all this time, me an' Ellen.' She spread her hands. 'What else could we do? We couldn't let the pore little mawther be turned out in the cold with nowhere to go but the Union – an' we wasn't goin' to let her end up there, not for nobody.'

Abigail gasped. 'You've kept her in the stable loft all this time and nobody knew?'

'Wilf know she's there. He empty 'er slops when 'e muck out the stables, an' we feed 'er out of our rations – which ain't over-much these days, I might say.'

'But what about my father – Mr Henry? He must have realized . . . '

'Beggin' yer pardon, Miss Abbie, but he's right there.' She pressed her thumb firmly on the seat beside her. 'That Mrs Markham rule the roost good and proper.' She shook her head. 'That ain't like it was when you was there, Miss Abbie. Me an' Ellen keep to our quarters as much as we can. We'd both 'ave left an' found other places but they ain't that easy to come by, 'specially there bein' the three of us, 'cause we couldn't go orf an' leave pore Hetty. So we jest hev to put up with it as best we can.'

'Oh, Daisy, I am sorry.' Abigail put her hand to her head in perplexity.

'I come to you, Miss Abbie, because thass gettin' a job to feed the girl. There's scarce enough for Ellen an' me an' Wilf, 'ithout hevin' to share what we get with the pore little thing.'

'Oh, Daisy,' Abigail said again. 'What a dreadful thing. Apart from anything else it's not right for Hetty to be imprisoned like that.' She sat staring at the geraniums and phlox blooming in the garden, but she didn't really see them, she was thinking only of the poor girl living hidden in the stable loft because she had nowhere else to go. And under her father's roof, too.

She stood up. 'I think it's time I paid my father a visit,' she said, her mouth set in a straight line.

'Oh, no, Miss Abbie, you better not do that. Mrs Markham 'ud send the lot of us packin' if she knew I'd bin to you.' Daisy looked horrified.

'Well, my dear, things can't go on like this. Something's got to bring my father to his senses. You go home now and leave it to me. I can scarcely make things worse, can I?'

'We could all end up in the Union,' Daisy said gloomily.

'I'll have you here with me before it comes to that,' Abigail promised.

'If you'd jest hev Hetty . . . '

'All right, Daisy. But I intend to speak to my father first.'

The next evening Abigail dressed carefully in her best dark blue silk and walked up to Hilltop House. No one would have suspected from her serene expression that her heart was hammering with nervousness as she rang the doorbell and heard it jangling in the depths of the house.

After a few moments Ellen opened the door.

'Is the master in?' Abigail demanded, ignoring the look of consternation that crossed Ellen's scraggy countenance.

Without a word Ellen crossed to the study and knocked on the door. 'A lady to see you, Sir,' she said hurriedly and then scuttled away, leaving Abigail to enter and close the door behind her.

Henry got to his feet, swaying a little. 'Get out!' he bellowed. 'Get out of my house! You know you're not welcome here!'

Abigail drew up a chair and sat down. 'Oh, Papa, don't you think the time for theatricals is past? It's over twelve years now and I'm a widow.' Her mouth quirked a little. 'A rich widow, at that.' She took off her gloves and laid them on the desk; it was covered in dust and littered with books and papers. 'You could say I've put my house in order and now I'm prepared to help you with yours.'

'How dare you! How dare you come here with such insolence!' He had difficulty with the last word and pronounced it 'isnolence'.

'Oh, sit down, Papa. And put that whisky bottle away. You need a clear head for what I'm going to tell you.' She watched him push the bottle a few inches across the desk, then she said, 'Did you know Hetty was still here? Living in the stable loft?' She hadn't raised her voice but had spoken in a conversational tone that somehow gave her words added impact.

Henry gaped at her, his jaw falling open as he leaned back in his chair.

'Ah, I thought not. And what else goes on under your nose that you're in ignorance of, I wonder?'

'You're lying. The girl's been gone six months or more.' Henry regained some of his old bluster. 'I dismissed her myself.'

Abigail went over to the bell pull and gave it a tug. Then she sat down again. 'Oh, yes, you dismissed her on some trumped up-excuse because your . . . housekeeper wanted to be rid of her. Although God knows why; she's harmless, almost half-witted and not exactly beautiful, so she could hardly have posed much of a threat to Effie Markham. But be that as it may' – she waved her hand – 'Daisy and Ellen refused to let the poor girl be turned out onto the streets to goodness knows what fate, so they've been looking after her in the stable loft. Right under your nose, you might say.'

'I don't believe you.' His eyes narrowed. 'You're just trying to wheedle your way back into my house . . . '

The door opened. 'Fetch Hetty, Ellen,' Abigail said without turning round.

The door closed again. 'Why should I want to wheedle my way back into your house, Papa?' she answered her father. 'Why should I be anxious to return to a place where I'm not wanted? I have a home of my own and two dear children, your grandchildren. I don't need you, Papa. Not any longer. But I suspect you need me.'

Henry automatically reached for the whisky bottle again to clear his head but Abigail got up and moved it further out of his reach. He frowned, obviously trying to gather his wits. 'I'm not well,' he mumbled.

'You're drunk,' she said unsympathetically.

There was a knock at the door and Ellen came in with Hetty. Henry stared at her as if he were seeing a ghost.

'We done the best we could by her, Miss Abbie,' Ellen said, apologizing for Hetty's appearance. The girl was filthy, her dress was in tatters and she scratched constantly. She peered round Ellen, looking from Abigail to Henry with hunted, fearful eyes, black and huge in her colourless face.

Abigail watched her father as he gazed unbelievingly at the girl. 'Yes,' she said, 'Daisy and Ellen showed a sight more compassion than you've ever done. They couldn't bring themselves to turn the girl out even though you didn't care. But then you wouldn't, would you? Look what you did to me!'

'I didn't . . . I would have . . . ' Henry, all his bluster and arrogance gone, slumped into his chair.

Abigail turned to Ellen. 'Take Hetty away, Ellen. Bathe her and find some clean clothes for her, and then give her a good meal in the kitchen.' She fished in her pocket. 'If there's nothing to eat there take this and go to Mrs Wrigley's and buy her a pie – and one for yourself and Daisy, too.' She smiled kindly at Hetty. 'Don't worry, Hetty, if you're not wanted here I'll take you home with me. Peggy can do with some extra help.'

Ellen and Hetty left the room. Voices were raised as they went down the hall and then the door burst open. 'Harry, what is the meaning of this? That girl is back! Do you hear me? That girl is back!' Effie Markham swept majestically into the room, stopping short as she saw Abigail. 'And who are you? What are you doing here?' she asked rudely.

That's not a very polite way to greet your employer's visitors,' Abigail said dryly. She felt in total command of the situation now and she realized what a long way she had come since her father disowned her. 'And Hetty is not "back", she's never been away. She's been . . . '

'Who are you?' Effie interrupted rudely. 'And what do you mean by sitting there all high and mighty, poking your nose into things that don't concern you?' She turned to Henry. 'Harry, what is this person doing here? Order her out. What are you, a man or a mouse?' She went forward. 'And will you answer me! Why is that girl back in this house?' She banged her fist on the desk to emphasize every word.

Henry struggled to his feet. 'I . . . they say . . . they tell me . . . ' He passed his hand over his face. 'She's been here all the time.' He spoke as if in a dream.

'He's ill,' Abigail said, getting to her feet.

'Rubbish!' It was not clear whether Effie was speaking to her or to Henry. 'She can't have been here all the time. Pull yourself together man, do.' She reached across the desk and grabbed him by the lapels. 'What *is* the matter with you? Aren't you master in your own house?' She gave him a violent shake and pushed him away.

He made a strange noise, neither a cry nor a choke but something between and fell back in his chair, his face like putty and his eyes glazed.

'He's ill,' Abigail said again. 'I told you he was ill but you didn't listen. Ring the bell, quickly.'

Effie gave him a frightened look, then with a panic-stricken little cry she turned and fled from the room.

Impatiently Abigail rang the bell herself and ordered Ellen to send Wilfred for the doctor. Then she loosened her father's collar and took his hand in hers, waiting for the doctor to come.

The doctor pronounced that Henry had suffered a heart seizure, and three men were called in from the street to help Wilfred to carry him upstairs to his bed. After she had made him comfortable Abigail went downstairs and gave a child a penny to take a note to her own house to tell them why she would not be back that night, and another one sixpence to deliver a message to Edwin at his lodgings on North Hill. It wasn't long before her brother arrived and when he had heard the story he sat with Henry while Abigail went on a tour of inspection.

The house was in a sad state of neglect, the bedrooms dusty and full of cobwebs and the drawing room swathed in dust sheets that were grey with dust. The silver in the dining room that she had always taken such pride in was tarnished and dull and the table looked as if it hadn't seen wax for years. Everywhere the curtains were faded and dust lay thick in the creases, and the carpets were threadbare. Abigail could have wept. She opened the door to the morning room. This was obviously the room they lived in. It was full of clutter and stank of perspiration and worse. In the armchair by the fireplace sat Effie Markham in a dress of cerise taffeta trimmed with green, eating an apple. Abigail stood in the doorway, looking at her father's mistress. How could he have taken this fat, blowsy creature to his bed? With her orange hair and painted face she looked every inch what she was. Abigail wondered briefly how many men she had 'entertained' in the house at Wivenhoe which her father had provided. Then another thought chased the others through her brain. How desperately lonely a man must be to seek the company of such a one; how sorely he must need to prove himself, to prove his manhood. Suddenly, she understood the insecurity that lay under her father's years of blustering autocracy.

All these thoughts flashed through her mind before Effie, staring back at her with an indifference that bordered on insolence, said, 'Is he all right? The old man?'

'No, he isn't all right. My father is very ill,' Abigail said with deadly calm. 'Too ill to have any further use for your services, Madam!' Her voice began to rise. 'So I suggest you pack your bags and GET OUT.'

Effie threw her apple core into the already littered grate and leaned over to select a chocolate from the box on the table, her heavy breasts wobbling unrestrained with the movement. 'Who do you think you are to order me about?'

'You know perfectly well who I am, so don't pretend otherwise,' Abigail snapped. 'Now, will you pack your bags and go, or do you wish me to call my brother? He's sitting upstairs with Father and he'll throw you out of the house with no compunction at all, I can assure you of that.'

Effie stopped chewing and a dribble of chocolate ran down her chin. 'You can't turn me out,' she said, suddenly uncertain. 'Where would I go?'

'That's your business,' Abigail said cheerfully. 'I'm sure you'll find some kind . . . friend . . . who'll take you in.' Her face hardened. 'But I want you out of this house within the hour.'

'The old man . . . '

'Never mind my father. You'll do as *I* say. Out of this house within the hour. Do you hear me?'

Effie stood up. She was taller than Abigail and with an attempt at dignity she swept past her out of the room, then ruined her exit by coming back for the rest of her chocolates. Abigail permitted herself a smile before going back up the stairs to her father's room.

He was lying propped up with the pillows in the big bed, his face as grey as the bed linen, but his eyes were open.

'Effie?' he whispered.

Abigail looked at Edwin and then at her father. 'Do you want to see her?' she asked.

A look of alarm crossed his face. 'No,' he whimpered softly, so that it was a job to catch his words, 'I wish she'd go. I wish I'd never let her come here.'

Abigail's face cleared. 'It's all right, Papa, she's going. She's packing her bags right now.' She sat down and took his hand in hers.

Edwin got up. 'I'll see her off the premises. Just to make sure she only takes what belongs to her. I don't trust that woman an inch.'

After he had gone Abigail sat in silence with her father for some time. Colour was beginning to come back into Henry's face and his eyes roved round the room. 'Am I going to die?' he asked at last.

'No, Papa, I don't think so.'

He gave a sigh. 'Thank God she's gone. She's led me a dog's life.' Then after a while. 'I don't know what I'm going to do. I need someone . . . '

'Don't worry, Papa. I'll look after everything till . . . '

'Till I'm better. Only till I'm better.' A brief flash of his old spirit returned.

She sighed. 'Oh, yes, Papa. Only till you're better.'

As she spoke the front door slammed on Effie Markham, the sound reverberating through the house.

After a few days Richard Cotgrove came to see Henry, and Abigail talked to him about the state of Chiswell and Son.

'It's been a combination of that woman and the whisky bottle,' Richard confided. 'Mainly the woman, though. I don't know what she's done with his money, but it's gone through her fingers like water.'

'She certainly hasn't spent it on the house,' Abigail said dryly. 'Nor on cleaning materials.'

Richard leaned forward confidentially. 'It's my belief she's salted it away against the day he tired of her. I shouldn't be surprised if she'd got quite a handy little nest-egg tucked away somewhere. She's not the sort to end up in the Union; she's far too canny for that.'

'But where does that leave Papa?' Abigail asked.

Richard shook his head. 'His position is a bit precarious, I'm afraid. But without her, and if we can keep him off the bottle, which shouldn't be difficult after the fright he's had with this illness, I think he'll survive.' He scratched his head with the end of his pen. 'But what about the servants? They haven't been paid for the past month. Will they stay, do you think?'

'Not been paid for a month? I didn't know that.' Abigail sighed. 'I'll talk to them. I'm sure they will stay, but they must have money for decent food. I'd no idea things were as bad as this. I shall have to keep an eye on everything from now on; to tell you the truth, although he doesn't realize it, I don't think Papa will ever be able to take a very active part in the business again.'

Richard smiled. 'I'll be very happy to work with you, Mrs Bateman.'

Abigail stayed at Hilltop House for a week, only going home for short visits to make sure her own house was in order.

'I've been thinking, Papa,' she said slowly one afternoon as she was sitting with Henry in his bedroom. 'Something will have to be done. I can't go on like this, running between the two houses, can I?'

It was a hot day and the windows were wide open to let in what air there was, together with the flies and the sound of horses' hooves and rumbling carts, which still carried in spite of the straw that had been spread on the road outside the house to deaden the noise. She sat by the bed, fanning away the flies as he lay propped up on the pillows, a diminished figure in the big double tester.

For a long time he said nothing. Then he turned his head towards her. 'No, you're quite right, you can't. I've been thinking about it, too.' Abigail had the distinct feeling that he couldn't wait to be rid of her. He went on hurriedly. 'But I must have someone. I need someone – a housekeeper . . . ' He paused and closed his eyes against the memory that word evoked. 'A proper housekeeper.' His eyes shot open. 'But it would have to be someone I could trust.'

Abigail nodded. 'Would you consider Sarah, my mother-in-law?' she asked. The question didn't come easily. She had spent a long time thinking about it, wondering what her father's reaction would be; whether in fact the very idea might bring on another attack, and she watched him anxiously as he considered her suggestion.

He didn't answer for some time, but lay there remembering a day twelve or so years ago when he had visited Sarah Bateman in her cottage to persuade her to stop the marriage between Abigail and her son. He could see Sarah now. Ironing, she'd been, and he could hear again the dignity and resignation in her voice. Contrary to his expectations she'd been no more happy about the union than he had. Against all his expectations, too, he'd come away from that meeting respecting – even admiring – the woman. She'd shown a surprising amount of perception and common sense. He signed deeply. But it would seem there must have been some kind of reconciliation between them or the girl wouldn't have made the suggestion she had. He was surprised. He would have thought Sarah Bateman was just as bitter about the whole thing as he was himself.

Abigail, watching him carefully, had no idea of the thoughts going through his mind and was beginning to fear she had made a dreadful mistake in even mentioning Sarah's name. 'It was only an idea, Papa,' she began, 'I daresay . . . '

'No, it was a good idea. I think Sarah Bateman would do very well,' he said. 'If she'll come.'

Sarah did agree to come, but not without persuasion. She visited Henry and stood at the foot of the bed, taking stock of the shrunken, balding figure lying there. Her mind, too, went back to their meeting all those years back. For the first time she saw not the strutting, bombastic Henry Chsiwell, arrogantly expecting his every whim to be obeyed, but an ordinary, frightened man. A man of spirit and independence who now needed caring for down to the last, most basic requirements.

'If I come I'll stand no nonsense, Mr Chiswell,' she said bluntly.

His eyes met hers in new, mutual understanding. 'I think we shall get along fine, Sarah,' he said, 'just fine.'

They both permitted themselves a slight shift of expression that passed for a smile.

Sarah moved in without fuss. Daisy and Ellen were delighted and set to with a will when she organized a thorough cleaning of the house, from top to bottom, working just as hard as they, with Hetty running back and forth with buckets of hot water. The house hadn't been so busy or cared for, nor so happy, since the day Abigail left it to marry Matthew, and she sighed with relief to think that things had settled down so well.

Abigail didn't regard herself as a sentimental kind of person, so she was quite unprepared for the feeling that hit her the day when, at her own suggestion, Guy wheeled Matthew's empty wheelchair up the hill for her father's use. The sight of the cushions that had supported Matthew's wasted body sent through her a sense of loss and desolation that was like a physical pain.

Wilfred had made a ramp so that the chair could be pushed down the steps and into the garden, and Abigail went to sit with Henry in the sunshine, hiding her own feelings under concern for her father's comfort.

But he said little beyond a grudging 'thank you' and seemed relieved when she got up to go.

After she had left Sarah came and sat in the chair Abigail had vacated.

'She's a good girl, Henry Chiswell,' she said abruptly.

'Who is?' He gazed down the garden.

'Your Abigail.'

He didn't reply, but began to tuck his rug more tightly round him. 'It's getting chilly . . . '

'Chilly, my foot. You're not going to change the subject like that. You're an old devil, Henry Chiswell; a stubborn, hypocritical old devil.'

'I don't know what you mean.'

'Oh, yes you do.' Sarah turned to face him. 'It's near on thirteen years since they were wed, Abigail and my boy Matthew. They didn't have things easy; neither you nor I wanted the marriage and we showed it. But we were wrong, Henry Chiswell. They had a good marriage. They loved each other. She cared for him after his accident with more patience than most would have shown – for he wasn't an easy man to nurse. Then when he died she shouldered the business. She's a fine woman, your Abigail, and you're a stupid, stubborn old fool not to recognize it.'

He plucked at his rug. 'I could drink a cup of tea.'

She folded her hands in her lap. 'I'll make you a cup of tea when I've had my say,' she replied. 'Your trouble is, you'll bear a grudge to your grave because you're too proud to say you're sorry; that you were in the wrong. It takes guts to do that. But life's short, Henry, you should realize that, since you nearly lost yours. It's time you put your house in order. Abigail has forgiven you and done what she can for you – what you'd let her – so why can't you forgive her? After all, she's had more to forgive than you.'

He turned on Sarah. 'Who says I haven't forgiven her? She comes and goes as she pleases. I don't stop her.'

Sarah snorted. 'Only because it suits you. Because you were afraid you'd be left alone. Oh, I can see through you, Henry Chiswell. I've only been here a couple of months but I can read you like a book. Any day now you'll be turning on her again, now that you've got your household sorted out, with me at your beck and call.' She was silent for a moment, then she added, 'Abigail deserves better than that. She's a fine woman, and I'm proud she's my daughter-in-law.' She sniffed. 'And if you'd got an ounce of sense you'd be proud to think she's your daughter.' She got up briskly. There, I've had my say. Now I'll go and make you a cup of tea.'

Henry said nothing, but watched her go back to the house, a tall, white-haired figure, her back still as straight as a young girl's. She was right, too, damn her. He hadn't really forgiven Abigail; he'd only suffered her presence because there'd been no one else to look after him. She'd nearly run her feet off, too, so that she could be there. She was a good girl, and it was true what Sarah had said, he had treated the girl shamefully. Unexpectedly, his eyes misted over.

'Oh, you've been an old bugger, Henry Chiswell,' he said aloud. 'There's no two ways about it, you've been a right old bugger to that girl.'

'I'm glad you've come to your senses at last.' Sarah had come silently back across the lawn and as she put the tea tray down on the table beside him she treated him to one of her rare smiles.

Abigail hadn't visited her father for some time. She had done what she could for him and now that Sarah was thoroughly in charge she sensed that he no longer wanted to see her. The thought saddened her. If his illness hadn't softened his heart towards her nothing would. Like Old Zac he was prepared to carry his grudge to the grave.

It was almost with reluctance that she eventually went to see him, quite prepared for the hostility that was returning with his recovery.

'Now he's got that chair he wants to spend all his time in the garden,' Sarah told her when she arrived. 'You'll find him out on the lawn.'

'He's improving?' Abigail asked.

'He's a changed man,' Sarah said mysteriously.

Abigail went through the house and down the steps beside the ramp Wilfred had made. Once again the sight of the wheelchair reminded her of Matthew and her eyes filled with sudden bitter tears. Henry looked round as she dabbed her eyes and blew her nose.

'It's the sight of the wheelchair that upsets you, girl, isn't it?' he said, his voice unusually kind. 'You were fond of that husband of yours, weren't you?'

She nodded, trying to compose herself as she sat down on the chair beside him.

He leaned over and patted her hand. 'I'm sorry, Abbie, my girl. I wronged you. You're a good girl, and I've been too bloody pig-headed to admit it.'

She looked up, surprise showing through the tears that still shone in her eyes.

He nodded. 'When a man gets as near to death as I've been, he starts thinking,' he said, 'because there's nothing much else he can do. I wronged you, my girl, and I admit it. I'm sorry.' He squeezed her hand. 'Can you find it in your heart to forgive me?'

She leaned over and kissed him. 'Thank you, Papa,' was all she could say.

'I've been such a fool,' he went on after a long silence.

'It's over now. It's all in the past,' Abigail said quietly, mopping up the tears which had begun to flow again as the result of his words, but he only shook his head.

'It's not just you, Abbie, and all the years I've wasted there. It's not even Pearl, poor lonely little girl. I never understood her, you know. Oh, I thought I did. I wouldn't listen to you and Edwin when you told me. But she was such a pretty little thing. I was so proud of her. I suppose I spoilt her; over-indulged her. I suppose that's why she turned out like she did. She thought she could have whatever she wanted, because that's the way I'd always treated her . . .'

Abigail laid her hand on his arm. 'It's in the past, Papa. It's no use blaming yourself.'

'No. I realize that. But it shames me. And it shames me, too, the way I've let the business go. My father built it up from an oyster stall on the quay. He worked his fingers to the bone to make a living at first but when he died it was a thriving concern and I promised him I'd make it even bigger. I did, too, at first, and I was proud of my achievements. But look at it now.' He sighed and shook his head. 'I got too big for my boots, that's the top and bottom of it all. I speculated. And lost. So I began to drink. Things didn't look so bad when I'd had a few glasses of whisky. And then there was Effie. She knew how to make me feel good; worth something. Your mother never . . . ' He paused and shook her head.

Abigail said nothing. The secrets, the problems, the disappointments of her parents' bedroom were not for her ears although she was more understanding, more tolerant, less willing to judge her father now that she was older and, she hoped, wiser.

He was silent for a long time and Abigail thought he'd worn himself out and gone to sleep. But after a while he began again. 'I feel so ashamed,' he said sadly. 'I feel I've betrayed my father and all he stood for. That's what hurts me most. To think I've betrayed my father and all he worked for.' He turned his head and Abigail saw tears glistening in his eyes. 'You've got a son, haven't you, Abbie?'

'Yes. William. He's almost twelve, now. And Laura is ten.'

'I'd like to see them, specially the boy. Will you let him come and see his old grandfather, Abbie?'

'Of course, Papa.' She hesitated. 'But I must remind you, he's a Bateman.'

Henry waved his hand and sighed weakly. 'Bateman. Chiswell. What does it matter, Abbie? What does it matter?'

# *Chapter Nineteen*

Abigail found that it mattered a great deal whether the name was Bateman or Chiswell, since, as well as being responsible for Bateman's Oysters, she had now, quite suddenly, been pitchforked into becoming virtually head of Chiswell and Son, too. Henry was no longer capable of making decisions himself and although Richard Cotgrove managed the business very efficiently, he needed someone to turn to when problems or difficulties arose. She found him a pleasant, hard-working man; as ever, smart in appearance and with a shrewd sense of business. Once Effie Markham and the whisky bottle ceased to be a drain on Henry's resources, Richard pulled things round with astonishing speed. Within two years it was beginning to be very profitable again.

Abigail often saw him. Apart from the weekly progress meeting which she held in her father's office, she saw him on his visits to Henry or when she went to check the transport of her own oysters or bloaters to London. Sometimes he would come to her with a problem concerning Chiswell and Son; and sometimes they would simply meet by chance as she made her way along the crowded quayside on her way to the warehouse. On these occasions he would stop, doff his hat, and stop to talk to her of the weather, the price of oysters, or the health of her children. It wasn't long before it began to occur to her that he was showing more than a passing interest in her welfare. At first she was amused, then flattered, even a little irritated, but as time wore on and his attentions increased rather than diminished she began to take him more seriously.

Then one winter's day, when she had been confined to the house with a heavy cold for more than a week, he called to see her, bearing a bunch of hothouse flowers.

'I missed you, so I asked your man, Sainty, where you were,' he explained. 'I don't wish to intrude, but I thought these carnations might cheer you a little, Mrs Bateman.'

'That's most kind, Mr Cotgrove.' She buried her face in the blooms. With these expensive flowers his intentions were unmistakable.

'You've surely not been working, Mrs Bateman?' He raised his eyebrows at the piles of bills and receipts that were strewn over the table.

She smiled a little self-consciously. 'A token gesture,' she admitted. 'I can never break myself of the habit of not wasting my time, although I must admit I haven't really done much work. I haven't really felt well enough.'

'I trust you are feeling better now?' He looked at her anxiously.

'Oh, yes, much better, thank you.'

'Perhaps . . . ' He gestured towards the papers on the table. 'Would you think it impertinent of me to suggest that I might help you? As you know I'm quite used to dealing with these matters, and you've helped me a great deal over the past two years.'

'Oh, but I couldn't,' she protested. Then she sighed. 'Yes, why not? I'm afraid they're in rather a mess. I've let them get behind, I'm afraid.'

He pulled up a chair to the table and rubbed his hands together.

'Then let's see if we can help you to catch up.' He smiled at her and she couldn't help thinking what a handsome man he was.

'Thank you, Mr Cotgrove.' She smiled back at him. 'Oh, dear, I've done nothing but say thank you, this afternoon. I must repay you for your kindness. Let me offer you tea.' She went over and pulled the bell to summon Peggy.

'That would be very nice, Mrs Bateman.' He paused in the act of sorting the bills from the receipts. 'But, since we've known each other for a long time now, would you do me the honour of calling me Richard? And may I call you Abigail?'

She stared out of the window. She knew exactly what his words implied. It was over three years now since Matthew's death and sometimes she had to admit she longed for the companionship of someone, for someone to share her burdens. And there were times when she worked quite closely with Richard. It would be so much easier if the two businesses could be run, if not as one, then side by side.

But she didn't love Richard Cotgrove. Oh, he was a pleasant enough man, but so different from Matthew. How could she expect to love this slim, elegant, almost effeminate man after being married to such an ebullient great bear of a seaman that Matthew had been before his accident? There was no comparison. Her mind turned to David. If only he would return. But he never would. Not after all this time. And it was foolish to cherish the hope that he might. He would never have stayed away all this time, with not so much as a word, not so much as an answer to her letters, if he had any intention of renewing their acquaintance. Renewing their acquaintance! What a stiff little term for all they had been to each other. Or had she dreamed it? Oh, what was the use?

She smiled. 'Of course you may, Richard.'

*

Abigail and Richard were married on the first day of January 1856 in St Leonard's Church. But this wedding was very different from the day she had married Matthew, some fifteen years earlier. For one thing the church on this cold, wintry day was packed with well-wishers, and for another Henry had insisted on being present, thus publicly giving his blessing on the union. Edwin wheeled him down the hill but the old man insisted on walking into the church. He leaned on his son's arm, a frail, docile figure, a far cry from the strutting, arrogant man who had turned Abigail out of his house all those years ago. And if the first thing Abigail saw as she left the church on Richard's arm was the empty wheelchair she gave no sign of the shock it gave her; the feeling of guilt; of betrayal to Matthew. Nor of the sudden fear that she might have made a terrible mistake. But there was no hint of any misgivings as the crowd wished the new Mrs Cotgrove well and showered her and her husband with rice and good wishes. She had chosen dove-grey silk for her wedding gown, with a wide crinoline that caused her new husband to joke that he could hardly get near enough to her to place the ring on her finger, Laura, now nearly twelve, was allowed to wear a crinoline for the first time, hers in a delicate shade of blue, and she pranced about excitedly and sat happily on her stepfather's knee; whilst William, grave but full of pride in his first grown-up suit, handed food round to the guests and Henry quietly nodded his approval from a position of honour by the fire. It was altogether a joyful affair and the bride and groom made a handsome pair as they stepped into the coach that was to take them to the railway station to catch the train to Ipswich where they were to spend a few days at the Great White Horse Hotel. Laura and William were going to stay at Hilltop House with their grandfather and grandmother so that Sarah, unreservedly happy at her daughter-in-law's re-marriage, could look after them. Everyone, including Henry, waved happily and blew kisses as the coach pulled away up the hill.

It was quite late when they arrived at the hotel. They were shown to their room and Richard said, 'I'll leave you to unpack your things, my dear. I'll go down to the bar for a nightcap. You only have to ring if there is anything you need.'

He kissed her briefly and left. When he had gone she smiled a little to herself. Dear Richard. He had no need to worry over her shyness. This time she had no fears or apprehensions over her wedding night. As she busied herself unpacking her trunk she recalled her ignorant innocence when she had married Matthew and the tenderness and understanding he had shown her, his gentleness towards her, for all he was such a big, bluff man. He had encouraged her to love with enjoyment, without reserve –the way she had later unashamedly loved David. The shame for that behaviour had come later and still haunted her.

She undressed and sat at the dressing table to plait her hair. It was still long and thick, the colour hadn't faded although now it was shot through with silver. She leaned forward and examined the fine lines round her eyes. It was no more than was to be expected in a woman of thirty-nine. Thirty-nine. Sometimes she felt as if she had been on earth for a hundred years. She finished plaiting her hair and climbed into bed to wait calmly for her new husband.

He was not long in coming and as he climbed in beside her she could smell the whisky on his breath.

She turned to him eagerly as he fumbled with her shift but as he transferred his weight to her she felt none of the hard masculinity she had expected, although his kisses were full of passion and promise.

'We are both tired,' she whispered gently, 'and drink is a great hindrance to lovemaking. Hold me close, Richard. In the morning things will be better.'

Without speaking he rolled away. He didn't hold her close as she had asked but turned his back and soon began to snore. She rearranged her shift and lay wide awake until the dawn crept into the room in a silent grey mist.

Contrary to her expectations things were no better in the morning, although he began their lovemaking with an energy and vigour that could almost be said to verge on brutality. But there was no culmination; no climax; no drowsy closeness afterwards in peaceful unity.

'It must be the strange surroundings,' she said. 'Things will be better when we get home, I'm sure of it.'

He didn't answer, but picked up a book and began to read.

They spent three days in Ipswich. They visited the docks where the big sailing ships were delivering grain from Australia and the colliers from Newcastie were disgorging their cargos of coal. They went to the Butter Market and looked at the famous Ancient House, with its richly carved timbers and pargeting, and they joined the throngs in Christ Church Park, walking over the gently sloping parkland to where the lake lay, black and sinister, before making their way back past the lovely red-brick Elizabethan house.

They made a handsome pair as they walked along together, he elegant in a long chesterfield and a tall top hat that he called his Lincoln, carrying a gold-topped cane and with his monocle screwed into his left eye; she in a rotonde trimmed with fur over her wide crinoline, her coppery hair visible under its fur-lined hood and her hands warm in a sable muff.

They never spoke of the fiasco of their nightly attempts at lovemaking and there was no hint of any inadequacy in the peremptory manner in which Richard gave his orders to the hotel staff and spoke to the cab driver who brought them back from a visit to the theatre. Abigail understood, without putting it into words, his need to assert himself, to prove his manhood where he could, and she was glad when the time came to return home, convinced that things would be better when they were settled into domesticity.

But here she was wrong. Things didn't improve at all when they returned to the Corner House to begin their life as a family with William and Laura. In fact, the more loving and patient she tried to be the worse things became until, after six months, he no longer even made any attempt to consummate the marriage and retired to sleep in the small room leading off their bedroom.

She felt hurt, rejected, unloved, but she hid her feelings and no one would have suspected from her behaviour that the marriage was not a complete success.

As for Richard, if he was unsuccessful in the bedroom he made up for it in the business. He worked long and tirelessly, driving himself and the men with him.

At the opening of the oyster season it wasn't on *Conquest* that he witnessed the first dredge; he was on the official boat with the mayor and corporation and he saw at close hand the silver oyster produced to check that the new oysters of the season were of good enough size. Abigail and William didn't care. They watched from *Conquest* with Josh, Guy and Tolley, together with Isaac and the new hands Reuben Carver and Jack Slack. They all had a merry time.

William had been allowed the day off school and he was in high spirits as they drank gin from the little glasses Abigail had bought specially for the occasion and ate gingerbread – larger pieces than those served on the official boat because Abigail and Peggy had made it themselves and had not stinted on the size.

'It'll be a good season this year, you mark my words, Missus,' Tolley said, raising his glass as the cry went up 'God save the Queen, the Mayor and the Corporation', and the flag was hoisted to a cheer from all the boats in the river.

'I hope you're right, Tolley,' Abigail said. 'We've already got twice as many orders as we had this time last year, thanks to Richard's advertising.'

'I don't know why 'e wanted to bother with all that advertisin' in the London papers an' all,' Guy said, munching his gingerbread noisily. 'We get near as many orders as we can handle without all that. An' it musta cost a pretty penny, I reckon.'

'It didn't cost any more to add our name to the advertisement for Chiswell and Son,' Abigail said, carefully omitting to add that after suggesting that they do this Richard had then charged Bateman's for half the advertisement. She gave a little laugh. 'Richard's motto seems to be expand or die, and he's quite determined that we shan't die.'

'Oh, no, the business 'on't die. There ain't no danger o' that,' Tolley said gloomily. 'But that ain't to say he 'on't kill us all strivin' to keep it alive.' He shook his head. 'We ain't all that happy, Missus, to tell ye the trewth. None of us ain't, with the way things are goin'. An' I might as well tell ye straight to ye face as say it behind ye back.'

'No call to worry the missus. Thass early days yet,' said Reuben Carver, a young, fresh-faced man with hopes of making enough money to be able to marry his sweetheart in the spring. 'We ain't even dredged our beds yet to see what we might stand to.'

'Reuben's right,' Isaac said. 'An' we'll hev the bloaters to fall back on, too. Ain't no call for you to fret, Missus. Not yet, anyways.'

Josh had said nothing during this exchange. He had never

liked Richard, Abigail knew that, but now that his little maid was married to the man wild horses wouldn't have dragged a word of criticism from the old sailor's lips. 'What I'd like to know,' Guy remarked, narrowing his eyes towards the official boat, 'is how the master managed to get hisself invited over there today.'

Abigail laughed. 'Mr Cotgrove knows all the right people, Guy. He's gone with Alderman Makepeace.'

'I 'spect the next thing we'll hear is that he's bin invited to the Oyster Feast in the Town Hall,' Jack Slack grinned. 'An' good luck to 'im, I say. With four little 'uns an' another on the way I can do with all the money I can get.'

'Then you'd best not go piddlin' what you do get up against the wall at The Anchor,' Isaac said in an undertone. 'If you was to go home sober a bit more often you'd give your pore ole woman a chance to wean one afore you shoved another up the spout.'

Jack roared with laughter. 'I see my ole darlin' don't go short o' nuthin',' he said. 'Nuthin' at all.' And he winked at young Reuben over Isaac's head.

Abigail knew she wasn't supposed to have heard that little exchange and her expression gave nothing away. But she couldn't help contrasting the obvious virility of all these men with the way Richard was. These men didn't need to prove anything; they didn't have to resort to violence to prove their masculinity; they knew they were real men. Their marriages were not the mockery hers was. For the first time she allowed herself to admit that her marriage to Richard was not at all what she had hoped for.

Jack Slack was right. Richard did receive an invitation to the Oyster Feast. It was held in the Town Hall and two hundred guests attended. All men, of course. Naturally he had a new suit of clothes and Abigail felt proud of him as he picked up his gloves and cane to leave in the cab that he'd ordered from The Castle Inn yard.

'We must keep up appearances, mustn't we, my dear?' he said with a smug smile as he gave her a dutiful peck on the cheek.

'Oh, yes, Richard,' she murmured with only the merest hint of sarcasm, 'indeed we must.'

But it wasn't long before the veneer began to show signs of cracking.

'I think we should move to a bigger house,' Richard announced one morning at breakfast. 'A nice house.' He looked round him. 'Something a good deal better than this.'

Surprised, Laura looked up from her porridge. 'I think this is a nice house. I like it,' she said.

'You speak when you're spoken to, Miss, and not before. I was talking to your mama,' Richard said sharply, giving her knuckles a rap with the back of his knife.

Abigail winced with Laura but she managed to keep her voice mild as she said. 'Oh, I don't know, dearest. I think this house is quite adequate for our needs.'

'Oh, really, Abigail!' Richard dabbed impatiently at his moustache with his napkin. 'Is that all you can think about? That it's *adequate* for our needs? Of course it's adequate, but have you no regard for our position? Our standing in the community?'

She smiled at him without guile. 'No, dearest. I have to confess I have more concern with the position of the house than our position in society. Where were you thinking this bigger house might be?'

'Lexden. Where those new big houses are being built.'

Abigail nodded. 'I thought so.' Then, deliberately, she shook her head. 'No, Richard, that's quite out of the question. I need to be near the Hythe for the warehouses and I don't want to be too far from Papa. He's much better now and he likes me to visit him as often as I can. I wouldn't see him much if we lived at Lexden; it's right at the other end of the town. I'm surprised you don't consider it inconvenient yourself. You have Chiswell and Son to think about, just as I'm concerned with Bateman's.'

'I don't want to go to Lexden. I want to stay here,' William said. 'I couldn't live that far away from the river. I'd die.'

'You'll live *in* the river if you speak to me like that, Sir,' Richard said, his temper rising at the unexpected opposition to his plan. 'Although it would do you good to be kept away from the quayside for a while, then your school work might improve. You can scarcely add two and two together and your handwriting is a disgrace. How old are you? Fifteen?' He picked up the bundle of books that William had put beside his chair ready for school and flicked through them. 'What's the good of teaching you Latin and Greek when you can't spell in English? Spell me chrysanthemum.'

William flushed. 'C . . .R . . . I . . . '

'See? There you are. As ignorant as a tinker's donkey.' Richard flung the books across the room. 'It's a waste of my money sending you to school.'

Abigail got up from the table and collected William's books and gave them to him. 'It's *my* money that pays for William's education, Richard,' she said, 'and although he hates school he's promised me he'll stay until his sixteenth birthday.' She nodded to William. 'It's not long now, dear, and you would do well to learn all you can while you're there. Education is never wasted and you are privileged to be sent to the Grammar School, even though it's a long walk for you each day.'

'It wouldn't be half so far from Lexden,' Richard said sarcastically.

'I don't care. I won't go to Lexden to live,' was William's parting shot as he went out of the door, his face dark and sullen.

'You'll do as I say, or I'll take my belt off to you.' Richard's face was equally dark.

'It's time for you to go, too, Laura,' Abigail, said, her expression giving no clue to her feelings. 'Have you got your sampler? And you have a piano lesson at Signor Anigoni's studio this afternoon, so don't forget your music'

'Sampler! Piano lesson!' Richard spat as the door closed behind her. 'What a waste of time and money. And the constant jangling of that piano when she's at home gets on my nerves. It's time she gave those lessons up and did something useful. Piano lessons are expensive.'

'Laura is a very gifted pianist,' Abigail said hotly, letting her temper show now that the children were not there. 'I won't have you belittling her talent just because you've no ear for music. And I know you've no ear for it because you can't even hold a tune enough to sing the hymns in church on Sundays. It's like standing next to a braying ass, standing next to you.'

'How dare you, Madam!' As Abigail had already discovered, Richard couldn't bear to be criticized and his face turned a dull red as he took a step towards her.

'I dare because it's true,' she retorted. 'Not that it matters. I don't care whether you can sing or not. But just because you don't appreciate Laura's gift don't dismiss it as unimportant.'

He got hold of her by the tops of her arms, gripping her until the flesh was bruised. 'If I say her piano lessons will stop, Madam, then they will STOP!' He let her go so violently that she staggered and nearly fell. 'I shall see Signor Anigoni today.'

'You will not!' she shouted. '*I* pay for Laura's lessons, not you. Her lessons will continue.'

He swung round to her, bringing his hand a stinging blow across her cheek. 'Don't you dare to defy me, woman! I'll show you who's master in this house.'

'That'll be a change. You've never managed to do so yet,' she replied, her voice full of scorn.

At that his eyes narrowed and he brought his fist round and punched her on the shoulder, knocking her right off balance. As she fell to the floor he put out his foot and kicked her. 'Now, who's master!' he said venomously and stalked out of the room.

Peggy came in as Abigail dragged herself to her feet.

'Are you all right, M'm? I heered a crash.'

'Yes, Peggy.' Abigail managed a smile and held onto a chair. 'I tripped over, that's all.'

'Hurt your face, by the looks of it, thass all red. Shall I get you some salve?' Peggy peered at her anxiously.

'No, thank you, dear. But I think, yes, I would like a cup of tea.'

Abigail sat staring into the fire as she waited for the tea. Oh, God, she thought, we've been married not much over a year and what have we come to? Tears began to trickle down her face.

# *Chapter Twenty*

When William returned from school he didn't go home but went straight down to the warehouse where Abigail was supervising the packing of the oysters, almost the last of the season. He said nothing about the morning's altercation until they were walking back up the hill together. At fifteen he was a big lad, nearly a head taller than Abigail and very like his father except for his coppery hair.

He looked down at her. 'He hit you this morning, didn't he, Mama? No, it's no use trying to pull your bonnet forward, I can still see the mark.'

'Oh, dear. And I thought I'd managed to hide it. Do you think Josh and Guy and the others . . . ?'

William put his arm round her shoulders. 'You don't have to worry about them. Mama. They wouldn't say anything. But it's not the first time, is it?'

She shook her head. 'No, it isn't.' She looked up at him. 'But I can put up with it, Will, really I can, as long as he doesn't touch you, or Laura.'

'You don't need to worry about me, Mama. He won't touch me, I'm as big as he is, and a good deal stronger, I daresay.

Anyway, he won't have the chance. I shan't be coming with you to Lexden. I've made my mind up on that.'

'You won't come, Will? But what will you do, then?'

'I'll go and live with Grandpapa. He'll like that, and so will Granny.' He turned to her. 'I couldn't come to Lexden, Mama. You do understand, don't you? I couldn't live that far from the river.'

She nodded. 'Yes, Will, I know exactly how you feel. I feel the same, myself. But if Richard says we must move, well . . . ' She shrugged eloquently.

'Oh, why did you marry that man, Mama?' he blurted suddenly. Then he hung his head. 'I'm sorry. But if only David hadn't gone away like that. He'd have looked after us when Papa died, I'm sure of it.'

She put her hand on his arm. 'Oh, Will, I'm sorry I've made us all so unhappy. But Richard seemed such a nice man when we first knew him. True, I've never really loved him, but I didn't expect to, not after Matthew . . . ' She paused, then went on, 'It seemed such a good idea. It meant it would be easier to keep an eye on Grandpapa's business along with ours. I thought Richard and I would work together.' She gave a rueful smile. 'I thought we might even be happy.'

'But it hasn't worked out like that at all, has it?' Viciously, William kicked a stone.

'Richard changed after we were married,' she admitted.

'Yes. We were all taken in by him, weren't we? Even Grandpapa. I know how he's tried to get his hands on Chiswell's and now he's doing the same with Bateman's.'

'How do you know that?'

'Uncle Josh and Guy and Tolley tell me things. Like how he goes on board to inspect the catch, to make sure they don't keep any back to sell off privately. Things like that.'

'They've never told me these things.'

'No, well, they reckon you've got quite enough to worry about.'

'Oh dear.'

'He keeps asking to go down river with them, too. He keeps saying he'd like a trip on the water, but they know he only wants to go to spy on them to see what they do. They keep making excuses so they don't have to take him.'

'Oh, Will, that's terrible. I'd no idea.'

'No, and perhaps I shouldn't have told you. But you don't need to worry, Mama, the men can handle Richard. He only sees what they let him see.' He grinned. 'I think they're waiting for some rough weather before they let him go with them. That'll make sure he never asks to go with them again, the bastard.'

'William! Your language!'

'I'm sorry, Mama. I shouldn't have said that. But it makes me so mad to think that he doesn't trust the men who work for us. Uncle Josh and Tolley and Guy are the salt of the earth. Oh, he's mean, Mama. He's so mean he'd scrape a farthing out of the gutter and not spoil his gloves.'

'Hush, Will, you mustn't say such things.' They reached the front door and Abigail looked over her shoulder as she fished for her key.

'I wouldn't say them if they weren't true,' William persisted under his breath, 'but they are, and I hate him.'

The house was silent when they went in. This was unusual, because Laura always spent the hour before supper practising the piano, and Abigail liked to sit and listen when she was at home.

She was taking off her cloak when Peggy came hurrying along the hall from the kitchen, her rosy face pinched with concern.

'There's some fresh cakes just out o' the oven, Master Will,' she said automatically to William. Then, 'Oh, M'm, somethin' dreadful's 'appened. Oh, it was dreadful. Terrible. I tried to stop it, but I couldn't.' She threw her apron over her face and began to cry noisily.

Abigail took her by the shoulders. 'Tell me, Peggy,' she demanded. 'It's Laura, isn't it? Tell me. Where is she?'

'Upstairs, M'm. In 'er room. But it ain't that, M'm, it's . . . '

William had gone into the drawing room. Now he came out and stood in the doorway, his face white with fury. 'Laura's piano's gone,' he said through clenched teeth. 'That bastard's sold Laura's piano.'

Abigail pushed past him into the room and stared at the space where Laura's pride and joy had stood, now only occupied by an untidy sprawl of music sheets. For a moment she stood there, hardly believing what she saw, then she rushed out of the room and up the stairs to Laura's bedroom.

The girl was lying face down on her bed, her dark hair spread untidily over the pillow and her body racked with dry, despairing sobs.

Abigail took her in her arms and held her close.

'It was gone when I came home,' Laura sobbed, her eyes red in her ashen face. 'There was nothing I could do. It was gone when I got home.' She buried her face in Abigail's shoulder. 'Oh, Mama, he's a dreadful man. I wish he'd go away. It was much better before he came here.'

'Hush now, you mustn't say such things.' Abigail stroked her hair and tried to calm her. 'You shall have your piano back, dear, never fear. I'll find out where he's sold it and I'll go and buy it back.'

'But it wasn't his to sell in the first place!'

'I know.'

'He said those awful things about my playing. They weren't true, Mama, were they? Signor Anigoni says . . . '

'Of course they weren't true, darling. You know that as well as I do.'

'He's jealous. Jealous because he can't do anything like that.' Laura wiped her eyes again and sniffed. 'I used to think he was nice. But he isn't. He's a monster.' Her eyes narrowed. 'I hate him.'

Abigail held her daughter close and stared at their reflection in the dressing table mirror at the foot of the bed. 'I hate him.' The same phrase from both children in the space of less than an hour. She put her hand up and touched the angry red mark on her own cheekbone. In her heart she knew that she hated him, too, and she was filled with despair.

Richard didn't come home until very late and he was in an ugly temper because he had been drinking. Abigail usually kept out of his way when he was like this because he often became violent when he was antagonized, but tonight she didn't care. She put on her dressing gown and went through to the next room, where he was alreadly blundering about getting ready for bed.

'What have you done with Laura's piano?' she asked quietly, her voice ominously calm.

He looked up from where he had sat down on the bed to take off his boots. His tie hung round his neck like a string and his collar was undone. 'I've sold it,' he said, with a grin that was more of a sneer.

'It wasn't yours to sell.'

'I can sell anything I like.'

'You had no right to sell Laura's piano. Who did you sell it to?'

'I sent it back where it came from.'

'Back to Mr Aggio?'

'That's right. I told him I'd had enough of its jangling. And so I have. It got on my bloody nerves.' His voice rose as he spoke and with the last word he flung his boot at her, hitting the wall beside her.

She took no notice, but still stood there. 'Will you go and buy it back tomorrow, Richard, or shall I? Of course, if I go, it will soon be all over the town that there is trouble between Richard Cotgrove and his wife; so if you want to preserve some semblance of a happy marriage you had better go yourself.' She still hadn't raised her voice.

He looked at her dully. 'I'm not going to buy the bloody thing back. And neither are you!' He flung his other boot at her. This one hit her on the temple and a thin trickle of blood ran down her face. 'There won't be room for it in the house at Lexden, anyway.'

'Oh!' She raised her eyebrows. 'I thought the house at Lexden was much bigger than this one.'

'So it is.' He frowned, trying to get his fuddled brain to match hers, that was so clear-sighted and coolly contemptuous.

'Not that it matters,' she went on, 'because I'm not moving from here. You can go if you like.' She turned to go back into her own room.

Suddenly he leapt at her, grabbing her by the shoulders and shaking her till her teeth chattered. Then he threw her to the floor. 'You're my wife!' he shouted, 'you'll do as I say! If I say we move to Lexden, then ... we ... move ... to ... Lexden.'

It was fortunate that he had taken off his boots because each word was punctuated with a vicious kick.

She rolled away and scrambled to her feet. 'That's right,' she panted, 'kick me. Show me what you really think of me. Don't pretend any longer that you care. Admit that all you married me for was so that you could get your hands on Bateman's; so you could manipulate it like you've manipulated Chiswell's, encouraging my father to drink so that he wouldn't see what you were up to. God help me, I didn't see what you were up to, either. But I do now.' She turned away from him. 'Go to Lexden, Richard. Buy your smart house with the money you've creamed out of my father.'

At these words he took a step towards her and caught her by the arms. She looked up at him, ignoring the pain of his fingers digging into her flesh. 'Oh, yes,' she went on, 'don't think I haven't realized what you were doing when you blamed Effie Markham for spending all his money.' She gave a mirthless laugh. 'Effie Markham! She wouldn't have had the sense. All she wanted was to be kept in clothes and a plentiful supply of chocolates. No, it was you, feathering your own nest, not her. It was no wonder you managed to pull the business round so quickly. All you had to do was stop helping yourself.' She wrenched herself free. 'Go to Lexden, Richard, I don't care. But don't think I'll come with you, because I won't.' She turned to go back to her own room.

'Of course you'll come. You've got no choice. You're my wife.' He spoke arrogantly.

She gave a scornful laugh. 'Only in name, Richard,' she said. 'Only in name.'

She guessed, quite rightly, that those words would incense him even further and he lunged at her, pulling her dressing gown off and tearing her nightgown to expose the flesh down to her waist. She didn't move, but stood watching as he unbuttoned his own clothing and then grabbed her again, bruising her breasts with angry kisses as he flung her onto the bed. She still made no struggle and as he pressed himself onto her she whispered in his ear, 'It's no use, Richard, is it? Why don't you admit the truth? It's not women you like at all, is it?'

He reared up and looked down at her, his face a mask of hatred. 'You can't prove *anything*.' But there was fear in his voice.

'I don't have to,' she looked up at him, 'I can see from your face that it's true.' She pushed him and he allowed her to escape from under him, still looking at her with absolute venom, but now it was tinged with fear. 'Oh, I'll keep your secret, never fear, Richard. I won't tell anyone. But you'll have to keep up appearances, too. There'll be no more violence in this house. If you as much as lay a finger on me again I'll tell the world what kind of a man you are. And *I'll* decide what's best for my children – without any interference from you. Another thing, there'll be no more talk of moving to Lexden. Do you understand?' She took a clean nightgown from the drawer and put it on while he sat on the bed, half-naked, fuddled and defeated. Then she went to the wash stand in the corner and poured water to bathe her face, coming up now into an angry blue weal. When she had done this she turned to him again. 'You do understand, don't you, Richard?'

He nodded dumbly.

'Will you go and get Laura's piano back tomorrow, then?'

He shook his head. 'No, you can go. Tell Mr Aggio it was a mistake. A misunderstanding on my part.' He put his head in his hands.

Abigail put her hand on his shoulder. 'It needn't be so bad, Richard. In fact, having a wife must make things easier. As long as you keep your part of the bargain I won't even mention what time you come in from your sickening –whatever you do; wherever you go.'

He shook her hand off and got up from the bed. 'Oh, leave me alone. You're not a wife, you're a bloody jailer.' He staggered back to his room and shut the door.

The next morning Abigail walked up to Mr Aggio's showroom in Head Street. If Mr Aggio's son thought there was anything strange in removing a piano from Mr Cotgrove's house one day and taking it back the next he gave no indication but merely suggested that when it was back in place it might be well to have it tuned. With the polite young man's assurance that the piano would be reinstalled and tuned by four o'clock that afternoon, Abigail left the shop.

And walked straight into Edwin.

'Abbie! What are you doing here at this hour of the morning? I thought you'd be busy at your warehouse,' he said, catching her as he nearly knocked her over.

She smiled. 'Just a little matter I had to discuss with Mr Aggio.'

'Not *another* piano!' he joked. Then he became serious as he peered into her white face. 'What have you done to your head, Abbie?' He frowned and took her arm. 'Come on, I'll take you to Bank's and buy you coffee and cream cakes. You look as if you could do with cheering up. I won't press you, but you can tell me all about it, if you want to.'

He guided her along Head Street, doffing his hat here and there to an acquaintance, and helped her to pick her way carefully across the road between the filth left by the carts, hansom cabs and other traffic. At Bank's he found them a table in a discreet corner behind a potted palm and said, 'There, now you can relax, Abbie,' before ordering the most enormous cream cakes and a pot of coffee.

'Oh, Eddie,' she smiled at him, 'you never change, do you?'

'I hope not, old girl. Now, what's the trouble? Do you want to tell Uncle Edwin? I won't pry, but you'll feel better if you get it off your chest, whatever it is. And I know there's something, so don't try to tell me there isn't.'

She smiled again. 'You could always see through me, couldn't you, Eddie?' she said sadly. 'So I might as well tell you.' She began by telling him about the piano and how she'd just been to get it back. As she had expected, he was incensed at Richard's behaviour. She hadn't intended to tell him anything more but somehow she found herself confiding everything, with no embarrassment over the most intimate details. It was a relief and in a way cleansing to be able to tell Edwin exactly what Richard was like.

He nodded when she'd finished, draining his coffee and pouring more. 'I'm not surprised, to tell you the truth, Abbie,' he said, pushing her refilled cup over to her. 'Cotgrove's got some strange friends, although there's nothing wrong that you could put your finger on; they're all too canny for that. Naturally, none of them are anxious to end up in prison; in fact, most of them are respectably married. Of course, that puts them above suspicion in the eyes of the public. But it doesn't help you, does it, old girl?'

Abigail sipped her coffee. 'No. But I have the upper hand now, Eddie,' she said calmly. 'He knows that I know, so he'll be afraid to put a foot wrong in case I betray him. He'll never strike me again, I'm sure of that.'

'Oh, Abbie.' Edwin covered her hand with his. 'To think it should have come to that! You haven't had all the luck in the world with your marriages, have you?'

'I was happy with Matthew. Sometimes I think I was happiest when we lived in Dolphin Yard . . . '

'In all that squalor? You can't be serious.' He sighed. 'I'm still fighting over places like that, Abbie. If only I could get the authorities to do something about the water supply. It's scandalous, Abbie.'

Abigail smiled. 'Yes, I read your latest article in the local paper. You'll have to be careful what you say, Eddie, or you'll find yourself out of a job.'

He sighed. 'Yes, the Commissioners have already complained.'

He bit into a second cake. 'But I shan't rest until there's piped water to every house and a proper system for flushing away the filth from the gutters and sewers. A big reservoir to provide water at pressure, that's what we need . . . '

'Oh, come on, Eddie. I can't see that ever happening.' Abigail got up from her chair. 'But I'll champion your fight for it – until you get thrown off the paper for going too far, that is.' She laughed. 'But thank you for cheering me up. You do me good, Eddie. I always feel better after I've seen you. I'm going to see Father now. I'll tell him I've seen you.'

Edwin groaned as he followed her to the door. 'Oh, no. Don't mention my name!' he said in mock misery. 'I was there last night and Sarah nearly turned me out because I got into an argument with him. She was afraid he'd have another heart attack, he got so agitated.' He grinned. 'But it does him good, keeps his brain alive. And it's all good-humoured.'

'Yes, his illness has mellowed him a lot.' Abigail held up her face for a farewell kiss. 'Goodbye, Eddie. And thank you.'

'The pleasure's all mind. I'm always happy to play escort to a lovely lady.' He placed his hat on his head at its usual rakish angle. 'Oh, and talking of lovely ladies, guess who I saw with a very nice-looking lady the other day? I must say I was quite jealous; it's almost the first time I've seen anyone I might have considered giving up my freedom for.' He shook his head. 'But, just my luck, she's already spoken for.'

'You mean another lucky escape,' Abigail laughed. 'But, no, I can't guess. Who was she with? Somebody I know?'

'Yes. She was with that chap, what was his name? He used to come and visit Matt. He was in the fruit trade. Oh, what was his name? David somebody or other. That's it. David Quilter.' He beamed at his cleverness in remembering.

But Abigail didn't smile back. 'In Colchester?' she managed to say, her voice coming out in little more than a croak.

'That's right.' Edwin didn't seem to notice anything amiss. 'They were walking down High Street together. I gather he's just bought one of those new houses in Lexden.' He took out his watch. 'I really must dash, Abbie. Shall I call you a cab?'

'No. No thank you, Eddie. I'd rather walk.' Numbly, Abigail turned away and Edwin went off, whistling, totally unaware of the bombshell he had just dropped at his sister's feet.

Abigail never knew how she found her way back. She walked blindly, her thoughts in chaos. David was back. In Colchester. But why had he chosen Colchester, of all the places in the world, especially now that he was married. What if she should see him? How would she react? Her heart was already hammering in her breast at the very thought of him, proving she had deluded herself in thinking she had forgotten him; deluded herself that he had merely been a substitute for Matthew; that she had only taken him to assuage a hunger that Matthew was no longer able to appease. She was forced to admit that it was not, had never been, that at all. She had loved him. She still loved him, God help her, even after all this time. But it was plain he didn't love her because he was married now. So why had he come back? Why? Why?

She didn't visit her father after all, but carried on down the hill to the water front. There was always something needing attention at either Chiswell's warehouse or Bateman's that would take her mind off thoughts of David.

The quayside was crowded as usual, with two people idly looking on for every one who was working, and she had to push her way through the motley crowd to reach Bateman's warehouse. *Conquest*, *Good Intent* and *Faith* were all tied up at the quayside and the men were in a huddle at the water's edge.

'No, Sir, we can't do with fewer hands,' Josh was saying. 'Beggin' your pardon, but you don't know what you're talkin' about.'

'Anyways, who'd you think you'd pay orf?' Guy asked. 'Each boat's got its own crew. They work together well. I can't see as anybody could be spared.'

'I hadn't decided that.' Abigail heard Richard's smooth voice and her heart sank. 'It's just that it seems you spend a great deal of time standing around with your hands in your pockets, all of you,' he went on, 'and I thought you could double up – if some of you weren't working on one boat you could go out on another, something like that.'

Abigail shouldered her way through to the little knot of men. There were the three senior men, Josh, Tolley and Guy, in their shabby sea-going moleskins and guernseys, and Richard, smart in a check suit, with his habitual rose in his buttonhole, his monocle firmly in place and his gold-topped cane in his hand. Suddenly, her temper rose at the idea that Richard, who never even got his hands soiled, should be trying to tell these men how to run their boats.

'You don't know what you're talking about, Richard,' she said hotly. 'You've never seen how they have to work, sometimes twenty-four hours and more at a stretch, wet through to the skin, without food or sleep, in the most appalling conditions. You wouldn't begrudge them an hour or two when the nets are mended and the boat made shipshape again while they wait for the tide if you'd seen what they have to do once they're at sea.'

'I've suggested that they should take me with them, enough times,' Richard said coldly. 'I might even be able to point out ways to make their tasks easier.' He gave a superior smirk. 'An ounce of brain is often worth a pound of brawn, you know.'

'In that case,' Josh said, his face devoid of expression, 'you'd better come down river with us termorrer, Sir. We're gonna start cleanin' the oyster beds read for the spat. Thass a heavy ole job, dirty, too, wrappin' lumps o' chain round the dredges an' then pullin' them acrost the beds to clear away the mud. But you come along of us. You see if you can tell us how to do it easier. I for one 'ud be glad to know how I could work 'ithout gittin' me hands cut to ribbons and me back fair broke in two.'

Tolley and Guy nodded in agreement. 'Thass six o'clock tide, so thass when we'll be leavin' so we go down on the ebb. Then we work through the next flood, stay down there all night an' come back on the flood next day,' Tolley said.

'Why do you have to stay down river all night?' Richard asked. 'Surely that's a waste of time.'

The three men exchanged glances that belied the patience in Guy's voice as he answered, 'I shoulda thought you'd 'ave realized, Sir, we can't get the boat back up here when the tide's out.'

'Oh, no, of course not,' Richard said hurriedly, 'I was forgetting.'

That don't do to forget things like that when you're on the water, Sir,' Tolley said amiably. 'You can git yerself into real trouble if you do.'

'What about you, Abbie? Would you like to come along, too?' Josh said. 'I know you like a trip down river and thass a long time since you've bin with us.'

'No, I don't think so, Josh, thank you, although it looks like being a lovely day for it. I've got quite a lot of work to catch up on.' Abigail turned to go into the warehouse.

'I see you bin walkin' into another door, Missus,' Guy said loudly. 'You got a rare nasty bruise on the side o' yore forrid. You'll hev to git yerself some spectacles, I can see that.'

She shot him a glance of warning as she put her hand up to her head. 'Yes, silly of me, wasn't it?' she said, stealing a look at Richard to see how he had reacted. But he had turned away and was busy making plans for his trip. 'I shall have to be more careful in future.'

By the time she had finished in the warehouse Richard had gone. She was not sorry because it was becoming more and more difficult to pretend that her marriage was a success. It was plain that the men guessed all was not well although she always maintained that she had fallen or walked into something to explain away the more obvious bruises.

She walked up the hill in the afternoon sunshine. On the way she stopped to buy daffodils from an optimistic flower-seller; few people at the Hythe had money to buy food, let alone flowers, and her cries were going largely unheeded. Abigail took the flowers into the churchyard and laid them on Matthew's grave. She knelt there for some time, a great sadness in her heart. She had loved Matthew, but not as much as he had loved her. He had loved her so much that he had taken his own life so that she would be free to love and be happy again. And what had she done? Thrown his sacrifice away by marrying Richard. It was all such a waste.

Slowly she got up and made her way home to the Corner House. As she pushed open the door strains of the 'Moonlight Sonata' reached her ears and she smiled. At least something was right with the world. Laura had got her piano back.

# *Chaqpter Twenty-One*

Richard paid off the cab and came in with so many boxes and bags that he had to enlist the cab driver's help to get them up the steps and into the house.

Abigail, sitting in the window working on the accounts, watched, but she didn't get up from her seat. He would come and show her what he had bought; he was like a peacock, he loved strutting around in new clothes.

It was ten minutes before he appeared. He was dressed in moleskin trousers and a seaman's guernsey, a cheese cutter hat and brand new leather boots. Over his arm were a set of black oilskins and a sou'wester.

'Oh, my God! What *do* you think you look like!' She nearly laughed, but stopped herself in time. He was a parody of a fisherman in his brand new clothes. Real fishermen had holes or darns in their guernseys, their moleskins were stained and their boots all scuffed and shabby. But Richard was apparently unaware of this and he looked inordinately pleased with himself.

'Well, I could hardly go down river in a suit,' he said defensively when he saw her expression.

'I expect the men would have found you things to wear, between them,' she said dryly.

'Ugh, no. I wouldn't want to borrow their dirty old moleskins and guernseys, they stink of fish. In any case, I daresay I shall be going again so it's as well to have my own gear.'

Abigail raised her eyebrows but said nothing. It was plain Richard had no idea what a day cleaning the oyster beds entailed.

The next afternoon, with Richard out of the way and the children at school, Abigail went to see her father. He was much improved now, thanks largely to Sarah's care and attention. She bullied him mercilessly and he revelled in it. It was amazing that after all the years of antagonism they could live in the same house, let alone in such harmony.

Henry was casting a desultory eye over Chiswell and Son's books. Richard allowed him to do this, knowing that it gave the old man a sense of still being in charge and assuming that Henry no longer had the stamina to do more than flick over the pages, without really noticing what was there.

But in that Richard deceived himself.

'I see they've taken two extra hands on the *Edith*,' he remarked by way of greeting.

Abigail went over and kissed him. 'I don't think so, Papa. The latest bee in Richard's bonnet is to cut down on the men. At Bateman's, at any rate. Let me see.' She took the ledger from her father. 'Ebenezer Hammond? I don't recall anyone of that name. Nor Tom Graves.' She frowned. 'I'll look into it, Papa.'

Henry looked at her over the top of the gold-rimmed spectacles perched on the tip of his nose. 'He's surely not up to that old trick – putting imaginary men on the payroll and pocketing their so-called earnings!'

'I wouldn't like to say, Papa, until I've looked into it.' Abigail handed him back the ledger and he closed it with a bang.

'Ah, he's a fly one, Richard Cotgrove. I used to think he was smart, but I've come to the conclusion he's not smart, but sharp, too sharp by half. He's cost me money, Abigail, in the past. I should never have trusted him.'

'And I should never have married him.' The words were out before Abigail could prevent them.

Her father looked at her sadly. 'Poor little girl. I always said you'd never marry. And here you are, twice wed.' He shook his head. 'And I doubt the second time had little love in it from either side.'

She lifted her head. 'I thought we could be happy, Papa. I didn't know what he was like.'

'And neither did I, child, or I'd have warned you.'

Sarah brought the tea tray in. 'Now, don't you go tiring him, Abigail. He may look hale and hearty but he's still far from well, you know.' She looked well and happy herself and had put on a little weight, which suited her.

'Ah, get away with you, woman,' Henry said, enjoying every minute of it as she plumped up his cushions and adjusted his rug. 'You fuss too much.'

'If I fussed less you wouldn't be here today,' Sarah retorted, 'and don't you forget it.'

'Oh, stop your blethering and fetch yourself a cup and saucer. I've been thinking over what I should do, and as Will is as much your grandson as mine it's only right that you should know.'

Sarah raised her eyebrows but did as she had been bidden. When she was seated and the tea poured Henry said, 'You hold Bateman's in trust for William, don't you Abigail?'

Abigail nodded. 'I have sole discretion over it until he comes of age, then it will be his. But that's several years away yet.'

Henry nodded. Then he said, 'I'm going to do the same with Chiswell and Son. I've thought about it for a long time and I've already discussed it with Edwin.' He waved his hand. 'I always hoped he would take over when I gave up but he's too busy belly-aching over the water supply and the sewage system. Why he can't leave things be I'll never know. We've never taken any harm from a bit of muck around the place. But there it is. He doesn't want the business and that's that.' He stopped talking and drank some of his tea to cover up the fact that he needed a break to get his breath back. 'William loves the sea, the boats, the business and everything about it. I'm right, aren't I?'

'Oh, yes,' Abigail said.

'He's just such another as his father and grandfather,' Sarah said, with more than a hint of pride in her voice.

'Yes, I thought so. I shall get old Holdaway my solicitor to come and see me. With your agreement, Abbie, we'll turn the two businesses into one – Bateman and Chiswell, and you can hold it all in trust for young Will.' He smiled grimly. 'I'll see that bugger Cotgrove doesn't get his hands on any more of my money, even if he is your husband, my girl.'

Abigail sighed. 'I should have been more watchful over Chiswell and Son, but it's taken me all my time to keep his fingers out of Bateman's. I'm afraid he's greedy for money.'

'He's a lot more things beside that. But you still have to live with him, my dear, so I'd better not say more.' Henry leaned over and patted her on the arm.

'I'm glad it's working out this way,' Sarah said thoughtfully. 'It was always intended that it should be Bateman and Chiswell, as I understand it, before Old Zac fell out with your father, Henry.'

'Chiswell and Bateman, it would have been,' Henry corrected.

'Bateman and Chiswell,' Sarah argued.

‘Oh, what does it matter, as long as both names are there?’ Abigail smiled.

‘That’s right,’ Henry agreed. ‘What does it matter? I’ll send Wilfred along to summon old Holdaway and I’ll sort it all out tomorrow.’

‘Thank you, Papa. You’ve made me very happy,’ Abigil said as she kissed him goodbye.

Henry chuckled. ‘I’ll bet that’s more than that husband of yours will say.’

A note from Edwin was waiting for her when she arrived home.

I’ve been given two tickets for the theatre tonight, some kind of variety, I think, and some chap who plays the piano extremely well. Dress yourself up in your glad rags, I’m taking you out on the town. If R. is likely to object, don’t tell him! I’ll pick you up at 7.30.

Eddie

She smiled. That was typical of Edwin. But ‘R.’ wasn’t going to object, because he was down river, probably in Brightlingsea Creek, in much less comfort than he was used to.

She was quite right. Richard was spending a far from happy day. It was cold on the boat, in spite of the warm April sunshine, and there was quite a breeze blowing.

The men were very pleasant; they showed him how to handle the ropes – they called them sheets – and it was soon plain why their hands were all calloused and horny; it only took one salt-caked sheet to slide roughly through his hands as the sail filled to leave them raw and bleeding. And he nearly broke his back heaving one of the four dredges overboard, heavy with the chain that was wrapped round it to drag the bottom.

‘Ye wanta try luggin’ ’em back over the side when they’re full,’ Tolley said with a grin. He hauled one up. ‘You hev to get your knee behind it an’ give it a sharp twist ... ’ He demonstrated deftly as he pulled the dredge over the side. ‘Like that.’

They emptied the dredge onto the deck and began sorting, throwing back the cultch and the oysters and setting aside the limpets and other rubbish. They used two long boards to gather up the cultch and throw it back overboard – another back-breaking job.

Richard found that he was expected to take his turn with the rest. It was no use complaining that his back ached, that his hands were sore, that he was wet through; because they simply looked at him, amazed that he even noticed such things.

‘There, thass a good job done,’ Josh said, throwing the last lot back into the water as the tide rose to the flood. ‘Now the bottom’ll be nice and clear for the spat. All right, boys, we’ll hev a brew-up an’ then we’ll try the wallet for a bit o’ fishin’, shall we?’

‘But surely it’s time to stop,’ Richard protested. ‘We’ve done a good day’s work, I should have thought.’

‘Ah, yes,’ Josh said, ‘but we can’t get back up river on the ebb, can we now, Sir?’

‘No, of course not. I realized that. But haven’t we done enough work for one day?’ Richard was tetchy. His boots were full of water and his moleskins were stiff from where he’d sat on a pile of nets that had been soaked by the spray. ‘But it’ll be getting dark before long. Don’t you ever sleep?’

‘Now an’ agin,’ Tolley said. ‘But we try not to waste wallyble time. We got an hour or two’s fishin’ yet, once we get outa the estuary. But I’ll go and brew up first while you others get the boat under way.’ He disappeared down into the cabin.

Richard managed to drink the thick, black brew that Tolley

handed him in a tin mug, but he didn't find it very appetizing. He was wet and cold, his hands were raw and the leather boots hurt his feet as they squelched with water at every step. He put on his oilskins in the hope that they would keep some of the cold wind out and tried not to think of the motion of the boat as he munched the doorstep of bread and hunk of cheese that had come up with the tea.

*Conquest* made good way with a beam wind and she was soon out into the estuary where, even on a calm day, the confluence of the two rivers, the Colne and the Blackwater, made the water choppy and unpredictable. Today, a fresh north-easterly had sprung up and the water was becoming more and more lumpy. Richard wished he hadn't accepted the tea and bread and cheese, and hoped he wouldn't be sick, especially as the scent from the fish stew that Tolley was cooking below kept wafting uneasily into his nostrils.

'Come on, lads, thass all ready,' Tolley shouted from the galley.

'Right, boys, heave 'er to and let's chuck the hook over, then we can all go down and eat together,' Josh called.

'Right-o, she's dug in,' Guy called back. He turned to Richard. 'Now come on, Sir, you'll want your share o' fill-belly, I'll be bound, to warm the cockles o' your heart.' He stood aside for Richard to go down the ladder to the cabin.

It was hot and stuffy down there from the coal stove and Tolley's old clay pipe, and the cupboard bunks were open to provide seats for them all. The air was blue with the stink of fish, stew, tobacco and wet oilskins. Tolley ladled a good helping of the stew he had made onto a saucepan lid and gave Richard a spoon. There y'are, Sir. Grip the handle 'tween yer knees so that don't spill with the motion of the boat.' He rubbed his hands. Thass a drop o' good grub. You git that acrost your chest, Sir, an' you won't take no harm.'

Richard sat down and took one look at the greasy mess in the saucepan lid before he changed colour. Silently, they all stood aside to let him rush up onto the deck and the clear, empty dusk of the breezy April evening.

Tolley picked up Richard's stew and tipped it back into the great iron cauldron. 'All the more for us,' he remarked, grinning into his whiskers.

Josh got up from his seat. 'I'll jest go up an' see after 'im.'

'Want any help, Gaffer?' Guy asked.

'No. I can manage.' Josh lumbered up the ladder.

Abigail was ready and waiting when Edwin arrived. She had put on her best dress of heavy green silk, a shade that she knew suited her colouring. The tight-fitting and off-the-shoulder bodice had a deep bertha of guipure lace and with it she wore a large cameo brooch and a gold pendant that enhanced her white neck. She had twisted green silk flowers to match her dress into her hair and her ivory filigree fan was tied with a green ribbon.

'My word, Abbie, you've done me proud. You look a corker,' Edwin said admiringly as he draped her soft white cashmere shawl round her shoulders. 'All the chaps'll envy me tonight.'

'You're a tease, Eddie,' she laughed. Nevertheless, she was pleased at his compliments and as he helped her into the cab she was determined to forget all her troubles for one evening and enjoy herself.

The theatre was crowded and Abigail found herself caught up in the mood of excited anticipation as she and Edwin were shown to their seats. The whole place was decorated in red and gold, with red plush seats and red flocked wallpaper on what little could be seen of the walls, and gilded columns supporting tiers of gilded boxes and galleries. The whole place seemed to glitter with the lights from the gas chandeliers.

There was a singer, an attractive young girl with a surprisingly full contralto voice coming from such a slight frame; a French conjuror and the accomplished pianist Edwin had particularly wanted to hear.

'I hope he'll play again in the second half,' he whispered to Abigail as they left their seats during the interval and went into the foyer for a little air. 'He hasn't played any Liszt yet and I'm told he's a great exponent of Liszt. Now, you stay by the window here and I'll bring you a drink.' He was obviously enjoying himself hugely.

Abigail stood fanning herself, watching the brightly coloured assembly and listening to the noise, the hum of talk over the almost continuous tinkle of female laughter, interspersed with the occasional loud guffaw from the men. Everyone seemed in high spirits.

'Here you are, old girl.' Edwin had elbowed his way through the crowd and he handed her a glass. 'And just look who I ran into! I told you he was in Colchester, didn't I? Look, your old friend, David Quilter.'

The whole place seemed for a moment to tilt at a crazy angle, but Abigail leaned against the window sill and closed her eyes briefly. When she opened them David was there, holding her hand and looking down at her.

'Abigail, how nice to see you again.' The formality of his words belied the look in his eyes, a look he was making no effort to hide as he searched her face for some answering glimmer. Yet his voice was smooth as he said, 'May I introduce my sister, Caroline? She's come to spend a few days with me, to help me settle into my new house. She goes home to Reading next Friday. Caro, this is Abigail. I've told you about her, haven't I?'

'Yes, indeed.' Caroline smiled at Abigail. She was about

twenty-eight, Abigail judged, tall, with a mass of thick, dark hair that she wore piled high on her head in a soft knot. She was attractive rather than pretty and her voice was low and husky. Edwin was already beginning to flirt gently with her.

All this she took in almost without realizing, and she even managed to join in the small talk, the discussion on the merits of the entertainment they had seen so far. But all the time she was aware of David beside her, his presence, his nearness, the tan that had not yet begun to fade, which left little white crow's feet when his eyes were not crinkled in laughter. She felt as if her world had suddenly been pitchforked upside down.

'Why not come and share our box for the rest of the evening?' David suggested as the bell went. 'There's only Caro and me and it would be a pity . . .'

'What a good idea.' Edwin put his hand under Caroline's elbow to escort her. 'I'm sure you two have plenty to talk about, too,' he said over his shoulder.

David and Abigail exchanged smiles. 'It looks as if my brother is determined not to let the grass grow under his feet,' she said.

'Wise man,' David commented and took her hand in his.

In the comparative privacy of the box they divided quite naturally into two pairs, Edwin sitting with Caroline and David beside Abigail.

'I've only just found out about Matthew,' David said in a low voice. 'Oh, Abbie, why didn't you write? Why didn't you let me know?'

'I did write, David, more than once. But you'd gone away and I didn't know how to get in touch with you.'

'But you knew I was going. I wrote and told you.' He took her hand in his. 'I didn't come myself because – well, I wasn't sure whether you would have forgiven me for . . . what happened at my house. I thought it best to write, and if you wrote back I would know you didn't despise me for the way I'd behaved.'

'The way *you'd* behaved!' The words came of their own volition.

He bowed his head. 'Yes. I watched every day for a letter, but it never came. In the end I agreed to go abroad for three years in the hope that I'd forget you. But I couldn't. And I know, now that I've seen you, that you feel the same. Why didn't you write to me, my dearest Abbie?'

Tears were running unchecked down her face as they both joined in the applause for something neither of them had even noticed. 'I didn't find your letter until you'd been gone for three months. Not until after Matthew was dead and we were taking down his bed,' she whispered as the next turn began. She dabbed her eyes and then fiddled with her handkerchief in her lap. 'He used to open the post and when he saw a letter addressed to me he must have put it to one side and it slipped down between the bed and the wall.' She gave a rueful, mirthless smile. 'Peggy, my little maid, was not all that diligent with her broom, I fear, and it just lay there, gathering dust.'

'Tell me' – he took her hand again – 'would you have asked me to come and see you? Or could you not have found it in your heart to forgive me?'

'Forgive you? When all the time I was thinking how you must despise me for my wanton behaviour?' She stole an incredulous glance at him.

'Oh, Abbie, how could I despise you for giving me the most precious memory of my life?' he said softly. 'But answer me. Would you have let me come to see you?'

She nodded. 'God help me, I would have welcomed you with open arms, even though I still loved Matthew.'

'And now?' She felt him move a little closer.

'Now? But haven't you heard that, too? I'm married again. A loveless match that I contracted for business reasons and because I was sure I would never see you again.' She spoke in a flat, dull voice.

He moved away slightly. 'Oh, God, what a mess. And to think I moved to Colchester when I came back to England so that I could be near you, could see you, could one day ask you to become my wife . . . ' His voice trailed off. 'I think it would be best if I went back to London, or somewhere. It doesn't really matter where. I've retired from my work and I've no need to seek employment. I made a lot of money whilst I was abroad which I invested because there was nothing to spend it on . . . '

'No, don't go away again.' She spoke in such a low voice that he could hardly hear her. 'Come and see me sometimes. The children will love to see you, Laura plays the piano exceptionally well now; I shouldn't be surprised if she makes quite a name for herself. And William will want to see you. He'll be a fisherman, like his father.' She was speaking quickly, the words tumbling over each other.

'And you?' His voice cut across her although he spoke in little more than a whisper.

The applause began again. 'I don't think I could bear it if you went away again,' she said quietly.

'But your husband? You say you are married again?'

She turned bleak eyes on him. 'Surely even Richard can't object to the occasional visit from an old friend of the family.'

Going home in the cab Edwin chuckled. 'Just my luck,' he said, without any sign of regret. 'I meet the most beautiful woman in the world, and not only does she refrain from giggling and fainting all over the place but she is prepared to hold an intelligent conversation on the merits of Liszt. And what do I find?' He smote his head dramatically with his palm. 'She's going back to Reading on Friday!'

'To her husband?' Abigail made a valiant effort to match his lightheartedness.

'No, to her elderly mother.'

'Well, then, there's hope for you,' Abigail smiled. 'Reading isn't a hundred miles away, is it? You could always visit her.'

'Yes, I suppose I could.' He brightened. 'And she's sure to come and visit her brother again because she said she liked Colchester.' He settled himself complacently in his corner of the cab. 'But I'm in no hurry. I'll take life as it comes.' He yawned widely. 'Oh, by the way, you did remember David Quilter, didn't you?'

'Oh, yes, Eddie. I remembered him.'

She didn't sleep. And in the cold light of dawn she realized what a terrible mistake she had made in inviting David to visit. It would be like twisting a knife in a raw wound every time he came, and ultimately they would both need, demand, more from their relationship. A love like theirs could not remain hidden, could not remain platonic. And Richard, whatever his own inclinations, would never stand for being cuckolded.

She got out of bed and lit a candle. Then she put on a wrap and sat down at her writing desk. The letter she wrote was long. This time there must be no misunderstandings, they must part but he must know that she loved him and that this letter was the hardest thing she had ever had to write. Tears blurred her eyes but she forced herself to write on and when she had finished she sealed it into the envelope without reading it through, lest she should have second thoughts about the way she had bared her heart.

She put the letter in a pigeon-hole in the desk and then dressed in her plain grey morning dress, pinching her cheeks in an unsuccessful bid to bring a little colour to her pallid face. Then she went downstairs to begin yet another day.

# *Chapter Twenty-Two*

Laura and William had nearly finished their breakfast when Peggy came into the dining room. 'There's a dirty little urchin at the kitchen door. Says 'e's got a message for you, M'm,' she said with a disapproving sniff.

Abigail got up from the table, the slice of toast in front of her barely touched. 'All right, Peggy, I'll come and see what he wants.'

The dirty little urchin Peggy had so disapproved of looked exactly like she herself had done before Abigail had rescued her from Dolphin Yard.

'What is it, boy?' Abigail asked kindly.

'Mr Josh from *Conquest* say can you come. There's bin a spot o' trouble,' the boy said importantly.

'Yes, I'll come right away. Peggy, give this lad a slice of bread and jam and see that Master William and Miss Laura get off to school in time. I'll just get my shawl.' She was on her way through to the hall as she issued her orders.

She was in no doubt as to what had happened. Richard had gone down river with the men and had acted in his usual know-all, tactless way and upset them all. Now she would have to use all her guile and persuasion to put things right. She'd always known it was a mistake for him to go, but he'd been quite determined. Nevertheless, she'd see to it that he never went again, upsetting men she had known and respected almost since her own childhood. Her fury with her husband was mounting with every step as she hurried down the hill and along the busy quayside.

Guy was on the quay, waiting to help her along the gangplank to *Conquest*, riding high on the full tide. Josh and Tolley were on deck. There was no sign of Richard. As she went on board they both snatched off their caps.

'Richard?' she said. 'Where's Richard? What has he done?'

Tolley led her to sit down on the hatch cover. 'He ain't come back, I'm afraid,' Josh said, his face wooden.

'Hasn't come back? You mean you put him off the boat at Brightlingsea?' She looked up at the three men. Their faces all wore the same wooden expression.

'No, Missus. We mean 'e ain't come back. 'E went an' got hisself drownded off the wallet,' Tolley said, his voice as wooden as his face.

'But . . . how? What happened?' She tried to gather her wits, but faintness threatened to engulf her. Someone thrust a mug of liquid into her hands and as she sipped it and felt its fire in her throat she realized that it was rum. But it cleared her head so that she could make some sense of what the men were saying.

'We was out near the wallet,' Guy was explaining, 'an' we was hove to. We put the hook – anchor – down an' we all went below for a bit o' grub to warm us.'

'I'd made a rare tasty fish stew,' Tolley put in.

'Well, the wind 'ud piped up by this time and the water was gettin' a bit lumpy, makin' the boat swill about a bit,' Guy said. 'We don't take no notice of it, but Mr Richard, bein' a landlubber . . . '

'He ain't used to it. He hadn't never bin out there afore,' Josh said. 'Like Guy said, he's a landlubber, when all's said an' done. 'E only had to get below an' smell the grub an' 'e was off up aloft again. He wasn't feelin' all that fancy, I don't b'lieve.'

Abigail nodded. 'He was seasick.' She licked her dry lips and took another sip of rum from hands that were shaking. She felt cold all over.

'I went up to see after 'im,' Josh continued, 'but he'd gone.'

'He worn't there,' Tolley added.

'Musta tipped over the side,' Guy said.

Abigail looked from one to the other. 'You mean he fell over the side retching?'

Thass what that look like,' they agreed, nodding.

'And you never found his body?'

Josh shrugged. 'Leather boots, thick guernsey, oilskins. He'd 'a' dropped like a stone. Worn't no chance o' findin' 'im. Specially in a fresh nor'easterly.'

'Shall I take you 'ome, Missus? We've told you all there is to tell, an' you don't want to be here when they come to take all the particklers. We've already told the harbour master, so 'e'll be along shortly.' Guy put out his hand to help her to her feet.

'Thank you. Yes. I must go and tell the children. They'll be . . . ' She stopped. They'd be glad. She couldn't say it aloud, but it was none the less true. In fact, it was hard to know who would mourn Richard Cotgrove's passing.

A sudden thought struck her and she looked at the three men in turn. Each one returned her gaze unflinchingly. There was no sign of sorrow or regret. Or guilt.

She turned away and allowed Guy to lead her back to the house. It was strange that she should have lost two husbands to the sea. And both by accident. But she was convinced that Matthew's death had been no accident, it had been suicide.

And Richard? The men had told their story. No one would refute it.

'Thank you, Guy,' she said as he left her at the door.

'Thass all right, Missus.' He looked her straight in the eye. 'You know we'd do anything for you.' He snatched off his cap briefly and then marched back down the hill, his head held high.

Abigail looked after him until he was out of sight. His step never faltered. Then, slowly, she went indoors to tell William and Laura. There would be no school today.

But there was something else to be done first. Her step quickened and she hurried up the stairs to her room. Taking out the letter to David she tore it into shreds and let the pieces flutter to the floor round her feet.